Dear Reader...

There's no place like England when it comes to romance. From the glorious cliffs of Dover and the lush green hills of country estates... to the grand courts of royal intrigue and foggy streets of London... England is a beautiful and timeless place that fires the imagination.

Tea Rose is a wonderful new line of novels that captures all the passion and glory of this splendid nation. We asked some of our favorite writers to share their most romantic dreams of England—and we were delighted with their enthusiastic responses! Whatever the period and style—adventurous, playful, intriguing, lusty, witty, or dramatically heartfelt—every *Tea Rose* romance is a unique love story with an English flavor and timeless spirit.

We hope you enjoy these special new novels. And please, accept the *Tea Rose* postcard as our gift to you, the reader, who makes all dreams possible.

**Sincerely,
The Publishers**

> P.S.—Don't miss these *Tea Rose* romances,
> coming soon from Jove Books...

Embrace the Night

by Elda Minger...

A marvelous Cinderella story with a touch of intrigue. A lovely servant girl finds romance in the eyes of a haunted Duke—and danger at a glittering London masquerade.

(Available in May 1994)

Sweet Iris

by Aileen Humphrey...

A playful romp through high society with a high-spirited girl who sparks scandal at every turn. Irrepressible Iris defies her family's romantic meddling—by forging an unlikely love of her own.

(Available in July 1994)

Tea Rose romances from Jove Books

PIRATES AND PROMISES by Anne Caldwell
EMBRACE THE NIGHT by Elda Minger (May 1994)
SWEET IRIS by Aileen Humphrey (July 1994)

PIRATES AND PROMISES

ANNE CALDWELL

JOVE BOOKS, NEW YORK

If you purchased this book without a cover, you should be aware that this book is stolen property. It was reported as "unsold and destroyed" to the publisher, and neither the author nor the publisher has received any payment for this "stripped book."

PIRATES AND PROMISES

A Jove Book / published by arrangement with
the author

PRINTING HISTORY
Jove edition / March 1994

All rights reserved.
Copyright © 1994 by Anne Caldwell.
Tea Rose is a registered trademark of Jove Publications, Inc.
This book may not be reproduced in whole
or in part, by mimeograph or any other means,
without permission. For information address:
The Berkley Publishing Group, 200 Madison Avenue,
New York, New York 10016.

ISBN: 0-515-11248-8

A JOVE BOOK®
Jove Books are published by The Berkley Publishing Group,
200 Madison Avenue, New York, New York 10016.
JOVE and the "J" design are trademarks belonging
to Jove Publications, Inc.

PRINTED IN THE UNITED STATES OF AMERICA

10 9 8 7 6 5 4 3 2 1

This book is dedicated in memory of
Stephen Ben Tyler, my childhood
sweetheart. For all the good times
when we were growing up and all the
wonderful memories he left behind.

PROLOGUE

THE Right Honorable Master Justin Tyler St. Clair tied his mount to the oak tree and wearily climbed onto the large rock. He considered this grove his special hiding place. And today Henrietta Parker had returned his locket, and his thirteen-year-old heart was broken.

He should have known. His mother had warned him that Henrietta only pretended to favor him, that her real interest lay in his older half brother, Quentin, the new Earl of Foxworth. But he was young and stubborn—and Henrietta was spoiled—and he had trustingly cast his heart at her feet.

It hadn't taken her long to trample on it, Justin thought. He knew he shouldn't, but Justin despised her for preferring Quentin's wealth and title. Although Quentin had yet to notice the young girl, Justin selfishly hoped Quentin would marry before Henrietta was old enough to capture his interest.

"Damn," he cursed.

Sabrina Smythe, known as Bree, stepped off the path into the clearing, overhearing his outburst. "Your mother would take away your fine horse if she heard you cursing like that," the little blond-haired girl scolded.

Justin eyed her skeptically. "You don't even know my mother." Ever since the little girl had come to visit her aunt and stumbled onto the grove and his secret place, she had made a pest of herself. This was his last day in England and he wanted to be left alone.

Bree laid her china doll down on the grass and climbed the rock. She was not put off by his shortness of temper. Sometimes he was kind and sometimes he wasn't, but most times he was kind. Especially when he treated her like an adult and regaled her with tales of his wicked half brother.

Bree understood wickedness and cruelty. Her nanny was cruel. Bree allowed a sigh to escape her as she stared up at her new friend. She could never be as brave as him. He never cried no matter how awful his wicked half brother treated him. He was so noble—a true knight—but at such times as this it was up to her to see that his armor didn't tarnish too terribly much.

"I am certain you mother would not be pleased if she heard you swearing—even if I don't know her."

"How would you know what my mother would think?"

"I may not have a mother of my own, but Nanny informs me daily on what displeases them. Besides, I am seven years old today," she said, tossing back her golden blond curls. "Papa says that's almost a grown woman. Why, he's even hired a governess for me. Miss Madelyne Montague. Doesn't her name sound ever so romantic?"

"Romantic!" Justin laughed a little at her sweeping assertion. "What would you know of romance?"

Bree straightened her shoulders. "Every woman knows of love and romance."

He started to brood again. "Have you ever loved anyone?"

Bree thought for a moment. She loved her pony, Juju, but she knew that wasn't what he meant. "I love my father," she said half to herself.

"When he dies, you will soon learn of how much he loves you in return," he mumbled half to himself.

PIRATES AND PROMISES

The sight of her knight's handsome face drooping into a frown saddened Bree's young heart. She hadn't meant to remind him of his father's thoughtlessness. Well she knew the story how everything was left to his wicked half brother. Heartsick, Bree reached out and touched his hand.

"I wish your father hadn't died so you wouldn't have to leave England. Virginia is so far away."

"No one cares if I leave," Justin snapped. "My own father certainly didn't."

As soon as the words were spoken, he was ashamed of his outburst. The girl hadn't done anything to deserve his bad manners.

"Now that Quentin is master of Foxworth, he will give Mother no peace if she stays," he said matter-of-factly.

Bree placed her hands on her hips. "Oh, those with titles are so heartless."

He was tempted to tell her that ladies who sought to marry men with titles could be just as heartless, but he kept silent.

"My grandfather is a viscount and owns a great deal of land, both in England and Virginia," he said instead, his chest puffing with pride. "They will be mine someday."

Just as suddenly, his shoulders drooped. "Unfortunately, he prefers to stay in America, where a title means nothing."

"Perhaps your grandfather doesn't care for his position here," Bree said in her best grown-up voice. "But surely the Americans respect it."

"A viscount is not as great a title as an earl."

"Does that mean so terribly much to you?" She elected not to mention that her own father was the Earl of Roxbury.

Justin scrambled to his feet and stared down at her. "Who would want to marry a man without wealth or title?"

"I would marry you."

He studied the girl's intent gaze. "You know nothing about me, not even my name. And I know even less about you."

"I will tell you my name."

Justin paced the length of the rock and back. "We've agreed not to tell our identities. I will be leaving England; we'll never meet again."

She tilted her head up to look at him. "If you insist on being stubborn, I won't tell you. But you may call me Princess until you leave," she announced regally.

"Princess?" he scoffed.

Bree climbed to her feet. "You needn't get short with me," she scolded.

Justin laughed. "But a princess?"

"I'm not actually a princess," she said, her blue eyes filling with tears. "It's what Papa calls me."

Justin felt like the lowest sort of worm. He handed her his handkerchief. "I'm sorry. I did not mean to wound you."

After a dutiful sniff, Bree accepted his apology. "You were merely upset because your half brother inherited everything," she said generously. "But you needn't be discouraged. I have faith in you. You shall go to America and make your fortune. Then someday you will return and show your awful half brother that—"

Justin's mind grasped upon the idea and turned it over and over. Others had gone to America to make their fortunes. Why not him?

"—and when you return, we shall be married," Bree continued, unaware she had lost her audience. "I think it should be on my eighteenth birthday. It would be ever so romantic and—"

Justin's lips curved in a smile. He would become so wealthy that even Henrietta would swoon at the sight of him. He would buy the largest estate in all of England and she would beg him to marry her then.

"—and we shall live happily ever after, just like in the storybooks Papa brings me from London. You may kiss me now if you wish," she finished, lifting her face dramatically to his.

Justin grabbed Bree by the arms. "Oh, Princess, you are wonderful. You have given me the perfect solution to my problem." He placed a brotherly kiss on her cheek.

"I shall make Havenwood the grandest estate in all of Williamsburg. Now close your eyes. I have something for you."

He fished in his pocket and pulled out the locket Henrietta had returned. "Here," he said, pressing the trinket into her hand. "Now you may call me St. Clair."

Before she could answer, he had slid from the rock and was gone. Bree stared down at the locket. "Oh, our pact," she breathed. Bree clutched the necklace to her young breast and whispered, "I shall keep your locket always, St. Clair. It will be our promise. I shall wait until you return, then we shall be married."

CHAPTER 1

THE young Virginian's handsome features twisted as he continued to listen to the nefarious crimes of his fellow card players. Justin Tyler, bored with his short visit to England, wasn't sure at what point in the conversation the idea occurred to him. Perhaps when the Duke of Westcliffe was boasting of the pretty little maid he had gotten in a family way, then had to dismiss. Or was it when his half brother, Quentin, told of the tenants he had cheated?

Not normally one to interfere, Justin told himself to forget what he had heard. The men were drunk and only embellishing their exploits for his benefit. The ten years he had been away from England had changed nothing. In their narrow minds, a poor American could never hope to compete with the power of a duke or an earl. They did not suspect he could buy and sell each one of them with the wealth he had accumulated over the last few years.

Despite his good intentions when the men grew more and more cocky in the telling of their lurid tales, a plan began to form in Justin's mind. The idea was ludicrous, of course, but if he had the time in which to carry it off . . . A pity he was returning home tomorrow.

"Your bid, St. Clair," the Duke of Westcliffe said.

PIRATES AND PROMISES

Justin smiled. What would they think if he were to tell them he no longer used the name he shared with his half brother?

"One hundred pounds," he announced casually.

The duke's hand shook slightly as he studied his opponent. Seeing Justin's cold stare, Westcliffe licked his dry lips. It was difficult to believe this dark-haired giant and Quentin were half brothers.

Justin leaned back in his chair. "Well, gentlemen, what's it to be?"

The duke glanced down at his cards. Normally he would not hesitate to bluff and see the hand out, but St. Clair had an uncanny way of knowing the true worth of his opponent's cards. The duke raised his eyes to the Virginian. The man not only shared the devil's dark looks, but his luck as well. Even the smile on the bastard's lips did nothing to warm the cold green eyes that sent a chill up one's back. With a loud grunt, he tossed his cards on the table. The others quickly followed.

Justin cocked a dark brow at the generous pile of coins they had surrendered so easily. It was a pleasant surprise to discover that Quentin and the others were not very astute in all their dealings. Not one of them had called his bluff.

"Gentlemen," he said, "it's time I left. I've a long ride ahead of me."

Groans went around the table as he gathered up his winnings.

"Justin, you can't leave now," Quentin whined. "It isn't often you join us at White's. Stay the week and take a later ship."

Justin knew the plea was not for his company. Quentin, along with the others, had dropped a fortune at the tables tonight. A fortune Justin was pleased to have transferred to his own purse, and the others were eager to win back.

"Sorry, gentlemen, but my business in England is finished, and I have a consignment of prime breeding stock to see to Virginia. Surely you will understand when I say I'd rather not trust their care to an indifferent crew."

"Horses?" Lord Struthers asked, finally showing an interest in something other than his wineglass.

"Some of the finest mares Montgomery's stables had to offer."

"Montgomery let you have some of his mares?" Quentin gasped. "Why I've offered the man twice what one of those mares is worth and he would not even discuss the matter."

"Perhaps he doesn't care for the management of your stables," Justin suggested, watching as Quentin's face flushed red. He moved back his chair and stood. "Thank you for allowing me to sit in on your game, gentlemen. Perhaps my next trip I won't be so pressed for time."

Despite the grumbling, Justin made his farewells and left. The hour was late and, after the smoke-filled room, the cool night air felt good. He raked his fingers through his dark hair before dropping them back to the pistol he carried in the band of his breeches. He could see his carriage down the way, his driver dozing on the box. Justin decided to walk the short distance.

The two men who waited in the alley were pleased. They'd have to be deaf not to have heard the snatches of conversations of the other patrons as they left White's. The American was the big winner for the evening. Normally, they would not have waited so near the door, but if the rumors were to be believed, the risk would be worth it.

A quick glance at the man leaving White's and they knew it had to be him, for there was no mistaking their prey. "A beaver felt and a cape as black as night with hair to match," their inside man had hurriedly whispered as he emptied the slops into the alley.

The leader pulled a sharp blade from his coat and stepped back into the darkness. Holding his breath, he listened closely for the footsteps of their pigeon. He motioned for his partner to look to his cudgel, then raised his knife.

When the American stepped into the head of the alley, they launched themselves toward the unsuspecting swell. But their pigeon turned at the sound of their footsteps, the

PIRATES AND PROMISES

warning in his stance and the readiness of his pistol freezing them both in their tracks.

The man was a giant. A black-haired, green-eyed devil of a giant. He stood like a statue from hell, the night fog curling around his black cape. Why hadn't they been warned their pigeon was actually a hawk?

The leader stuck his knife behind him and managed a toothless grin. "Evenin', guv'nor," he said with a nod, then scurried past the tall American.

"Wait for me," his cohort called behind him.

Justin settled his pistol back in the folds of his cape and smiled. The thieves had thought him an easy target.

Even so, the episode served to quicken his steps to his carriage. He'd ride after all. He signaled the driver, then stepped inside.

He had expected to sleep on the ride to Portsmouth, but his mind kept reviewing the path the conversation had taken once tongues had been sufficiently loosened with the steady refill of the wineglasses. It was obvious the five other players at his table cared little for his opinion of them or they wouldn't have talked so freely. Quentin he could understand. His half brother had never made a secret of his prejudices toward Americans. But what had motivated the others?

His earlier idea kept returning, but he shook it off. Even if his ship wasn't leaving in the morning, it was none of his concern. Seeing his mares safely to Virginia was his goal—another step in establishing Havenwood as one of the richest estates in all of Virginia.

He pulled his beaver felt down and stretched out his long legs to the opposite seat. He was pleased with all he had accomplished in the last ten years.

A warm ocean breeze swept through the common room of the Duck and Ale as Justin lifted his glass for another swallow of the warm brew. A freak summer storm had sent his ship, the *Seahawk*, limping back to Portsmouth with the mainmast broken.

It would be at least two weeks before the repairs were completed and they would be ready to set sail again. Business at the inn was unusually brisk and Justin had been fortunate to secure rooms for his manservant and himself. He considered returning to London, but the thought of whiling away the hours at the card tables had no appeal.

He took another sip of ale, his attention wandering to the locals at the next table.

"Highwayman got ol' Lord Wilihand's purse last night, 'e did," the skinny farmer was saying.

His companion leaned forward, his voice low. "As much as he cheats his tenants, his purse could use a little lightenin'."

"Rumor has it, it scared 'im so bad, 'e wet 'is breeches," the farmer said with a chuckle and a broad wink. "A right nice comeuppance, I'd say."

Justin's lips twitched. Casually, he set the liquid to swirling in his glass, then took another swallow. It appeared Quentin's acquaintances were not the only peers needing a lesson.

The idea that had been nagging him since the card game was again in his thoughts. Perhaps it was time Quentin and his friends had their pockets lightened. Perhaps some of their corruption should be rewarded in kind. He stood and tossed a coin on the table and went in search of his manservant.

Justin sat at the small writing desk and glanced out the window of his room at the late afternoon sun. In a couple of hours it would be dark. If he wished to put his plan into motion, he must hurry.

"Can you have everything by nightfall?" he asked as he handed his servant a bag of coins.

Higgins scratched his bald head and carefully reviewed the list. "It'll take some doing but I'll have it here."

Justin could tell from the sparkle in Higgins's eyes the idea appealed to him. "I'm counting on you, Higgins."

"When have I ever disappointed you?" the manservant asked on his way out the door.

Justin didn't bother to point out that Higgins's interpretations of Justin's instructions, more often than not, took a creative path all their own. But despite that, Higgins was loyal.

He poised his sharpened quill over a fresh sheet of parchment. Living in America had given him a taste for fair play. Given the short time, he might not be able to wield the sword of retribution for everyone, but it would give him great satisfaction to try.

The Duke of Westcliffe would be leaving for London tonight for his weekly game of cards. He would be the first, Justin decided as he made note of the names of the men at the card game. With another dip of the quill into the crystal inkwell, he added another list opposite the first. These were the ones who had been hurt by Quentin's friends. After tracing a bold circle around the first name, Justin laid his quill aside.

He wasn't sure he remembered where the duke's estate was located. But, no matter. There would be plenty of places on the way to stop and obtain directions.

It took the rest of the afternoon to formulate his plans. Justin had no more than finished with the last of his preparations when Higgins shoved open the door. The small man stood, framed in the doorway of his bedchamber, his thin sides heaving.

"Good Lord, Higgins, why were you running?"

"Even with . . . the generous bag of coins, the bloke . . . didn't want to part with his bloody breeches. But I've got 'em," he shouted, waving the seaman's bag over his head.

Justin began unbuttoning his shirt. "Good work. Now help me dress."

"Wait till you see what I have," Higgins said as he crossed the room and emptied the bag on the bed. Proudly, he held up a large-legged pair of trousers for Justin's inspection. A frayed rope dangled from the gathered top.

Justin plucked the dark blue sailor's breeches from Higgins's fingers and inwardly groaned. Higgins seemed so pleased with his choice of costume, it was difficult to tell him it wouldn't do. It wouldn't do at all. Justin would have to postpone his plans until tomorrow evening.

"I'm supposed to be a highwayman, not a sailor," Justin pointed out.

"Don't you see?" Higgins asked. "You can walk the docks freely and no one will know you're a highwayman." He paused in thought. "Lessen, of course, you happen to meet up with the big bruiser I snatched this garb from," he added with an embarrassed glance.

Justin's brow furrowed. But he didn't point out that his caper as a highwayman was not destined for the dock areas.

He thumbed through the rest of the articles to see what would need to be replaced while Higgins waited patiently. Justin had to admit Higgins had been thorough . . . right down to the small jeweled dagger.

He sighed. He only had two weeks to complete his scheme. Perhaps the costume would do for one night.

Higgins helped him dress. Despite Justin's earlier reservations, the loose breeches gave him a freedom of movement he would need. Justin stood back and studied his image in the mirrored glass over his washbasin. "You've done a fine job, Higgins," he said.

Higgins ran his hand thoughtfully across his chin. "You say these men know you?"

"They're Quentin's friends, not mine. But, yes, if they get a close look at me, they'll know who I am."

Higgins rummaged through the room's only cabinet for a few minutes, then returned with one of Justin's shirts.

"You'll be needin' to cover your hair then."

"Must we use my new silk shirt?"

"It's the only dark one you have," Higgins said, shoving the shirt and dagger at him.

Reluctantly, Justin took them. "Banishing boredom certainly has its disadvantages," he mumbled.

It didn't take long to cut a large square and wrap it around his head, tying the corners behind his ear as he'd seen the sailors do. Then he cut a long, narrow strip. Holding it up in front of him, he lined up the sections he'd need to slit for his eyes. A few cuts and the holes were made.

Finished, he stuck the dagger into a sheath secured to the band of his breeches. "I look like a damn pirate," he cursed at his reflection.

Higgins walked around him, studying his employer from all angles. "You'll scare the breeches off that duke," he cackled. "That you will."

Justin couldn't help but smile. "If I do, I'll bring them back for you, Higgins. Turnabout is fair play."

Higgins beamed. "A pair of them fancy breeches would sure be nice."

Justin arrived at Westcliffe just as the duke was leaving and was forced to follow for over two miles before they passed through an area that suited his purposes. The driver ignored his warning shot, but the chase was short. The heavy coach took a corner a tad too wide and the wheel dropped into a hole, breaking the carriage's axle. The coach had just stopped when the duke's footmen scattered into the bushes.

Justin's horse pranced nervously up beside the duke's disabled coach. Once getting his mount under control, Justin placed his back to the full moon, then waved his pistol in the air. The driver dropped down from the box. Justin almost felt sorry for the small man, but he had more important matters to worry over. He tossed his dagger to the driver and instructed him to cut the lead horse loose.

The driver's hands were shaking so much at the sight of the tall, dark man that the dagger slipped through his fingers. But a quick glance at the highwayman's rigid jaw sent him scrambling to recover the knife.

Justin leaned down and tapped his pistol on the carriage window. "Out of the coach, Your Grace."

Silence. Nothing but the soft whisper of the wind as it played across the silk ties of his mask. Justin waited. Still no movement from inside the coach. With enough force to rattle the windows, he struck his boot against the door.

"Out, I said!"

The squeal from inside the coach told him his prey was unhurt, just hoping to play possum.

"We're coming out," the duke whined. "Don't shoot. We're coming out."

When the duke shoved his guest out before him, it was clear he thought to give the impression that his young companion was the owner of the fine carriage. Not bothering to mask his disgust, Justin waved the stranger aside, then leaned down to catch the duke's eye.

"Hand over your purse, Your Grace."

After much bluster about highwaymen and the shortage of hangmen's nooses in England, the duke finally reached into his vest pocket and pulled out a small leather bag.

Justin laughed at the offer. "The other one," he growled.

"This is the only one I have," the duke protested, shoving the pouch at the highwayman.

Leaning closer, Justin looped the drawstrings over the end of his pistol and lifted the purse from the duke's hand. "My, my, Your Grace," he said, "were you expecting to win every hand tonight?"

Justin was pleased to see the Duke of Westcliffe had the courtesy to blush.

After depositing the purse in his saddlebags, Justin waved the pistol at the driver. "Turn the horse over to His Grace, then crawl inside the coach and find the plump purse your *noble* employer attempted to hide."

The duke started to object, but the uncompromising posture of the highwayman caused him to reconsider. He took the reins from his driver.

"Unless you plan on walking the entire way, you might want to mount that nag you're holding," Justin suggested.

"I'll wait for my driver, if you don't mind."

"Have it your way."

Justin leaned forward and casually rested his arms across the neck of his horse. Seeing the duke's uneasiness, his lips slid into an easy grin. "Did I say that you will be coming with me?"

The muscle along the duke's jaw twitched, but he offered no comment. The other man's cold, detached view of the situation intrigued Justin.

Except for the stranger's light gray eyes, he appeared to be a younger, thinner version of the duke. Justin raised a dark brow. Odd, he had only now noticed the uncanny resemblance. From the conversation around the card table, he knew the duke to be unmarried and wondered who had warmed the other side of the old man's blanket often enough to persuade the duke to acknowledge the fruitful result of their lovemaking.

Justin nodded to the stranger. "Another of your by-blows, Your Grace?" he asked politely. Neither man answered, but he could tell from the look of surprise on the duke's face that the possibility had not occurred to him. But not the stranger. Justin would be willing to wager he knew, and from the hatred marring the man's handsome face, he was not pleased his secret was out.

The air was thick with tension by the time the driver stepped down from the coach. Hesitantly, the man held up the purse. "Here it be," he said, not sure he wanted to move any closer to the highwayman's huge steed. Taking careful aim, he tossed it at the thief's outstretched hand.

Justin caught the leather pouch neatly. "Ah, this is more like it. Now help His Grace mount, then hand the reins to me."

"Where are we going?" the duke demanded.

"To pay a gentleman's debt."

It took the better part of an hour to reach the small village that bordered the duke's estate. Once there, they skirted the line of shops until they reached the tavern nestled among the trees on the far side.

"Don't even consider calling for help," Justin said easily.

The duke only grunted as they nudged their mounts close to the stone building.

Only the hoot of a disgruntled owl told of their presence. While they waited, the tavern door swung open with a bang, plunging a shaft of light across the dark road.

"Home with ye, Moses," a thin figure said, gently pushing a wool cap down over the farmer's ears and guiding him out the door.

Mumbling about the lack of hospitality, Moses stumbled his way across the road and Justin was forced to pull the horses up short to avoid their stepping on the old man.

"Farmer!" he shouted.

Moses swung around. "Bloody feet don't know how to work anymore," he grumbled by way of an apology to the strangers.

Moses may have been drunk, but he was agile enough to catch the coin the dark stranger tossed his way. Curiosity drew him close to the big black horse. The story of meeting up with a highwayman ought to bring at least one free drink for the telling.

"What ye be a-wantin'?" he asked, prepared to give the masked man anything he owned, which wasn't much since most of what he earned went to replenish his supply of ale.

"You can rest easy, man. We'll only be needing directions for now."

Moses eased up on his toes and tried to get a glimpse of the gentleman hunkered down on the far plug. "Ye're asking the right man then. I knows everyone w'at be anyone 'ereabouts."

"We're looking for a maid that used to work at Westcliffe. She'll be carrying the duke's bastard."

Moses stifled a snicker. "Ye'll 'ave ta do better than that, pirate. The ol' duke leaves more 'an 'is share in the family way."

"It would be the young one he turned out a few weeks back."

"That'd be Nellie," he said. "She's living out behind the old stables. 'Er father wouldn't let 'er back 'ome, w'at with 'er disgracing 'erself and all."

"Thanks, old man," Justin said, nudging his mount forward.

They had passed the stables on the way in and it would be too far to backtrack now. But Justin was tempted to spur the horses to a gallop, if only to see if the duke could keep his seat. A mouthful of English soil might be the proper physic for someone who considered himself a prime stud.

But unfortunately that wasn't the type of justice he had planned. He reached over and untied the duke's hands.

"Down, Your Grace!" Justin ordered.

With the careful deliberation of one long unused to straddling a horse, the duke slid off the broad back of the carriage horse. "You're not leaving me here, are you?" he whined.

"I have decided the maid might not be so very pleased to see you again."

Justin smiled down at his prisoner. "Now off with your clothes."

"Are you mad?" the duke bellowed.

Pulling out his pistol, Justin pointed it at the duke. "Are my instructions truly so difficult to understand?"

The duke swallowed the lump that threatened to choke him and quickly began unbuttoning his shirt, his eyes never leaving the barrel of the pistol. "I'll see you hang for this!"

"That was certainly one of the options I considered for you."

A sickly pallor etched the duke's thin lips and he continued to undress in silence. Naked, he stood shifting uneasily in the cool night air.

"Hand me up your breeches," Justin said. The duke gave him no argument.

Justin pointed the pistol down the village road. "Now off with you." He grinned down at the naked man. "Oh, and I'd not be seeking help from anyone along the way if I were you. I rather imagined you walking all the way back to Westcliffe in the altogether. I'll be keeping a close eye on your every step and I know you wouldn't want to disappoint me. Besides which, with your reputation, I doubt there would be a tenant of yours who would open their door to you."

The duke started off. Gingerly running from one shadow to the next, he made it past the first thatched hut before Justin fired the pistol. Curtains were cautiously raised and doors opened as the sleeping village woke to the sight of the Duke of Westcliffe running through the streets as naked as a newborn babe.

A deep chuckle rumbled in Justin's throat and he turned the horses for Nellie's shack behind the stables. The healthy bag of coins should give her a fresh start.

After fastening the frog at the neck of her spencer, Lady Sabrina Smythe tugged the snug jacket in place. Then, retrieving her soft leather gloves from the clutter of her dressing table, she pulled them on. "Maddie, I shall be back before anyone knows I have left."

The young woman's governess, who had been patiently awaiting this moment, set her needlework aside and stood. She crossed her sturdy arms before her and glared down at Bree. From the top of her charge's golden-blond curls to the tips of her tiny pink slippers, Bree was a captivating bundle of stubborn determination, but Miss Madelyne Montague could be just as stubborn. And she was larger.

"Your father said it's not safe to be traveling at night these days and you are not to go anywhere until after this madman is caught."

"Stand aside, Maddie. I'll not let the threat of some highwayman masquerading as a pirate keep me from going to Foxworth."

"Not as long as your father pays me to see to your welfare."

"Obviously, he doesn't think it's too dangerous since he left us here alone while he ran off to London. I think he made up the pirate story to keep me here. Well, it won't work. I plan to personally confront Quentin with my refusal. I shall not marry the fiend even if he is the Earl of Foxworth and I shall tell him so myself."

"Bree," Maddie scolded, "you can't truly be certain the earl is a fiend. You only know a few wild stories you were told as a girl."

Bree tapped her foot impatiently. "We've been over this a thousand times. Papa won't listen. It's up to me to tell the earl I can't marry him."

The rash of robberies by the pirate in the area worried her more than she cared to admit, but a promise was a promise and Bree would do what she had to to keep it. "I won't marry anyone but St. Clair."

"The Honorable Mr. St. Clair," Maddie scoffed. "He gives you a locket and promises he'll come back and you wait for him for ten years."

"Is Foxworth any more worthy? He's only marrying me for the dowry my father bribed him with."

"Would you prefer he did not provide you with a dowry?"

"Yes, for then Lord Foxworth would be looking elsewhere for another plump purse to pillage. He's no better than Lord Monford in my new book, for he only wished Lady Hatfield's inheritance."

Maddie's gray eyes darkened. "I have been too lenient with you, young lady," she said. "I should never have allowed those books in this house. They've done nothing but fill both of our heads with romantic nonsense. Now they have you believing St. Clair is a noble knight who will suddenly appear and carry you off to America with him. Take a lesson from me. There are few loves that are as perfect as those we read about."

Bree stared in fascination at the woman who had been more than a governess to her for the past ten years. "You were once in love?" she asked, surprised at the revelation.

Maddie lowered her gaze at Bree's close scrutiny. "Once."

"Why did you not tell me about it?"

How could she explain that her own wish for love was as hopeless as Bree's? Maddie looked away. "It was a long time ago," she said brusquely. "It's over now. Things of the past are best forgotten, so it's no wonder your father has decided it's time he took you in hand."

Bree raised a finely arched brow. "Father has decided someone else needs to take me in hand and he hopes if he pays enough money he will be able to relinquish the responsibility to Foxworth."

"You mustn't talk as if your father doesn't love you," Maddie admonished. "Why, he sends you the loveliest gifts from London and he writes you most every week. There aren't many young ladies as fortunate as you."

"I'm well aware of my father's love for me, Maddie. I rank well below his London haunts and his cronies. He . . ."

Bree paused in thought. She had almost told of the letters she had written as a child, asking her father to please tell her why he had suddenly gone away and begging him to come home again. They were letters her father had ignored. She stubbornly swallowed the tears that burned the back of her throat.

"In all honesty," she continued calmly despite the tightness in her chest, "I would have to say he has placed me somewhere between his new hunter and his hounds."

Maddie wished she could have argued with Bree, but there wasn't much point. The only way to defend Bree's father would be to reveal the mystery behind his remaining in London and it was not her place to repeat the vicious gossip. Maddie's only task now was to help temper the ways of a stubborn and determined young woman. But even after ten years, Maddie wasn't sure how much, if any, influence she had over the headstrong Bree.

"Perhaps your father doesn't wish his daughter to pine away for someone who will never return. After all, it was a long time ago and you were both children."

Common sense told Bree it was foolish to cling to her dreams, but the woman in her knew that her destiny lay with St. Clair. To give up the promise would mean that she had no one who loved her.

"He'll come for me, Maddie. I know he will."

PIRATES AND PROMISES 21

Her words tore at Maddie's heart. "This is all my fault, Bree. B-being hopelessly in love once, I'm afraid I encouraged your romantic fancy." Maddie wiped away a tear that slipped down Bree's cheek. "We got a lot of enjoyment out of our fantasies, but we're both older now and we can't let our foolish childhood promises ruin our lives."

"I'm marrying St. Clair, Maddie," Bree stubbornly repeated.

"You don't even know whether he's alive or dead. At least wait for my cousin's letter from Virginia. For all we know of him, St. Clair might very well be married already."

The notion was too close to Bree's unspoken fears for comfort. "I don't want to argue with you, Maddie, but I've waited long enough. Your cousin is too busy with her duties at the Winghams'. She'll never have the time to find him for me. In the meantime, I must deal with the earl's offer of marriage."

"You're just as stubborn as your father, but it will do you no good. With as much money as your father has offered to settle on Lord Foxworth, there is no chance of him releasing you of the alliance."

"I don't plan on asking, Maddie. I will *tell* him the way it is to be. He is the one with no choice in the matter."

Maddie let out a dramatic sigh. "If you've set your mind to this, then I'm going with you."

As soon as the Earl of Foxworth saw Sabrina dragging her governess from the coach, he knew why she'd come. He had the butler show them to the drawing room, where he joined them. Although Miss Montague took a chair a discreet distance from them, Quentin was disappointed Sabrina had felt the need to bring her along. The blond beauty was known for bending the accepted rules of conduct and he'd hoped she would attempt to slip away on her own when she learned of the engagement.

He tried not to let regret show on his features, but the disappointment of not having the opportunity of sampling the fare before the wedding was great. Just having her sit across from him conjured up delightful images of running his fingers over her ripe, young curves. Why, the very thought set his loins to aching, and once he had taken her to his bed, her father might be persuaded to part with even more of his wealth to ensure the marriage.

With the companion's disapproving eyes on him, he curbed his lecherous thoughts and reached for the cord to ring for a footman.

"Would you or Miss Montague care for some refreshments?" he asked.

"No, thank you, Lord Foxworth. Maddie and I have only a few moments. I've come about your offer of marriage."

Justin's two weeks were almost up, and Quentin was the last on his list. Although he had derived great satisfaction from righting another wrong, he was happy to be done with it. Quentin's retribution was the easiest. All had gone as he planned. Memory had served him well and the bag slung over his shoulder was filled with a goodly portion of the family jewels.

He let himself out the study door and along the garden wall. From the lights in the drawing room, Quentin must have a late guest. As soon as he heard his brother's voice, Justin knew where he would leave the dagger which had become his trademark after the first robbery. He eased up to the open French doors.

"I've come about your offer of marriage," he heard the vision in pink say.

Something stirred inside Justin at the image across the room. Her hair was the color of soft-spun gold; her eyes, the bright blue of a clear spring morning. With the rose-petal glow of embarrassment on her ivory-smooth complexion, she was exquisite.

He found his gaze dropping to trace the outline of her slim waist, then traveling up again, slowly taking measure of the generous breasts that pushed provocatively against the snug fit of her bright pink spencer. As if she felt his eyes on her, she defiantly squared her shoulders, sending an ache through him.

So this was the countrified morsel of delight Quentin was bragging to his cronies about. Money . . . and beauty. A pleasing combination. Much more than Quentin deserved.

But what was she doing away from home at night with only her governess to lend her countenance? She looked far too innocent for Quentin's tastes. But then Henrietta had been innocent too, before she had married Quentin. A year as his wife and she had taken her own life. Justin still felt a pang of regret for poor Henrietta's fate.

Justin raised the dagger to take aim at the family crest on the wall next to Quentin's head.

"I cannot marry you," the young woman finally said.

Justin lowered the dagger when Quentin's brows snapped together in anger. Ah, so his half brother was about to lose the little golden plum.

"That is not what your father led me to believe," Quentin said with slow deliberation.

Bree eyed the earl coolly, searching his face in hopes of stirring her childhood memories of St. Clair, but it had been too many years since that day in the grove. The only memories the earl stirred were the stories of his cruelty St. Clair had painted so vividly.

She tossed her head defiantly. "My father is obstinate, Lord Foxworth. He refuses to acknowledge that I am pledged to another."

"Your father told me of your infatuation." Quentin leaned forward and Justin had to listen closely to hear what was said.

"My first wife had a silly obsession for another also. Trust me. It is something I can make you forget in time."

The cruel smile on Quentin's lips told Justin how his brother intended to accomplish his boast. His fingers closed over the dagger and he considered the possibility of accurately sending the dagger to a more appropriate target. But the girl stood abruptly, blocking his aim.

Bree was furious. Forget! She would never forget. The details of St. Clair's features may have grown dim, but the feelings he had stirred in her heart were as strong as ever. "I cannot speak for your dead wife, Lord Foxworth, but I can assure you I take my promises very seriously. Good evening, my lord."

Quentin grabbed her arm and Maddie was immediately out of her seat. "Stay where you are," he ordered the older woman.

Maddie opened her mouth to scream, then closed it when the earl threatened to break Bree's arm.

"You forget yourself, Lord Foxworth," the golden-haired beauty said as Quentin pulled Bree roughly against him.

"You'll leave when I've had my say," he growled.

"Her father will hear of this, Lord Foxworth," Maddie said.

"Hush!" the earl demanded. With Miss Montague glowering at him, Quentin turned back to Bree. "You won't need to waste your time telling your father. I'll make certain he hears of it myself." He grinned at his triumph. "After your unorthodox little visit, I'm sure he'll agree that a hasty wedding will now be in order."

"I'll never marry you, you . . . you black-hearted . . . toad!"

"You don't seem to understand, my dear. If you don't marry me, I shall take great pleasure in seeing that no one else will have you." He twisted her arm behind her, forcing her up against him. "You see, my dear, either way, you will be mine."

"You're saying I have no choice," Justin heard her say. But even as he heard her words he knew her calm acceptance was a facade. It was the only thing that held him from breaking in on the scene.

Suddenly Quentin released her. "I'm pleased to see we understand one another."

While Bree rubbed her arm, she deliberately allowed her small embroidered reticule to fall to the floor. Quentin bent to retrieve it for her. Before he could straighten, she grabbed up a bronze statue that rested on the table beside her and brought it down over Quentin's head.

"Oh, Bree. What have you done?" the governess screamed when Quentin fell to the floor. "You've killed him."

"Nonsense, Maddie, I—"

But her denial froze in her throat as a large figure lunged through the garden doors. He was a giant man, tall, with broad shoulders. A dark figure swathed in black, his eyes glittering green orbs behind the slits of his mask.

"The pirate," Maddie breathed, then fainted at the highwayman's feet.

Justin leaped over the woman's prone form and vaulted for the drawing room door. Thankfully, he had just enough time to turn the key before a servant tried the knob.

"Out the garden doors," he said over his shoulder as he knelt beside Quentin.

"Is he dead?" Bree whispered.

Justin stood, towering over her. "I thought I told you to leave." He meant to scare her, but she stood firm.

"My governess. She's fainted. I can't just leave her here."

"I admire your concern, but once that footman reports the noise and the locked door, the entire household will be here, so I don't think you have to worry about the earl accosting your companion. He's hardly in any condition to ravish a woman. Now go!"

Bree laughed nervously.

Even her uneasy laughter was as clear as the ring of fine china and it took him a moment to remember that they had yet to escape.

"Come!" He grabbed her wrist and pulled her to the door.

Bree braced her feet stubbornly against his. He continued to pull, but only managed to bunch the carpet where she had dug her heels in.

Justin tossed the dagger, leaving it quivering in the floor by Quentin's head. "Damn!" he cursed as he leaned down to pick her up. "I said to come with me."

His powerful arms were like a vise and it was all Bree could do to catch her breath. "I'll n-not g-g-go without M-Maddie," she managed to get out.

Justin paused in the garden to retrieve the bag of jewels. "I could always leave you behind to hang," he said, threatening to drop her. "But it would be a shame."

Her blue eyes widened. "They would hang me?" she whispered as she clung precariously to the front of his black cape.

"This isn't something you can expect the servants to keep to themselves."

As if on cue, the drawing room door splintered open.

Bree threw her arms around his neck. "I've changed my mind," she said. "I'll *allow* you to abduct me after all."

CHAPTER 2

BREE watched the highwayman as he secured his loot to the saddle of his magnificent horse. "Of course, you realize I'll need my own mount," she said. "Something with a little spirit. I truly detest a plodder. And do make certain the saddle is clean. I wouldn't want to soil my gown."

Justin turned to her in disbelief. "Is there anything else you require before we continue to flee for our lives?"

"Don't get nasty. This is my new gown and I don't wish to ruin it. After all, no one but the earl has seen me in it. And that hardly counts."

"I could always leave you here and you could wear it to your hanging."

"My, but we are testy, aren't we?"

When he opened his mouth to protest, Bree raised her gloved hand and waved her dismissal. "Go ahead. I shall watch over your mount until you've returned."

"Well, Lady . . . ?"

There was no point in providing the scoundrel with the information that her father was a man of wealth and position. "*Miss* Sabrina Smythe," she lied. "Bree to my friends, but you may call Miss Smythe."

"Well, *Smythe*," he said, swinging her up onto his horse,

"as I see it, your gown's going to get a mite rumpled, but your neck will be intact."

He was pleased to see her clamp her mouth shut. If it weren't so important that they put some distance between them and Foxworth, he'd almost be tempted to kiss that stubborn line from her jaw.

Placing his foot in the stirrup, he swung up behind her. She didn't so much as flinch when he reached around her for the reins.

It felt good to have her wedged between his arms. Family jewels and a fiancée. He had done well tonight. Quentin would be furious once he came around. Not only had he lost a good deal of the family jewels, but his little golden-haired rabbit had slipped the snare. The thought brought a smile to Justin's lips.

He flicked the reins. The woods were thick behind Foxworth and Justin was forced to pick his way carefully through the trees until they reached the road on the far side. Once there, he gave his mount free rein and they thundered down the country lane.

Even though Smythe's manners left much to be desired, he owed it to the young lady to see her home before he returned to Portsmouth. He hoped the servants were not certain who'd been to visit, so she could escape trouble. But her family was probably influential enough to keep her from harm. He urged the mount on. It was at least an hour's ride to Southampton and he needed to get a prudent distance between them and Foxworth before he slowed their pace.

Miss Smythe's person wasn't making her rescue easy. She sat stiff in his arms, the rose scent of her blond hair filling his nostrils. Common sense told him he was acting out of character... that he should set her down at the first village he came to, but the mere touch of her shoulder rubbing against his chest brought other ideas to mind. He'd best remember he was a wanted man with no time for seductions. Yet, a man was entitled to a few lustful thoughts.

They rode on in silence. Discovering she liked the feel of

PIRATES AND PROMISES 29

his strong arms around her, Bree relaxed against his chest. Strangely, she felt unafraid. Left to her own devices most of the time, it was an unexpected pleasure to find someone else had taken charge of the situation.

Intrigued, Bree ventured a peek at her rescuer. A shame he wore a mask. Yet a handsomely chiseled jaw and a span of broad shoulders set her imagination soaring as to what it would be like to further the unlikely acquaintance.

This was so like the romantic tale she had read only last week. In one fell swoop, Sir Henry, the hero, had rescued the fair maiden from the wicked hands of the villain and carried her off to his castle. She gave forth a deep sigh. If only this were St. Clair and not the pirate, he would take her back to his home in Virginia to be married and live the rest of their lives in happiness.

"Where are you taking me?" she finally asked once her rescuer slowed the horse to a sedate pace.

Despite his better judgment, Justin leaned toward her. "To my bed," he whispered.

With her face flushing a becoming shade of pink, she glared up at him. Even in the pale moonlight, her blue eyes were strikingly beautiful.

"Don't get your petticoat in a pucker," he said at her indignation. "It was a jest."

Shifting toward him, Bree studied his masked face. "You're not much of a gentleman, are you?" she asked soberly.

He smiled. "Have you met many highwaymen who are?"

The night breeze had picked up, ruffling her neat curls. She used her finger to spear one back in place. "If you put a real effort toward it, do you think you could be gentleman enough to tell me where you are taking me?"

His grin broadened. "I could, but then I was never one for putting myself out. I suppose that's why I took to stealing."

"You're not even attempting to cooperate," she scolded.

Damn, but he did enjoy kindling the fire in those blue eyes!

"I thought you might get a tad upset if I told you I was going to sell you to the first dandy who came along with enough funds to finance my way to America."

"You're what?" she demanded.

"A pox of a situation, isn't it?" he said, shaking his head. "If you were a man, I could get more selling you to one of the captains in need of a crew, but you're a woman. Since you are so puny and all, I can only hope to get enough coins to cover my passage."

"Perhaps it's not too late for my father to exchange me for a man," she muttered to herself. "He doesn't appear to particularly care for what fate granted him anyway."

He knew from the bitterness of the words, he shouldn't tease her so, but the defiant tilt of her chin tickled his fancy and he leered down at her. "I have nothing against your compensating me in other ways."

Her blue eyes darkened dangerously. "With me so puny," she spat out, "I would hardly think it worth the effort."

He was pleased to see her courage hadn't deserted her. But what would she do if he kissed her? he wondered, then leaned forward to find out.

He had barely lowered his head when she bunched up her fist and hit him squarely on the nose.

The blow was surprisingly effective. "Why did you do that?" he said fishing for his handkerchief.

Bree squared her shoulders. It would not do to let him see how terribly he had frightened her. "I thought you were going to kiss me," she said.

"I was."

"Then you should know why I hit you."

He daubed at his throbbing nose. "It hurts like hell," he growled.

"It is small punishment in comparison to the royal beating Nanny gave me when she caught me kissing the stableboy when I was eight."

"Anyone caught kissing the stableboy deserves to be beaten," he offered as he lowered his handkerchief. "I'm bloodied," he said, half shocked.

PIRATES AND PROMISES

"I'm not surprised," Bree said, a hint of a smile in her voice. "I'm quite clever with my hands."

Justin eyed her warily over the handkerchief. "Can you manage to hold your fists for a while?"

"Are you going to try to kiss me again?"

"Hell, no!"

"Excellent, because I have decided that if you are going to America, I shall be going with you."

The horse sidestepped uneasily under the sudden tightening of the rein, and for a moment Justin concentrated on bringing him around. What had started out as a simple plan to spoil Quentin's wedding was becoming extremely complicated.

"You're going home," he growled. "To your father. It's time he took you in hand." He waited for her to ask him how he knew who she was, but she merely slumped against his arm.

"You are not the only one of that opinion, but my father is not home," she said dejectedly, then just as suddenly straightened. "Besides, I can't go there. They'll come for me. And hang me," she added.

"Don't be silly," Justin said. "Quentin's not dead."

"Not dead!" Bree twisted toward him. "Then you lied to me?"

Justin wasn't about to make the same mistake twice and kept a close eye on her clenched fist before he answered.

"Not exactly," he began. "Quentin would have hanged you himself for striking him as soon as he came to. You are fortunate I took you away."

"It's merely a reprieve," she sighed. "My father will still force me to marry Lord Foxworth."

She looked so forlorn, Justin wanted to reach out and pull her back against his chest. He caught himself in time. "Does your father often mistreat you?" he asked.

She lifted her face to his, the moonlight playing in her hair. It seemed all too easy to forget this was the same woman who had hit him. She appeared so . . . vulnerable.

Bree looked up into his masked face and considered telling the pirate that her father rarely put forth the effort to visit anymore, let alone gather together enough emotion to actually abuse her. Yet the thought of airing her problems in front of a stranger somehow went against her upbringing.

"Even though my father is away a great deal of the time, I know he loves me dearly," she lied, "but lately he's gotten this notion in his head that I need a husband to keep me in line."

Justin had no difficulty believing that. His nose still smarted from her punch. Yes, he could see how she could be quite a handful for anyone. Lord, he'd probably done Quentin a favor abducting her as he had.

"Did you hit your father too?" He knew it was silly, but he had to ask.

She looked at him as if he were crazy. Then she suddenly grabbed the front of his shirt, and he instinctively pulled away.

"You must take me with you," Bree demanded.

"Oh, no I won't," he said, trying to pry her fingers from the front of his shirt. "Now let go of me before this horse unseats us both."

"Promise you'll take me with you."

"No!"

Bree relaxed her hold. "Why not?" she asked, bitterness spilling out in her words.

Free at last, Justin tried to put his shirt back in order. "Smythe, when I took you from Quentin, I had only two things in mind—to rescue you and to ruin his chance of wedding you. I had no intention of adopting you."

"Then you think I should have to marry the earl?" she snapped.

Justin was no fool. He could see her anger building and did a quick assessment of the position of her hands before putting forth his argument. "I don't think anyone should have to marry a man such as Quentin. And," he added, raising his hand to stave off her objections, "America may be more civilized than your countrymen are willing to acknowledge, but it is no place for a young lady alone."

Her face broke into a radiant smile. "But I won't be alone," she declared. "The one I am pledged to lives in America. Once I get there, we shall be married."

Justin's brow creased in a frown. "You're pledged to another, yet your father is forcing you to marry Quentin? I thought you were putting Quentin off."

She didn't think it wise to tell him the pledge was not her father's, but her own. "Quentin is an earl. And quite wealthy," she explained.

At the forlorn note in her voice, a wound that Justin had thought long since healed twinged with an old, familiar ache. Time had not changed anything. Wealth and position were still everything.

"Then why are you fighting the marriage?" he asked, bitterness brimming within him.

"Because Quentin is a cruel and wicked man."

Justin pulled his mount up. "Has he hurt you?"

Although the masked face was in shadow, Bree could feel his anger and was surprised at its intensity. "N-no," she stammered. "But then I did not have to be one of his victims to learn of his cruelty."

Justin had heard enough. With a tug on the reins, he turned the horse.

Bree was afraid to ask, but she had to know. "You've changed your mind about taking me home, haven't you?"

"I shall get you to Portsmouth. From there you can secure passage to America if you are determined."

He handed her the reins, then reached up and untied the silk mask. The knotted scarf covering his head came next. It felt good to have them off, he thought, running his fingers through his mussed hair. He felt her eyes on him and smiled.

Bree found herself staring at the pirate, and it took all her efforts to return his smile. The man was breathtakingly handsome. His hair was every bit as black as the silk scarf that had covered it, and his eyes, sheltered beneath the thick, black brows, were a deep, dark green. Almost as green as she remembered St. Clair's to be. But where St. Clair's face had reminded her of the sculptured lines of an Adonis, the pirate's was blessed with the rugged lines of a warrior. She took a deep breath and handed the reins back to him. It was fortunate her heart was spoken for.

"It isn't too late to change your mind," he pointed out.

Bree tucked herself against his shoulder. "No, I shan't change my mind," she stated. "I am going to America."

Bree traced the outline of the locket that hung between her breasts. A stab of anticipation plunged through her. It was true. She would finally be seeing St. Clair again. The dream that had been with her for so many years was about to become a reality, and it frightened her a little.

She closed her eyes and relaxed with the gentle sway of the horse. Tomorrow would take care of itself. For now, she was happy.

As the miles passed beneath them, Justin wondered at her silence. He had expected at least a thank-you. Was she having second thoughts about what she was giving up?

He looked down at her bowed head and realized she had fallen asleep. With some difficult maneuvering, Justin managed to cover her with his cape.

What had he tangled himself up with? He was right to tell himself that he was only protecting her. He knew Quentin would not give up looking for Miss Smythe, and if she could not count on her father for help, she was as good as married to his half brother.

But what was he going to do with her once he got her to Portsmouth? He couldn't take her on to Virginia. She knew him as the pirate and he'd be in a devil of a fix if she lost her temper again and decided to turn him over to the authorities.

Although he was fairly certain his identity was safe as long as she felt in need of his help, he continued to wrestle with the problem. If he took Smythe to America he would need a plan whereby she would be under his control. But then he doubted the hellcat who'd bloodied his nose could ever be under anyone's complete control.

Still, taking Miss Smythe to America was out of the

question. He had set more important goals for himself and had other pressing matters to deal with at home. For the last ten years, he had helped his grandfather turn Havenwood into one of the wealthiest estates in all of Virginia. Also, when he returned, he planned to propose to Regina Wingham. It was a mere formality for the whole of Williamsburg had paired the beautiful Miss Wingham with Justin since her first ball two years ago.

Justin had done nothing to discourage the gossips. It was a well-known fact Mr. Wingham was willing to put up a prime piece of pastureland as part of Regina's dowry and it was a section Justin had long had his eye on for the new mares. He couldn't allow an association with Miss Sabrina Smythe to be made public and put an end to his plans. Besides she had her own fiancé.

As if she'd read his thoughts, Smythe snuggled protectively against him in her sleep and surprisingly enough he liked the feel of her lying against him. Quentin's fiancée. Perhaps there was justice in this world after all.

All too soon they arrived at Justin's lodgings at the inn. Dressed as he was he could not rouse the innkeeper to secure another room. She'd have to share his.

"You are a blackguard and a scoundrel," Bree shrieked.

Justin ducked the candlestick she threw at his head. "Be reasonable, Smythe. There were no more rooms available."

Bree sat on the bed, her legs tucked under her as she searched for something to throw. Finding nothing else close, she grabbed one of the pillows and tossed it. He didn't even bother to duck, but let it bounce ineffectively off his broad chest.

"Did you have to put me in your bed?" she shouted.

Justin doubted she even realized the restraint it had required of him to lie next to her and not touch her. Even now with her rumpled gown, and her curls spilling in disarray about her flushed face, she was quite a temptation. But he knew how fierce she was and intended to keep his distance.

"You're carrying on as if I had taken advantage of you. You were asleep. As long as I stayed on my side of the bed, what did it matter?"

"It does matter. What am I to tell my betrothed when I see him?"

He grinned at her. "You could tell him you slept with a highwayman."

"I fail to see the humor in this," she stated, sweeping the hair out of her eyes. "Because of you, I'm ruined."

Justin crossed his arms over his chest. "Don't try foisting this on me, Smythe. First you almost kill Foxworth, then you insist upon running off with the pirate. My dear, you were ruined before you slept in my bed."

He was right, but she wasn't about to let him off so easily. "Couldn't you at least have slept on the floor?" she demanded.

"No, but I could have bedded you down with my manservant," he shouted back.

Bree rose up on her knees and grabbed the other pillow, her blue eyes two orbs of crystalline fire. "You mean to tell me you have a manservant?"

Justin grinned broadly at the pretty little minx. "Being a highwayman doesn't mean you can't enjoy a few luxuries."

"And he has his own room?" she asked, wanting to be fair and obtain the facts first. At least he had the grace to look a bit discomfited, she thought, but it would not atone for his unspeakable behavior. "Well?"

Justin shrugged. "*He* does what I ask. He's entitled to his own room."

She tossed the other pillow. "You could have slept with him instead of me."

"Not me. The man snores."

If she had had a pistol, she would have shot him. The man's gall was beyond anything she had ever known before. Didn't he realize what it would mean if St. Clair were to learn that she'd shared another man's bed? He would think she had betrayed him.

PIRATES AND PROMISES 37

"What must I do to get my own room?"

As soon as she saw the mischief dancing in the pirate's green eyes, she knew it was the wrong question to ask. He stepped forward until he towered over her. Her breath all but lodged in her throat as he leaned down, his gaze locking with hers.

"You could be my servant," he said, a broad grin stretching across his tanned face.

Bree met his insolence with disdain. "You would enjoy having me at your beck and call, wouldn't you?"

"It would get you to America," he pointed out.

She didn't answer but he could see that she was considering the offer. Like the majority of her countrymen, she was not aware of the vast territory America covered. More than likely she thought once she stepped ashore it would be only a matter of hours before she found her betrothed and he rescued her.

"It won't take long to draw up an agreement," he offered. Maybe taking Smythe to America wouldn't be so bad after all.

"You're saying that if I am willing to be your servant, you will get me to Virginia?"

"Ah, so your lover is from Virginia," he said.

She lowered her head, but not before he saw the bright pink that flooded her cheeks.

"He's not my lover," she mumbled, embarrassed that the word was certain to mean more than her innocent arrangement with St. Clair. "He's my betrothed."

Bree ventured a look at the pirate. Should she tell him St. Clair's name? What if he should know of him? A familiar knot formed in her stomach. Worse still, suppose St. Clair had forgotten the promise. Suppose he was already married as Maddie had suggested. Her father had warned her that she was putting too much faith in a childhood promise. This pirate would surely enjoy telling her what a fool she was.

Justin watched the myriad of emotions that crossed her face. There was something she wasn't telling him. For whatever reasons, her father obviously didn't approve of the betrothal. More than likely because the fiancé was an American, Justin thought, the old resentment surfacing again. He only hoped it wasn't one of his neighbors.

"What is your betrothed's name?"

Without hesitation, Bree borrowed her book's hero. "Sir Henry," she lied.

Bree stared at her reflection in the mirrored glass over the washbasin. She had lied about St. Clair's name and the lie told her more than she really wanted to face at the moment. All these years, she had vehemently defended her reasons for clinging to an impossible dream. Now when it came to explaining the special relationship to strangers, her faith in St. Clair's promise was so weak that she felt the need to lie. Yet wasn't it more important to insure that the pirate didn't tell her beloved she had shared a bed with another?

No matter how hard she tried to justify her actions, tears filled her eyes at her own treachery. But there was no returning now. The pirate was right. By fleeing with him, she had closed the doors behind her. Her only hope was to reach Virginia and find St. Clair. But first, she had to get passage to America.

The pirate's solution had some merit. But, of course, it would never do to strike such a bargain with him. Besides, he had merely suggested it to harass her. Surely there were others traveling to America who would be overjoyed to obtain the services of a maid. Why, the Winghams had come clear across the ocean to obtain the services of Maddie's cousin to be governess to their daughters. And Miss Humphreys in *The Tattered Dream* had managed to support herself with such a position. Bree was certain she could handle the duties of a governess—or perhaps even that of a lady's maid—until she found St. Clair.

Her plan of action settled, Bree turned her efforts to making herself presentable. Using a damp cloth, she smoothed out the wrinkles of her rumpled gown as best she could. Her hair caused her the most problems. For the life of her, she couldn't coax the stubborn strands

PIRATES AND PROMISES 39

back into the wreath of curls, and the hair hanging loose about her shoulders only served to call attention to the truth of her seventeen years. Frustrated, she gathered the curls and secured them with a ribbon she had carefully removed from the front of her gown.

Now where did one go to seek a prospective employer? She would ask the pirate but she doubted he would be of much help. Other than sending up a breakfast tray for her, she had heard nothing from the man since morning.

Stay in the room, indeed! How did he think she was to find a way to Virginia sitting in her room? Where was he, anyway? More than likely out disposing of his ill-gotten gain.

His indifference to her concerns was disheartening, but what more could she expect from a highwayman? Like the heroine, Miss Humphreys, she would have to look to her own resources to find a position.

From the noises drifting up from the docks, there certainly should be enough merchants to whom she could present her plan. She would approach the ships' captains first. They would know who might be on their way to America.

With that goal in mind, Bree left the inn to seek an employer; but before she had gone very far the lascivious leers and crude remarks the men made cooled her optimism. Didn't they know better than to treat a lady so deplorably? With her head held high and a mutinous gleam in her eye, she marched by them. Bree refused to be deterred by the fear that churned in her stomach. She had to find a way to leave England, or she'd be forced to return home and marry the despicable Lord Foxworth.

It wasn't until she boarded the third ship that she learned from the chief mate of someone who might be able to assist her. Mr. Tremble, a wealthy merchant, and his family would be leaving for America in two days. Luck was with her. They were residing at the same inn.

Returning to the Duck and Ale, she sent a note up to the merchant, then took a table in the corner of the common room. It was difficult to ignore the whispers of the other occupants, but she focused her attention on the activities outside the window as she waited for Mr. Tremble to join her.

"Miss Smythe?" asked a round, little man who approached her.

She nodded that he take a seat, but he remained standing.

"I'm somewhat baffled by your note," he said, his cheeks suddenly flaming red between the muttonchop whiskers. "I did not advertise for a lady's maid."

Bree gave him a warm smile, hoping to put him at ease. "Sir," she began, "I find myself in an awkward position. I am without funds and it's imperative that I get to Virginia as soon as possible. I was hoping that you could assist me."

His friendly smile faded. "I do not lend money to strangers," he snapped.

"You misunderstand, Mr. Tremble. It would not be a loan. I am willing to work as your wife's maid until I've earned the cost of my passage."

The frown on his face told her the idea lacked sufficient appeal. "If you have children, sir, I would make an excellent governess. Or a nanny," she offered in hopes of changing his mind. "Sir, I will be willing to take any position you might have available. I must get to Virginia."

She was heartened by the sudden smile on his face.

Pulling out the chair across from her, he sat down. The frown he had worn until now curved up in a smile when he leaned forward. "Any position, you say?"

She lowered her eyes at his bold perusal. *He wonders if I'm too young for the position,* she thought. Drats, she hoped it wasn't that of a cook. With her inexperience, she'd be fortunate not to poison the family. But she couldn't afford to allow him the opportunity to question his decision.

She held out her hand to him. "We have an agreement then?"

The gesture appeared to cause him undue embarrassment and when he didn't take her hand, Bree dropped it back in

PIRATES AND PROMISES   41

her lap. "Sir," she said, her voice low as she leaned forward. "I must have this position."

Mr. Tremble mopped his damp brow and looked quickly around him. "Miss Smythe, this is not the place to discuss the particulars. My wife and daughter are shopping, but they might return at any moment. With it being my wife's birthday..."

He shrugged his shoulders as if that explained everything. Well, it certainly didn't explain anything to her. Americans were undoubtedly difficult to understand.

"Your wife's birthday?"

He searched the room behind him. "Yes," he finally said, "it wouldn't do for her to discover... you understand..."

A surprise? Of course, for his wife's birthday. Bree smiled brightly. "I understand perfectly," she said. "I'm willing to begin my duties at your convenience."

With a broad smile, he jumped out of his chair. "Give me a few hours to find a room, then..." He paused at Miss Smythe's apparent confusion. He must be handling this poorly. True, he was not accustomed to making such arrangements in this manner, but, all in all, her reaction was most baffling. "You do realize you can't stay here," he said. "My wife and all."

"Yes. Yes, of course. It wouldn't do to give it away."

"Excellent," he said, breathing a sigh of relief. Life had suddenly taken a wonderful turn. With a pretty little thing like Miss Smythe as his mistress, his associates would finally grant him the respect he deserved. What did it matter that his destination was New York and not Virginia?

"I'll leave a note with the innkeeper as soon as I've secured your room."

CHAPTER 3

....

JUSTIN wearily climbed the stairs to his room. After exercising the new mares in the morning, he'd spent the rest of the day trying to find Bree safe passage to America. It wasn't a simple task to find a suitable individual to act as companion to a young, unmarried girl, but he had finally stumbled onto the perfect solution. An elderly parson and his wife, along with their flock, were leaving for America within the week and, in less than four hours, the good parson would be coming to collect Bree. Justin would be more than relieved to relinquish his responsibility for the little spitfire.

A broad smile suddenly tipped the corners of his full lips. Having met the dour couple, he was hard-pressed to decide who would be more vexed with the arrangement—Bree or the parson and his wife.

When he opened his bedchamber door and discovered the room empty, the confident smile quickly died. Where was Bree? He searched the wardrobe and looked under the bed but she was nowhere to be found. A tight band of worry circled his chest. Surely she hadn't left the inn.

The thought sent Justin hurrying from his room and down the stairs. If she had, it might take him hours to find her and the *Seahawk* was due to sail at dawn. He had worries enough with Higgins being gone so long. But at least there was an excuse for his manservant's absence. He had to dispose of the jewels before he could distribute the funds among Quentin's tenants.

Justin slowly shook his head at his callous thoughts. Higgins could take care of himself. But Bree was a naïve young woman who would be free game for the riffraff that roamed the docks.

"Have you seen a young lady in a pink gown leave here?" he asked the startled innkeeper.

"I may have," the man answered smugly, a knowing grin lifting the corners of his thin lips.

Justin grabbed the front of the innkeeper's shirt. "Answer me!" he shouted. "I must find her."

With the gentleman's fingers tightening on his shirtfront, the innkeeper decided prudence might be the wisest tactic. "One moment, sir," he muttered as he stretched to reach beneath his counter. Finding what he wanted, he straightened. "The lady dropped this," he said.

Justin tore the note from the innkeeper's fingers. "Miss Smythe" was scrawled across the soiled paper.

"Will she be staying another night?" the innkeeper asked with a sly grin.

Having no wish to satisfy the innkeeper's curiosity as to the contents of the note, Justin stepped away before opening it. The words written across the cheap white parchment upset him more than he thought possible. Bree was to meet someone in the room overlooking the wharf at the Blue Maiden Inn.

A knot tightened in his stomach. The place was a haunt for prostitutes and drunken sailors. Why would Bree be meeting someone there? Only a fool would go there without a weapon to protect his back and his purse.

Before he set out, he checked the prime on his own pistol, then hurried from the inn. Bree was more than enough temptation for a gentleman to forget his manners. It didn't bear thinking of what would happen to her at an establishment such as the Blue Maiden. She would be gobbled up as a succulent morsel before she reached the stairs.

* * *

The wharf was busy with stevedores loading and unloading the ships and Justin had to fight his way between the livestock and large crates of merchandise.

"The little fool," he kept muttering to himself as he stepped around the lazy sailors that lounged against the doors of the taverns and shops. It would be a miracle if Bree even made it to the inn. Every type of lowlife he had ever come across appeared to have crawled from the alleyways.

As he stepped through the doors of the Blue Maiden, all his fears were realized. Everyone had gathered at the bottom of the stairs, their interest focused on the sounds coming from the bedchamber overhead.

Lewd calls followed Justin's progress as he shoved his way through the crowd and mounted the stairs. The Blue Maiden was known for its drunken brawls and the commotion should have netted not so much as a raised brow. Bree's entrance must have caused quite a stir to have captured everyone's attention.

Suddenly, all went quiet upstairs.

Justin hurried up the last of the steps and down the hall, checking each room as he went. When he finally pushed the door to the last room open, he found a short, stout merchant standing amidst a shower of coins, clutching his nose.

"You've bloodied it!" Tremble wailed.

A livid Bree faced the merchant. She leaned forward, her hands on her hips. "It's no more than you deserve for thinking I'd be anyone's mistress, much less yours!" she shouted with all the outrage of an indignant angel.

"You said you'd do anything for the price of passage," the merchant whined.

"A maid—or even a governess—yes, but not that," she screamed at him. "You're nothing but a lecherous old man to have thought otherwise."

Justin leaned against the doorjamb and crossed his arms over his chest. He couldn't for the life of him banish the smile that tipped the corners of his lips.

PIRATES AND PROMISES 45

"Do you intend to punch all of England before you leave?"

Bree spun around. "What are you doing here?"

"You dropped your sponsor's note."

"Mr. Tremble is not my sponsor," Bree hissed, turning to bestow another frown on the merchant.

"I'm not anymore," Tremble said as he stooped to gather his coins. "You may have her with my blessing."

Stepping forward, Bree placed her slippered foot on the merchant's hand. "You were never my sponsor," she said through clenched teeth. "And I'll thank you to remember that, my good man."

Tremble tried to pull away but Bree's foot held his hand tightly against the floorboards.

"You'll be leaving the coins, of course," she added, leaning down and fixing him with a stern eye.

"They're mine," Tremble protested.

"You brought me here under false colors, sir. For that you owe me my travel expenses."

The merchant's face reddened in anger. "What travel expenses?" he shouted. "The inn is down the way and you walked here."

Bree calmly set to placing the pleats of her gown in order. "I refuse to be penalized for a temporary shortage of funds," she said, squaring her shoulders. "Had I the coins, I would have hired a carriage and you would have had to reimburse me. Now kindly dispense with this petty bickering and hand me my money." She punctuated the request with a heavy stomp of her foot on his hand.

The man grunted but quickly gathered the coins with his free hand and offered them to her.

"Thank you, Mr. Tremble," she said sweetly after removing her foot and letting him rise.

The merchant hurried past Justin, a curse curling his lips.

"Inform your wife she has a new lady's maid," Bree shouted after him.

Justin pushed away from the doorframe. "Oh, no you

don't," he said. "You wouldn't make it out of port before he had you in his bed."

Bree raised her head from counting the coins. "I need not worry about that possibility now. I read a book, *The Handmaiden's Prayer*, in which Mr. Morton made unwanted advances to Lady Meade and Lady Meade threatened to tell his wife. Well, Mr. Morton left her to her duties quickly enough then."

"You're talking about a novel you've read?" he asked, somewhat confused.

"Yes, *The Handmaiden's Prayer*. Isn't that what I just said?"

"Trust me, Smythe, they don't put bounders such as Mr. Tremble in books for young ladies."

"Oh, but they did," she insisted. "There was Mr. Morton, then Mr. Williams. He was in—"

Justin grabbed her by the arm and pulled her from the room. Her hair, loosened from its ribbon, fanned about them, swirling over Justin's hand. The silkiness of it startled him, sending any number of his own lecherous thoughts spiraling through him. Unfortunately, he could think of a few romantic scenes himself. Upset that she could so easily discomfort him, Justin tugged all the harder at her arm.

"You read too many books, Smythe," he growled. "And until I can turn you over to someone I can trust, you're coming with me."

"No," she protested. When he didn't slow his pace, she was forced to tap him hard on the shoulder. "I need a room and this one was paid for."

He said nothing, but continued to tug at her arm. Certain he was bent on ignoring her wishes, Bree tapped harder. "Unhand me this minute, you . . . you . . . you pirate!"

At her careless use of his newly acquired identity, Justin stopped suddenly and Bree stumbled into his back. He turned to her, his eyes a dark green under his furrowed brow.

"I'll not leave you here for any drunken sot with the coin for a bribe to secure the key to your room. You may not have read that in one of your novels, but it would surely happen nonetheless. Now come along before I raise my hand to you."

Each time she recalled the cheer that had burst forth from the patrons of the Blue Maiden at the pirate's announcement, a warm blush flooded Bree's face. The man had embarrassed her for the last time. And, if that weren't insult enough, he had dragged her back to the Duck and Ale as if she were some misbehaving child. Then he had the gall to lock her in his servant's room.

Well, he needn't think this would change anything. She'd as soon work her way to Virginia scrubbing the decks of a ship rather than stay with him. But first, she would have to get out of this room.

After a careful search of the bedchamber, Bree realized the only way out was the window. She smiled to herself. It was what the heroine of *The Wayward Miss* had done. The pirate would not be so quick to ridicule her novels if he ever discovered how helpful they had become.

Determined that the distance from the window ledge to the cobbles below was not going to deter her, Bree ripped the sheets from the bed and tore them into narrow strips. Finished, she then tied them together in hopes of lowering herself to the ground. When the improvised rope proved to be a tad short of a safe escape, she tugged it back up and added the manservant's garments. That should be enough, she told herself before tossing it out the window. The triumphant smile quickly faded when the entire bundle slithered over the window's edge.

"Oh, no!" she cried, leaning out the window. In her enthusiasm to be gone, she had tossed the line out the window without securing the end to the bed. Frustrated, she watched as the cloth rope coiled on the ground below.

Upset with herself, she checked the drawers of the chest again in hopes of finding more of the manservant's clothes. But her efforts were of little use. Her inspection didn't even turn up so much as an extra stocking.

Bree tried the door again, but it was still locked. She pounded on the wood panels and screamed at the top of her lungs, but no one came. There was no telling what the pirate had told them belowstairs that caused them to ignore her cries for help. He had certainly called her enough uncomplimentary names on their way back from the Blue Maiden.

She raised her hand to strike the panels again when she heard a key turning in the lock. Surprised, she stepped back as the door swung open. A man, thin as a lake reed, stood with his mouth ajar at the sight of her.

"Well, tadpoles and turnip greens!" he exclaimed, finally recovering from the shock. "How did you get in here?"

With a quick curtsy, Bree breezed past him. "I've finished with the room, sir," she said, then paused outside the door. "Your bath should be up in a moment. You'll find the clean linens on the washstand."

A thought suddenly occurring to her, Bree paused in her flight. With a sweet smile on her lips, she turned back to the man. "If you toss your clothes out, I'll see that they're washed while you bathe."

"T-thank you," Higgins stammered. The staff had certainly improved since he had left that morning. A pretty chambermaid and a hot bath to boot. After being on the road since dawn, he could certainly make use of it. He began undressing.

Where was Higgins? Justin wondered for the hundredth time. The sun was beginning to set and the man had yet to return. And with Smythe on his hands, he didn't have time to look for his missing manservant.

His gaze scanned the common room once again. With nightfall, the Duck and Ale was beginning to fill. Thank goodness Bree's caterwauling had finally stopped. Another hour and the innkeeper would have demanded he remove her from the premises. It was upsetting enough that Bree's screams had scared off the parson and his wife, but he'd not appreciate having to spend his last night in England sleeping curled up on the docks.

PIRATES AND PROMISES 49

A smile touched Justin's lips. He had to admit, the lady might not use the best of judgment, but she had spunk. Miss Smythe and Quentin would never have survived a marriage. Bree was not one to conform to complete obedience in anything and Quentin demanded nothing less. Justin would have dearly loved to have witnessed the attempt at such a union. She'd have bloodied Quentin's nose for certain.

His smile suddenly faded to a frown when he envisioned her curled up in his bed. Not that he considered himself old at the age of three and twenty, but he couldn't recall the last time someone so young had struck his fancy. Damn, but the lady had an uncanny way of sneaking into his thoughts of late. Yet, what did he expect? The flawless cream of her complexion was what poets had waxed eloquent over for centuries. And her hair . . . like liquid gold.

Perhaps the memory of carrying her to his own room was still too fresh in his mind. When he held her in his arms, the light pink muslin of her gown did little to disguise her narrow waist or the ripe, full curves of a generous bosom. The thought of someone else casually availing themselves of those tantalizing attributes was enough to set his blood to boiling. It would be a sin to sample the fruit, then toss it aside. Smythe's charms warranted more than a quick tumble in the sheets. The passions he suspected were hidden deep within her needed the patience and experience of a competent lover to bring them to the surface, not the bumbling efforts of some insensitive clod.

Smythe was like a fine, spirited mare, he decided. She needed the guidance of a special handler to bring out her full potential. The delicate but firm hands of a groom to run the soft cloths over her long limbs. The . . .

Justin's mouth suddenly went dry and he motioned the barmaid for another drink. But the strong brew did not cool the fires building within him. He only had to close his eyes to feel again the silky strands of her hair wrapping him in a cloud of flaxen gold, and he knew that if he continued to dwell on the image the temptation to take her with him when his ship sailed in the morning would be too great to ignore.

"The supper tray is ready," the barmaid said as she refilled his glass. "Do you wish me to take it up to the young lady?"

"No!"

When the maid frowned at his sharp reply, Justin tossed her a coin to apologize for his bad manners. "I'll take it up myself," he said, then lowered his voice and added, "She's having another bad day."

The maid smiled her understanding. The lie about the fragile condition of Bree's sanity had spread quickly through the staff. He knew it hadn't been the gentlemanly thing to do, but he couldn't trust Bree to stay in the room.

By the time Justin had finished his drink, the maid had returned with Bree's supper tray. Justin squared his shoulders and started up the stairs. Taking the tray to Bree was a waste of time. Since he had left her to fume in Higgins's room, he knew where it would end up. On him. But he had to at least make the effort.

All was quiet when he stopped outside Higgins's door. He pulled out the key and inserted it into the lock, but before turning it, he tapped lightly on the heavy oak door.

"Smythe?" he called. "Smythe, I have—"

The door opened suddenly and Higgins peeked from behind it. "I thought you'd never come," he muttered accusingly.

Justin pushed his way into the room and set the tray on the stand beside the bed. "What are you doing in here? And where's Bree?"

"If you mean that pretty little wench in the pink gown, she took my clothes."

"She did wh—" It was then Justin noticed that Higgins remained behind the door. "Come out here, man," he ordered. "We don't have time for this tomfoolery. I've got to find that woman before she takes it in her head to turn me in to the authorities."

PIRATES AND PROMISES 51

Higgins inched from behind the door, his face a bright red. "She took my fancy breeches, she did."

"You let her take your clothes?"

Higgins hung his head and mumbled, "She tricked me."

He looked so pathetic standing there that Justin knew he couldn't give vent to the laughter that threatened to erupt. "Well, hurry and dress," he said, coughing discreetly into his hand. "You can't expect to get them back hiding in this room."

"She took all my clothes," Higgins mumbled.

"At least cover yourself until I can find something for you."

"With what?" he bellowed. "She pitched everything out the window, I tell you. The linens, the counterpane. Even the rug by my bed."

"Everything?" Justin frowned as he took in the stripped bed. "I'll get something from my room."

"I doubt you have much left yourself," Higgins said solemnly as Justin turned to leave.

Justin started for the window, but Higgins stopped him. "No point in looking. Some alley waif carried them off over an hour ago."

Justin left Higgins's room, but in a few moments he was back carrying a bundle of clothes and the rope of sheets Bree had used to lower herself from Justin's window. "That little she-devil tossed everything but the highwayman's costume," he ranted, pacing the narrow room and waving the dark trousers. "She knows good and well I can't make use of these. Not while everyone's searching the countryside for the pirate."

He stopped in front of Higgins. "The *Seahawk* will be carrying another passenger when she sails, Higgins. The lady wants to work her way to America, does she? Well, I suddenly find I have need of a maid. A blue-eyed, golden-haired maid. Passage, for a contract of indenture. She won't be wiggling out of the agreement either. I'll draw up the papers myself while the innkeeper finds something for you to wear." His green eyes darkened. "We'll not return until we find her and get the papers signed, and you can damn well wager your last coin that the signature on them will be hers."

They searched for Bree most of the night. Justin roused innkeepers from their beds and drunks from their sleep, but no one had seen her. As a last resort, he returned to the Duck and Ale and dragged the lecherous merchant from his sleep, demanding he tell them where he had hidden Bree. Mr. Tremble swore his innocence and Justin believed him.

But where was he to look now? The first pale light of a false dawn was already painting the eastern sky. He would have to supervise the loading of the mares soon. What would he do if they hadn't found Smythe by the time the *Seahawk* was scheduled to sail? He couldn't just leave her here. If they didn't find her soon, he would have to send Higgins ahead with the horses.

He raked his fingers through his hair. Was it possible she had decided to return home? If you kept to the old road, Southampton was not that far away. But it did not ease his conscience. She would have been better off married to Quentin than she was roaming the docks—or the dark countryside. As soon as his mares were loaded aboard the *Seahawk*, he would go to Southampton.

A foot nudged her backside and Bree awoke with a start.

"Best get a move on," one of the older stableboys called to her. "Lord Richards will be 'ere before ye wipe the sleep out of yer eyes and 'e'll be wanting that fine stallion of 'is ready."

Bree crawled out of her bed of straw and, with a mournful groan, stumbled to her feet. The stall of a public stable was not the most comfortable of bedchambers, but at least she'd had the place to herself.

She stretched her weary bones and glanced to the small window. It wasn't even light yet. Why couldn't Lord

Richards wait until she'd gotten a decent night's sleep? Didn't he realize she would function a great deal more efficiently once she'd rested properly?

Catching the lad eyeing her suspiciously, Bree lifted her hands to her woolen cap. She was relieved to find it was still in place. "What are you staring at?" she demanded.

"Yer a girl," the lad accused.

Bree's eyes dropped to the front of her coat. It was open and her breasts pushed shamefully against the thin cotton shirt beneath. She should never have unbuttoned the jacket but her breasts had ached so at the restraint. Why did the pirate's manservant have to be so painfully thin?

Bree looked back to the stableboy, her eyes narrowing as she took stock of him. She'd lose her new position for sure if the lad went to Lord Richards.

Lowering her voice as best she could, she shoved her face close to his. "Ain't you ever seen a freak o' nature before?" she growled.

The lad's eyes widened. "Ye mean, yer a boy and you growed a pair of apple dumplings?"

"A family curse, it is," she said boldly. "Goin' to have the cutter chop them off soon as I get the coin."

"Oh," he breathed, his mouth as round as his eyes. "I never seen a boy what be a woman afore."

When he reached out to touch her breasts, Bree reacted without thinking.

"Ow!" he bellowed, holding his nose. "Why did ye do that?"

She squared her shoulders in indignation. "You'd not touch a woman's breasts and I'll not 'ave you touching mine."

The lad backed off from the note of authority in her voice.

"And you'll not be telling anyone about me breasts," she added as she fastened the edges of her coat. "Have to keep me job if I'm ever to be rid of them."

The boy reluctantly agreed. He started to tell the lad he'd pay the ha'penny he'd been saving to get a glimpse of them, but remembered his nose and thought better of it. But he found his eyes following the lad as he tended to his chores.

His constant attention was wearing on Bree's nerves as she pulled the leather halter over the stallion's neck. What would he say if he noticed her slippers beneath the overlong breeches? She had been fortunate to have been hired to watch over Brutus. The big bay stallion had been trying his handler's skills when Bree spotted them yesterday. Anyone with half a brain could see the man was afraid of the horse. Unfortunately, Brutus knew it also and was taking advantage of the fact to test the groom's mettle.

Bree loved animals and detested the spoiling of the big bay by the incompetent handler. Before she took the time to think of the consequences, she had hurried up to the horse and grabbed the reins. Within moments, the animal was quieted and Bree was hired onto Lord Richards's staff.

It scared her to think if she hadn't come along when she did yesterday, she might have been forced to return to the pirate. The unsettling effect he had on her was more frightening than the antics of the stallion.

"Will ye be going to Jamaica with Lord Richards?" the stableboy asked.

Jamaica wasn't Virginia, but at least it was closer than she was now. "Brutus be me work now," she answered. "I'll be going with 'im."

"I'd 'elp ye with the brute but I've got me own 'orses to tend to," he said. "There be a wee bit o' grain in the large bins. Lord Richards done paid 'ard coin for the privilege o' boarding and graining, so ye've a right to it."

Bree waited until the lad was busy with his own chores before selecting a small wooden bucket from one of the shelves overhead. Filled with dust, discarded cloths, and bits of broken harness, it was obvious the pails weren't put to much use. Bree made her way to the back of the stables and dumped the contents of the bucket onto the pungent-smelling mixture of straw and manure someone had piled by the door. Using the sleeve of her borrowed jacket, she wiped the bucket clean, but she soon found she needn't have bothered. The grain wasn't much better.

PIRATES AND PROMISES

Bree sifted the dust and chaff out as best she could before scooping a small amount of oats into the bucket.

The bay had been watching her progress and nickered softly when she approached his stall. "A light breakfast for you this morning," she whispered to the stallion as she reached up to rub his neck. "Hopefully the quality of the ship's fare will be worth the wait, boy."

Bree picked up a soft cloth and rubbed the horse's coat while he ate. By the time she finished, Lord Richards's man had arrived with her instructions. She was to take Brutus to where the *King's Lady* was docked. Once she had him aboard, the ship's crew would see to the stallion's confinement below deck.

If she could hide the fact that she was a woman until the ship sailed, it wasn't likely they would throw her overboard at that point. With no way to be rid of her, she could surely convince them that her talent for being able to handle the big stallion was worth the price of her passage.

Bree tied the lead rope to the bay's halter. His ears pricked forward as he watched her out of the corner of his eye. By the time they were ready to leave, the stallion seemed to be all manners. Bree called softly to him and he stepped in behind her. It was difficult to believe this was the same horse who had sorely tried the groom's patience only last evening.

Despite the early hour, the docks were busy. Bree worried that the noise would upset the bay. Yet he didn't appear to notice. She stopped a stevedore to ask directions to where the *King's Lady* was docked, but Brutus's constant circling made it difficult for Bree to concentrate on the directions. And when the bay reached down to nip at her, she barely managed to step out of his way before his teeth closed on the shoulder of her coat. The bad manner of the night before returned.

"Enough, my fine friend," she scolded. "We'll be there soon."

But the large horse continued to tug impatiently, almost anxiously, at her tight hold on the lead rope and Bree's arms began to ache at the strain. If not for the crowded dock, she would have never been able to hold him. A shame there wasn't the time or the place for a hard ride. The bay certainly needed something to take the edge off his pent-up energy.

Suddenly Brutus stopped his circling. The large bay stared over the heads of the crowd, his body trembling. Bree went to his head, but even that didn't appear to calm him. Something down the way had captured his interest and, whatever it was, it had the bay's full attention. She reached up to stroke his nose.

"It's all right, boy. I'm here. Nothing's going to hurt you."

His eyes widened and he tossed his head. Bree quickly scanned the docks to see what had upset the horse, but there was only the hurried activity of the loading and unloading of the ships. Why would that suddenly bother the horse?

The bay stood trembling beside her, the cool morning breeze off the water whipping through his mane. All her calming words had no effect. Before she could stop him, he rose on his hind legs, pulling the lead rope from her fingers. His wild scream pierced the air. It was a scream filled with hatred and it curled around Bree's heart.

She reached for the rope as he came down, seizing it only moments before his hooves touched the wood planks of the docks. He lunged forward and Bree was forced to run with him. Angry shouts were hurled at her from both sides as workers jumped out of the path of the big stallion.

The docks were too crowded for the bay to get into his stride but Bree was having the devil's own time keeping up with him. Desperately she clung to the rope as she ran by his side. Stumbling now would mean falling under the crushing power of his hooves. Just when she thought she would have to let go of the rope, he stopped and Bree found herself amidst a small herd of startled mares.

Again, the stallion reared and issued his savage cry.

The dock noises hushed as everyone turned to watch the enraged beast.

"Secure the bellyband and get Nighthawk into the hold.

I can't risk a fight now," she heard a familiar voice shout. "I'll take care of the mares."

Bree froze. The pirate's stallion stood poised on the deck of one of the ships. Despite the cross-ties his handlers had on his halter and the huge leather band that circled his powerful girth, the big black stallion rose on his haunches and issued his own shrill challenge to the newcomer.

There was no holding Brutus. He pulled the rope from Bree and charged through the frightened mares.

"Get that horse in the hold!" Justin shouted again as he hurried down the gangplank to head off the rogue stallion. He was almost to the bottom when he realized he had no weapon.

The bubbling tar pots hanging over the hot brazier at the edge of the dock drew his attention. The rank substance was used to seal the decks of the ships which anchored at the busy port and the pots were seldom left to cool. Grabbing a long stick from the hot fire, Justin waved the flaming torch at the stallion.

Bree held her breath as Brutus slid to a stop in front of the tall pirate. The bay screamed his fury as the black stallion was hustled from sight. Rising once more on his haunches, he struck out at the torch, but with the odoriferous tar replacing the scent of the other stallion, Brutus soon lost interest in getting past the pirate. He turned instead to claim his mares. Boldly he circled his scattered harem.

Now was Bree's opportunity. She would get the lead rope while the mares distracted his attention. While careful to keep her back to the pirate, lest he recognize her, Bree moved slowly toward the stallion.

Justin gripped the torch in his hand. What was the lad thinking? Only a fool would try to step between the stallion and his prize before the bay's temper cooled. He tossed the dying torch aside and grabbed a whip from one of the sailors who had helped with the mares.

"Stay back, boy!" he shouted as he made his way around the mares.

But the mares were frightened by the bay and Justin soon

found himself caught in the middle of the restless herd. Across the backs of the mares, he could see the lad had fallen to the same fate. If he didn't reach the boy soon, they'd both be trampled.

The fury of the stallion at the invasion of his herd only served to excite the mares further. Before Justin could get to the lad, the boy stumbled and almost fell. Justin gasped at the soft golden curls that tumbled from the woolen cap.

"Smythe!" he shouted. "Get out of there!"

But the stallion's attention was also drawn to Bree. The mares were his and he wasn't about to stand idly by while they were taken from him. His fury was kindled anew and he pushed his way into the herd.

Ears laid back, he savagely bit at the mare that blocked his path. She squealed in pain and bolted past Bree.

With the mare gone, Bree stood facing the bay. Alone. She stared back at the giant stallion. His eyes were those of a demon, his nostrils flaring with hatred. There would be no calming the stallion with soft words this time. He was crazed with his need to claim the mares.

Bree's cry of anguish caught in her throat as the stallion reared above her. She closed her eyes; but, before the hooves could reach her, someone pushed her aside.

She opened her eyes again to find the pirate driving the bay back with a short whip.

"Fetch someone to get the mares on board," he shouted at Bree, but she couldn't take her eyes off the battle before her.

Stubborn determination was pitted against raw hatred as the tall man faced the huge animal. Warily they circled one another, each looking for their opportunity.

The bay finally lunged, his teeth bared.

Tossing the whip to Bree, Justin stepped to one side and grabbed the stallion's halter. With the grace of a dancer, he swung up onto the bay's broad back.

The crowd roared its approval and even Bree had to admit she was impressed at the ease with which he had taken command of the situation.

"What goes here?" a man demanded as he stepped forward. "What are you doing atop my horse?" He turned and searched the crowd. "And where's my stable lad?"

Justin was having his own problems keeping the bay calm and was losing his patience. "Only a fool hires a boy to care for a rogue such as this," Justin tossed back.

Lord Richards drew his shoulders back in indignation. "Brutus is no rouge."

"Come take charge of him, then."

Lord Richards's face pinked. "A-as s-soon as I find my lad," he stuttered.

Justin leaned over the horse's neck and snarled, "You either take charge of this animal now or I'll order my man to drop him where he stands."

Lord Richards paled at the sound of a hammer being pulled pack on a pistol. "You'd shoot my horse?" he wailed.

Justin glanced over the man's shoulder at his manservant. "Higgins, hand me my pistol."

"O-oh, but you mustn't!" Lord Richards blustered.

Bree couldn't let this happen. Brutus getting loose was all her fault. She hurried up to the pirate. "The bay is my responsibility, sir."

Justin straightened and arched a questioning brow at the gentleman. "You let a mere slip of a girl handle your mounts?"

Lord Richards felt his face grow warm. Except for the long hair, the wench did look a lot like the lad he had hired last evening.

"Lord Richards," Bree pleaded. "Don't listen to him. I can handle Brutus."

Justin smiled down at her. "Indeed, you've just demonstrated as much."

"Brutus was the perfect gentleman until your mares—" Bree clamped her mouth shut.

Justin's grin broadened at the pink glow of embarrassment that stained her cheeks. "Until my mares what?"

The man was beyond anyone she had ever met. He knew she needed this position if she was ever to get to Virginia.

"Until your mares cast a—a lustful craving on him," she blurted out, her blush deepening.

Justin threw back his head in laughter and those close enough to hear joined in.

Bree turned to Lord Richards. "Please, my lord, I must have this job."

Lord Richards only stared at her. His hope that the lad would appear and take Brutus in hand crumbled. He'd look all the more a fool to turn the stallion over to this girl.

A short, shabbily dressed servant moved past him and handed a pistol up to the tall man on his horse. Lord Richards stepped forward. Now that Brutus had calmed, he'd have no trouble getting him to the ship. "You'll not be shooting him now, will you?"

Those dark green eyes bored through to his soul.

"Give me a reason not to."

Lord Richards didn't care for the way the man's lips slid so easily into a sneer. "I'll see to him myself."

"I've decided that's not sufficient," Justin said. "The horse attacked me. He's uncontrollable."

Bree stepped around Lord Richards. Letting her anger get the best of her, she glared up at the pirate on the horse. If Brutus were destroyed because of her, she would never forgive herself. It galled her to know the pirate was more than likely aware of it too. She had half a mind to threaten to reveal his identity, but highwaymen were hanged.

"Sir, there's no reason to shoot him now," she stated instead.

The stallion danced under Justin's tight hold but Bree refused to back away. It was plain to see she felt responsible for what had happened. Justin smiled to himself. A gentleman would never take advantage of a woman in distress, but when had he ever considered himself the gentleman?

"The papers I drew up, Higgins," he snapped. "And a quill and ink."

CHAPTER 4

BREE held the papers clenched tightly in her fist. "And if I refuse to sign them?"

Justin cocked the pistol. "Then I shoot the horse and you're left without a position."

"She doesn't have one now," Lord Richards protested loudly. While most of the time he was afraid of the bay, he didn't want the horse destroyed. The stallion had cost him a small fortune. "I'll pay you for any damages, just give over my mount."

Bree chewed thoughtfully on her lip as she studied the pirate. His green eyes hadn't wavered once since he had met her gaze. He didn't even appear to care that he was upsetting Lord Richards, and she found herself again comparing the tall, dark man to St. Clair. A foolish notion, to be sure, for there could be no comparison. The St. Clair she remembered would never be anything but a gentleman and the pirate would always be a rogue. Much like the stallion. But would the pirate truly kill the horse? The stubborn set of his jaw told her she'd best not call his bluff.

Her eyes dropped once more to the papers. He expected her to sign them. A seven-year indenture. Her only consolation was that he would then be obliged to take her to America.

Her blue eyes narrowed. "You can make me sign these now, but as soon as we reach America, I intend to buy back my freedom. Is that understood?"

It was difficult not to smile at her naïveté. There was no doubt in his mind that she thought her lover would provide the coin to purchase her papers. She didn't realize he intended to keep her so busy she'd never have the opportunity to search for her betrothed. He laid down the pistol and nodded his agreement.

At Justin's acquiescence to her unlikely demand, Higgins quickly dipped the quill into the crystal bottle of ink he had borrowed from the captain and handed it to Bree. Seeing her confusion as to where to set the papers as she signed them, Higgins bent in front of her and offered his back.

She was a right sassy miss and she may have ruffled Tyler's feathers, but Higgins held no grudge. She was the first woman he had known who stirred something other than indifference and contempt in Tyler, and Justin's grandfather had certainly paraded enough of them through Havenwood. The old viscount would be pleased that someone other than the spoiled Miss Regina Wingham had caught Justin's attention.

"I allowed ye to talk me into reoutfitting me ship to suit yer needs and those of yer horses, Mr. Tyler, but I'll not be taking a woman aboard me ship!" the captain bellowed. "And that's that."

Bree couldn't hide her grin at the sight of the two men—one tall and one short—facing off. If not for the fact that the pirate needed the ship, she was positive he would have had no qualms about reaching over and squashing the captain like a troublesome gnat.

An early morning breeze ruffled the pirate's dark hair and it set Bree to wondering what it would be like to run her fingers through the thick black curls. Justin Tyler. Even knowing his name, she still thought of him as the pirate. She smiled openly at the withering glance he tossed her way.

It would take more than that to dispel the fantasy that had taken over her thoughts.

Her eyes dropped to his mouth. Surely Nanny's dire warning about kissing a man was nonsense. Although the pirate's scowl matched that of the ugly captain's, the man remained disturbingly handsome and Bree found her thoughts sensually tracing the edges of his full lips. A shame she'd felt the need to punch him before she'd had a chance to feel the firmness of them against hers.

"She'll be no trouble," Justin lied.

The captain stubbornly crossed his arms over his broad chest. "Trouble or no, a woman's bad luck aboard a ship. With all her sashaying atop the decks and her feminine ways, she'll be a distraction to the crew and I'll not be risking me vessel for no man."

"How much will it take to lay your superstitions to rest, Captain Tibbs?" Justin asked calmly. He then stood quietly until the man had finished with his spitting and sputtering. Pulling out his coin purse, Justin poured a large portion of the contents into the captain's hand.

"A woman's still a curse to any ship," he argued. But with the gold in his fingers, his earlier conviction had gone out of his words.

One by one, Justin added more coins to the offer and Tibbs greedily licked his lips as he watched the pile grow.

"Me men won't like it," he said.

With another withering glance directed at Bree, Justin plopped the remaining contents of the purse into the captain's large fist. "Perhaps the sharing of a few of these will alleviate their concerns."

After pouring the coins into his own purse, Tibbs quickly tucked them into the front of his shirt. "Their concerns be damned! The *Seahawk* be me ship and they'll do as I say."

Bree didn't know whether to be relieved or distressed at the pirate's success. To be sure, she'd get to America, but how much humble pie would she be required to eat on the way? If the pirate's scowl was any indication, she'd be as fat as a Christmas goose by the time they reached the shore.

The pirate pulled at her coat sleeve. "We'd best get you below deck before Tibbs has a change of heart."

Adopting a subservient attitude, Bree followed him meekly across the deck to the stairs that led below. He didn't hesitate, but grabbed the rail and began climbing down. Bree peered over the edge. The steps were nothing more than a crude ladder leading down into darkness.

"What are you waiting for?" he shouted up at her.

Bree stepped over onto the rung. She hated heights with a passion, but she'd not let him know. She tossed her small bag over the edge. With a deep breath, she closed her eyes tight and scurried down into the cavernous hole. Her foot coming down on a suspicious lump stopped her cold.

"Damnation!" Justin bellowed from below as he pulled his hand out from beneath her slippered foot.

Bree lost her tenuous foothold. Frantic, she wrapped her arms around the ladder and clung for dear life. She was going to die. Even now, she could feel her hold slipping. She was being sucked down to her death without ever having seen St. Clair again.

"Will you let go so I can help you down!" Justin said as he continued to pull at her.

Bree opened her mouth and let go with a bloodcurdling scream. "I'm falling. I'm going to die."

Justin stepped up another rung and reached up to pry her fingers loose. "I won't let you fall," he coaxed. "But you have to release the ladder if I'm ever to get you down."

"I'll die," she wailed.

Carefully, he moved up until he had his body wrapped around hers. "Trust me. I'll not let you die."

Bree looked back over her shoulder. "You promise?" she demanded.

He grinned at her. "Why would I let you fall and give up the right I've reserved to murder you on my own?"

Excellent, he thought. The fire was back in those blue

eyes. "Now we'll move together, Smythe," he said. "With each step I take, you take one also."

The secure feeling of being cradled against him helped ease the tension in Bree and she unwrapped her arms from the ladder. He took the first step, but when his lean body moved slowly down hers, she gasped with a different fear. Her entire being tingled with a mixture of strange emotions. Emotions that raced unchecked through her.

"Now, you step down," he prompted her.

She took another deep breath, then lowered her foot to the next rung. It seemed so natural to slip into the snug cocoon his body formed for her. Yet, the thoughts that tumbled through her head were anything but familiar.

"Now I shall step down," he whispered.

His words were a warm caress against her ear, but somehow Bree managed to follow his lead. With each sensual brush of their bodies, she found it more and more difficult to keep her thoughts from straying to forbidden fantasies. By the time they reached the bottom, Bree was a bundle of contradictory emotions. The old fears Nanny had instilled in her warred with the new desire.

When Bree turned from the ladder, the pirate didn't step back and she found herself caught against his broad chest. Instinctively, she knew that to raise her eyes to meet those compelling green ones of his would be a mistake, but before she could review the possible consequences she found herself drawn to them. Even in the dim light that came from the small opening above, they had a startling effect on her.

Her mouth suddenly went dry and her heart seemed to pick up a beat, then thundered uncontrollably against her ribs when he reached out to undo the fastenings on her coat. Mesmerized, she could do nothing but watch him. When he finished, he tucked his hands under the edges of the borrowed coat. Slowly he ran his fingers across the outline of her collarbone, then pushed the woolen garment from her shoulders and down the length of her arms. By the time it fell to the floor, Bree found she was holding her breath in anticipation, for he had kindled a fire in her every bit as bright as the one that blazed in his seductive eyes.

She trembled as he lowered his head to hers. Despite the unbridled desire in his eyes, his lips touched hers with a gentleness that surprised her. Entranced, Bree slid her hands up his muscled arms and behind his neck. Despite all the warnings Nanny had beaten into her, Bree boldly returned the kiss.

With a soft moan, Justin gathered her to him. She felt so good, he thought, as he slid his hands down her slim back. Not even Higgins's shirt could hide the ripe curves of her young body. It was rare for a woman's kisses to set his heart racing so. Hungrily, he crushed her to him.

Bree stiffened at his tight hold and attempted to pull away. Yet he didn't release her. With the expertise of a master, he nibbled at the edge of her lips. To be sure, she was enjoying the kisses; but when he moved his hips wantonly against hers, she knew it was like the bay with the mares. She'd thrown a lusting on him she might find a bit difficult to control. Even so, there surely had to be more to losing one's virtue than an innocent kiss.

But instinct told her there was nothing innocent about the pirate's kisses. Was a kiss all it took to become a fallen woman? Bree moaned at the thought.

When their kiss deepened, Bree's entire body tingled with the unfamiliar longings. Determined to put an end to the seductive downfall of her reputation, she turned her head from the pirate, but he merely moved his lips to her exposed ear.

This was nothing like the novels she and Maddie had smuggled into the house to read. His whispered breath was sending enticing little chills dancing up and down her body and the temptation to let him continue was strong. But even without Nannie's warning, she had read enough of the books to know that if the heroine let a man take too many liberties before marriage, something awful would befall her. It was never too clear what the liberties were, but his bold touch more than enlightened her as to what they might be.

Even now his hands had found their way under her shirt.

Panic seized her as his hand covered her breast. She would have to put a stop to this. But it was so difficult to concentrate with the waves of delicious anticipation that coursed through her.

Bree suddenly stiffened. What would she do if she were to find herself in the family way? Wasn't that why the heroes and heroines of her books always married after they kissed?

The pirate would never marry her. Highwaymen never married. She was certain there must be some kind of highwayman's code that said they were never to take a wife.

But in spite of her growing anxieties, when Justin lowered his mouth to her open shirt, Bree couldn't hold back the moan of pleasure that escaped her lips. Somewhere in her mind she could still hear the sounds of activity overhead. Footsteps hurrying back and forth, shouts of command, yet she remained lost in time at the base of the ladder, cradled in the pirate's embrace while he had his way with her.

This must be part of his code, a distant portion of her mind whispered when he swept her up in his arms and carried her down the dark companionway to the room at the end. Weren't highwaymen required to take helpless women to their beds and have their way with them? She was sure she had read that very thing somewhere.

The thought that she was one of many somehow did not sit well with her, yet she couldn't manage the words to tell him to put her down. Instead, she laid her hand on his broad chest, enjoying the emotions that laced her body with forbidden desire.

When they reached the cabin, the pirate kicked the door shut behind them, then stood her on the floor beside the bed. As if he could read the doubts that still gnawed at her, he bent over her and laid a moist trail of persuasive kisses along her neck and into her hair. Before she could gather her thoughts, she found her arms around his neck once more, her body leaning boldly against his. She gasped as his teeth bit into the sensitive lobe of her ear.

Her heart thundered against his. Good heavens, what if he planned to ravish her? Why, he might be raping her this very moment and she was too inexperienced to realize it!

Any fool knew that no matter how intriguing the experience might be, you didn't allow a man to rape you. Why, it was the most awful of awful things that could happen to a young lady.

She dug her fingernails deep into his back. She had to get him to stop. Highwayman code or not, he had wreaked havoc with her emotions long enough.

"Yes, my little golden witch," he whispered in her ear, his hand once more seeking her breast. "Let me see those fires you keep hidden so well."

Bree opened her mouth to protest but before she could get a word out, he covered her parted lips with his. The kiss was no longer a gentle teasing thing, but a devouringly seductive act that left her weak and trembling in his arms.

Bree was shaken by the devastating effect it was having on her will to put a stop to this. Even though the memory of Nanny's beating threatened to choke her, she was too overwhelmed to fight what he offered. With a cold chill of recollection, Bree flinched as the whip of her childhood struck her over and over again in her mind. A kiss. A child. A kiss. A child.

Just when she thought there was nothing more the pirate could do to her, his tongue slid into her mouth. Sensually, it teased, alternately coaxing, then exploring the depths. Bree found her own tongue mating with his as she welcomed his bold caresses, hoping they would shut out the hurtful images of an earlier punishment.

Despite her efforts to shut out the memory, a tear slipped quietly down her cheek, leading the way for others to follow. There was no help for her now. She was a fallen woman. She had betrayed St. Clair. Sweet, gentle, sensitive St. Clair. And if she didn't stop this soon, she would be left with a child with no father—just like the upstairs maid.

Justin pulled away. "Why are you crying?" he demanded.

"You won't marry me," she blubbered.

Justin's green eyes snapped angrily. "Why the hell should I marry you?"

"T-to g-give our child a name," Bree answered between sobs.

He grabbed her by the shoulders and held Bree from him. "What child!" he bellowed.

Placing her hands on her hips, Bree lifted her tearstained face up to his. "You were about to rape me and you can ask that?"

Justin dropped his hands from her shoulders. "Rape?" he asked, confused. Child? What on earth was she talking about? Could it be her "betrothed" had left her pregnant, and she was wanting to accuse him?

At the sudden narrowing of the pirate's eyes, Bree choked back her words. He looked angry enough to strangle her.

Justin grabbed the edges of her shirt and pushed it from her shoulders. Her breasts were full, the nipples still swollen. She tried to step away, but he pulled her roughly to him, his hand plunging into the band of her breeches to examine the validity of her claim. He'd not have her shoving her bastard off on him.

Despite his anger, he could still feel the stirrings of passion when his fingers caught in her tangle of curls as his hand swept low across her belly. If she were with child, she had yet to show the signs. Her stomach was firm, but flat.

"How long has it been since you were with your lover?" he demanded, removing his hand.

Nanny *had* spoken the truth. A kiss had gotten her pregnant. She could see it in his eyes. The warmth of embarrassment flooded her and she pulled the edges of her shirt together.

"How dare you!" she screamed up at him. "Any child I had would be yours, not St. C—"

Bree bit down on her lip. She could not believe how close she had come to telling him of St. Clair. The pirate's face was livid with anger.

"St. Clair? You're carrying Foxworth's child?"

A wrenching disappointment twisted Justin's gut. The

child was Quentin's. "Perhaps I should send you back to him."

Bree's relief that he had mistakenly thought her slip was a reference to the earl was short-lived at his solution to her dilemma. He meant to return her to Lord Foxworth.

"No! Oh, please no," Bree begged. "You cannot mean to leave me here with him."

"You'll drop your foolish claim that your child is mine?"

Bree lowered her eyes from the anger she saw in his. It didn't matter if the pirate stubbornly refused to claim his responsibility for the kiss. She could never marry the earl. Not even to give a child a name.

"Y-yes," she reluctantly agreed.

Justin closed the stall door on the mare. "She'll be needing some of your special salve, Higgins. That bay left an ugly gash on her right side."

"I'll get to it as soon as I secure this last mare."

Justin widened his stance to brace himself for the swell that rocked the ship. The captain had waited only until the last horse was lowered into the hold before he shouted instructions to weigh anchor. It had taken all of their efforts to get the frightened mares into the row of stalls that ran the length of the hold before the ship had reached the rough waters outside the snug harbor.

The welfare of the mares should be his first concern, yet Justin's thoughts kept straying back to Bree. He could still feel the warmth of her in his arms, the softness of her lips, the honey sweetness of her mouth, the way her full breast filled the palm of his hand.

"Damn!" he cursed under his breath. He should have set her ashore. To spirit away Quentin's bride-to-be was one thing, but to deny him the knowledge of his own child was quite another.

Although this sudden surge of conscience where his half brother was concerned baffled him, Justin couldn't get past the fact that by assisting Bree in her escape, he had also robbed the child of its birthright. At one time in his life

Justin had foolishly coveted what Quentin had. Now Bree was denying her child the same riches.

Justin tossed down the cloths he had used to clean the cut on the frightened mare. Someone needed to show Bree the error of her ways and it might as well be him.

Bree studied herself in the silvered glass over the washbasin as her mind reevaluated her dilemma. Surely Nanny had to be mistaken. Yet, Nanny was not the only one to have hinted at such a thing. What of the upstairs maid who had gotten in the family way and everyone had whispered how she was seen kissing the footman only days before she was condemned as a fallen woman? But Maddie had said the maid shouldn't be held accountable for falling victim to a man's kisses and had insisted the girl be allowed to keep her position.

A noise at the door drew her attention. Bree spun around to face the tall figure she saw silhouetted in her mirror.

Ask him, she told herself. He would surely know. Yet, she couldn't make herself say the words that might betray her ignorance—and youth. Better to maintain the facade of a woman of experience.

"Oh, it's you," she said with a casual air she was far from feeling.

"Yes, it's me," Justin growled. Taking her by the arm, he pulled her over to the bed and sat her down. "I don't want you saying a word until you've listened to what I have to say."

Despite the fierce scowl he bestowed on her, Bree nodded politely. It was obvious that after some thought, he had decided marriage was the honorable thing to do, even for a highwayman.

"Foxworth may not be the best choice of husbands," he began.

Bree's blue eyes narrowed.

"But you must think of your child," he continued. "Quentin is wealthy and if the child is a boy, there's the title to consider."

Her fists clenched, Bree stood to face him. "You wish me to pass yo—"

"But you said—"

"No, you said," she shouted up at him, her fist punctuating the statement on his chest.

Justin backed down from her fury. "Then who is the father?"

Bree clamped her mouth shut. She'd not give him the opportunity to laugh at her. "You can believe me when I say any child I had would not be the Earl of Foxworth's."

"Whoever the father might be, you must make him own up to his responsibilities. You cannot cheat your child out of all his father can give him."

Bree eyed his nose thoughtfully, thoroughly confused but not willing to let on.

"You needn't fret," she said bitterly. "The father has no wealth to give a child." Her blue eyes ruthlessly raked his tall frame. "And no prospects for any in the future."

Odd, how one look from her had him feeling like a child who had just been caught pulling off the wings of a beautiful butterfly. He did not appreciate the role she had cast him in.

Justin cupped her defiant chin in his hand. "Fortunate for you I am obligated to see to your well-being for the next seven years."

Bree did not care for the broad grin that curved his sensual lips as he calmly turned and left the room. Determinedly, she swallowed the hot tears that burned the back of her throat as she reached up and removed the locket. With a trembling sigh, she stuffed it in the bag with her dress. The pirate didn't even realize his kiss had destroyed her dreams. She could never marry St. Clair now.

CHAPTER 5

LUNCHTIME came and went, but the pirate didn't return. Bree hadn't eaten a thing since breaking her fast the previous day and her stomach was beginning to protest. She paced the room once more, stopping at the small desk tucked into the corner. She should have sent a note to her father before leaving England, but then when had her safety ever mattered to him? He had loved her once—when she was young.

It wasn't until after her eighth birthday that he had suddenly grown cold and moved to their house in London. She had written him often then, begging him to come home. She had even written the letters at a desk much like this one. And he had ignored them all.

Bree ran her hand over the freshly oiled surface of the desk. While she knew nothing about ships, she would venture a guess that the desk, and everything else in the cabin, was new. Though the room was much smaller than her bedchamber at home, the cabin boasted a lovely oak wardrobe, a nightstand, and a matching bed which appeared to be built into the wall. At the foot of the bed, next to the cabin's one small window, was another smaller wooden cabinet, topped with a fine porcelain washbasin and mirrored glass. Built into the corner beside it was an odd-shaped privy with an ornately carved wooden lid and matching porcelain knob. New brass rails trimmed the table, highboy, and desk, as well as the shelves above them.

Whoever had decorated the room had thought of everything. Blue velvet curtains at the one small window matched the lace-trimmed coverlet on the bed and the bright hooked rugs that all but covered the brightly polished wood floors. All in all, the room appeared too luxurious for a man whose plumpness of purse depended on a successful night's raid. Being a highwayman looked to be a profitable profession, for someone had certainly taken great pains to see to the comfort of the pirate, and she couldn't imagine the captain doing it without just compensation. But then, it was none of her affair, she told herself. It was a shame the same courtesy did not extend to the pirate's guest.

Where was Justin anyway? Didn't he know she was hungry? Several times she walked to the ladder that led aboveboard only to be turned back at the thought that she would have to climb it on her own.

The cabin, although quite nice, appeared to shrink each time she returned. She would go raving mad if she were forced to spend the next six to eight weeks staring at those four walls.

Giving up on anyone bringing her a lunch tray, Bree selected a book of sonnets and carried it to the bed. She'd give anything if she had one of her novels to while away the hours.

She was nothing more than a coward, Bree told herself as she stood at the base of the ladder once more.

Placing one foot on the bottom board, she stared longingly at the square of light above her. It was ridiculous to let a mere ladder get the better of her. Eventually, she would have to get over her fear of climbing the wooden steps or she would starve to death. She couldn't spend the entire voyage confined below deck relying on an inconsiderate highwayman.

Grabbing the side rail, Bree stepped up on the bottom

PIRATES AND PROMISES

rung. Once there, she pressed her body firmly against the wooden steps. Without looking up, she knew she had only accomplished a small victory. She had counted the steps enough times to know she still had twelve more to go.

The bottom ones were easy, she told herself as she lifted her foot to take the next step. It wasn't as if there were a great deal of distance between each rung. As long as she didn't look down, she'd do fine. And with only eleven more, it shouldn't take long.

Bravely Bree loosened her death grip and lifted her foot. Her slipper had barely touched the next step when the ship lurched to one side and Bree found her feet swinging free.

"Lord have mercy!" She heard a shout from down the companionway, then the sound of bare feet running toward her. The ship gave another lurch and she found herself on the floor, staring up into the wide eyes of the cabin boy.

"Are ye 'urt, miss?"

Bree shifted on the hard floor. Her pride and her backside hurt something awful, but it wasn't a subject you discussed with a man, even if the man were actually a lad who looked no more than three and ten. She started to stand when the ship was rocked with another wave and Bree slid across the companionway.

The lad reached down to her. "Grab me 'and," he instructed.

He took her fingers in his. Then bracing his bare feet against her slippers, he pulled her up.

Samuel stared at the beautiful young woman. Even though Captain Tibbs had told him about Mr. Tyler's maid, he had wanted to see her for himself. He had been cabin boy on the *Seahawk* for more than seven years now and had never known the captain to allow a woman aboard his ship. Women were a curse. Didn't the Bible say as much? He didn't read himself; but when the captain was in his cups, he quoted the Scriptures often enough.

A knot suddenly tightened around his heart. Samuel glared at the woman. Had the captain also been taken in by this blue-eyed witch?

"A maid who can't keep 'er pins beneath 'er should be a-stayin' in 'er cabin," he said with a scornful twist of his mouth.

Bree eyed his dirty feet. She was hard-pressed to decide which hurt more, her pride or her backside. Her pride won out.

"Perhaps if I had as much tar between my toes as you do, I wouldn't find myself sliding with each wave," she pointed out.

Samuel frowned at the pretty maid. "The captain said as 'ow ye 'ad more fire in yer eye than any servant 'e ever seed. Said Mr. Tyler'd be better off a-leavin' ye in England for all the good ye'd be a-shinin' 'is boots and all."

"Captain Tibbs said that, did he?" Bree asked calmly while her blue eyes blazed with an irrefutable proof of the captain's astute observation. "Well, you may tell your good captain he'd do well to look to the competence of his own staff before he judges that of another. The day is more than half gone and I have yet to be served my lunch."

"Served, ye say?" Samuel turned the thought over in his mind. "Ain't heared of a servant being served afore," he mumbled to himself. Maids served? No, ladies were served. Even he knew that.

His small, dark eyes suddenly narrowed suspiciously, reminding Bree of a rat one of her spaniels had once cornered in the stables. "It need not be much," she hurried to say. "A small loaf of bread with a wedge of cheese ought to do nicely."

She paused a moment to reconsider what it would take to appease the deep rumblings of her empty stomach. "And a few slices of venison, a small dish of vegetables, and a cup of hot tea," she added.

"And per'aps ye'd also be wantin' a bowl o' thick cream and fresh strawberries and a glass of champagne to wash 'em down with," he sneered.

Bree squared her shoulders at his impertinence. "There is no need to be rude. The pi— Mr. Tyler paid dearly for my passage. The least the captain can do is see that my meals are adequate. I shall wait in my cabin. You may serve me there." She turned and left him standing in the companionway.

Samuel watched her until the door was closed. "I'd wager me last coin ye not be Mr. Tyler's servant, but 'is doxy. Well, ye'll be gettin' no better than the rest of us," he hissed. "And ye'll be a-fetchin' it yerself. Captain Tibbs don't abide no tarts aboard 'is ship."

With his hand on the cabin door, Justin hesitated. He had purposely stayed away from Bree, and even though he knew it was necessary for his own peace of mind, it still nagged at his conscience. She swore the child did not belong to his half brother, but he couldn't rid himself of the vision of her lying in Quentin's arms, her silken hair wrapped around their entwined bodies.

"Damnation!" he cursed. Not since Henrietta Parker had Justin envied Quentin's unerring luck with women. Perhaps it was returning to England that had reopened the wounds he had once thought healed. Yet, did it really matter what had stirred up the old jealousies? If the mere thought of Bree with Quentin could revive the resentment he had once harbored for his half brother, then it was past time Justin took his own wife and put an end to the demons that had haunted his youth.

Like every aspect of his life, the choice of his bride was carefully planned to further the goals he had set for himself. And Miss Wingham, along with her handsome dowry, was in his plans. As soon as the ship docked in Virginia, he would pay a call on Mr. Wingham and ask for Regina's hand in marriage.

But there was plenty of time to think about that. Right now he was tired, dirty, and hungry. The captain was still upset about having a woman aboard his ship and had offered no assistance to insure the mares would have a safe trip across the ocean. Higgins and Justin had had their hands full settling them in, and all he wanted now was water to wash the dust away and a place to lay his head. With that in mind, he shoved open the cabin door.

The room was filled with the glorious colors of a dying sunset, but Justin's attention was immediately drawn to Bree. She lay across the bed, fast asleep. Although she still wore Higgins's clothes, the snug shirt and overlarge breeches only served to stir his imaginings of the soft, feminine curves he knew to be hiding beneath them.

Taking the time to wash his face and hands did not curb the desire that nagged at him and before he realized he had crossed the room, he found himself standing over her. She certainly looked young curled up on the coverlet with her golden hair lying across her ivory cheeks. Justin sat on the edge of the oak bed and gently brushed the soft curls aside. Despite his gentleness, she woke.

Bree stared up at the dark-haired figure that leaned over her. The fading light from the small window above them bathed his dim features in a strange aura of colors, but there was no hiding the green eyes that seemed to caress her with the love her heart craved.

"St. Clair," she breathed.

Justin felt the old jealousies twist his gut. "I'll see that you're returned to Foxworth on the first available ship," he said bitterly at the love he saw in her eyes.

Bree's dream quickly became a nightmare when she realized the man sitting on her bed was not St. Clair, but the pirate. How could she have made the awful error? Now he thought she had mistaken him for the earl and was threatening to send her packing again.

Bree scooted up on the bed. "You can't send me back," she stated. "The earl is terribly cruel and after what I've done, he would surely beat me. And when I die from the awful scars he'll leave on my broken body, it will be on your conscience."

"Quite a story, but I'll not argue with it," Justin said as he continued to search her face. "Quentin was never one for forgetting a slight."

Bree met his intense gaze. "You speak as if you know him well."

PIRATES AND PROMISES 79

Justin couldn't resist running his fingers down her flushed cheek. "Too well for my own peace of mind," he said half to himself.

"But you stole from him," Bree persisted.

Justin cupped her chin in his hand. "And that upsets you?" he asked gruffly.

Refusing to be intimidated by the anger she saw in his eyes, she met his gaze defiantly. "Not particularly," she answered bravely. "It merely brought to mind a few puzzling thoughts."

Justin's eyes darkened. "Such as?"

Bree felt her courage slip a notch. "Obviously the earl has displeased you in some way."

"The earl has displeased more than me. But pray, continue. What else is it that puzzles you?"

His seemingly conciliatory manner did not fool her. She could feel the tension emanating from him. Tilting her chin defiantly, she proceeded. "While I'll concede the items you took must have netted a handsome profit to have purchased such fine mares, it still has me wondering if it is customary for a highwayman to steal from someone he knows."

Justin's brows dipped in a frown. "Why do you assume the mares were purchased with the earl's jewels? Is it not possible that I purchased them with my own funds?"

Bree's easy laughter filled the small cabin. In anger, Justin grabbed her by her shoulders and pulled her toward him. "I fail to see what you find so amusing. The mares *were* paid for with my own coin."

"Despite what you might think, Mr. Tyler, my attic is not to let," Bree said, her blue eyes brimming with laughter as she looked up at him. "Even I know a highwayman has no funds other than what he takes from someone else."

"The coin was mine," he said, wondering at his need to make her understand. It had been a good many years since Justin had felt it necessary to prove his wealth to anyone. He hadn't known Bree a week and already she was stirring up all the old insecurities he thought he'd outgrown.

Justin told himself wealth meant nothing to him anymore.

It was only people like Quentin—and Henrietta Parker—who put so much value on possessions. But still he couldn't keep from trying to explain.

"Everything the pirate took was returned to those to whom they *rightfully* belonged," he said. "I kept nothing."

Bree studied him thoughtfully. He seemed earnest—as if he were telling the truth . . . "Not a single farthing?" she finally asked.

Her close scrutiny was unsettling to say the least. Justin tightened his grip on her shoulders. He didn't know whether to shake her or kiss her.

"Not a single farthing," he stated firmly, still not sure why he was trying to convince Bree of something that held no consequence. The skepticism in those blue eyes told him she would never believe the truth.

"As you say," she answered coolly. "Then being so wealthy and all, can you explain why a lunch tray was not provided for me?"

Justin dropped his hands. A lunch tray? What did that have to do with the amount of his wealth?

"*I* dined quite well," he lied.

"Well, I dined not at all."

Fascinated by the way her blue eyes darkened in indignation, Justin almost dropped his teasing. For, if truth be known, Justin had walked away from the captain's table without partaking of the meal. His loss of appetite had to do with the dark stranger who had boarded only moments before they had left the docks. Nicholas Thurston. Although he looked and acted the part of a gentleman, there was something about the man that did not sit well with Justin. He couldn't help thinking he had met him on an earlier occasion under less amiable circumstances.

"A shame you could not have joined us," he said. "Since you are a servant, that was out of the question. But you need not fret. Lunch was rather disappointing. I doubt that you would have cared for the cold beef and cheese."

Bree's stomach growled in protest.

"Now the supper provided was more to my liking," he

lied with a broad smile, for he hadn't eaten that meal either. "Succulent chunks of beef swimming in an exquisite sauce, tender asparagus, and—"

He caught her raised hand before it reached his face.

"Who taught you to be so ready with your fists?" he demanded. "Surely your father did not condone such unladylike behavior."

"My father was not around often enough to condone much of anything," she reluctantly admitted, then bravely squared her shoulders. "But you deserved it—leaving me here to starve, then bragging about your own feast."

"I did not leave you here to starve. The door was not locked. There was nothing to stop you from going to the galley for your meals."

"And how was I to get there?" she asked. "I could not get beyond the ladd—" Bree snapped her mouth shut as his full lips curved in understanding.

"Ah, the ladder," he said sternly in an attempt to stifle his amusement. "How very remiss of me to have forgotten." The prospect of helping her up the wooden steps greatly appealed to him. He grabbed her other hand and pulled her to her feet. "Come along then. We shall see what we can beg from the cook."

"Can you not bring me something here?" Bree protested.

Justin continued to drag her toward the door. "I have not the least idea what would satisfy your palate." He stopped suddenly and turned to her. "Why, the cook might try to fill your tray with eel's eyes and rat's liver."

He watched her soft pink lips twist into a sneer.

"Eel's eyes and rat's liver? Surely, even you could come up with something a bit more believable."

He grinned sheepishly. "The eel's eyes were a bit much, weren't they?"

Bree raised a delicate brow. "And the rat's liver?"

"Oh, with the amount of rats on this ship, it's a distinct possibility."

Bree suddenly paled. "Rats?" she asked as she quickly stepped into the security of his arms, her eyes suddenly searching the dark corners of the room. "There are rats aboard this ship?" she gasped.

To be sure, Justin had yet to see one, but most ships were known to house a rat or two in their hold. "Most certainly," he answered, enjoying the feel of her in his arms. "But you need not worry, they rarely come out until dark." He smiled as she glanced apprehensively at the fading sunset coming through the cabin's small window.

She snuggled against him. "I don't believe I wish anything to eat after all," she replied meekly.

Justin's conscience twinged again. While he would have liked to keep her tucked intimately in his arms, he knew she must be hungry.

"Come along," he said with a notable sigh of regret. "You must have something to eat and it's a long wait until morning."

"But the rats," Bree protested.

Justin took both of her hands in his. "You'll find them only in the hold," he admitted as he pulled her to the door.

"But you said—"

"Let's not dawdle," he replied, quickly changing the subject. "If we hurry, perhaps we can secure a portion of the beef before it is gone."

Bree's hunger won out over her need to clarify the misunderstanding and she let him guide her out of the cabin and down the long companionway to the ladder that led to the upper deck. Despite her earlier determination to overcome her fright, she stopped at its base, her feet refusing to take the first step.

Justin moved up behind her. Reaching over her shoulder, he grabbed the ladder. When she didn't more, he curled his arm around her slim waist and lifted her.

"Put me down," she screamed. "I've changed my mind. I'm not hungry after all." A low rumble gave lie to her protest.

"It would appear that your stomach does not agree with you," he pointed out. "Now, no more of this nonsense. Take hold of the ladder before I drop you."

PIRATES AND PROMISES

Bree immediately did as he asked. Once she found her foothold, she wrapped her arms around the wooden sides. Eyes tightly closed, she clung to them.

"Move up," Justin instructed.

"No-o-o," she wailed. "I'll fall."

Justin pried at her clamped arms. "You're not even trying."

Having her death hold dislodged, Bree scrambled down the two steps. White-faced, she glared up at him. "I'll remain down here," she shouted.

"That's ridiculous. You can't spend the entire trip in our cabin."

"I can and I will! And if you won't bring me food, then I'll starve." She turned and marched away.

"Then you'll starve," he shouted after her.

Bree quickened her pace when she heard his footsteps behind her, but by the time she reached the cabin door, he had caught up with her.

"You're being childish," he said as he took her arm and pulled her around, forcing her to face him.

Her retort died on her lips at the cold mask of suppressed anger he wore.

"You're going up that ladder if I have to beat you all the way," he said between clenched teeth. "This trip is too long for you to spend it below deck."

She backed from him, her fear of the ladder eclipsed by her fear at his anger. Having spent her entire life under the supervision of her father's servants, Bree had never been forced to do anything against her will before. Childish indeed! She would show him.

With stubborn conviction, Bree squared her shoulders, stepped around him, and once more walked the long companionway to the ladder. She hesitated only a moment before grabbing a firm hold and proceeding up the ladder. She could hear him coming after her, but she couldn't bring herself to look down. Instead, with each trembling step, she concentrated on the fading light above her. Climbing a ladder wasn't so terribly difficult, she bravely told herself.

Each step, no matter how unsteady, brought her closer to her goal. But despite all her efforts of encouragement, her pause after each rung lengthened noticeably.

"Would you care for my help?" Justin called out as he followed her.

Bree hurried up the remaining steps. It wouldn't do to accept his brand of assistance. Her last encounter in his arms had proved disastrous enough. She'd not risk another. With relief, she stepped over onto the deck. Having reached the top, her legs suddenly gave way and she sat down hard on the wooden planks.

Justin found her there. Gently, he gathered her trembling body against his. "I'm sorry," he whispered into her hair, "but I know of no other way for you to overcome your fear."

"Sorry! You're sorry!" Bree pulled out of his arms. "Of all the—"

Justin caught her fist. "Oh, no you don't," he said. "You'll not be bloodying my nose again."

They struggled, Bree's anger growing. "You beast!" she declared. "How dare you touch me!"

Having gotten the upper hand, Justin couldn't resist his urge to tease. "For the next seven years, I own you, Smythe," he said.

At the pirate's devilish laughter, Bree panicked. Kicking and screaming, she fought his hold on her. Somehow she managed to get to her feet, but he was right beside her, pulling her against the hard planes of his massive chest.

"Damn!" Justin cursed as her struggles threatened to tumble them over the edge of the hatch. Shifting his weight, he brought them both crashing back down onto the deck. Quick to take advantage of her momentary incapacitation, Justin rolled atop her.

"Get off me," she said through clenched teeth.

Recalling her unerring skill with her fists, he grabbed both her hands and pinned them over her head. "Perhaps I like where I am," he teased, enjoying her delightful squirming.

"Harlot!" a dark figure bellowed.

PIRATES AND PROMISES

Justin twisted around to see the captain and Mr. Thurston standing over them. Releasing Smythe's hands, he climbed to his feet, then turned to help Bree up.

"Good evening, Captain Tibbs," he said.

Tibbs ignored Justin. With an unsteady swagger, he approached Bree. "I'll not 'ave this jezebel working her wiles on the men aboard me ship."

"I am not a—"

"Save your lies for someone else," he shouted, waving an empty mug in her face. Boldly, he stared at her body. "I seed wha' I seed. Ye was a-tryin' to seduce Mr. Tyler. And on me own deck, ye was. 'Ave ye no shame?"

Bree's face flushed. "Me!" she choked out. "It was not I. Mr. Tyler is the—"

"Hush!" the man bellowed, spewing his rum-sodden breath in her face. "I know all about yer kind, I do. Harlots every one of ye. The Bible speaks of yer wicked doin's and I'll not 'ave the likes of ye cavorting atop me decks. If ye can't contain yer lustful ways I'll set ye aboard one of me dinghies and tow ye the rest of the way to America."

Bree was positive she heard the pirate chuckle and threw him one of her most scathing frowns. He merely smiled at her discomfort.

"Captain Tibbs," she said. "I—"

He waved his fist in her face. "I'll not be arguin' with the likes of ye."

Bree opened her mouth to give him a much-needed putdown when she felt Justin's hands on her shoulders. Before she could object, he stepped around her and took the captain by the arm. They walked away, leaving her fuming. She glared at their retreating figures. It was apparent from the bowed heads and the exchange of coins, the pirate was once more being forced to appease the captain's misgivings.

A soft curse caused Bree to turn around in time to see the look of disappointment on the cabin boy's face as he stepped out of the shadows.

Samuel had not missed the lustful way the captain had looked at Sabrina.

He stretched up on his toes and shoved his face close to hers. " 'E should throw ye to the sharks," he whispered gruffly. "Yer kind belongs with the fishes."

Before Bree could defend herself, he turned and left. Goose bumps crawled along Bree's arms as she stood staring at the empty shadows. Although he was gone, Bree could still feel the shroud of hate he left behind.

Nicholas Thurston observed the byplay with interest. So that was the way it was. Satisfying the captain's . . . needs must be the boy's responsibility and he was worried the pretty little wench was planning to take his place in the captain's bed. He almost smiled at the absurdity. If the lady was destined for anyone's bed, it would be his.

Nicholas reached out and took her hand. "I'm sorry you had to see the captain like this," he said, boldly brushing the back of her hand with his lips. "Too much drink sometimes does that to a man."

The red-haired stranger's intense gaze startled Bree as much as his actions. Even though the smile on his lips appeared genuine, his eyes were a disturbing frosty gray, as silver as the full moon.

"Then Captain Tibbs should learn to drink in moderation," she answered with a coolness that matched what she had glimpsed of his soul.

After casting a glance over Bree's shoulder to where Mr. Tyler was finishing up his dealings with the captain, Thurston released her hand and bent gallantly at the waist.

"I defer to your superior judgment, my lady," he said. "Now if you would but choose to seek me out should you become bored . . ."

He purposely left the balance of the invitation up to her imagination. Having planted the words designed to intrigue her, he turned and left.

Bree stared after him. The man was handsome enough, she decided, but he didn't have the same staggering effects on her as the pirate. Perhaps she should take him up on his offer anyway and devote some time to the perplexing concept.

"Stay away from him," Justin whispered as he stepped up behind her.

"Is that an order?" Bree tossed over her shoulder.

"It's more than an order. It's a warning." Justin watched as the man disappeared into the captain's quarters. "Mr. Thurston says he's from Williamsburg, yet I have never heard of him."

Bree turned her head. "Williamsburg?" Why had he mentioned Williamsburg? "And do you know everyone in Williamsburg?" she asked, surprised at how calm she sounded.

Justin's lips curved in a smile. "Anyone who's worth knowing," he said.

When the embarrassing warmth his comment evoked flooded her cheeks, Bree was relieved the pirate's attention appeared to be occupied with the captain's unsteady progress. If he was telling the truth, did he also know there was no Sir Henry? But it didn't really matter now. Unless forced to, she would never admit to her own fabrications.

CHAPTER 6

BREE finished the generous meal, then shoved her plate aside. She had eaten so much she felt as if her stomach would burst. While the cook had been less than gracious when asked to prepare another meal, Bree had to give him his due. The food had proven quite tasty.

Hoping to avoid Justin, who had stepped out on deck to smoke his pipe, Bree quietly made her way back to the cabin alone. She wanted time to reflect on what he had said about Mr. Thurston. But before she reached the ladder to her cabin below, the pirate caught up with her.

"Would you care for a walk about the deck?" he asked.

Bree eyed him suspiciously. "Are you planning to toss me overboard?"

Justin leaned toward her. "As much as you've cost me, I'll admit the idea has crossed my mind."

Before she could offer her protest to his ungentlemanly behavior, the corners of his full lips lifted in a wicked grin.

"Don't get your hackles up, Smythe. I'll not be tossing you overboard, nor allowing you to jump. You'll not get out of our contract that easily."

Although a tightness closed over her heart, Bree refused

PIRATES AND PROMISES

to let the pirate intimidate her. Boldly she shoved her face into his.

"Kindly do not judge me by your standards, pirate. For I am neither the thief nor the liar that marks the characters of you and your cohort. You have my written word that I will serve you for the next seven years and I fully intend to abide by our agreement." She answered his grin with one of her own. "That is, until Sir Henry redeems my papers."

A stab of desire pierced Justin's body. Serve him, she would. After all, he was no longer dealing with a virgin, but a woman who had experienced the fiery passions of a man's touch. He had no qualms about her sharing his bed. To be sure he would have to woo the obstinate miss, but that only made the game all the more delightful.

Justin brought his hand up to cup the delicate line of her beautiful jaw. Forcing her gaze to once again meet his, he ran his thumb across her soft lips. "I think it only fair to warn you that you might as well abandon this ridiculous idea that your betrothed will redeem your papers once we land in America."

"I will not," she said bitterly. "As soon as I step ashore, I shall seek him out. Sai—Sir Henry shall reimburse you for your expenses and then I shall be rid of you."

"Ah, but then you have forgotten one very important fact, my little chambermaid."

Bree glared up at him. "Such as?" she asked boldly despite the man's overpowering presence.

"Such as a small matter of opportunity. Since you are an indentured servant, I may choose to have you at my beck and call at all times. It will hardly afford you the opportunity to visit Sir Henry."

Bree jerked away from him, almost falling across the cargo hatch in her efforts. "You lied to m—"

The words died in her throat as her attention was suddenly drawn to movement along the shadowed wall of the galley. The cabin boy had been spying on them again.

"Damn!" the pirate cursed, also spotting the cabin boy lurking among the shadows. "That little water rat appears to be following us, more than likely waiting for something to report to the captain." He grabbed Bree's hand and pulled her to the ladder. "Let's get you below before Tibbs decides he wants to dip into my purse again."

Putting aside her fear of falling down the ladder, Bree stubbornly refused the pirate's help. Determined to conquer her fear and the confusing array of sensual longings the pirate evoked in her, Bree stepped down into the dark passage. With shear stubbornness, she made it to the base of the ladder unassisted.

Once her feet were safely planted on the floor, Bree hurried along the hall to her room. In her absence, someone had straightened the cabin and lit the two oil lamps that swung from brass hooks secured in the ceiling. After a cold night tossing and turning on a mattress of straw, the bed with the corner of its coverlet folded down looked most inviting.

Bree moved to close the heavy oak door behind her, but she was not quick enough. The pirate's tall frame filled the doorway. His compelling gaze as he lowered his head to enter sent a river of warmth coursing through her. Bree backed across the room only to find herself next to the wooden bunk, her knees threatening to crumble beneath her. She could only pray that the sea beating against the ship was loud enough to disguise the wild racing of her heart. But Justin appeared not to notice her embarrassment and proceeded to make himself comfortable.

Removing the black cape from his shoulders, Justin hung it on the peg beside the door. "I see Higgins has been here," he said casually.

The pistol came next and Bree tried not to stare as he eased it from the broad band of his breeches and placed it on the room's only table.

Even though he turned his back to her, Bree knew he was working with the buttons on his white linen shirt. Surely he did not intend to spend the night here. When he turned back to her, the fire in his sea-green eyes confirmed her fears. The undeniable lust sent another rush of warmth washing over her.

PIRATES AND PROMISES 91

Bree managed a swallow of cool air. "Y-you can't sleep here," she finally choked out.

Justin arched a dark brow. "Where do you propose I sleep?"

"Anywhere but here."

"You forget. This is *my* room."

"Then you must secure another for me."

"This is not an inn, Smythe. There are no extra rooms to be had."

"Your manservant?" she ventured to ask.

"Is bedded down with the horses."

Bree reached down and stripped the coverlet from the bed and headed for the door. "Then if you will kindly give me directions, I will join him and leave you to your sleep."

Justin grabbed her arm. "You cannot mean to spend the night in the hold with the animals."

His words were low, a hint of a threat hovering on the sharp edge of them. In spite of the tremors that threatened to reduce her knees to a watery mush, Bree glared up at him.

"Surely your manservant would protect me should my safety be in question," she stated coldly. "But if I were to remain here, who would come to my rescue?"

She was relieved when he saw fit to drop her arm and step away, but the smile that trembled on his lips had her questioning her small victory. With a great deal of pomp, he bowed before her and bade her follow him.

Bree frowned. Of course, it was so like him to mock her for being a coward. But she'd not let his opinion upset her. All that mattered was that she reach Virginia and find St. Clair without tarnishing her reputation further. After what had happened between her and Justin, there was no longer a question of marriage, but St. Clair was her only hope of escaping the pirate's demands—demands she was beginning to suspect included more than the duties of a household servant.

Justin took one of the lanterns from its hook and led

the way. After hurrying to catch up with him, Bree followed meekly down the companionway, past the ladder and through a small door at the end. A rush of fresh air swept past her, but as soon as the door closed behind them, the cool air pooled at their feet.

They appeared to have stepped into a room of cavernous proportions for the lamplight did not reach much beyond the handrail of their walkway. She squinted to see in the dim light.

"Where are we?" she whispered.

"The 'tween deck. It's just above the hold."

"And the r-rats?" she asked, moving closer.

Justin grinned down at her. "Not here. They would be down with the animals."

"You're just saying that to frighten me from spending the night there," she accused.

He shrugged. "Have it your way."

"I shall. Even if they are there, I would rather take my chances with them."

Each step they took announced their presence with a hollow echo. Bree strained to hear the sounds of the horses—or the stirrings of a rat. But she only heard the muted clamor of the ocean waves as they licked the sides of the large ship. She hoped the pirate knew where he was going, but she refused to question him further. His answers might be more than she wished to know at the moment.

Bree tried not to look beyond the circle of lamplight that bobbed across the rough boards at her feet. She suspected that to step to the edge would confirm her suspicions—the boarded walkway that hugged the hull of the ship was somehow suspended above a vast open space that would set her knees to quaking. But the pirate did not give her much opportunity to dwell on her fears. His long strides forced her to hurry after him or be left in darkness. She vowed once she got off this ship, she would never again submit herself to this terrible punishment. No more ladders. No more walkways. If she didn't have a good solid foundation under her feet, she wasn't going to go anywhere.

The discovery that the walkway had suddenly become a landing of what appeared to be a broad stairway surprised Bree. The steps to her left ascended to a large square opening that was covered with a crosshatch of slats. Moonlight fell through the tiny square openings and spilled its vague pattern on the broad wooden stairs.

"Where do the steps lead?" she asked nervously.

"Down to the bottom of the hold," he mumbled as he quickly descended another set of stairs to the next landing.

Bree hurried to catch up. "I meant the stairs going up," she demanded. "Where do the stairs going up lead?"

"Up!" he shouted over his shoulder, then turned to the left.

Bree followed. When she stepped down into the hold, the strong smell of manure was so overwhelming she forgot about the stairway.

Down the center of the room a series of stalls had been erected. Suspended over each one was a set of large rings to which a series of heavy ropes had been tied. The ropes were part of a large, elaborately woven bellyband that wrapped each horse snugly, giving their hooves minimal contact with the straw-covered floor of their stall. A cross-tie device allowed them to reach their hay and water and also helped keep them from being slung against the sides of their stall should the ocean become rough. The pirate had certainly seen to the comfort of his animals.

As Bree moved closer, she could see that the stalls for the horses were a new addition to the hold. The wooden sides gleamed golden in the lamplight compared to the aged wood that made up the small compartments along the ship's hull that held several fat pigs and two crates of chickens. The stalls that weren't filled with livestock were filled with hay, straw, and bags of grain.

"Where will I sleep?" she asked.

Justin grinned at the woebegone tilt of her lips. "This was your idea, not mine," he reminded her.

Bree glared at him. "I have no other choice, pirate," she said before turning from him.

"Ah, but you do," he teased as he followed her from one stall to the next. "I am more than willing to share my small bed with you."

A particularly large pig caught Justin's attention and he stopped to inspect it. A fine animal, he thought. He would have to remember to ask the captain who would be receiving the shipment. He leaned closer. He certainly hoped the presence of the livestock didn't mean the captain had a penchant for fresh meat instead of salted. He could always use another breeder such as this.

When the pig suddenly took exception to the unwanted attention and lunged at the wooden rails, Justin quickly stepped away. "I wouldn't ask to bed down with this one if I were you, but perhaps one of the other pigs will not mind sharing its lodgings."

Bree stopped. Her shoulders stiff, she turned back to him. "Anything would be preferable to sharing yours," she said bitterly.

A wicked grin swept across his face. "Each to their own tastes, Smythe. Me, I much prefer a warm, willing wench to that of a slab of bacon."

"If warm and willing are your requirements, then you'd do better with your slab of bacon. At least your belly would be filled. Which is more than I can say for your bed."

Having bestowed her thoughts on the subject, Bree turned and walked away. She didn't have to look back to know that he was following her. Every nerve in her body seemed attuned to his presence.

"Now that I've found the stalls, you may feel free to leave," she said without turning around.

Justin stepped up beside her. "I was taught that a gentleman never abandons a lady in need."

"A gentleman?" she asked, arching a delicate brow. "And what would you know about being a gentleman?"

"Didn't I tell you? In certain circles, I have been set up as the example other young men should strive to follow."

Bree stopped beside a large pile of straw. "I can see how you'd want to keep that particular lie to yourself as long as possible," she said absently as she picked up the wooden pitchfork and began pulling at the towering stack.

"You are a younger son, no doubt," she tossed over her shoulder. "With no other prospects than wedding some wealthy merchant's spoiled daughter and living the rest of your life off the earnings of his distasteful enterprises, I can see how a gentleman might decide to turn to the noble life of a highwayman."

"You can put away your sarcasm, Smythe. I might have been a younger son once, but that's changed now. I don't have to marry wealth, nor do I have to depend on the inheritance of an indifferent father. I worked hard for what I have, which is more than you can say for the Earl of Foxworth and his friends."

The depth of the bitterness in his words surprised Bree. She stopped rearranging the straw and stared at him. The change that had come over Justin was frightening. Hate, bitter and overflowing, appeared to have etched a destructive trail of malice along the ruggedly handsome lines of his face. For a fleeting moment, Bree could envision St. Clair pacing the rock in the meadow dealing with his own cache of bitterness.

Concerned, she reached out and touched his arm. "Do not let your hurt cloud your future. Take hold of your destiny and carve out a life for yourself that will put these demons to rest."

When Bree realized he was looking at her with a new respect, she almost wished the words had been her own. In truth, she had borrowed them from one of the books she had read. Perhaps Maddie was right. Perhaps she was trying to live her life through the characters in her books instead of facing her own loneliness.

"Are you offering to help?" he asked with a teasing grin.

Bree's heart skipped a beat. His dark handsome looks were enough to make a woman forget the rogue he was.

There was no doubt about it. Justin had a way about him. A way that set her body to tingling. A way she'd do best to avoid.

"A true man doesn't need anyone," she stated.

He ran the back of his hand down her cheek. "You're wrong. A true man is one who admits his needs."

Bree was just on the point of noting how sensitive he seemed when she spotted the suspicious light in his eyes.

He bent close to her. "And a woman's task is to . . ."

Bree cast him a wary glance. "Yes?"

"I think you know the answer to that one, Smythe," he said, his voice low and husky. "In case you've forgotten, I'll be in our cabin waiting to refresh your memory."

He turned and walked away, leaving Bree fuming. She might be his servant, but what he hinted at was not part of her duties. The gall of the man. If he expected her to come to him, he was in for a great surprise. As far as she was concerned, he could spend the rest of his days waiting in the cabin.

The ship lurched and Bree felt the hot bile rise in her throat again. The air was thick with the smell of the animals and just taking a breath made Bree's stomach knot in protest. After spending most of the night ridding herself of a super which had gone sour, Bree was surprised there was anything left to cause her such distress.

Her nanny's warning about a kiss came scurrying back with a vengeance. The upstairs maid had suffered a similar malady. "Morning sickness," everyone had whispered in hushed tones. Heaven help her! This couldn't be happening, could it? Surely a kiss couldn't cause all this.

When Bree heard the sound of footsteps, she curled up on her straw pallet and let the silent tears run unchecked down her cheeks. All she wanted to do was die, but she was so sick she knew she'd have to get better just to have the strength to accomplish it.

The footsteps stopped beside her. "I brought you some coffee," Higgins said, thrusting it at her.

PIRATES AND PROMISES   97

"Go away," Bree sobbed.

"Mr. Tyler said it's time you got up."

Bree lifted her head. "I don't think I can."

Higgins took one look at her, then wedged the hot mug of coffee between two sacks of grain. "Here let me help you," he said as he shoved a pail toward her.

Bree would have given anything to have been able to send him away, but she knew she was too weak to help herself any longer. At least Higgins seemed to have forgiven her for taking his clothes.

"You're as green as scum on swamp water," he said, lowering her back onto the straw bed.

Bree wished he hadn't used that particular image. It had an immediate effect on the contents of her stomach and Higgins was forced to assist her again.

"You've never been on a ship before, have you?" he asked.

She shook her head no.

"Takes a while to get your sea legs," he offered. "A lot of people get seasick their first time."

Seasickness? She closed her eyes, relief soaring through her. Of course, how stupid not to have thought of it before. Her illness could just as easily be the inexperienced sailor's malady.

"If you're one of the lucky ones," he continued, "it will pass in a few days."

Bree opened one eyelid, then let it drop. "I don't think I'll live long enough to find out."

"You'll not be dying and cheating me out of seven years of service," said a voice above her.

Bree didn't have to open her eyes again to know the pirate had come looking for her. That deep voice could belong to no one else.

"It's no wonder you're sick," he said as he picked her up, blanket and all.

Bree struggled against him. "What are you doing? Put me down this minute."

"Lie still," he ordered. "The odor down here would make

anyone in your delicate condition dump their dinner."

"You put that so elegantly," she said, trying not to dwell on the fact that he had acknowledged that she might be with his child. She closed her eyes tightly.

"Are you referring to the fact that you lost your supper or my mention of your condi—"

"Never mind!" she interrupted. Why hadn't she ever asked Maddie about babies and such? The answer to that was simple enough—Maddie was such a proper lady. She would have more than "dumped *her* dinner" if Bree had asked. Not only would she have refused to answer, but she would have lectured Bree for no less than a fortnight on the appropriate subjects of conversation for young ladies.

"Always a lady," Bree mumbled to herself.

Justin stopped his climb of the stairs. With a dark brow raised, he looked down at her. "Ladies don't go chasing their lovers across the sea. Besides, how do you plan on explaining the child, or did you foolishly hope to palm it off on him too? Because let me tell you—"

Movement from up above caught his attention. Justin looked up in time to catch a glimpse of the cabin boy turning from the top of the stairs. He frowned. The captain must have told the lad to keep an eye on them. There was no other reason he could think of that would have the cabin boy walking the deck at this time of the morning—especially with the captain's breakfast still to be looked after.

"Well, you've gone and done it again," he accused. "If Samuel heard you, you may not have to worry about whether I might be tempted to toss you overboard. The captain will do it for me."

Bree was too weak to give him the put-down he deserved. "Another attempt to scare me?" she somehow managed.

"Keep in mind, I don't have enough coin to cover the captain's price of having a fallen woman aboard his vessel."

At the moment, Bree almost wished the captain would have her tossed overboard. Anything to rid her of this malady.

PIRATES AND PROMISES

* * *

"Whoa there, Samuel," Nicholas said as he grabbed the filthy boy by the shirtsleeve and swung him around to face him. "Where are you going in such a hurry?"

"I've got something to tell the capt'n."

From the gleam in the boy's eyes, it didn't take much to suspect the information was about the enticing little morsel of womanhood Nicholas had met last evening. The captain and the boy had talked of nothing else since they had set sail. Determined to know for certain, he laid his arm across the boy's shoulder and led him away from the captain's door.

"Tibbs is in no condition to hear anything at the moment. So what say you tell me what has you so excited."

Samuel eyed Thurston skeptically. "And why should I be a-doin' that?"

Nicholas pulled a coin from his pocket. "Because I'm willing to pay you for the information." He held the coin just out of the boy's reach. "Think on it carefully," he continued. "A secret can be shared many times before it is no longer a secret, but the offer of this coin only comes once."

With a short jump, Samuel grabbed the coin out of Nicholas's hand. After a quick look around, he leaned close.

"I jus' seed Mr. Tyler carrying that tart," he whispered. "Real close they was. And 'e tried to tell the capt'n she was 'is servant," he added.

Nicholas cocked a dark brow. "Ah-h-h, so you're saying they're lovers."

Samuel nodded his agreement.

Nicholas was not put off by the fact that Miss Smythe might be the noble Mr. Tyler's light-skirt. To his way of thinking, it only improved his own chances of getting her into his bed. Once a woman abandoned her virtue with one man, she became easy prey for the next man to come along with smooth manners and sweet words, and no one could say Nicholas's words weren't the smoothest and sweetest to be had. Besides, he had discovered years ago that he much preferred the bed of an experienced woman. Virgins expected the man to be honorable and honor was one trait Nicholas never intended to lay claim to.

The only thing that threatened to thrust a stick in the spoke of his wheel was the boy. The way the captain already viewed the beauty's presence, this little gem of information might very well have the captain turning the ship back to port. That would not do.

"Would another coin buy your silence?" he asked.

After glancing over his shoulder to assure himself that no one was close enough to overhear, Samuel cocked his head to one side and grinned. "Ye want I should keep it to meself?"

Until I've tired of her, Nicholas thought. "Let's say at least for the next few weeks."

Nicholas was not one for rushing things. A few weeks should be more than enough time. After all, a woman too easily coaxed to one's bed wasn't worth the effort.

"A jezebel!" the captain shouted as he pounded on the open Bible before him. "I've taken a jezebel aboard me ship."

Managing to hold a grin in check, the cabin boy nodded solemnly. He was pleased he had managed to slip away from Mr. Thurston before he was tempted to take the bribe. The captain was every bit as upset as Samuel hoped he would be.

"I knew she was a 'arlot the first moment I laid eyes on 'er, sir," he said, hoping to add fuel to the captain's burning anger.

The captain stared down at his rum. "I've made a pact with the devil and God will punish me for this. Mark me words, boy, we'll never make it to Virginia. God will lower his mighty fist and crush me ship into a thousand splinters."

Samuel's eyes grew large. "We be cursed all right."

The captain took another generous swallow from the jug

of stout rum which hadn't left his side since they had set sail. He had let himself accept a bribe. Blood money it was—and they'd all die because of it.

A shadow passed the window and Tibbs found himself staring out at the tall Virginian. "Look at the way he carries her," he sneered. "He'll be bringing down God's wrath on us all. There won't be a piece of the *Seahawk* left big enough to say we was here."

"Ye could 'ave 'er thrown overboard," Samuel offered. He refilled the captain's near empty mug. "Then maybe we could slip by God unnoticed."

The captain's head bobbed up. He may be drunk, but he wasn't drunk enough to toss the purse until he'd emptied all its gold.

"You don't understand, lad," he said as he thumped the opened pages of the Bible. "God says to forgive the 'arlot and not cast the first stone or . . ."

He rolled his eyes heavenward, trying to remember just how it went. "Anyway, it says we 'ave to give 'er a chance to redeem 'erself. 'Elp me up now, lad. I need to talk to Tyler about this."

Justin could feel his purse growing lighter with each staggering step the captain took toward him. The man was drunk! Justin would have made himself scarce if it hadn't been for Bree. She needed the fresh sea air to rid herself of her queasiness.

"Tyler-er-er," the captain slurred, "need to speak with ye."

Justin set Bree down with her back propped against one of the hatches. Tucking the blanket firmly around her, he whispered in her ear. "If you open your mouth and cost me so much as one more coin, I'll up your indenture by five years." Having given the warning, he turned his attention back to the captain.

"In pri-i-vate," the captain added, tugging at Justin's sleeve, but he wouldn't budge.

After all the coin the pirate had already parted with, Bree

was surprised to see him stand his ground this time. His jaw was like granite, his eyes hard emeralds of green. Obviously there was a point beyond which you did not push the pirate. The captain must have sensed it also for he wasted no time in dropping his hand from the pirate's arm.

"What do you want, Tibbs?" the pirate finally asked.

The captain positioned himself between Justin and Bree. He couldn't trust Tyler not to mention the coin he had already accepted for the woman's passage and had no wish to have his men overhear.

With his back to Bree, he leaned close to the Virginian. "The woman," he whispered harshly. "I can't 'ave a 'arlot walking me decks, Tyler. Unless she repents and turns from her evil ways, she is to stay below deck."

"A harlot, you say?" He could see the blanket shifting wildly on the deck behind the captain. "Well, well, I can't say as I can argue the point with you." He waited until the words sank into the captain's foggy mind, then continued. "Unfortunately, the lass is sick and I'll not have her soiling my quarters with her supper. Until she's better, I will leave her here and let the sea wash away the evidence of her gluttony."

He would have heard Bree's determined denials had not Tibbs taken exception to Justin's blatant disregard for his wishes and started shouting, "Ye'll e-e-either take her below now and see that she stay-s-s-s there or I'll be returning the both of ye to England."

Bree managed to scoot over enough to see around Tibbs. Justin hadn't so much as lifted a brow at the captain's warning, but Bree could feel his anger fill the space between them. Like some wild untamed animal waiting to pounce, the pirate loomed over the drunken man. One didn't need to hear the growl to know the threat was real. Instinct had a way of painting its own vivid portrait of danger.

When the pirate finally spoke, his voice was low and even. "Do that and I'll see that all ports in Virginia—and the other states—are closed to the *Seahawk*."

"And how are you to do that?" the captain sneered.

"You forget, Tibbs, we Virginians stand together. All I need say is that the *Seahawk* is an English ship and when the captain discovered me to be from Virginia, I was cheated out of my paid passage."

Tibbs had seen enough of the Americans to suspect that Tyler might be right. He had found them to be a disgustingly proud lot—ready to start a brawl over the least slight. He had seen tempers along the wharves flare on more than one occasion over incidents as minor as who had first dibs on a whore's favors.

Tibbs quickly scanned the deck to see how much his men had heard. Everyone appeared to be occupied with their tasks, but one could never tell. It wouldn't do to let them think the Virginian had gotten the upper hand. He'd lose his men's respect.

He leaned close to Tyler and had to brace himself to keep from toppling over on the man. "Ye wi-i-i-n for now, Tyler," he managed to say, "but if she causes any trouble aboard me ship I'll 'ave 'er tos . . . tos-s-ssed overboard."

CHAPTER 7

"YOU called me a harlot," Bree said through clenched teeth.

Justin bent toward her and rearranged the blanket. "Will you at least wait until the captain's out of hearing?" he growled. "In your condition, I couldn't very well say you were a virgin, now could I?"

Bree blinked back a tear that had suddenly sprung to her eyes. "You make it sound so . . . so . . ."

"Cut, dried, and packed away? These things happen. A kiss . . . and well . . . then . . ."

When he met her horrified gaze, he couldn't bring himself to put her moment of weakness into words. She still looked an innocent.

"I truly am sorry," he said. "I shouldn't have brought up your past indiscretions when you're feeling so poorly." He fussed with tucking the blanket tighter. "This sea air should help rid you of your . . . ailment. From all I've heard, this should only last through the morning, then I'll see that you get a nice hearty lunch."

Bree didn't care about lunch. "Go away," she said, turning from him. He had confirmed her worst fears. A kiss was all it took. She curled up into a ball and listened to his footsteps as he walked away.

All this time, she had clung to the hope that what Nanny had told her was all a bunch of nonsense. "A kiss and then..." A few short words from the pirate had twisted her heart into a knotted bow.

Bree woke to the sound of men arguing.

"Ye do it," one of the them shouted. "I'll not be havin' the devil's curse on me."

Bree raised her head. The wind had picked up and dark clouds boiled across the heavens, covering the sun. Two men stood over her, but it was difficult to see their faces in the darkness of the gathering storm. When she sat up, the men backed away. It was almost as if they were afraid of her. Due to the captain's silly superstitions, no doubt. Well, she didn't care anymore. She felt so much better. Not only was the queasiness gone, but she was hungry again.

"Where's Mr. Tyler?" she asked them.

" 'E's below with 'is 'orses, miss," one of them said.

The second man peeked around his friend. "If ye would be a-thinkin' of movin' to one side a mite," he suggested, "we could be a-lowerin' that canvas afore the wind sweeps us back to England."

His comrade backhanded him in the gut. "Not that way, you overgrown whale."

Pasting a smile on his face, Otis turned his attention back to Bree. "What Ned 'ere means to say is if it wouldn't be too much trouble, ma'am, we'll be needin' that there rope you was restin' your... your... your sweet 'ead on," he finished in a rush.

"Isn't that what I said?" whined Ned.

Bree moved the blanket aside and tried to stand, but the ship tossed so violently that she soon found herself sprawled on the deck in a most unladylike manner. Ned rushed forward to help her, but his friend held out his hand and stopped him.

"I'll be doin' that, Ned," Otis offered generously, swaggering up to Bree. "I be more e-muned to the devil's curse than ye be."

Leaning down, he held his hand out to her. "Grab ahold, miss, and I'll 'elp ye to yer cabin."

Bree rescued her blanket from a gust of wind, then gathered her legs beneath her. "Devil's curse," indeed. She had half a mind not to accept the man's help, but knew she'd have a difficult time making it below on her own. She took his hand.

"All hands ahoy!" a cry came, sending a chill up Bree's spine.

They hadn't gone five steps when she heard Ned's wail behind them. "What about the sail, Otis?"

"Lower it, ye fool, before the wind—"

The ominous sound of canvas ripping halted his words. With a curse he brushed Bree aside and ran back to Ned. "The captain's going to 'ave us swinging out on the jibboom for this," he shouted over the wind.

Three bells signaled the alarm. As Bree clutched the rail, two men seemed to appear out of nowhere. With frantic haste, they untied the ropes and lowered the sail. The weight of the canvas uncurled the ropes from their place on the deck. The sail Ned was struggling with had almost reached the crossbar when the rope broke in Otis's hand, setting the sail loose in the wind. His shouts brought more men who worked diligently to help contain the billowing canvas.

Bree backed away from the chaos. The same sail that had earlier aided in their journey was now a demon set loose from hell. The wind caught the heavy material, hurling it at the men. A sailor grabbed the rail in time to keep from being swept over the side.

"Get below!" someone shouted, but Bree continued to watch in horror as the giant canvas whipped in the wind. So caught up in the drama, she didn't flinch when she was grabbed from behind.

"I said get below," Justin shouted. "And quickly, before the captain decides to pitch you overboard while no one's watching."

"This was not my doing," Bree said.

She looked so lost and bewildered, Justin could almost

feel sorry for her. "Try explaining your innocence to a man who has submerged his entire faculty of reason into a tankard of rum."

"It is not my fault that the captain dips too freely in his cups."

Justin tightened his hold on her arm. "And it's not you who ends up delving out your coin to appease his conscience. Now unless you have sufficient means to cross his palm when he gives vent to his next tirade, you'd best take my advice and get below."

Finding his grasp too secure to shake off, Bree lifted her head to the wind and marched beside him as best she could to the steps that led below to the hold.

"I can't believe you would begrudge me a few measly coins," she said, pouting as they started down the steps.

Justin stopped short and swung her around to face him. "You consider a hundred pounds a few measly coins?"

"My companion, Maddie, gets more than that just to see that I am kept entertained. Surely a successful pirate such as yourself could afford such a paltry sum."

He glared down at her. "How do you know but that those few measly coins were not all I had left?"

Justin was surprised to see her blue eyes widen in alarm at his question. She certainly had a way of picking away at his conscience.

"Were they?" she breathed. "Because if you are short of funds, I'm sure my fiancé—"

"That would be Sir Henry," he offered.

"Yes, S-Sir Henry," she answered after lowering her eyes to the front of his linen shirt. "I'm sure he will be forever grateful to you for bringing me to him and—"

"And he loves you so dearly, he will reward me handsomely for returning you to his arms. Is that it?"

"There is no reason to mock me, Mr. Tyler. Sir Henry is a man of honor, which is more than I can say for—"

"Me?" he finished for her. "I am truly looking forward to meeting this paragon of virtue. A shame our destination is Williamsburg, for I—"

"Williamsburg?" Bree could not mask her pleasure. "We will be landing in Williamsburg?"

"So the noble Sir Henry is residing in Williamsburg, is he?" Justin asked as he tugged at her arm.

Bree was relieved the darkness settling overhead kept him from seeing the telltale blush that warmed her cheeks.

"But of course you know of him," she said with a great show of innocence as she continued down the steps. "You've bragged of knowing anyone who is anyone in the town, and with Sir Henry living on one of the estates on the outskirts, you're sure to have met him."

Justin searched his memory, but could not come up with a face to match the name. The thought that Sir Henry was not a gentleman after all crossed his mind. The man had more than likely elevated the true status of his position to impress the beautiful Miss Smythe. And Miss Smythe had naïvely accepted the man at his word. She wouldn't be the first young lady to have her head filled with dreams while a bounder such as Sir Henry relieved her of her innocence.

Now he understood the reasons behind her father's attempt at a hasty marriage to Quentin. In a few months, the truth about her condition would be evident to everyone. If anyone deserved to feel the sharp edge of the pirate's revenge, it was the perfect *Sir* Henry.

They had reached the first platform when the lightning struck, filling the hold with its eerie glow. Justin turned and confronted her.

"Which plantation does this *gentleman* reside at?"

Another bolt of lightning lit the area. Bree caught her breath at the anger revealed on Justin's handsome face. His eyes had darkened until they were a reflection of the storm clouds that boiled overhead. Green lightning with black thunder at its core. Bree's heart picked up a beat. How could an image so cold bring such warmth to her body? She tried to move away.

"Which estate?" he asked again.

The only estates she knew of in Virginia were St. Clair's

and the one Maddie's cousin had gone to and she wasn't about to name either of them.

"Sir Henry is a very private man and I'm certain he would not wish me to discuss him with strangers."

The pirate's lips lifted in a sneer. "I'm sure he wouldn't. To do so might lead you to find out that the gentleman doesn't exist."

Bree didn't have to ask to know that the embarrassing heat that lanced her body had turned her face a bright pink. Justin knew of her charade—or thought he did. Bree started to protest when another deafening clap of thunder sounded overhead. It was answered by screams from the hold.

"Damn!" Justin cursed when the ship pitched precariously. The mares. Pushing past Bree, he took the remaining steps two at a time. It wasn't until he reached the bottom that he realized Bree was following.

"Go up to the cabin," he shouted over his shoulder. "It's not safe down here."

Ignoring the pirate's orders, Bree continued down the steps. With the crew busy with their own duties aboveboard, he would need all the help he could get. She might not know much about caring for horses on a ship, but she knew the slings they wore offered little protection against the fierceness of these winds.

But she was not prepared for the pandemonium that greeted them when they reached the hold. The sow Bree had named Aphrodite for the size of her large brood had fallen against the door of her stall, breaking the hinge and shattering the chicken crate Bree had placed outside her door. Chickens and piglets were everywhere—in the narrow aisle, in between the hooves of the frightened mares, and in the straw where Higgins was jabbing frantically with his long-handled, wooden-tined fork.

A healthy thrust of Higgins's fork and he dislodged a fat rooster from the top. With the ungainliness of a rock that had sprouted wings, the squawking bird took flight. When it flopped from stall to stall trying to reclaim its balance, the mares went crazy, screaming and plunging at their ties.

"That chicken's supper tonight," Higgins said, but it was the squeals of the piglets that concerned Bree.

Justin would be of no help to the small animals. All his efforts were focused on trying to calm the big stallion. Bree didn't know what to do. If Aphrodite didn't round up her brood quickly, the matter would soon be put to rest by the thrashing of the mares' hooves. But trying to rescue the wiggly creatures would be next to impossible. Unless . . .

Bree grabbed up another one of the forks from the hook on the stall and joined Higgins in stabbing the prickly straw bedding and carrying it to the mares.

"Mr. Tyler wants a straw wall beside the mares," Higgins shouted. "But be careful you don't stab 'em with the tines while you work."

The ship tipped and the mares swung like giant pendulums against the sides of the stalls, their hooves barely missing the piglets. "Help them," Bree cried.

"There is no help for this. The sea is too rough."

Not willing to see the little ones trampled, Bree tossed her forkful to the back of the second stall. It landed on one of the piglets. Offended, he shook off the prickly stalks and ran squealing back to his mother. Another one followed. Bree smiled and hurried back to the towering heap. If she could work fast enough, perhaps she could aid in saving Aphrodite's little ones as well.

Once Justin had calmed the stallion, he grabbed one of the forks and helped. The next hour, Bree worked harder than she had in the entire seventeen years of her life. She not only managed to get the piglets secured, but assisted with the mares as well. Although the cool air of the storm filtered down into the hold, sweat poured from everyone's brow.

Once finished, they stood back to survey their work. They had done a fair job, but the tossing of the great ship only scattered their carefully stacked walls beneath the hooves of the mares.

"What we need is something to hold the straw against the sides of the stalls," Justin said as he rested his arm on the top of his wooden fork.

"Blankets?" Bree suggested.

"Blankets would do it. If we had enough to drape over the walls between the stalls, it would help hold the straw in place."

"You may have mine," Bree offered.

Higgins held tightly to the wooden slats of the pigsty behind him. "One won't do," he muttered. "We'd need every blanket on board this old tub."

As soon as the words were out, the three looked at each other, a broad grin of a shared conspiracy spreading across their faces.

"The crew deserves to have their blankets filched," Higgins pointed out. "Not a one of them has ventured this far below yet. Not even to feed the other animals. Don't know how the captain thinks they're going to survive the crossing."

"I suspect whoever was assigned the task has little liking for our aromatic cargo and the captain hasn't been sober long enough to notice," Justin said before lifting the corner of his lips in a wicked grin. "What say you both to the pirate making a little raid on the ship's store?"

Bree felt her heart swell with pride at the notion of being included in the caper. "I say the pirate has more than paid for his share of the blankets this trip. What say you, Mr. Higgins?"

Higgins seemed to think on it a moment. "I say you have a right tidy way of lookin' at things, Miss Smythe," he said with a grin.

Justin tried to ignore the radiance that lit Bree's face, but the beauty of her smile was enough to light the hold without the oil lanterns. Knowing such thoughts were dangerous, he busied himself with collecting the wooden pitchforks and returning them to their hooks. Finished, he placed his arms casually across the shoulders of his two helpers.

"Then I say we be about collecting on the luxuries due this paying passenger while the good Lord keeps the storekeepers busy."

Swept up in the excitement, Bree was more than willing to follow. She had always been one to create her own schemes. Never had she been included in anyone else's. All her young friends were much too stuffy to dream the wonderful dreams that made her life bearable.

Bree frowned. If she were honest with herself, she would admit that other than Maddie, she had few true friends. It was another reason why St. Clair had come to mean so much. His promise of returning was the only thing worth holding onto through the years—especially when her father's London pleasures claimed his attention. St. Clair had provided her with the hope that one day she would be loved and she'd never let that hope die.

When they reached the level where the crates were stored, Justin turned to the right. Bree and Higgins stumbled after him. Although the ship continued to sway, he hurried along the rows of roped crates as if he already knew his destination. With the storm raging outside, the hold was dark and the pirate carried the only lantern. If it hadn't been for the great flashes of lightning, Bree would have surely lost her way.

Justin didn't stop until he reached a door at the end of the ship. Without knocking, he pushed it open and entered the large room. The fury of the storm had scattered everything that wasn't fastened down and Bree had to watch her step as she followed the pirate into the room.

A gust of cold air sent a shiver skittering up her back. One of the windows had worked its way open and hung precariously by one hinge as the wind and the rain swung the frame violently back and forth on its tenuous moorings.

"Gather the blankets," the pirate shouted above the storm. "And hurry. We mustn't be caught now."

Bree wanted to ask him if they wouldn't find themselves in equally hot water once the theft was discovered, but she withheld the comment. Securing the horses against injury was more important.

She had stripped several bunks when she felt a tap on her shoulder. Terrified they had been caught, Bree let out an unladylike yelp. With her heart pounding and the woolen prizes clutched firmly to her bosom, she turned around.

PIRATES AND PROMISES 113

It was only Justin grinning from ear to ear at her fright. Relief washed over her only to be replaced by anger. The man had scared her on purpose. If the blankets had been knives, she would have thrown them at him.

"With what Higgins has, this should be enough," he shouted, still maintaining his devilish grin. "If we need more, I'll come back later."

Bree pushed past him, making sure her first step was firmly planted atop his boot.

"What the—" she heard from behind her.

It did her heart good to see the light wobble in tune to his limp as he carried the lantern high behind her. The sway of the ship made progress slow between the stacked crates. Bree eyed the ropes that held the huge wooden boxes in place. One frayed rope and the entire cargo could come tumbling down on them.

A flash of lightning lit the stairway, almost blinding Bree as she stepped onto the wooden platform. Thunder rumbled and the ship lurched in its wake, throwing Bree against the far stair rail. With her arms full of the borrowed blankets, she lost her footing and tumbled toward the open stairway below. Somewhere, as if off in the far distance, Bree heard Justin's shout. "Take the lantern."

All Bree's years of fearing heights culminated in that one moment. She couldn't see the steps. She couldn't feel the fall. She couldn't breathe. Rough hands clasped her tightly and wouldn't let go. Someone was shaking her.

A slap across her face sent splinters of colored lights shooting through her head. Taking in her surroundings, Bree gasped for breath. She was balanced on the edge of the step, wrapped in the pirate's arms. Her cheek smarted in the worst way.

"You hit me," she shouted up at him as he pulled her from the stairs.

Justin grinned down at her. "Only thing I know to do for hysterics," he said. "That, or throw a bucket of cold water over your head, and I didn't have time to fetch one."

He loosened his hold on her, then reached down for the

scattered blankets. Once he had them stuffed back in her arms, he turned her around to the stairway. "Now do you think you can make it below without my help? I have mares to attend to."

Determined to manage on her own, Bree settled her hip against the rail and stomped down the remaining steps. Well, let him attend to his mares. They obviously meant more to him than anything else.

Still upset, Bree fumed to herself while the men set about fastening the blankets over the rails of the stalls. Other than making sure the ends were secure, there wasn't much skill required in the feat and the woolen squares hung with all the dignity of a vacated cocoon.

It was Bree's task to fill the misshapen cubicles with straw. She knew it was imperative for the mares' safety that she work quickly but it was all she could do to keep her own balance. Each lurch of the ship threatened to send her scrambling across the floor.

Using the rope that kept her breeches from dropping around the tops of her slippers, Bree tied herself to the end of the first stall. Then kneeling, she scooped up a generous handful of the straw and stuffed it into the hole between the stall slats and the blanket. Soon she had the cavity filled. Untying the rope, she moved to the next rail, then anchored herself again.

The mare, frightened by the sudden appearance of someone crawling before her, squealed and struck out. Bree slid back as far as the rope would allow and fell. She gasped when the hoof missed her head by only inches. Crawling back on her hands and knees, Bree glared up at the mare.

"I'm only trying to help, you ungrateful bag of—"

A boot tapping on the floor near her hand ended Bree's unladylike tirade. With a sense of dread, she allowed her gaze to wander up the snug breeches, past the white linen shirt, to the dark scowl on the pirate's face.

"My intention was to calm the mares, Smythe, not start a war."

Bree scooted up next to the stall. "Tell that to your

high-stepping friend here," she said as she reached up to stuff a generous handful of straw in the makeshift sleeve. "She was the one that became hysterical and declared this to be a battle. Perhaps you should consider a slap to *her* face," she added bitterly.

He held his hand down to her. "I'm sorry, Bree," he said so politely that Bree accepted the olive branch and rose in his arms. "You had stopped breathing and looked so frightened I didn't know what else to do."

His hooded eyes held hers and Bree found herself drowning in their dark green depths. How could she remain upset with him when his gallantry reminded her so much of her storybook heroes? Standing close to him, she wondered if, after all these years, St. Clair stood as tall as the pirate or if his shoulders were as broad.

Without warning, the pirate lowered his gaze to her mouth and Bree wondered if he was going to kiss her. She parted her lips in anticipation of his touch.

Her breeches! They were sliding down. Hoping to stop their descent, she threw herself against him. The breeches stayed put but another heat took the place of the one caused by her embarrassment. His nearness burned through her. She was afire with it. When she heard a moan rise from deep within him, she knew he too was torn by the temptation she had innocently offered.

Bree grabbed at the top of her breeches, but before she could move away, the pirate stepped back. "You go to the other end and help Higgins. I'll finish here."

A cold, empty knot formed in Bree's stomach, but she did as she was told. No one stands next to the raging fires of forbidden passion and does not get burned, she told herself. No one but me.

"She's a curse on us all, I say!"

The captain's voice seemed to bounce off the small cabin's walls, hitting Bree's aching head from all sides. She vaguely remembered the storm stopping in the hours just before dawn, but not before she had been gripped with a bout of morning sickness again. Sometime later, Justin had carried her to his bed. She didn't know what had happened after that. She had been too sick to care.

She could hear the pirate calmly telling the captain to keep his voice down.

"This is me ship and I'll say what I please," the captain roared.

"You can't blame the storm on a woman. Only God has a say in that."

"And he's punishing me for allowing ye to bring 'er aboard. I want that woman off me ship!"

"And how much is it to cost this time?" she heard the pirate ask. Bree lowered the blanket she had pulled over her head.

The captain stood with his face shoved up at the pirate. "Ye can't bribe God with the color of yer gold," he slurred.

Justin pulled some coins from his pocket. "I'm not bribing God, I'm bribing you."

Bree could see the captain licking his lips in anticipation of getting the coins. "Are ye paying for the damage she caused last night?" the captain asked.

"I'm paying the last I have. If you take it, I must have your word this will not be brought up again. Miss Smythe continues with us and no more threats of throwing her overboard."

The captain grudgingly took the coins. "No more threats," the pirate stated firmly. "Miss Smythe continues with us."

"Captain! Come look!"

The shout interrupted Justin's demands.

"What is it?" Tibbs asked.

"A ship!"

With one last look to the bed, the captain turned and ran down the companionway. Justin turned to Bree. Another ship? Another way for the captain to rid himself of his nemesis? The cry of the second mate hung like a black omen between them.

CHAPTER 8

THE ship stood dark and ominous against the morning sky. She was tall, long, and sleek, and built for speed. Painted black from stem to stern, she was the color of death—the specter of every sailor's nightmare. The absence of a flag proclaiming its country of allegiance told as much as if it had flown the telltale flag of the black skull and crossbones from her mast.

At the whiteness of his second mate's face, the captain pushed his men aside and staggered to the rail. Well aware of his authority, he rudely grabbed the spyglass from the mate's trembling fingers.

He didn't need to see the letters painted boldly across the stern to feel a chill curling up his back. The body of a dead man swinging from the crow's nest more than accomplished the task. He only knew of one ship that displayed its crimes so arrogantly. Tibbs took a deep breath, swallowed hard, then lowered the glass.

It was the *Black Lady*, the most notorious of all pirate ships. The *Seahawk* was no match for the cannons that lined the pirate ship's decks. The knowledge went a long way toward sobering a man up.

"Is she catching up with us?" Tibbs shouted up to the sailor atop the mainmast.

"Nay," he returned. "She keeps a nice safe distance, she does. Our cannons can't reach 'er if she stays there. Bidin' 'er time, I'd say, Capt'n."

With the threat of the pirate ship hanging over him, the coins Tibbs had accepted from Tyler seemed to grow warm in his pocket. The devil's price for guilt. If he had thought to question the Lord's curse for bringing a harlot aboard before, what he saw now put all doubts aside.

"This is all Miss Smythe's fault," Tibbs muttered to himself.

He'd set her adrift now if he thought he could keep his crew from learning of the bribes he had already accepted from Mr. Tyler. Anyone but Tyler he would have silently eliminated, but you didn't toss someone like him overboard. There would be an investigation. Charges would be filed. He did too much business with the merchants in Virginia to risk that. Damn Tyler. He knew it too.

As if the fog had finally cleared from his rum-soaked brain, the knowledge of what he had been doing to Tyler hit Tibbs like a gale force. No matter what he tried to tell himself, it was blackmail plain and simple. Mr. Tyler was a man of influence in Virginia. What would happen to the trade Tibbs had built with the merchants if it got out that he had been squeezing coins out of Tyler because Tyler had dared bring a trollop aboard? A captain might have total say on his ship, but the merchants' trade was his livelihood. Dare he hope Tyler would not mention it to the others?

"It's the woman!" one of the sailors shouted. "First the storm, then this."

Tibbs's heart sank as he heard the accusations echoed among his men. He turned to find Tyler and the woman standing behind him. The dark arched brow told him that Tyler was calling his bluff. If he sided with his men, they would learn of the bribes and he was likely to have a mutiny on his hands.

"Get the woman below, Tyler," he growled. "You don't want the pirate scum on that ship to see 'er and decide they want to board because they've been too long without a piece of skirt?"

Justin took the spyglass from the captain and lifted the long tube to his eye. With it, he could see the pirates scattered along the decks of the black ship. Even though he suspected the other ship to have a glass as powerful, he was certain with the clothes Bree wore and the dim morning light, anyone that far away would have a difficult time determining that Bree was a woman, but he wasn't going to put forth an argument now. Handing the spyglass back to the captain, he took Bree's arm. With the crew claiming her to be a jinx, she would be safer out of their sight anyway.

"Down to the cabin," he commanded.

Bree pulled out of his grasp. "You don't believe this nonsense, do you?"

Justin watched her a moment through narrowed eyes. Short of picking her up and carrying her, there was only one way he knew of to get her below without a fight.

"It doesn't matter whether I believe it to be nonsense or not," he said. "I can't risk them coming aboard to get you and finding my mares."

"Your mares?" she choked. "He's trying to condemn me as some sort of witch and you're concerned with the welfare of your mares?"

With a telltale smile pasted firmly on his lips, Justin couldn't risk meeting her gaze. He chose instead to look over her shoulder. "I don't see why that should surprise you. You yourself said I was inconsiderate and overbearing. So let's have no more quibbling over this. Get yourself down to the cabin and stay there until this pirate ship takes its interest elsewhere."

"Aye!" the captain said, adding his opinion to that of Justin's. He leaned down to whisper something to the cabin boy, who had come aboveboard to see what the commotion was all about. When he finished, he turned back to Bree.

"I'll have Samuel escort ye below."

Bree stiffened with indignation. "I don't need *his* help,"

she said. "I know the way." With that, she swung around and walked away.

"I'll go with 'er," Otis offered, then hurried after her before the captain could call him back. Ned trailed after them.

Otis didn't speak until they were safely below. "Beggin' yer pardon, miss, but if ye could but learn to keep ye temper under ye bonnet when ye're in the captain's vicinity, ye might fare a bit better."

"But he's such a toad," Bree tossed over her shoulder.

She could have sworn she heard Ned snicker, but when she turned to see, Otis appeared to have taken Ned in hand and squashed any humor the sailor might have derived from her comment.

Otis smiled knowingly at her. "I can't be arguin' with that, but Capt'n Tibbs doesn't take kindly to 'avin' 'is orders questioned in front of 'is men."

Bree continued walking down the narrow companionway. "I'll keep that in mind for the future, Otis, but for now excuse me if I consider the man a coward and a fool."

She stopped in the companionway, knowing her two escorts would be forced to do likewise. With hands on her hips, she turned back.

"Didn't you hear him whisper to Samuel to hang a cross on my cabin door?"

"Can't say as I did, miss," Ned answered quickly, "me bein' on the far side of the deck, so to speak. But I can see where that might tend to irritate someone as delicate as ye. Why, me an' Otis—"

Otis cut off Ned's speech with another back-handed punch to the man's plump ribs. "She ain't talkin' to ye." Otis paused a moment to clear his throat. "W'at Ned means to say is me an' 'im don't think ye be 'alf the witch the captain makes ye out ta be."

Half? Bree didn't know whether to be angry or touched. She chose the latter. "I guess I should thank you for your belief in me," she said as she opened the door to her cabin.

"Weren't nothin', miss," Otis declared with a big smile on his face. "Everyone knows a woman be a gentle creature. Why, she'd 'ave no call to try to outsmart a man, now would she?"

"Unless the man were the captain or Mr. Tyler," she mumbled to herself as she stepped into the cabin and closed the door.

She had barely crossed the room when she heard a loud knock. Before she could open the door, Justin let himself in.

"What are you doing here?" she demanded. "I thought you would be with your precious mares."

"I would be," he shot back. "But I've come for my pistol. If those pirates decide to come aboard, the captain will need all the weapons he can muster."

Fear, like a heavy stone, seemed to have lodged in her heart. "Do you really think they will try to board the *Seahawk*?"

"I don't think they'll attack immediately. They're merely trying to determine our weaknesses for now. With the *Seahawk* carrying my mares instead of the usual crates, she might not be riding as low in the water. If they think we're not carrying a full cargo, they might go their own way. It's up to them now. They'll have to decide if they think we're worth their efforts. If they do, they'll attack."

Frightened by the grim lines on the pirate's face, Bree ran the short distance between them and flung herself into his arms. "I'll do anything you ask," she wailed. "Just don't let them take me."

Justin looked down at the top of her blond head in amusement. If he had known it only took the threat of pirates to bring about her humble obedience, he would have introduced the possibility sooner.

He wrapped his arms around her and pulled her close. The thin shirts between them did little to hide Bree's firm breasts pressed invitingly against his chest. Although earlier he had resolved to ignore the temptation, Justin could feel his own body responding to her nearness. He rubbed his fingers along the small of her back and, for a moment, he considered taking advantage of the situation.

It would be so easy to carry her trembling body over to the bed. He would lie down beside her. Comfort her. And then . . .

Walter Bishop stood in front of the large mahogany desk and wished he were anywhere else but Lord Foxworth's study.

"You were right, gov'nor," he said. "Lady Sabrina was with the pirate. Stayin' at the Duck and Ale, they were."

Quentin's gray eyes narrowed. "And did you bring her back with you?"

Walter looked to his boot tops for encouragement. But his action accomplished nothing. Once he'd taken proper measure of the pirate, he'd quickly abandoned any plans he'd fostered of snatching the young lady.

"The highwayman took her aboard the *Seahawk*," he finally mumbled.

Quentin's fingers curled around the silver top of his walking stick. "And you let her get away?"

The deceptive calm in his question lured Walter into lifting his head. What he saw dried his mouth up like a winter apple. Hell's bells. He was in for it now.

"Beggin' your pardon, Lord Foxworth, but—"

Quentin stood. Raising the cane, he brought it down on the desk in front of the short man. Papers went flying. Unconcerned with the mess, Quentin leaned across the desk and glared at him.

"There will be no begging my pardon or anyone else's. You've been in my employ long enough to know I pay for the best and I expect the same." Quentin sank back down in the deep leather chair behind his desk. "Now get out!"

His feet rooted to the floor, Walter twisted his cap into a tight ball. "I did find out where the ship was bound, my lord," he offered, hoping to redeem himself.

Quentin lifted a dark brow. "Well, out with it."

"The ship set sail for America. Virginia, I was told."

"Virginia?" Quentin repeated. Caught up in his thoughts for revenge, he tapped the end of the walking stick against his free hand for a few moments.

"Well, well. So she thinks to lose herself in that godforsaken land with her lover, does she? I think it's time Lord Smythe learns where his daughter has gotten off to. Then, of course, I shall play the saddened fiancé. Being of such a generous—and forgiving—nature, I shall also volunteer to go to Virginia and bring her back. My half brother, being a Virginian himself, might even prove to be of some help. What do you think, Walter?"

Although Walter was basically a bully and a coward, he relished hearing of the punishment of others and smiled for the first time since entering Foxworth's study. "Not having met your half brother, I can't rightly say, but you'll find her. And when you do, she'll regret having played loose with you, Lord Foxworth. That she will."

The sadistic gleam in Walter's eye only served to heighten the sense of exhilaration growing within Quentin as he plotted his revenge.

"On your way out tell my butler I have a message for him," he said coolly, dismissing the man.

He'd have him instruct his valet to pack immediately. No one got the best of Quentin St. Clair without paying the price.

Justin strode the quarterdeck in frustration. He had had Bree in his arms and his conscience had balked at the idea of taking her.

Damn! It wasn't as if she were a virgin. Bree was not new to the passions of lovemaking. If truth be known, she'd more than likely be pleased to rekindle them with him.

Yet, even as the thought crossed his mind, Justin knew the real reason behind his not taking advantage of the beauty in his arms. With the threat of the pirates hanging over them, Bree was terrified. He'd not have her turn to him for comfort only. When she came to him, he wanted her to bring her soul.

As if he could banish the pirate ship by merely wishing it away, Justin looked out over the water, but the dark ship was still hovering just out of range of the *Seahawk*'s cannons. At first, Captain Tibbs had tried outdistancing the pirate vessel, but he had quickly learned that the big black ship was capable of equal speed. When the *Seahawk* slowed, so did the pirate ship. With stubborn persistence, it matched them furlong for furlong. How many more days would it be before the captain of the *Black Lady* called an end to these cat-and-mouse games and attacked?

Bree dipped her handkerchief in the bowl of tepid water, then dabbed at her face and neck. Since the storm, the weather had grown unusually warm. It was hot enough to bake bread in the tiny cabin. It didn't help that she continued to be sick the better part of each day. Eight days, in fact. Eight days and she was still confined to these stifling quarters.

She lifted the limp strands of her hair off the back of her neck and wondered if the pirate ship would ever stop following them. She didn't know how much longer she could stay cooped up like this without going stark raving mad.

At least Justin had not insisted on sharing the cabin with her. Other than the few times he came to take her above deck after dark, she saw little of him.

He had even allowed her to wear her pink dress. Even though she had to don the shirt and breeches for her nightly walks aboveboard, wearing the gown during the daylight hours made her feel like a woman again.

The captain had instructed Samuel to see to her needs and the lad never let a moment pass that he didn't let her know of his displeasure with the arrangement. Justin had warned her to ignore the cabin boy's manners and remain civil for he no longer had sufficient coin with which to soothe the captain's anger. Bree didn't want to think about how much she had cost him so far.

At the knock on her door, Bree stiffened. She wasn't in the mood to smile politely while Samuel continued to taunt her with his sly innuendos about her unorthodox relationship with the pirate.

With a frown on her face, she pulled the door open. "If you've come to—"

The words died at the sight of Mr. Thurston standing in the companionway, a warm smile on his handsome face.

He removed his hat. "It will be dark soon and I've come to persuade you to join me for a walk about the deck."

He presented the image of the perfect gentleman, and Bree couldn't help but respond to his easy manners. She knew she must look a fright, but he didn't seem to care.

"I don't think I'd be fit company for anyone at the moment, Mr. Thurston," she said, lifting her hand to straighten a stray strand of hair.

"Miss Smythe, you look as fresh as a rosebud," he said with a slight bow.

His smile should have put her at ease, but it only served to make her more aware of her untidiness. "I don't—"

"Don't say you care what Mr. Tyler would have to say on the subject," he interrupted, "because if you do, let me put your concerns to rest. Mr. Tyler is once more occupied with his precious mares."

At her continued hesitation, Nicholas almost turned and left, but the thought of her lying writhing beneath him in the throes of an uninhibited passion urged him to try again. He reached out and tipped her chin up.

"It would be a waste to allow Tyler to keep you hidden away the entire trip," he teased.

Bree did so want to get out of the cabin. It was the only time she could rid herself of the squeamishness that continued to plague her. "Perhaps a short walk . . ." she said with a sigh.

Nicholas held his arm out to her. "I certainly hope you find the company intriguing enough to allow me to persuade you to have supper with me tonight."

"I don't think—"

Nicholas stopped and turned her to face him. "What am I to do with you, Miss Smythe? Is Mr. Tyler the only gentleman allowed the privilege of enjoying your company?"

"No, it's merely..."

Nicholas lifted a dark brow. "It's merely that he has a prior claim on your affections?"

"Heavens, no," she said. "Mr. Tyler and I have an unusual... business relationship. That is all."

"I'm pleased to hear that, Miss Smythe."

He had taken her arm again and Bree was finding herself warming to the stranger. Justin Tyler could certainly learn from the man's gallantry.

The last ribbons of a brilliant sunset were dropping into the sea when they reached the deck. With a sigh, Bree leaned back against the stair rail to watch. Despite the stunning colors, her attention was drawn to the ominous silhouette of the ship that clung like a giant black shadow to the south of them.

When the colors faded and night wrapped them in darkness, Bree ventured closer to the rail. "Will they ever stop following us?" she asked.

Nicholas stopped. "At least they are keeping a proper distance," he said as he waited for Bree to turn toward him. Once he had captured her undivided attention, he continued. "If they knew of the rare treasure we carry, they would not have spared us so long."

Bree dropped her gaze to the rail. There was no mistaking the admiration in his voice, nor in the glance he bestowed upon her. The gallantry of a gentleman. It was something one of the heroes in her books would have said. It was something she could envision St. Clair saying. The thought tore at her heart. Even after everything that had happened between her and Justin, could she truly tuck away her dreams and never take them out again?

Her traitorous body might long for the highwayman's touch, but her heart would always belong to St. Clair, she stubbornly reminded herself. No matter what havoc Justin wreaked on her senses, she must never lose sight of her love for the man who had filled her dreams all these years.

"Thank you," she said quietly.

Nicholas placed his hand over hers. "There's no need to thank someone for saying what they believe."

Bree stared down at his hand. Nothing. She felt nothing. If she could resist this man's advances and sweet words, surely she could offer the same resistance to the pirate's.

"What are you doing up here dressed as you are?"

Not having heard Justin approach, Bree was startled by the harsh words. "I . . ."

Nicholas pushed away from the rail. "If you must know, Tyler, I asked Miss Smythe to accompany me for a walk about the deck."

"She knows the rules. She doesn't wear her gown when she comes aboveboard."

Nicholas purposely let his gaze travel down the pink gown. "I must say, I see nothing amiss in the manner in which Miss Smythe is dressed. As black as the night is, I don't understand why you are creating such a fuss."

"I don't expect you would," Justin answered gruffly. He had finally recalled where he had met Thurston before. The insolent perusal the man had given Bree had triggered the memory that had been hovering at the edge of Justin's consciousness since the beginning of the trip.

That night in England. Thurston had been the gentleman traveling with Lord Westcliffe when Justin had abducted the duke. It was no wonder he was forever catching Thurston staring at him in puzzlement. The man was probably attempting to recall why Justin appeared familiar.

Justin grabbed Bree's arm and pulled her toward the stairs. Lord help them all if recognition were finally to dawn on Thurston as well.

At the pirate's rudeness, Bree started to pull from his grasp, then thought better of it. His green eyes were like frozen emerald nuggets—cold enough to frost her flushed cheeks.

Tired of his high-handed ways, Bree refused to lower her gaze from his. The pirate might still have the power to embarrass her but she was becoming accustomed to his poor manners and exchanged glare for glare.

"We can't run the risk of someone from the *Black Lady* getting a glimpse of you," Justin stated firmly as he met Bree's hard stare. "So for the safety of all of us, you will go below and change."

Nicholas stepped forward. "No polite request, Tyler, just a command?" he asked.

Bree stepped between them. "Mr. Tyler's manners may be in desperate need of renovation, but in this instance, he is correct. I do need to change. However, it's a shame he couldn't have been more of a gentleman about it." Having delivered the set down, Bree turned and walked away.

"I shall await your return," Nicholas called after her.

Justin wanted nothing so much as to pick the dandy up and toss him over the side. It was apparent that if he hadn't come along when he did, Thurston would have placed his hand someplace more intimate than atop Bree's fingers.

Justin clenched and unclenched his fists in anger. Even knowing Bree would never be a match for Thurston's smooth brand of charm, he almost wished he hadn't interrupted the little tête-à-tête. Chances were Bree might have bestowed the popinjay with one of her swift punches.

"Stay away from her," Justin warned.

Nicholas leaned back against the rail. "I wasn't aware that Miss Smythe was spoken for."

"She's not. But I hold the papers on her that says I have the right to decide how her time is spent."

"How very fortunate for you," he said with a lazy drawl.

Justin's lips twisted into a grin. "Yes, it is, isn't it? And, the most fortunate thing about it is that you aren't on her schedule of duties."

Bree was still mumbling silent curses at Justin's surly behavior when she reached the cabin. So she had forgotten to change into her shirt and breeches before she went above. It wasn't as if she'd done it to annoy him.

She started undoing the ties on her gown. "I'd be willing

to wager he's not made a mistake his entire years," she mumbled.

The door slammed behind her. "You'd lose the bet," Justin said. "I've made numerous mistakes, but I find my biggest mistake was ever rescuing you from Quentin."

"I didn't need your help," she tossed over her shoulder.

"Given the manner with which you attract trouble, there is probably a lot of truth in what you say."

She didn't even bother stepping behind the screen, but continued to undo her gown. "You can always surrender the papers I signed."

Seeing the difficulty she was having with the gown, Justin stepped behind her to assist. "I've considered it," he said, helping her undo the remaining ties, "but after all the coin I've paid out on your behalf, the gesture would be too costly."

Bree spun around. With a tug at the sleeves, she pulled the gown from her shoulders. It fell to the floor around her ankles. "Your precious coins," she snapped, stepping out of the circle of folds. "Is that all that occupies your thoughts?"

The sight of her creamy white breasts straining against the lace edges of her chemise when she bent to pick up the gown set Justin's heart to racing. Damn, he wanted her, but the image of her in Quentin's arms rose like an evil apparition before him, dashing his burgeoning lust with the cold water of reality.

The mere thought of her married to Quentin still tore at his gut. Justin took her by the shoulders and pulled her roughly against him. Would he never be able to shake the image?

"What occupies my thoughts is you, Smythe," he said bitterly, before huskiness lowered his voice. "Don't you know what having you near does to a man?"

At the strange look in his eyes, Bree's mouth went powder dry. "I . . ."

"Don't you know that when I see you all I want to do is toss you across that bed and claim you for mine?"

Claim her? What was he saying? The desire building in the green depths of his eyes hinted at something more than the indenture papers he held on her. The Something Awful? Bree trembled at the thought of an unknown fate more dreadful than the results of his kiss.

"You wouldn't," she said with more conviction than she felt. "I belong to . . . someone else."

"Your Sir Henry?"

Bree swallowed against the curtness of his question. "Y-yes," she choked out when he grasped her by the chin.

"Don't delude yourself into thinking that it is your Sir Henry that keeps me from taking you to my bed. Your only protection is my knowing that Quentin is the one who occupies your heart."

Justin stiffened at the anger that had taken hold of him. Afraid of what he might do, he released her so quickly she almost fell.

"I'd not share my horse with the bastard, let alone my mistress."

Justin had to get away from her before the destructive thoughts got the best of him. The only hope for them both was the fact that Quentin was safely tucked away in England, so he'd not have to worry about the possibility of killing his half brother.

CHAPTER 9

IT was dawn but the sun was not yet warm enough to burn off the wisps of ground fog or dry the heavy dew still clinging to the grass. The two gentlemen and their seconds crossed the deserted meadow. There was no physician—no onlookers. Dueling was no longer considered fashionable and to be caught meant having to flee the country.

When the box of weapons was presented, Quentin leaned over and selected his pistol from the set, then handed it to his second for a closer examination.

Although Quentin appeared calm, he seethed with mounting fury. Lord Smythe's reaction to Walter's findings had come as quite a surprise. Never would he have guessed that the old man would have taken offense to him investigating Sabrina's disappearance. The things he had accused Quentin of were not to be ignored.

It hadn't mattered that Quentin had denied everything. The old man foolishly raged on until the entire night's clientele at White's knew of the charges. He had left Quentin with no other choice but to challenge him to the duel.

With his back to Smythe and his pistol pointed skyward, Quentin started pacing, but each step only served to fuel the anger already burning within him until he could no longer see the need to contain the fire. He stopped at the agreed fifty paces.

"One." Lord Manly, the young man acting as Mr. Smythe's second, shouted out across the quiet morning. "Two."

Quentin turned and fired.

"You fired before the count," Lord Manly gasped. When he reached Smythe's still form, he bent to examine the wound. Blood poured freely from his friend's shoulder. Foxworth had cold-bloodedly shot and killed Lord Smythe.

Lord Manly grabbed the earl's unfired dueling pistol. Lord Foxworth deserved to die for the cowardly behavior he had displayed. Slowly Manly rose to his feet and turned to face St. Clair, the pistol clutched at his side.

"You, Lord Foxworth, are no better than a coward. A gentleman waits for the count of three."

Manly raised the pistol, but before he could take proper aim, a shot rang out. The young man stared down in horror at the hole in his gut. St. Clair's second. He hadn't thought to watch the man.

"Excellent shot, Walter," he heard Lord Foxworth say before the blackness of death overcame him.

Quentin started toward Smythe when a movement at the far end of the meadow caught his eye. A carriage was coming.

When Bree returned aboveboard, she was relieved to discover Mr. Thurston gone. After her confrontation with Justin, she was in no mood for pleasantries. Her head was pounding and all she wanted was to beg a cup of hot tea from the cook to soothe her frazzled nerves.

The wind had come up and Bree had to hold on to the rail as she made her way along the deck. Other than Pheps, the chief mate, standing at the wheel, she didn't see anyone. It was obvious from the lack of activity that the captain must be closeted in his cabin again with his jug. She only hoped the cook hadn't taken to shirking his duties in the captain's absence like most of the crew.

PIRATES AND PROMISES

It seemed to take forever to make her way to the galley, but if the lights blazing from the window were any indication, she was in luck. The cook was working late.

Bree heard the voices before she got to the door. With her hand on the latch, she hesitated. She had no wish to run into the captain. When a burst of laughter erupted behind the closed door, Bree relaxed. The captain had to be elsewhere for she knew he wouldn't tolerate anyone enjoying himself. She pushed the door open, then almost fled when all eyes turned toward her.

Mr. Thurston, the cook, and several rough-looking sailors were hunched over the room's only table, their cards held possessively against their chests.

"I only came for a cup of tea," she whispered huskily.

Nicholas held his hand out to her. "Come join us." When he saw her hesitate, he added gallantly, "Even in those unlikely rags, you look most beautiful."

Before returning his smile, Bree looked warily around at the others. With all the time her father spent at the tables in London, she knew how much men valued their game of cards.

"I didn't mean to interrupt," she said.

"Nonsense. Cook here will get you a cup of tea." Nicholas pushed one of the men off the barrel beside him. "Tom needs to get back to his duties anyway. You come sit beside me. I'm teaching these barbarians the fine points of a gentleman's game of cards and they are beating me at it—frightfully so, I might add. But with someone as beautiful as you beside me, perhaps my luck will change."

The scowl on Tom's face as he left the room told Bree she had made another enemy among Tibbs's crew, but curiosity kept her from turning down Mr. Thurston's invitation. After Nicholas had been so gracious as to place his lace handkerchief on the barrel for her, Bree could do nothing else but take her place at the table.

Nicholas shuffled the cards. It was time he reclaimed the coins he had allowed the other players to win. Bree's presence was all he would need to distract the men from the sudden shift in their luck.

"Have you ever played before, Miss Smythe?" he asked as he dealt the next hand.

"No, but my companion warned me that many have lost their fortunes at the tables."

"And also made them," he said with a sideways glance at her. "By the time we reach Virginia, you could be a very wealthy young lady."

Ah, now he had her interest. Another lamb to fleece, he wondered, or merely a means of repaying Tyler for his high-handed rudeness earlier? Of course, there was always the possibility of winning something other than a few paltry coins. There had been more than one lady who attempted to reclaim her markers by way of sharing her feminine charms with him.

"I will teach you the game, if you like," he offered.

He could see by the light in her blue eyes that she was intrigued by the idea. The sparkle was enough to take a man's breath away.

"I'll even stake you a few coins to make it interesting."

Bree frowned. "I don't know if I should, Mr. Thurston."

He didn't listen to her protests, but dealt her in. At first, he put aside his intent to recoup the funds he had allowed the others to win to assist Bree, but it was soon evident that Miss Smythe had a real talent of her own for the cards and the next few hours seemed to sail by as he surrendered his place to sit at her arm and watch her take hand after hand.

The cook tossed his cards down on the table. "I'm out," he said.

Bree looked to the other men in turn as they placed their cards down and nodded to pass. With a smile, she scooped up the small pile of coins on the table.

"This is delightful," she said.

Nicholas leaned back in his chair. Things had not gone as he would have liked. Bree now held all the coins he had planned on winning for his own purse. "A lady does not gloat over her abundance of luck, my dear."

Contrite at her lack of sensitivity, Bree looked at the

others apprehensively. "I'm sorry," she said. "I did not mean to win so much."

"Nor does a lady apologize, my dear. Winning, like everything else, is something you accept as your due."

His preaching on her manners was beginning to annoy Bree. "Shall we play another game?" she asked.

Nicholas reached in front of her and gathered up the cards. "I think you have taken enough of these gentlemen's coins for one evening." He stood and looked around the table. "Perhaps tomorrow evening. What do you say? Miss Smythe will give you the opportunity to redeem your losses tomorrow evening."

After a few surly ayes, Nicholas held his arm out to Bree. He may not have been able to win back the money he had lost earlier, but he had every intention of seeing that Miss Smythe compensate him in other ways.

"Shall we take that stroll I promised you earlier?"

Bree dumped the last of her winnings in the leather pouch she had won from the cook and took Mr. Thurston's arm.

The moment the carriage came to a stop, Maddie pushed open the door. She didn't wait for the footman, but jumped down. Lord, please let him be alive, she prayed as she knelt beside the still figure stretched out on the wet grass.

"Manly?" Edward asked when she touched him.

Maddie thought her heart would burst. He was alive.

Kneeling on the grass beside him, she gently pillowed his head in her lap. "Help me get him into the carriage," she shouted to the footman.

"Manly?" the question came again.

Maddie looked to the driver who had walked over to Lord Smythe's second. At the solemn nod, she closed her eyes against the tears that threatened. "I'm sorry," was all she could say.

"St. . . . Clair shot . . . before the count," Edward said between ragged breaths.

Maddie pushed a stray curl from his forehead. "Hush now. I promise when we get you home, I will send word of St. Clair's crimes to the constable. But for now, you need to save your strength."

With a heavy sigh, he collapsed in her arms.

When Justin saw that the game was breaking up, he stepped back into the shadows. He had been watching for hours through the smudged galley window, telling himself it meant nothing to him if Bree chose to spend her free hours playing cards with Thurston, but he envied the easy friendship they seemed to have slipped into so quickly.

When the door opened, Thurston had a smile on his face and Bree on his arm. Keeping to the shadows, Justin followed them.

"Do you know what you are going to do with all your winnings?" Nicholas asked, guiding Bree along the moon-washed deck.

"Oh my, yes," she answered without hesitation. "I'm saving it to pay Mr. Tyler for my freedom."

The comment brought a wry grin to Justin's lips. Bree might have been the winner for the evening, but little did she know, winner or no, there weren't enough coins on the entire ship to tempt him to hand over her documents of indenture.

Thurston paused at the rail. "With such a worthwhile goal, I will have to see to it that you are invited to the game every night."

Justin was not close enough to hear Bree's reply, but her soft laughter brought a frown to his lips. He didn't care for Thurston and from all he'd observed the feelings were reciprocated.

The dislike didn't stem from the fact that Thurston was attracted to Bree, he told himself. After all, what man on the ship wasn't? There was more to it than that. It was almost as if Thurston struck up the friendship with Bree for no other reason than to annoy Justin.

The frown brought a furrow to his brow. Unfortunately, Thurston's plan was proving successful. Justin was annoyed. No, Justin corrected himself, he wasn't merely annoyed. He was furious.

PIRATES AND PROMISES

He reached them before they had gone two more steps. Drawing back his fist, Justin pulled Thurston around. "I said to stay away from her, Thurston," he warned as he hit the dandy.

Bree stared down at the unconscious man. "Only you are allowed to punch someone?" she asked.

Justin took her by the arm, but didn't say a word until they reached the cabin. "Must you play cards with that bounder? Can't you find anything else to occupy your time?"

Angry, Bree turned on him. "What would you suggest? I've cleaned the cabin until it shines. I've read every book on your shelf and let me tell you there weren't many of them worth reading."

This was getting him nowhere. The fire of anger in her eyes only served to light his own fires of passion. Numerous ideas came to mind of how she might spend her free time, but he knew without asking that his offer that they spend it in the bed behind her would be turned down. "If I can find you another book, will you promise to behave yourself?" he asked instead.

"It depends on the book. I don't care for just any old one. It must be a romantic story of—"

"You want me to find a book filled with romance on a ship of uneducated sailors?"

Bree cocked her head to one side and smiled up at him. "It would keep me away from the card table."

Justin returned her smile with another frown. Smythe was an enchantress when she set her mind to it.

"If there is one to be had, rest assured it will be in your hands by morning."

He didn't locate one until three days later, but the book was all she could have hoped for. *The Baron's Vixen*. The heroine, Miss Lucy, had blond hair much like her own, and of course, she captured the baron's heart.

Checking her reflection in the mirror, Bree frowned at the sight of her straight blond hair. Even though she lacked the curls of Miss Lucy, she would have been blind not to notice that the seamen seemed to glance at her more often than they did at their cards. Mr. Thurston—Nicholas—had told her she should take advantage of their interest and flirt with the men. It would only help add to her winnings, he had assured her.

If only the wind didn't blow the curl out of her hair. It really needed washing, but what was the sense of washing it if she had no way of curling it. What she needed was . . .

Bree spotted the pirate's white linen shirt hanging from a wooden hook on the back of the cabin door. It had been hanging there for two days now. She thoughtfully fingered the soft material. With this hot weather, the pirate really had no need for it. He wouldn't even miss it, she told herself as she lifted it off the hook.

It didn't take her long to cut it into the narrow strips she needed. Once finished, she grabbed up the washbasin and started for the door. Drats! Someone was sure to stop her before she got to the galley to refill it with fresh, warm water. She might as well try to make do with the cold water left over from her morning wash.

Attempting to wash her hair proved to be harder than she thought. The washbasin wasn't large enough to accommodate the long strands all at once and Bree was forced to wash them a section at a time. When she finished, her hair was a series of knots and tangles and it took her the better part of an hour to smooth the unruly locks.

Using the pieces of linen, she tied each strand up into a little curl. She couldn't wait to see the look of approval on the men's faces—nor the surprise on the Justin's when he came to escort her to the galley. She'd even risk wearing her pink gown.

The look on Justin's face was everything she had hoped for. He took her by the shoulders and turned her around, then gallantly held his arm out to her.

"May I?" he asked.

PIRATES AND PROMISES

Trying not to look at his bare chest as she smiled up at him, Bree rested her fingers lightly on his arm. He didn't even seem to notice that she wore the gown.

"Most certainly, sir," she said in a low whisper.

She was pleased with the way Justin couldn't take his eyes off her as they made their way down the companionway. She had never felt so beautiful before. The thought that she was being rather disloyal to St. Clair crossed her mind, but the beguiling smile on the pirate's lips shoved the doubts aside. She was only trying to stay on his good side, she told herself.

When Justin paused at the end of the hall and turned to her, she wondered if she'd gone too far. If the hungry look in his green eyes didn't vanish soon, it was evident he was going to kiss her again. Even knowing it was wrong didn't curb the delicious ache spreading through her body at the thought.

The kiss was necessary, she told herself. This one would not take her by surprise. She could study it and decide if the warnings about it were true . . . and what it was about the first one that had bothered her so. Yes, another kiss and she could not only shove the memory of the other one out of her mind once and for all, but she would put the silly things her nanny had told her aside.

She watched in fascination as he lowered his head to hers. She had thought herself prepared, but when he dug his fingers into her back, bringing her up against the solid warmth of his naked chest, she knew she was mistaken. He touched his lips to hers and there was no holding back the wanton moan that tore from deep within her.

Somewhere in her consciousness she knew he was undoing the back of her gown. The teasing seductiveness of his velvetlike kiss warred with Nanny's warning, but she couldn't summon up the words to stop him. The tiny ties were no protection against the skill of his fingers and it wasn't long before her back was exposed to his touch.

The knowledge that she should pull away dimmed, for his kiss was no longer a gentle coaxing thing but the demanding right of a lover. The hauntingly wild taste of it took her breath away. It was too late to pull away now. He had already set her body to trembling with desire.

The kiss deepened. Her lips parted at his demands and his tongue slipped in. She knew her heart had stopped beating for no one could live through such ecstasy.

Instinctively, her hips moved against his. The innocent gesture seemed to bring a new urgency to his kiss. His hand sought out her breast and Bree was certain she was going to be damned for this unsanctioned pleasure. Never had she imagined that a kiss could light so many fires within her. An ache like no other spread though her, burning until it scorched her clear down to the secret recesses of her womanhood. It was no wonder her nanny had warned her about the evils of a kiss.

Suddenly, the muscles in Justin's arms tensed and he released her. "It's rather difficult helping to fasten the ties on your gown this way," he said coolly as he turned her around.

Bree started to protest when she saw the cabin boy at the top of the steps watching them. "Perhaps I should have Higgins help me," she somehow managed to mutter.

"Never mind, I think I have it now." He checked to see if Samuel had gone about his duties, but the lad still stood as before, silhouetted against the dark sky.

"It's turned cool," he added. "Wait here for me. I'll get my shirt and be right back."

Bree nodded numbly, her traitorous body still crying out for the fulfillment of the passions he had aroused. How had she let it go this far? Wasn't St. Clair the one she loved? In Justin's arms it was difficult to keep that in mind.

"Where's my shirt?" she heard him call from the cabin. She glanced to see if Samuel heard. He hadn't moved.

"I used it," she called back. "You'll have to wear another one."

Justin stepped into the door of the cabin. "I don't have another one."

Even in the pale light of the moon, Bree was sure she

could see a smile on the lad's face. He was listening to everything the pirate said as he went back to searching the cabin.

"You cut up my shirt!" Bree heard the shout all the way down the hall. "Why did you cut up my shirt?"

She could hear the frustration in his voice. It was understandable. It echoed her own. She hurried down the companionway to warn him that Samuel was still listening.

"If you weren't in the family way," he shouted, "I'd take you over my knee and give you a spanking you'd not soon forget."

Bree cringed. Samuel would have to be deaf not to have heard him.

"She's what?" Tibbs shouted.

Samuel threw out his chest. "He said if she wasn't in the family way—"

Captain Tibbs didn't let him finish. He slammed his mug down on the oak table. "It's no wonder the good Lord thought to rain 'is anger down on us. Not only did Tyler bring a 'arlot aboard, but 'e planted his bastard seed in 'er."

"Are you going to set her afloat?" Samuel asked eagerly.

"I should set them both off me ship," he said, "but I won't. But don't think Mr. Tyler will be gettin' away without God's punishment. Take a couple of men and 'ave them bring the sinners to me. I'll be on the quarterdeck."

The door slammed with a bang and the captain was left to his rum. Stiffly he rose from the table and fetched his Bible. As he saw it, there was only one way for Tyler to atone for his sins.

"Marry her!" Justin looked from one man to another. But there was no help. The captain's decisions were law. "Why should I marry her? The child's not mine."

Tibbs looked to Bree. "Is that true? Does the child belong to someone else?"

Bree couldn't bring herself to look at Justin. If she was in the family way, he was the father. Yet, his denial wasn't as to whether she was to have a child, but that the child was his. What was she to do? He'd hate her no matter what she said. There was no holding back the tear that slipped down her cheek.

The captain grabbed her arm. "Who is the child's father?" he shouted at her.

A sob escaped Bree's throat. "No one's touched me but Mr. Tyler," she mumbled in shame.

"That does it! Ye'll marry 'er tonight, Tyler, or I'll put the both of ye afloat. It's either make a 'onest woman of 'er or ye can take ye chances with the captain of the *Black Lady* out there."

Justin grabbed Bree's arms and shook her. "Tell him the truth, Bree. I'm not the father of your child."

Bree's head remained bowed. She refused to even look at him.

Heaven help them both, she was going to stand silently by while the captain married them.

The anger that had been building with each word of the ceremony threatened to suffocate Justin. Bree stood with her head bowed beside him, seemingly unaware of what was happening. He wanted to take her by the shoulders, shake her and scream that marriage was forever.

How could Bree have done this to him? He knew she wanted a father for her child, but she had blatantly ignored the fact that it was not his responsibility to fill the position.

"Ye are now man and wife," Captain Tibbs announced proudly.

With the words, Justin grabbed Bree up in his arms and swept past the suggestive grins of those who had witnessed the wedding.

He didn't bother lifting the latch on the cabin door when he reached it. With a swift thrust of his booted foot, he kicked the oak door open.

Bree was going to be sorry that she had ever crossed him. He may not be the father of her child, but what she didn't realize was that she was now his for the taking.

CHAPTER 10

BREE cried out when Justin tossed her onto the bed. With her heart in her throat, she ventured a peek up into his dark green eyes. He looked angry enough to strangle her.

"Take off your gown," he growled at her. "And be quick about it."

Bree scooted back on the bed.

Justin frowned, but started undressing. "Don't look at me as if I'm some sort of insect you've pinned to a board. This marriage was not what I had in mind, but then that never mattered, did it?" He leaned down toward her. "You've finally gotten what you wanted, now I'm going to get what I've wanted since you threw my clothes out the window and ran away. Revenge. Thanks to you, we're married and I've a right to claim it."

His indignation gave her courage. "You didn't expect me to lie to Captain Tibbs, did you?"

"No, I expected you to tell the truth," Justin said. He tossed his boots in the corner, then started unbuttoning his breeches. "But since you persist in this little fantasy of yours, I might as well reap some of the rewards of your imagination."

Although the heat of passion was plainly reflected in his eyes, Bree kept her eyes focused on his face. She didn't need to look to know that his unbuttoned breeches were the only thing that stood between her and his nakedness. She dared not let her gaze wander, even in curiosity.

"What are you planning on doing?" she asked, her voice a raspy whisper.

He continued to stare down at her and, at first, she didn't think he had heard her question. A battle of some sort appeared to be taking place inside him. Then suddenly, he reached out and stroked her cheek.

"What would you like me to do?" he asked, taking her hand and helping her from the bed.

Before she knew it, she was standing in the circle of his arms. A lump began to form in her throat. Just his touch left her breathless, an unexpected warmth spreading wildly through her body, and she didn't know why she couldn't shake it. How could she tell him what she wanted when she didn't know herself? How did you explain something you knew nothing about?

"A kiss?" she suggested.

Justin pulled her up hard against him. "That's a start," he whispered.

Before she could protest, his lips came down on hers. Bree stiffened in his arms. This was no gentle seduction, no persuasion, only a cold need. From the fierceness of his kiss, there was no doubt that he was still punishing her for not lying about the child. Bree struggled against him. "Justin, please," she pleaded.

He pulled away.

"There is no need for you to take your anger out on me."

"And pray, who should I take it out on? Captain Tibbs?"

Bree glared up at him. "That would seem the logical choice. After all, this marriage was not my idea either."

"It was your idea," he reminded her. "Ever since that first kiss, you have tried to foster someone else's child off on me."

"But the kiss . . ." Bree hated the blush she felt warming

her face. It was too late now to wish she had had someone explain the ways of . . . of that sort of thing more thoroughly.

"What about the kiss?" he asked. He looked confused.

Until now it never occurred to her that he might not realize what happens with a kiss either. He seemed to know everything. And his kisses. He appeared to be so experienced with them. Bree frowned when she realized the significance of her discovery.

My heavens, the man must have been going blithely through life bestowing his kisses everywhere, not knowing the consequences of his actions. He might have fostered any amount of children in his wake. Someone needed to point this out to him.

Bree stepped back. "Did no one ever tell you that you can't just go around kissing whomever you please?"

He smiled at her embarrassment. "My grandfather did warn me that not every young lady would take kindly to it. But up until now, I've had no complaints."

Bree couldn't believe they were having this conversation. It was obvious that even her scanty information on the subject was greater than his.

"Justin," she started. Bree dropped her gaze to collect her thoughts. The sight of his open breeches brought her eyes racing back to his.

"Mr. Tyler," she said, hoping the formal address would chastise him for his ungentlemanly behavior. "If you go around kissing every young maiden you encounter, England will soon be filled to overflowing with your . . . your . . . offspring."

"Bastard children, you say?"

Ignoring Bree's gasp, Justin pulled her back in his arms. Once he had her tucked securely up against him, he began to rub his hips suggestively against the front of her. It didn't take him long to find the ties at the back of her gown and start to undo them.

"You and I both know . . . it takes more . . . than a kiss to accomplish that, now don't we?" he said between kisses.

"More than . . . ?" Bree pulled back so she could search his face. Somehow what he seemed to be suggesting with the sensual movement of his hips made more sense than her nanny's explanation. Even now the strange sensations he stirred in her body sent out a warning she couldn't deny, but she had to know for sure.

"But your kiss . . ." she began.

The reason behind her confusion suddenly hit him with the force of a hammer. Surely no one was naïve enough to think a kiss would . . .

Justin searched his memory. Had he ever been that young and inexperienced? Suddenly, he didn't care. His heart soared with the possibility he was right.

He folded her tenderly in his arms. "You thought I had gotten you with a child that first time I kissed you, didn't you?"

Bree wanted to die. He would think her a fool. As she tried to think up an appropriate answer, she felt his kiss on the top of her head. All the days of worry fled and Bree couldn't stop the tears of relief that spilled from her eyes. Numbly, she nodded her answer.

Justin's heart filled with unexplained joy. He hugged her to him. She was his. Only his.

"There's so much more to it, love," he whispered into her hair. "So much more. And I'm going to thoroughly enjoy teaching you."

The warmth of his words sent white-hot fires of desire spiraling unchecked through her. She could feel his fingers unfastening the last of her gown's ties. The anticipation was as intoxicating as his touch.

Slowly, but firmly, his hands massaged the tension from her back. Bree laid her head on his chest. She knew she should put a stop to this, but it had been a long time since she had felt loved by anyone. She closed her eyes and lost herself in the unfamiliar sensations.

"Yes," he whispered as he leaned to turn down the wick on the oil lamp. "Just relax and I'll show you everything there is to being a woman—my woman," he added proudly.

He eased the gown from her shoulders. Next, he gently tugged it from between them and sent it on its way to the floor. The thin chemise came next.

Bree sighed. The hair on his chest felt rough against her naked breasts. Rough, but steeped in the warmth of his tanned skin.

"Hold me," she breathed against him. "Hold me and don't ever let me go."

Justin cradled her slim body next to his. She was making it difficult to remember he must go slowly. He didn't want to hurt her, but if she kept this up much longer it was going to be an impossible feat.

Until now he had never been called on to practice restraint. Women had always come eagerly into his arms. He was a demanding lover and they reveled in the part they played in satisfying his needs. With Bree, it would have to be her needs—her wishes.

With her breasts pushing tantalizingly against his chest, he once more ran his hand firmly down her back. Her response was immediate. He could feel her heart racing, her breath become short, labored gasps. He almost stopped breathing himself when she arched her back, laying her body wantonly against the length of his.

Leaning them both to one side, he pulled the blanket from the bed. Take it slowly, he reminded himself as he picked her up and laid her across the sheet. Then, he stepped back and bent to finish undressing.

The moonlight shining through the small window shimmered across the surface of her nakedness. Skin of blushed ivory, Bree was like a delicate piece of fine marble that had been carved into sensual perfection by the talented hands of a master craftsman. And she was his.

In his haste to join her, Justin stumbled trying to rid himself of his breeches. Heaven help him. His hands were even shaking. What was it about this woman that threatened to unman him?

Bree was no light-skirt. She was his wife and he could see that he was not the only one affected by what was about to happen. Bree might be young and innocent, but there was no mistaking the desire that laced her half-closed eyes.

Justin slipped into the bed beside her and all his insecurities vanished when she modestly covered her breasts. He was the teacher here; Bree, his pupil. He meant to introduce her to all the wondrous secrets of lovemaking he had learned himself.

His eyes never leaving hers, Justin took her hand and wove her fingers with his, then raised her hands over her head. Her breasts pushed invitingly up at him. Not yet, he told himself as he eased over onto her, his chest covering hers.

Bree closed her eyes. All her dreams of romance and St. Clair came flooding back to her. Justin's hands caressed her hot body and she thought she'd die from the need he provoked in her. St. Clair would have made her feel like this, she thought. St. Clair would . . .

The pirate's kiss spun her down into a world that had held her prisoner in its fantasy for the last ten years. She was no longer lying with Justin, but with her love—St. Clair.

Gently . . . ever so gently . . . Justin reminded himself as he tasted the appealing fullness of her mouth, but when she hungrily returned his kiss, he knew she wanted more. Instinctively, he realized it was unwise to give in to her now and drew away.

Her hair, like molten gold, curled around his fingers. Moonlight cast an ivory glow on a body blushed with the fires of passion he had kindled within her. With tender persuasion, he placed a kiss on each closed eye. When she didn't open them, he returned to her lips. Unable to hold back, he kissed her with a thoroughness he hoped would tell her of the wild delights to come. It brought forth the desired results. Bree rose beneath him, a moan escaping her bruised lips.

At her eager response, Justin lost the last tenuous hold on his self-control. She was his wife and she wanted him.

It was time to take what she offered and give her what she needed.

Justin shoved his knee between her legs and moved to cover her.

"St. Clair," she whispered huskily in his ear.

Justin stiffened. Was it possible he'd heard her right? Had she really spoken his brother's name? Justin rolled off her.

Bree's fantasy evaporated with the absence of his warmth. Confused, she sat up. "St.—" She bit her lip, cutting the revealing name off unspoken.

"Go back to your dreams, Bree," Justin said gruffly as he reached for his discarded breeches. "Let me know when you're ready for a man."

He hurriedly slipped into his breeches. He didn't bother buttoning them. All he wanted to do was get away before she saw the blood dripping from the knife she had shoved into his heart.

Bree lay in bed staring at the ceiling. Her body, her arms—her heart—felt so empty. It had all seemed so real. She was lying in St. Clair's arms, then he had walked out on her. But it hadn't been St. Clair. It had been Justin. And Justin had left her.

Perhaps it was fate. Her father—now the pirate. Even her dream of St. Clair had fled. Bree drew her knees up to her chest. The bed seemed so empty and cold. Was no one ever to love her again?

Yet if she was honest with herself, she would admit she didn't deserve Justin—or St. Clair. Thinking back, she knew what she had done was wrong. In her foolishness, she had betrayed both Justin and St. Clair. Justin may not have wanted to marry her, but he had. And she had lain in his arms and thought of St. Clair.

Everything had gone so wrong. After thinking on it, she decided the blame lay with the pirate. His nearness had made her question her love for St. Clair, driving her nearly to distraction.

But did it truly matter whose fault it was? What mattered was she was now married to Justin. Even though he would never understand, she couldn't simply set all her dreams aside and accept this marriage. The memory of St. Clair's promise had been with her for too many years. It was all she had the long lonely years she had spent with no one to talk to but Maddie and the servants. No, she couldn't give up on all that. At least not without talking with St. Clair again.

Maddie dipped the cloth in the cool water. It had been days since the duel and still Edward tossed and turned with fever. Having wrung out the cloth, she placed it on his fevered brow.

"B-Bree."

Maddie fought against the tears that stung her eyes. Lord Smythe had done nothing but call for his daughter since he had been brought home. "She'll be here soon," she lied, knowing it was the only thing that would allow him the rest he needed so desperately.

Ever since coming to Roxbury Towers to be governess and companion to Bree, Maddie had harbored a secret affection for Lord Smythe. The fact that one of his discarded loves had spread the vicious lies that had driven him off to London had turned out to be a blessing in some respects for Maddie. Had he stayed, he would surely have guessed the secret of her affection.

If Maddie could only go back in time, she would strangle Lady Tatterall for spreading the nasty rumors about Lord Smythe being too close to his daughter. An unhealthy relationship, she had hinted maliciously. It had all been in spite. It was the *good* lady's reason for the earl not succumbing to her efforts to bring him up to scratch.

In the end the reasons hadn't mattered. Devastated at the thought the rumors would be believed, Lord Smythe had taken off to London and left the raising of his daughter to Maddie. Bree had thought her father no longer loved her when, in truth, he was afraid to show it.

PIRATES AND PROMISES 151

* * *

Justin stood at the rail watching the moonlight dance across the ocean waves. The pirate ship still followed in their wake, a constant reminder that their fate was still undecided. It didn't help to lighten Justin's already dark mood.

Why didn't the captain make his move? It was as puzzling as his wedding night with Bree.

Damn, he was tired. But how was he expected to get any sleep when all he could think of was Quentin's name on Bree's lips. While it was true there was no rhyme or reason to the actions of women, he would never understand why she spurned Quentin's advances if she wanted him so much. Why, she had actually appeared frightened when he had threatened to return her to his half brother.

Perhaps like most women, she wanted Quentin, but only on her terms. Had she thought to pique his interest by turning him down? Bree was just young and naïve enough to think her youth and beauty was all that was needed to bring the Earl of Foxworth under her spell. Little did she know, Quentin bowed to no one's wishes but his own.

A glimpse of the *Black Lady*'s sail caught his attention. Was it his imagination or was the *Black Lady* closer than he remembered? The pirate ship was still staying to the south of them, yet he could have sworn the gap between them was broader earlier in the day. He looked again, taking note of the distance. Was it possible the *Black Lady* had moved closer without anyone noticing?

Although the wind had come up, the pirate ship wasn't running at full sail, but then neither was the *Seahawk*. Unless the pale moonlight was playing tricks on his eyesight, the ship was gaining on them.

"Come and get us," Justin whispered to himself. "Take your blasted cutlasses and come aboard. I'm ready to draw someone's blood."

Perhaps running one of the blackguards through would purge the devils that haunted his heart. Even as the thought crossed his mind, clouds covered the moon and the night fell dark. Perhaps his wish would come true.

Justin looked to Pheps, the chief mate, who had the wheel, but the man appeared half asleep. He glanced up to study the thick blanket of clouds overhead.

If the crew was quick, it just might work. They might be able to slip away from the pirate ship before the clouds uncovered the moon.

Justin swung around and grabbed the first sailor he could find. "Get the captain, man."

Otis tried to pull away. "Not me. I've learned to keep me distance when the capt'n be in his cups."

"He's drunk again?"

"Tighter'n Aunt Bessie's white blouse," Otis said grimly.

Knowing how sound carried over the water, Justin leaned close. "The *Black Lady*," he whispered. "It's moving up, but if we hurry, we might be able to slip away while the clouds are covering the moon."

Otis gave him a broad grin. "I'm in," he said, keeping his voice low. "Do you want me to spread the word to raise all the sails?"

With the strong breeze that had picked up, it would soon carry them away from the ship that echoed their every move, but something stopped Justin.

Once the captain of the *Black Lady* found them missing, he was certain to know what they had done and would raise his sails in pursuit. No one knew the speed of the huge craft. They might find themselves no better off by morning. No, there was a better plan, but even if it proved successful, he'd still be facing the captain's wrath come morning.

"Otis," he whispered. "I'll take care of Pheps. You spread the word to lower all the sails."

"But—"

"Think about it, man. With our sails down and this gale, the *Black Lady* will soon be out of sight. When the moon comes out and her captain finds us gone, he'll think we slipped away from him and spend all of tomorrow trying to catch up with us."

PIRATES AND PROMISES 153

Otis's face lit up with a grin. "And he'll be leavin' us behind."

"Exactly."

"You're a right smart man, Mr. Tyler."

Justin frowned. The captain was certain to have other views on the subject. Once Tibbs found out what he'd done, there'd be hell to pay.

"Don't give me any credit yet," he said. "We still have to lower these sails without making a sound. If the captain of the *Black Lady* so much as has the slightest clue as to what we are doing, he may decide to come alongside and board us now."

"You don't need to worry about us, Mr. Tyler. We'll get 'em sails down without a whisper of noise."

Justin gave Otis a healthy pat on the back. "We're all counting on you."

Otis's chest swelled with pride. Nothing had ever been left to Otis's skills before and it pleased him that the American trusted him enough to give him the chance.

"We won't be lettin' ye down," he said. "If this works, we'll all be a-singin' yer praises come mornin'."

"Don't be practicing any songs. We don't know whether the plan will succeed yet."

The problem of the sails taken care of, Justin walked to the steps that led up to the poop deck. He had climbed half of them when he heard the crash behind him.

"Sorry, Mr. Tyler," he heard Otis whisper loud enough to carry the length of the ship.

Justin cringed when Pheps, alerted to the sudden change in the ship, leaned around the big wheel to see what might have happened. Justin could barely make out his silhouette against the dark sky.

"What's going on?" the seaman shouted to Justin as the ship slowed yet again.

Justin hurried across the poop deck. Before he reached Pheps, the ship lurched to one side as another sail hit the deck.

"What the—"

Otis was doing better than Justin had hoped. If his guess was anywhere right, the wind would soon push the *Black Lady* several furlongs ahead of them.

He hurriedly explained his actions to Pheps. The darkness did little to hide the relief that was evident in Pheps's face. The strain of the last fortnight was showing on everyone.

"Captain Tibbs will not be for likin' this," the little man warned. "He's none too pleased with you as it is."

"If the plan works and we elude the *Black Lady,* tell him you were the one to order the sails lowered. If it fails, then place the blame with me."

Pheps might be the captain's flunky, doing most of the work with none of the credit, but he was no fool. The American's plan had all the earmarks of being successful. He smiled up at Mr. Tyler.

"I think it best if we just lower them sails and sit 'ere for a spell," he said. "Then w'at say you, we swing a bit north?"

Justin smiled broadly. "Excellent, Mr. Pheps. It's a good chief mate that makes a wise decision."

Bree reached for the blanket. The cabin had grown decidedly cooler in the last hour. A tremble coursed through her body, but it was not from the cold. Justin may have left, but there was no doubt that he would return to have his way with her.

Yet, where was he? Scarcely had the question formed in her mind than the door opened. Outlined against the lantern burning in the companionway, his frame seemed to fill the doorway. She didn't have to see his face to know it was him. No one on the ship could match his height, nor his overpowering presence.

He didn't say a word, but closed the door. In a few strides, he was across the room. Bree closed her eyes as he began undressing. She tried to keep her breathing even so he would think her asleep, but between the pounding of her heart and the trembling of her body, she knew she wasn't very successful.

"Move over," he grumbled as he lifted the blanket and climbed in beside her.

Bree moved as far away as the narrow bed permitted, but he was having none of it. He reached out and pulled her to him.

"You needn't worry that I'm going to claim my rights," he said as he threw his leg over her. "I merely want to get warm."

It was too dark to see his face, but his voice told her he was still angry. "How do I know I can trust you?" she asked, careful not to move.

"Because I want this marriage even less than you do and as soon as we land in Virginia, I'm going to my solicitor and request he start annulment proceedings."

An annulment? Lady Camille in *The Heart Speaks* got an annulment from the dastardly Lord Seals when he had forced her into a runaway marriage. But the author had been very specific in pointing out that it was possible because they had not shared a bed. But after her ignorance concerning the kiss, she wasn't about to ask him about this.

"Will this annulment take very long?"

"Long enough" was all he would say. Bree wanted details. Well, perhaps not a whole lot of details. The pirate seemed to take undue delight in what he thought to be his education of her into the mysteries of men and women.

"If we're to get this annulment," she finally ventured to ask, "should I be sleeping in your bed?"

He snuggled closer. "I rather like having you warm it for me," he said, his voice a soft whisper against her hair.

Bree struggled to sit up. "Perh-haps I should le-eave."

He pinned her beneath his arm. "I don't think that's wise," he said. "If Captain Tibbs suspects you don't intend to honor the wedding he so graciously performed to save us all from the wrath of the man upstairs, he might decide we'd both be better off overboard."

"Why would he do that? He married us. That should be more than enough to satisfy him."

"Let me just say he'll not be in the best of moods when he awakes."

Bree wished she could see his face. "What happened? Did someone hide his rum?"

"No, although someone needs to." He traced a pattern of small circles up her bare arm. "I've rid us of the pirate ship tonight, but I don't think the captain will be too pleased."

"That's w-wonderful," she said around a big yawn she couldn't manage to stifle.

"Such a show of enthusiasm, my dear."

Bree ignored the barb. "But why won't Captain Tibbs be pleased?" she asked.

"With the captain having complete authority aboard his ship, me taking care of the situation without his permission might be viewed in the wrong light." He tucked her tighter against him. "Thank goodness Pheps saw my way of things. Now go to sleep while you have the chance."

He settled his nakedness against her and Bree was suddenly wide awake. She lay still and tried not to think about the lean, hard body lying next to hers, but the strange feelings of need she had experienced earlier sprang to life.

Why hadn't anyone warned her? People were no different than any of God's other creatures. The pirate had thrown a lusting on her. It was almost like a disease. Once you were touched with the urge to mate, there was no cure. No cure but the one God had given them and that was to give in to what came naturally. But she was not one of God's animals, she told herself. She was a person and a person should not be plagued with the same uncontrollable needs. Yet all she wanted to do was . . . but then he hadn't bothered showing her, had he?

Bree turned to him and his arm tightened around her. She started to push away, but the steady rhythm of his breathing told her it wasn't necessary. He was asleep, but lying intimately in his arms only deepened the ache growing within her.

Bree took a deep, steadying breath. The thin cotton nightshirt Higgins had fashioned for her suddenly felt hot and constraining. She considered taking it off and lying next to Justin's cool body. Just the thought of her nakedness lying next to his sent another rush of raw emotion shuddering through her.

She knew she was a fool to dwell on such things, but Justin had opened up a whole new awareness of herself. She no longer felt like a child perched on the edge of womanhood. Somewhere along the way she had slipped off and become a woman with a woman's needs, and as a woman she wanted to explore these strange new feelings.

Drat him anyway. Each temptation he offered only served to lessen her resolve that St. Clair was the only man for her. Where had all her stubborn conviction flown? She was like a leaf blowing in the wind. A leaf that wanted more than a snug bed in the corner of a sheltered courtyard. She wanted to tumble to the edge of time . . . in the pirate's arms.

Could she? she asked herself as the idea swirled around in her thoughts. What would it hurt? Justin was asleep and would never know. Careful not to wake him, she eased his arm from where it lay at her waist. Next she lifted the cotton nightshirt over her head. Bree gasped in surprise when the movement caused Justin to shift in his sleep, bringing his arm back across her.

Bree lay quietly. Perhaps she should stop before curiosity proved to be her downfall. But when Justin didn't wake, she grew more confident and turned into his arms. All she wanted to do was reexperience the need he had awakened in her earlier—experience it and study it.

But lying next to him proved more potent than she had imagined. His body was no longer chilled and the warmth of it seemed to draw her nearer. The ache was back, seeping into the edges of her being. Like an itch that needed scratching, it prompted her to rub her body wantonly against his.

A low moan came from the pirate. When his arm closed tightly around her, Bree froze. Her body was crushed against his, her heart racing. Calm. Remain calm, she told herself. Breathe easy. He's not awake, only close. If she remained perfectly still, perhaps he would return to his dreams.

Seconds passed, then minutes. Justin still seemed on the verge of waking. Bree yawned. She had certainly learned her lesson. She'd not let her curiosity get the better of her again. As soon as she could remove herself from his arms, she'd put that nightshirt back on and stay on her own side of the narrow bed.

Another yawn captured her. She didn't know why she was so sleepy all of a sudden. The coolness of the cabin should have been keeping her awake, but then lying naked in Justin's arms provided all the warmth she needed. If she closed her eyes, she told herself, she could imagine again that she was lying in St. Clair's arms. Loved and being loved.

Bree yawned again and closed her eyes. She tried hard to concentrate, but for some reason she couldn't hold on to the images of her future with St. Clair that she had so easily conjured up all these years. Despite all her efforts, she couldn't re-create the earlier fantasy. She was all too aware that it was Justin's arms she lay in this time.

CHAPTER 11

"YOU get back in bed," Maddie shouted as she hurried to set the tray down. "Dr. Jones will have my head if he learns of this."

Edward knew the smile he gave her was weak, but if Maddie knew him at all, she would know it was genuine. He was well aware of her tireless dedication in nursing him, but it was time he got up and took care of matters himself. And finding his daughter before Lord Foxworth did was at the top of his list.

"Has Grant returned?"

"Your man of business said he would be up as soon as you've finished your breakfast," she offered with a stern eye to the bowl of untouched broth.

Edward sank back down on the bed, but he wasn't about to be put off. "Was he able to secure passage on the *Queen's Way*?"

Maddie didn't bother stifling the deep sigh that hovered on her lips. "He was," she said, retucking the napkin into the front of Lord Smythe's linen shirt. Finished, she stood over him, a smile teasing the corner of her lips. Although she disapproved of what he was about to do, she was pleased to see that making the plans had put color back into his pale cheeks.

159

After taking the chair next to his bed, she picked up the spoon and began feeding him. "Dr. Jones and I have decided that since you are determined to be buried at sea, we shall come along to attend your funeral," she teased.

"And Grant has approved of this?"

"He has even secured three additional cabins for the momentous event. One for himself."

"I have nothing against the three of you accompanying me as long as you aren't too disappointed when I live."

Maddie smiled down at him. It was all she could do not to reach out and touch his hand.

"Should you survive the trip to Virginia," she said, spooning him another portion of the hot soup, "I promise not to begrudge you the accomplishment."

A fire seemed to light his blue eyes and Maddie was reminded of Bree's stubborn resolve to hold on to her own dream of marrying St. Clair. The two were a lot alike in their single-minded determinations.

"I shall find her, Maddie," he said, "and if she's still of a mind to marry St. Clair, I will do everything in my power to see that the American is aware of the honor she would be bestowing on him." He paused, his eyes growing brighter. "And then I shall find Lord Foxworth and kill him."

The weak morning light was making its way through the cabin's small window when Justin woke to the feel of a woman in his bed—and in his arms. Bree. This was the way he dreamed of her. Warm and naked.

Her head lay on his arm, her hair a golden pillow of curls for them both. Even knowing what she'd done to him didn't keep his traitorous body from responding to her nearness. Heaven help him, but the ache was even more powerful than the night before. Unable to resist, he trailed his hand up her side, past her slim waist, then he cupped her breast while his thumb sought the sensitive nipple.

Justin wasn't prepared for the tortured sigh that escaped his lips. He couldn't believe how much he wanted her and how little she wanted him. It was evident Quentin was the only one to interest her and she had not hesitated to reveal that fact on more than one occasion. Then who was this Sir Henry? Another love?

Yet, if that were true, why had she removed her clothes now? If she had undressed merely to tease him, she was playing a dangerous game. Thoughtfully, he continued to rub his thumb across her nipple. It pleased him to have it spring to life under his touch. When the gesture brought forth a soft sigh from Bree also, Justin found himself holding his breath. He didn't want to wake her. But he needn't have worried for she soon resettled against him under the blanket.

He should take her, he told himself. After all, she was his now. But teasing did not mean she meant for him to have what she so boldly flaunted.

Justin's green eyes narrowed. Bree was naïve, but was she so naïve as to not be aware of what her nakedness would do to him?

Frustration, then anger, fought with his conscience. Strangely enough, it was that very same anger that kept him from claiming his revenge.

He wondered if this was a trap. If so, Bree must have thought to seduce him into changing his mind about consummating the marriage. Why else would she be lying naked beside him? For some unknown reason, she must have concluded there were more advantages to remaining married to him than to seek the annulment.

Careful not to disturb her, Justin pulled his arm from beneath her head and slipped out of bed. As he dressed, he found his attention repeatedly drawn to the gentle rise and fall of the blanket with each breath she took. The prospect of returning to bed was tempting, but he managed to muster sufficient anger to keep himself from leaning down to recapture the breast that teasingly thrust itself against the woolen cover.

"Damn!" he cursed to himself. It was obvious she thought to play him for the fool. If he stayed much longer, he'd soon be falling in with her plan of seduction and find himself with no recourse but to remain married to the little vixen. The last he'd heard annulments weren't easy to come by for those who consummated their vows and it was more important he kept his wits about him. A man couldn't have two wives and he already had his choice safely tucked away in Williamsburg.

Bree lifted a weary eyelid at the slamming of the door. Surely it wasn't morning already. It seemed as if only moments had passed since she had closed her eyes and waited for the pirate—

Justin!

Bree shot up in her bed, but the cool air of the cabin sent her scrambling for the blanket that had fallen from her naked shoulders.

What must he think of her? She had dropped off to sleep without the nightdress and Justin had surely discovered it when he woke. Bree's face grew warm at the embarrassing possibility. How would she ever explain that she merely wanted to see what it felt like to lie next to a man?

Frantically, she looked for the discarded nightshirt. It didn't take her long to discover it lying under the blanket where she had pulled it off last evening. Ignoring the cold, she tossed the woolen blanket aside and crawled from the bed. She reached for her chemise, then decided it could do with a washing. Although she doubted the pirate would be returning anytime soon, she wasn't about to have him discovering her in this embarrassing state of undress again. She'd wear the gown without it.

She had no problem getting into her pink dress, but securing the ties at her back was proving a mite more difficult. After a series of complicated twists and turns, she managed all but the ones that were either too low or two high to reach.

She looked wistfully at the long white linen strips she had used to curl her hair. If she hadn't cut up the pirate's shirt, she could have worn it to hide the gap. Now she would be forced to stay in the cabin until Justin came looking for her.

Bree plopped down on one of the oak chairs. Sure that everyone had deserted her, Bree was surprised by the knock on the door. "Who is it?" she called. She wasn't about to let that traitor, Samuel, in.

"It be me, miss . . . Mrs. Tyler," Higgins said through the door. "I've brought something for breakfast."

Bree had the door open before he finished. "I'm starved, Higgins. What did you bring?"

He crossed the room and set the tray on the room's only table. After he removed the napkin, he stepped back.

"Found an egg one of them chickens laid up in the straw and I had Cook prepare it for you. Then we have salt pork and I even managed to get a slice of his fresh-baked bread and a wedge of cheese."

Bree leaned over the tray, closed her eyes, and took a deep breath. "Oh, Higgins, you're wonderful."

"Look in the covered bowl," he said. "Cook made some stewed apples in honor—"

The sight of Bree's gaping gown caused him to pause but a moment.

"—of your wedding," he finished.

Bree peered over her shoulder to see what had distracted Higgins. The gown. She had forgotten all about the gown.

"Would you mind fastening it up for me, Higgins? I had much better luck with the ties yesterday, but today I seem to be all thumbs."

"Certainly, Mrs. Tyler," he said.

He sounded so stiff and formal that Bree set the napkin back on the tray and turned to him. "I would rather you call me Bree if you wouldn't mind." He looked so stricken Bree was certain she had offended him. "Unless you would rather not," she thought to add before turning her attention back to her breakfast tray.

"It's not that, Miss B-Bree," he stammered. "It's well . . . I'm afraid I'll . . . What I mean to say is you have nothing between you and your gown and I'm afraid . . . well, my fingers might slip and I might touch your back. And I wouldn't want you to think I was . . . you know, fast," he finished in a rush.

When Bree glanced over her shoulder, she had to bite down on her lip to keep from smiling at the bright pink blush that covered his weathered face.

"As long as your fingers haven't turned into ice like the cabin has, I think I can manage to endure."

"Oh, turnip greens, Miss Bree," he said as he thrust his hands up under his arms. "They're ever bit as cold, but if you were to wait a small while, I'll have them warmed."

"Nonsense, Higgins. They can't be any colder than I am with the back of this gown open to the elements."

Higgins dropped his hands. "I'm sorry. Didn't think about that, Miss Bree. I'll have you tied right and tight in no time."

When he finished, Bree picked up her cup of coffee. "Has Mr. Tyler had his breakfast yet?" she asked with what she hoped was a deceptive casualness.

"He's taking his with the captain and that Mr. Thurston." Higgins smiled down at her. "We shook loose of the pirate ship during the night," he added with a touch of pride, then lowered his voice to a whisper. "It was all Mr. Tyler's doin' too."

She looked at him over the rim of her cup. "The captain?" she asked. "What did he have to say concerning the matter?"

"Too deep in his cups to notice, I would imagine."

Bree swallowed her sip of coffee. "Justin's part in this would be something best kept to ourselves, Higgins," she advised.

"You need not worry yourself on my account. What between seeing to the needs of them mares and Mr. Tyler, I don't have time for the tellin' of any stories."

Storytelling? If Higgins had worked for Justin for any length of time, he would surely know everything there was to know about him. Odd, she had never thought to ask Higgins about what working for Justin was like. He was probably her only chance of finding the answers to all the questions that plagued her.

"How long has Mr. Tyler been a highwayman?" she asked bluntly.

"Much too long."

Bree picked up her spoon. "And how long have you been with him?"

Higgins busied himself with straightening the room. "Almost ten years now," he mumbled, hoping his lack of enthusiasm would put an end to the questions. Justin had told him of the annulment he would be seeking once they landed in Virginia and he didn't want a tearful woman on his hands.

Bree tapped the shell of her egg. "If you've been with him as long as all that, you should know where we'll be staying in Williamsburg."

Higgins turned the question over in his mind. He couldn't recall Justin mentioning it when he talked with him this morning. Knowing of the change in Justin's plans, he doubted Tyler had any intentions of taking Bree to Havenwood. Not only did the little lady know too much about Justin's activities as a highwayman, but she might take exception to the fact that Justin still had hopes of marrying another woman.

"You'll have to be puttin' that question to Mr. Tyler," he finally said. "He hasn't told me his plans."

Bree scooped another spoonful of egg out of the shell. "Surely he's told you what he needs the mares for," she said before taking the bite.

"Aye, he has. Mr. Tyler plans on improving his line of racehorses with them mares."

Bree dropped her spoon in surprise. "Mr. Tyler breeds racehorses?"

Tadpoles and turnip greens! Miss Bree was so easy to talk to he'd almost given Justin's identity away. He'd have to redeem himself, and fast.

"You might say that, Miss Bree." He couldn't look her in the eye for fear she'd know he was stretching the truth.

"Mr. Tyler, what with his business and all, he doesn't have a place to keep them mares. So he takes them down New Orleans way." Higgins paused a moment to gather his thoughts.

He had the mares in New Orleans. Now what would Justin being doing with them there? A smile lit his face when he thought of the answer.

"Mr. Tyler, he does a lot of business with the big plantations," he said, spinning the tale. Justin was forever teasing him about the creative slant he tended to put on things. Well, this was one time he should be pleased with Higgins's special talent. "They're right proud of their horses down there," he continued, "and Mr. Tyler—well, he'll see they pay top dollar for this here shipment of prime ones."

The answer somehow disappointed Bree. She had hoped the pirate was going to do something worthwhile with the mares. If she was any judge of horseflesh, and no one could say she wasn't, the mares were of good stock. Her father would have paid handsomely for any one of the mares, but selling them to others was not what she had hoped Justin had intended. With the right stallion and good training, the foals could make a man's fortune—or a woman's.

She took another sip of coffee, then focused her attention on finishing her breakfast without any more speculation. If Mr. Justin Tyler wanted to sell away his chance to become a wealthy and respected gentleman, it was none of her concern. Unless . . .

Justin was having much the same thoughts as he looked out to sea. Who he was and what he'd done were no concern of Bree's. Once their ship landed, he was off to see his grandfather's solicitor. He had no intention of letting this marriage continue one moment longer than necessary.

As he looked out over the endless waves, his dark brows came together in a frown. It was bound to take a few days before the solicitor could draw up the necessary papers and what was he to do with Bree until then? It was obvious he couldn't take her to Havenwood. All he needed now was for his grandfather to get wind of the marriage. The old man had been harping at him for years to take a wife and would probably do everything in his power to keep them together. And since the old viscount had never approved of the arrangement Mr. Wingham had proposed, he wouldn't be very sympathetic to Justin's breaking up his marriage to Bree so that he could marry Regina. No, a swift annulment would be best—for himself and Smythe.

He had no more than solidified his decision when he caught a glimpse of pink out of the corner of his eye. Like every man on deck, Justin turned to watch her progress. Unbound hair, as golden as sun-ripened wheat, swirled like a gossamer curtain about her slim shoulders as the wind caught the silken strands up in its bold grasp. The loose curls made the perfect crowning touch for the tempting morsel of womanhood that moved so sensually beneath them. His scrutiny soon dropped to the full breasts that strained against the thin pink fabric of her gown. Lust came burgeoning forth with the memory of how the perfect globes had filled his hand, the dusky nipples responding readily to his touch.

With slow deliberation, he lowered his eyes, allowing his attention to drift lazily down the front of the pink gown, past the tiny waist to where the breeze had plastered the pink material along the length of her long, slim legs. With each step, the skirt shifted but did not lose the captivating outline of her slim body. Justin took a deep breath and let it out slowly.

How could God have been so heartless as to put the guileless soul of someone such as Bree into an alluring body much more suitable to that of a courtesan? But then when had anything concerning women ever made sense? Their choices in husbands certainly didn't. First Henrietta Parker, now Bree. Both of them had preferred Quentin to him.

He glared down at her when she stopped in front of him. "What are you doing out here, Bree?"

She was not about to let his rudeness put her off this time. "I have a proposition to put to you."

Although he was determined to remain stern with her, the corner of his lips lifted in a grin. "And what might that be?" he asked, letting his gaze drop to the snugness of her gown.

When his green eyes darkened with passion, Bree wanted to slap the smile from his face. "It's not what you think," she growled up at him.

Justin leaned down. "I'm not sure I'm interested then."

"Well, get interested!" she shouted, punctuating her demand with a sharp stamp of her foot.

The fire in her eyes only served to rekindle his own desire. If this continued, the rest of the trip would be nothing short of hell. He turned back to the railing.

"What's your proposition?" he asked.

She looked out to sea. "These mares you have."

Justin didn't say anything, but continued to watch the sunlight frolic across the waves.

"I know good stock when I see it," she continued. Now she had his attention. "Well, I was thinking there must be a lot of wealthy landowners in Virginia who would love to have mares as fine as yours."

"More than you know," he mumbled. If the mares proved out as breeding stock, he'd have some of the finest horses in all of America.

"So what is your proposition?"

Bree took a deep breath. "I think it's time you turned your efforts to something other than robbing others."

"You think to reform me, do you?"

His casual treatment of her suggestion irritated her. "I think you should keep the mares, look to increasing your stock, then sell the colts for a handsome profit."

Justin lifted a dark brow. "Raising horses takes land—and money, my dear. Where would a poor thief such as myself get that kind of blunt?"

"You will have enough coin once you sell my indenture papers to my fiancé," Bree boldly brought to his attention. "Besides which, if I am treated properly for the rest of the journey, perhaps I can persuade him to help finance the project. Perhaps . . . as your partner?"

PIRATES AND PROMISES 169

"Ah, yes, the exemplary Sir Henry. The man with the plump pockets. He would become my partner? And what happens to my mares if you can't find him?"

Bree bristled at his cynicism. "Don't look at me with that frown on your face. I only thought to help you on the path to becoming an honest man. Must I also think of all the little troubling details?"

"Feeding the mares is not a troubling detail. It is mandatory if you hope to have anything to sell."

His cynicism was beginning to tax her patience. "Everyone says your precious America is abundant with land for the taking," Bree added sarcastically. "Couldn't we find a small piece to run your mares until my fiancé redeems my papers?"

"If you truly wish to reform me, it will take more than the locating of your Sir Henry."

Bree didn't like the sudden darkening of his green eyes. "Such as?"

Justin touched the side of her cheek with the back of his hand. Her sun-kissed skin was like warm silk. "How genuine is your concern for me, my little princess? I wonder."

The pet name struck her like a cold gust of wind. It had taken her until the age of eleven to realize the hollowness of her father's endearment. She had cried for days. Angered, she swatted at his hand.

"I play no one false coin, pirate," she said through clenched teeth, ignoring the twinge of guilt for her own greed in the project.

What of my brother? he thought, but didn't voice his contempt. He would rather punish her in his own way.

"And are you willing to place actions to that noble claim?"

The smile on his full lips spoke of more than just disbelief, it was an unmistakable challenge of her ability to carry it through. She couldn't let it pass.

Her gaze met his. "Yes! Within reason, of course," she added.

"Is that to be your way out, my little princess?"

His mockery raked her already taut nerves. Bree's eyes

narrowed to angry slits. "Put a name to your demands and let's be done with this petty bickering."

"Partners," he said without hesitation. "Not with Sir Henry, but with you."

The pirate and her, partners? Of all the things he could have offered, she had not expected this. Dare she accept?

"And my contribution is . . . ?"

"Until Sir Henry redeems your papers, you will care for my household and help with the mares. Without complaint," he added. "In that manner, you not only may have a share in the venture, but can see to my total reform at the same time."

"Partners, but not as man and wife," she stated.

Didn't she realize that what he wanted from her did not always require the benefit of clergy? In fact, bedding the vixen would be most pleasurable—after he had secured the annulment.

"Not *as man and wife*," he assured her.

Bree studied him a moment. With the sardonic smile that lingered on the corners of his mouth, she knew she must be missing some vital point, but what it might be continued to elude her.

"And you will secure the annulment?"

"I will secure the annulment."

She still didn't trust him. "And you agree to sell my papers to my fiancé?"

"Him and him only," Justin stated.

Bree held out her hand. "Then we have an agreement, pirate."

"Justin," he corrected her as he took her hand. "You have agreed to help make my fortune . . . and save my soul, and I have agreed to allow you to try."

Bree smiled at his teasing. "You're right. It may certainly prove to be an impossible endeavor."

Justin watched the gentle sway of her hips as she walked away.

"Impossible, yes," he whispered. "With you close to me, there is no hope to save my soul."

CHAPTER 12

TRUE to her promise, Bree was up bright and early the next morning. She dressed in Higgins's shirt and britches, straightened the small cabin, then fetched hot water for Justin's morning shave. And all without a word of complaint.

She wished she could read the book Justin had found for her again, but there would be time for that later. First, she would show him that she was capable of holding up her end of this partnership.

The day proved an endless series of chores. First, the horses had to be fed and watered. Then Higgins cleaned the stalls and placed the soiled straw into large canvas bags. Once he had a cubicle swept, Bree relined it with fresh straw.

They had no more than finished caring for the horses when Justin informed her he had purchased the "particularly fine" pig lounging in the far stall and would she be so kind as to see to the beast's comfort while he brushed down the mares.

The "particularly fine" pig turned out to be the one Bree called Grump. His manners were such that even Aphrodite turned a cold rump to him from her pen. Bree wouldn't doubt that the pirate had only purchased the pig to irritate her, but she gritted her teeth and said yes.

But the beast wasn't at all of a cooperative nature. Not only did he refuse to move aside when she tried to clean his home, but he had such an intimidating manner about him that Bree decided he could very well live in his filth. So when Higgins wasn't looking, she tossed the new straw over the wooden rail onto the old and hoped the pile grew so deep that the fat old porker would soon find it too difficult to walk.

Finished, Bree stabbed her pitchfork into what was left of the pile of straw, then flopped down beside it. Tired, she leaned back on the prickly mattress. Every bone in her body ached, even her toes. It was no wonder. The satin slippers offered little protection. Given the scuffed condition of the delicate material, they didn't look to be faring much better than the rest of her. There was no hope that the slippers would last until the *Seahawk* reached Virginia. She closed her eyes. She could only hope she would.

"I've hauled all the canvas bags to the top of the stairs for you," Higgins said, overly loud.

Bree opened one eye. "May I present them, along with my regards, to Justin?" she asked.

Higgins ignored the devilish grin. "Now don't you be a-doin' anything to rile Mr. Tyler," Higgins warned.

He had never known a person to get caught up in so much trouble before. Bree was forever doing the wrong thing. Her so pretty and all, he'd have thought she didn't get into such tangles.

"You ask one of the captain's men to help you," he added. "And don't be gettin' into no mischief. The bags shouldn't be too heavy. Just drag them along to the stern. Make sure the wind's to your back, then give the straw a toss."

Bree cocked her head to one side. "And what will Justin be doing?"

"I'll be there as soon as I can," Higgins said, deliberately ignoring her question. "Mr. Tyler, he needs me to find him a shirt. Seems some idiot cut his to shreds."

Idiot?

"Is that what he told you?" she asked, trying to maintain a hold on her temper.

Higgins shook his head solemnly. "Don't it beat all? It's a sad thing when a man's clothes aren't even safe."

He suddenly dropped his gaze to the shirt and britches Bree wore. "Beggin' your pardon, m-miss," he stammered, his face growing red. "Sometimes there's a call to be a-borrowin' a man's things."

Bree nodded her acceptance of his apology. "I'll have these bags gone by the time you're back," she said.

Higgins was pleased with her willingness to help, but he was also relieved to get away before he said anything else to embarrass himself. Yet he couldn't help thinking he had missed something important in his instructions.

Otis hurried to catch up with Bree as she struggled with two large canvas bags. "Let me 'elp ye, Mrs. Tyler."

"Thank you, Otis. I asked some of the others but the captain claimed they were too busy with their own duties to be able to assist me."

Otis took a quick look around. "Then we'd best 'urry afore 'e finds something to busy me 'ands and I can't 'elp either."

"These are the last ones, but they seem to be the heaviest of all," Bree said, dropping one of the bags on the deck and lifting the other up to the rail. With a heave, she dropped it over the side.

Otis picked up the last one and tossed it after the other, then stood, watching it slowly drift away.

"Beggin' yer pardon, miss, but weren't that man of yers only emptying these 'ere bags afore?"

"Emptying?" Bree tried to remember exactly what it was that Higgins had said. Something about hoping her back was to the wind when she dumped them.

Otis continued looking over the edge. "Aye, I'da swore the last time 'e brought these up, 'e only tossed the straw."

Bree looked down over the rail. Heaven help her, what had she done now? "You think they might have more bags down below?"

Otis started to answer when he spotted Higgins returning. He touched Bree's hand. "I'll see what I can find," he offered before slipping away.

Higgins marched up to her. "Beg your pardon for bein' so late," he said. "I had to—"

He suddenly paused and searched the deck. "Where are the bags?"

"I dumped all the straw for you," Bree said with her brightest smile, hoping to distract him.

Her efforts failed miserably. Higgins paid no attention, but walked a small circle, looking behind kegs and around coils of rope. "Where did you put the empty bags?"

Bree's smile faded and she solemnly pointed out to sea. A ripe autumn apple couldn't have grown any redder than Higgins's face.

"No!" he wailed, then ran to the rail and looked down. A lone canvas bag bobbed in their wake. Like a drowning man, it gasped a final breath, then sank below the surface.

"You drowned my bags," Higgins said, turning to confront her.

Bree had meant to be brave, but what with all that had happened lately, her lower lip had its own ideas and set to trembling. "I only meant to help. And you did say to toss them."

Higgins slowly, but firmly, clenched and unclenched his fists. "The straw, not the bags. Why would I have you toss the bags?"

"Because they smelled?" Bree ventured to ask.

"Smelled! What did you expect from a shi . . . straw bag? Workin' with horses is always a smelly task."

"And you had best grow accustomed to it," Justin whispered behind her.

Bree swung around. There he stood—his bronzed chest bathed in sunlight. "Where's the shirt Higgins was to get for you?" she demanded.

PIRATES AND PROMISES 175

He flexed his arms. "Does my nakedness bother you?" he asked.

The provocative huskiness of his words sent a shiver of desire scrambling up her spine. She glanced to Higgins, but he had slipped away.

Bree took a long steadying breath. Sharing a bed beside the giant lent wings to lustful thoughts every time she saw him. Standing close as she was, she could almost feel the heat of him lying next to her—the passion he would draw from her. Her heart skipped a beat. What was happening to her?

"You should have the decency to cover yourself in the presence of a lady."

"A lady?" he mocked. "A lady does not lie in the arms of one man with the name of another on her lips."

So that was it. He was upset because she had whispered St. Clair's name. She knew trying to apologize would not help. After all, how could she explain what the childhood promise had meant to her all these years? How could she explain that St. Clair's was the only kindness she had known? A promise of love she had so desperately needed. Until now.

The revelation surprised her and she studied Justin as if she were seeing him for the first time. When had this happened? When had she turned from her childhood dreams and placed her heart in the pirate's keeping?

"I—"

Bree caught her bottom lip between her teeth. There was nothing she could say. Even if she did explain St. Clair, Justin didn't want the marriage. He didn't want her—not for all time. The partnership he offered was all she could hope for.

It was time she quit trying to live in the storybook dreams she created for herself. She was no longer a young girl. The pirate had touched the woman in her. He had pulled her from her sheltered cocoon of denial and sent her soaring on the wings of a butterfly. It was up to her now to fly.

Bree stepped close. With her hand on his chest, she

peeked up at him through lowered lashes. Perhaps with the right enticement, he might review his decision. After all, an annulment could always be canceled.

"Perhaps I need someone to make me forget my past indiscretions," she said in what she hoped he would take as an invitation.

Justin cupped his hand over hers and looked at her so intensely, Bree thought her heart would burst. Those eyes. Those dark green eyes. So much like the ones that had haunted her dreams all those long, lonely years.

Justin swallowed against the dryness in his throat. She was offering him everything he wanted—everything but her heart. It shouldn't matter, he told himself. He wasn't one who looked for love in his bed companions, but somehow he needed it with Bree. It took all his willpower to take her by the arms and set her from him.

"Offer it to me again, Bree," he said. "Offer it to me once I have the annulment and you have nothing to gain by our coupling."

Nicholas smiled to hide his annoyance as he dealt the cards. Tyler stood beside him; the man's unwelcome presence was clearly placing a pall on the evening's game. Although Tyler hadn't said a word, Nicholas could tell from the frown on his face that he didn't care to have Bree gambling with the crew. But Nicholas wasn't interested in Tyler's opinion of the matter. Even before the wedding, Nicholas had formed a dislike for the tall Virginian and it pleased him to no end to cause Tyler such displeasure.

He smiled across the table at his pretty prodigy. While he himself was oftentimes forced to resort to cheating in order to win, Bree had a natural talent for the cards. If only he could convince her to leave Tyler and come with him, they'd soon empty the plump pockets of the wealthy landowners of Virginia.

"Your bid, Bree," he said, deliberately using her Christian name to taunt Tyler.

Bree twisted her lips into a grimace. If she raised the bid

too high, most of the players would throw in their cards, but she had such a terribly good hand she hated to waste it.

A glance at the small pile of coins lying on the table told her the pot certainly wasn't worth the hand she held. "Four shillings?" she offered.

The groans around the table told her the bid was too high. Bree knew she was getting greedy but she hated to be cheated out of the earnings this hand deserved.

"Gentlemen," Nicholas said. "The lady will be more than happy to take markers against your wages." He leaned close and touched Bree's hand. When he saw Tyler stiffen, he purposely trailed his fingers along the back of hers. "You wouldn't mind waiting until the men receive their pay in Virginia, would you, love?"

Bree smiled brightly. "No, of course not."

Justin placed his hand on the table and looked to the other players. "Mrs. Tyler may accept your markers, but do you really think it wise? With her run of luck lately, you'd do better to count your losses and return to your duties. At least you won't be working the rest of the voyage to pay your debts."

Chairs scraped the floor as the men pushed back from the table.

"Don't listen to him," Bree shouted. "I could just as easily lose and you'd be holding my markers."

Justin leaned down until his face was level with hers. "And might I ask how you would plan on redeeming your markers?"

"Well, I . . ." The men had stopped in the doorway. "I would . . . You know you could . . ."

"Not me, Bree. I pay no one's gambling debts but my own."

Bree glanced toward the door. The men were leaving. "There was no need for you to cover my markers," she said through clenched teeth. "I wasn't losing."

Justin turned over her cards. "Perhaps not this hand, but you could just as easily lose the next."

"Not Bree," Nicholas tossed in. "She's a true winner."

Justin straightened, dwarfing Nicholas's scant six feet. "*My wife* will always be a winner to me, Thurston. She doesn't need to prove it by taking the hard-earned coins from a handful of lovesick sailors."

Bree blinked away the tears that had sprung to her eyes. It was the first kind thing she had heard from Justin lately.

"Truly, Justin," Bree breathed. "Do you truly think that?"

He took her hand and pulled her up from her seat. "Truly, Bree."

She smiled shyly at him. Things were going to work out just like the book he had given her. She could feel it. St. Clair would still have to be told that she could no longer marry him, but those things happened. Besides, he hadn't bothered to contact her the last ten years.

What was important was that Justin had finally fallen in love with her. If he didn't still have her hand clasped tightly in hers, she would have stopped to say a prayer to thank God for the change he must surely have wrought in her. She was now somebody someone could love and it was all she imagined it to be.

She ventured a glance at Justin. Even with that frown that appeared to be permanently etched on his features, he was so handsome. And he loved her. She blinked away a tear. Someone finally loved her.

When they reached the steps to the hold, Bree couldn't wait any longer. She tugged at his hand and pulled him over to the rail. "Tell me again," she insisted.

Justin just stood there as if confused by the request.

Bree chuckled at his denseness. Men had such short memories. "Tell me you love me," she said as she moved into his arms.

Bree's heart froze as time seemed to stand still while the silence between them appeared to go on forever. What was wrong with him? He looked mad enough to strangle her.

"Justin?" she whispered.

"I don't love you, Bree," he said, his lips curved in a bitter grin. When she reached for him, he dropped his hands, turned, and walked away. Bree wanted to die.

* * *

How did one get over being such a fool? Justin asked himself as he turned once more on the empty bed. The night had grown dark and he could no longer see the blanketed figure asleep on the cabin floor. It had been two weeks since he had walked away from Bree, but, if he closed his eyes, he could still see the hurt in her soft blue eyes.

He'd cursed himself a thousand times, yet he couldn't bring himself to right the wrong. Every time he started to apologize and admit that he might—that he had feelings for her, strong feelings, he would remember the passion in her voice when she had whispered Quentin's name on their wedding night.

Damn! Why couldn't he just put his own pride and hurt aside and take what she was offering? But that was the problem. She could offer her body, but what he wanted was her heart. A part of it would always belong to Quentin, and he could never accept that.

The cabin suddenly seemed to fill with the sounds of Bree's gentle breathing. He closed his eyes, hoping to somehow close out the memories as well. But Bree was everywhere, haunting him, teasing him.

Justin had to get away before he went mad. He reached for his clothes. A walk on deck would soothe his troubled mind.

He had one leg in his breeches when a wave picked up the ship and set it back down again. A loud thud followed, accompanied by a cry of pain.

Bree! Justin tossed his clothes aside and dropped off the bed. He found her sitting on the floor beside the table, rubbing a lump on her head. He ignored her protests and helped her to her feet.

The ship lurched again and when he reached out to keep her from falling, she tumbled into his arms. She didn't say a word, but stood trembling against his braced legs. He knew it was a mistake to keep her there, but he couldn't bring himself to let her go.

Knowing full well the trap he might be walking into, he wrapped his arms around her and held her close. Her soft sigh against his naked chest was like a whisper of desire that cut deep into his soul. He leaned down to kiss her, then changed his mind.

Quentin—and his own plans—would always be there, pushing him away from her. He held Bree from him. He didn't need the light from a lantern to tell him she was seeking to catch a glimpse of him, trying to see what was on his mind—and in his heart. Hell, he didn't even know the answer to that himself. All he knew was that he wanted her lying beside him when he woke. It was the only thing he would allow himself now.

Leaning down, he lifted her over the edge of the box bed and gently laid her on the tangled sheet. "You'll be safer here," he said before crawling in beside her.

Bree moved close. "What would you say, if I told you I don't want to be safe?"

Justin shoved the blanket down between them. "I'd say that bump on your head needs looking to," he answered gruffly.

As soon as he said the words, he wished he could take them back, but it was too late. She had already turned her face to the wall. He had hurt her again.

Why did he constantly say the wrong things when he was with her? He had to be the biggest fool ever born. He wanted her every bit as bad as she seemed to want him and as her husband he had a right to her pleasures, yet he knew to accept what she offered would not only put an end to his dreams, but lay his heart open to her scrutiny. The dreams for his future—and the future of Havenwood—were what mattered, he bitterly told himself. Carrying them for ten years was more than enough proof of their importance.

The lie kept him awake long after Bree had fallen asleep. But the sound of the rain beating down on the deck overhead kept him company—and the knowledge that restraint would secure him the annulment.

The marriage had ruined everything. There was no doubt

in his mind, if not for it, Bree could have been lying in his arms now, flushed with a night of their lovemaking. He would have wooed her until it happened. Bree was a vulnerable and trusting young woman—the type most susceptible to an unscrupulous man's attentions. He buried his face in her hair. One such as himself.

In fact, as naïve as she was, it might even be possible to have her and the annulment too! He pulled the blanket from between them and tucked her close. Justin made up his mind then and there. If she ever offered herself to him again, he would take the risk and not turn her away.

Day followed day and Bree continued to help with the horses. Since the captain was indisposed most of the time, discipline on the ship became lax and Otis and Ned took to assisting her with her tasks when they had a free moment from their other duties.

It was soon apparent that the sailors had spotted their missing blankets draped over the stall rails, but not one of them made a comment on the discovery. Justin wondered if it was due to the fact that Tibbs was certain to place the theft at Bree's door or that the unrelenting heat from the last few days made the use of the blankets unnecessary.

Jealousy tore at Justin's gut at the two men's attentiveness to Bree. He lay awake nights and dreamed of cutting their hearts out and feeding them to the sharks that circled the ship of an evening.

A smile came to his face when he recalled the captain's sudden appearance in the galley. He had been livid. The card game had been canceled and the men sent back to their duties. Justin was pleased. At least Bree would be spending less time with the men and more time with him.

Although she slept beside him now, Justin found himself wanting more. He wanted the hands that stroked the necks of his horses to be stroking him. He wanted the soft soothing melodies she sang to be for him, not the mares. Most of all, he wanted her to repeat her offer. But she didn't.

Justin spent the long, sleepless hours before dawn longing to reach for her, longing to pull her into his arms, but there was no going back. No chance of wiping those hurtful words away and pride kept him from telling her they were lies. He had thrown all his chances away with her and he knew it.

Unable to sleep one night, Justin decided he might as well see to the mares. Higgins had noticed a few of them were off their feed and he didn't want to risk losing any. Careful not to wake Bree, he dressed and went below.

It wasn't until he reached the hold that he noticed the difference in the sway of the ship. No longer did it have the rolling motion of a ship running with the waves. Now it tipped gently back and forth, as if it were tied to the dock. He considered going aboveboard to question the oddity when he heard a shout coming from the other end of the line of stalls. Not recognizing the voice, Justin moved cautiously toward the circle of light. The sound of another man joined the first, but he still didn't recognize the voices; the words were mumbled and too low to be heard.

With care, he eased the pistol from the band of his breeches. He had taken to carrying the weapon since the *Black Lady* had appeared on the horizon and this was one time he was pleased with his decision.

The light from the lantern momentarily blinded him when he stepped from behind the last stall.

"I'll wager two farthings," a man said. Groans rose from around the small circle of players.

Feeling a bit foolish for his thoughts, Justin returned the weapon to its place. It was only a few sailors, along with Otis, Ned, and Higgins indulging in a game of cards. At least Thurston wasn't there.

"Gentlemen," he said with a nod.

" 'Ello, gov'nor," Otis answered. "Care to try yer luck? The stakes ain't worth the splinters we've been collectin' in our backsides, but the company's friendly."

Before Otis had finished with his offer, two of his companions moved aside to make room. They were correct about one thing. Without Thurston, the company appeared to be amiable. With a shrug, Justin pulled out what was left of his coins, then lowered himself to the wood floor.

"What about the captain's orders about not playing cards?" he asked.

Otis shuffled the cards. "I only 'eard 'im mention that it was not to be in the galley."

"Flat out like a beached whale, he is," Ned chirped up.

Justin grinned at the true reason behind the game. Perhaps he would enjoy playing after all. "Can't say as I can contribute much," he said as he dumped out the gold coins onto the planks. "The captain has taken a liking to lightening the weight of my purse lately."

The comment brought forth a few snickers from his fellow players, but Otis's frown soon squelched their impertinent manners.

Justin cocked a dark brow at the newly acquired respect for the little man, but Otis only smiled smugly at the questioning glance.

"Damned cheeky," Justin mumbled to himself as he picked up his cards. Dipping into the man's pockets would please him to no end.

CHAPTER 13

"THE sails haven't cupped a breath of air all evening," Otis announced as he returned from a pressing duty on deck.

A nervous glance passed between the small group of sailors. Without a breeze, the ship was at the mercy of any wayward current that happened to pass their way. If the *Seahawk* bobbed around lifeless in the water for too many days with no winds, the water—and possibly the food—would not last until they reached Virginia.

Death sat on everyone's shoulder until the winds picked up. As if a command had been issued, one by one, the players turned their cards over and filed up the steps.

Justin did some quick calculations of the amount of feed left for his mares. He was pleased he had insisted on the extra hay being loaded aboard. He could only hope the captain had made the same provisions for the crew's and passengers' welfare. With the surplus fodder, his only worry was fresh water. If it looked to be running low, the captain would not allow any for his mares.

"Higgins, if the winds don't pick up by this afternoon, cut the hay feedings. And there will be no more grain until I say."

PIRATES AND PROMISES   185

"You think we might run out?" he asked as he dumped back the portion of oats he had measured out for the feed bags.

"No, too much grain with a shortage of water and the mares will all be coming down sick. With the extra allowances I made there should be hay for at least two more weeks. After that . . ."

Higgins handed the feed bag to Justin. "You think we'll be stranded that long?"

"Who knows what God might have in store for us? This trip appears to have been cursed with more than its share of bad luck and I think it wise to prepare for the worst."

"Miss Bree?"

Justin glanced to the stairs as he helped rehang the leather feed bags. Thank goodness she had yet to come down.

"If we have problems, it won't be Bree's fault, but Tibbs would have everyone believe she was the cause," he said, a deep frown etching his forehead.

"The men seem to have formed a liking for her," Higgins offered.

"Their coming to know her was definitely to her advantage. She certainly appears to have woven a spell around them, but if she continues to reign the winner at the card games, all that may change. It wouldn't be the first time losers have blamed their poor card-playing skills on a curse."

Higgins handed another feed bag to Justin and nodded sagely. "I can almost see that little rat dropping, Samuel, telling the men that very thing."

"Unless the wind picks up in the next day or two, I see no other hope for the situation than keeping her occupied with her other duties. Perhaps then we can keep her from the captain's notice."

Nicholas placed his hand over Bree's. "You need not worry. I've already spread the word. The game will be in my cabin this evening."

Bree glanced around the galley to see if anyone else had

noticed Mr. Thurston's unwanted gesture. It was difficult to ignore the prickling of hairs on the back of her neck at the gentle squeeze of his hand, but she needed to learn to put the little nigglings of fear aside. After her wanton reactions to the pirate's advances, she was merely a little shy about the innocent gestures.

After all, it wasn't as if Mr. Thurston had invited only her to his cabin. There would be any number of others to keep them company. Besides which, with her small hoard of coins beginning to grow quite handsomely, she wasn't about to turn down an opportunity to add to her cache. It was too much to hope that she would win enough to redeem her papers from Justin, but at least she would be close.

Even so, she watched with trepidation as Justin approached. If only he didn't have to be so tall—and so overwhelmingly handsome. It was the green eyes, she told herself. All he had to do was look at her, then cock a dark brow, and he released a bevy of butterflies in her stomach that defied all of her attempts at control.

"What manner of trouble are you brewing today, love," Justin whispered as he bent to kiss the curve of her neck.

Bree would have pulled away, but she knew he only did it to annoy Mr. Thurston. When no one else was about, Justin treated her with the cold reserve of a tutor she had once had.

"Mr. Thurston has arranged for a game in his room tonight," she said.

Thurston stood at the darkening of Tyler's countenance. "Until then," he said.

Justin watched Thurston leave the galley before taking a seat next to Bree. "Do you think that wise?"

"Nicholas says—"

"So it has become Nicholas now, has it? How cozy."

Bree frowned at him. "Nicholas says," she continued firmly, "that Captain Tibbs may have put a halt to us playing cards in the galley, but Nicholas may do whatever he pleases in his cabin."

PIRATES AND PROMISES

Justin leaned across the table. "And what pleases him, Bree? You?"

The accusation was too close to Bree's own earlier suspicions to contain the blush that threatened to give her away. Angered with both Justin and herself, she slid back her chair and stood.

"As long as I please someone, what should it matter to you?"

He let her walk away. She was right. It shouldn't matter, but it did. He could manage to maintain his distance from her most of the day, but when Bree was with Thurston, he had to be at her side. The thought of remaining in his cabin knowing she was sitting beside that bounder was too much for him to endure.

He sipped his coffee, his mind picking at the memories best left hidden in the dark corners of his mind. Realizing that Bree was capable of stirring this jealousy within him did not put him in the best of moods. It only made his temper worse.

It was so simple to tell himself that dwelling on such things was a waste of his time, but it was hard to forget the soft, innocent kisses that drugged one's senses—and the body that fit so snugly against his. Everything about her drove him wild with need. If he closed his eyes, he could almost feel the pearl silkiness of her skin beneath his fingertips. The thought tore a shuddering breath from him.

Warm, wet wine with the richness of thick, sweet cream. That was Bree. But Bree didn't love him. She loved Quentin. For her own good, he'd have to see to it that she never saw his half brother again.

Quentin pushed the plate of meat aside. They expected him to eat this? Not only was it impossibly tough, but it was reclining in a layer of congealed fat cold enough to turn the strongest of stomachs.

Carefully Quentin catalogued the indignities he was forced to endure on this miserable trip. He fully intended to extract proper compensation when he finally located Sabrina. The wedding must come first, he had to repeatedly remind himself. Without Sabrina's inheritance, none of this would be worth it.

With nothing else to occupy his time, Quentin's thoughts kept returning to the duel. The appearance of the carriage still nagged at him. Had Lord Smythe told someone of their meeting? The possibility wouldn't have caused him more than a moment's worry if it hadn't been for young Lord Manly.

Quentin's friends would understandably look the other way over the unfortunate death of Lord Smythe, but he would be called to account if he could offer no valid explanation for the death of Smythe's second. His only consolation was the fact that there was no one other than Walter who could lay the crime at his feet.

Maddie lifted the cup of tea to Lord Smythe's lips. "Dr. Jones is very pleased with your progress. He says if you wish, you may go up on deck today. The warm sun should do you good."

"I *wished* to go days ago," he snapped.

Edward had been cooped up in the tiny cabin for weeks and wasn't about to pass up an opportunity to express his views on the outrage. "Jones fusses over me worse than some damn nanny," he said. "He had better pray I'm never around should he find himself in this position."

Maddie chose to ignore his outburst. "Now, now, Lord Smythe. You must admit you would never have survived your wound if it hadn't been for him."

Edward reached out and took her hand. "The truth is, I would never have lived if it hadn't been for you." He loved the way she blushed at his compliments. It almost made him feel young again. "After nursing me all these weeks, the least you can do is call me Edward."

"Edward," she said as if trying the taste of it on her tongue. "If you don't think it would cause a scandal, I think I'd like that."

"To hell with the gossips. I've had enough of trying to please them."

Maddie couldn't hold back a smile. "Then you're going to talk with Bree."

"If she'll allow me to."

Bree vowed she would never talk to another man. They were all acting like children and she told them so. Justin had stomped off with one of those murderous looks darkening his face merely because she had managed to win a few personal items from one of the sailors. Bree would have been pleased with her ability to rile Justin had not the triumphant grin on Mr. Thurston's been every bit as disturbing.

While Bree didn't care for Justin's high-handed way of telling her that from now on she was to forgo her gambling, Bree suspected Nicholas had deliberately baited the pirate when he had objected to her winning the seaman's slicker. What other excuse was there for mentioning that she had already won no less than four shirts, three pairs of serviceable breeches, two pipes, three tubs of bathwater, and a whip?

Well, she didn't care about Justin's views on her gambling. More than likely he was merely worried that her winnings would enable her to redeem her papers and he would lose the services of his personal slave.

Convinced this was the true reason behind his unreasonable demands, Bree retrieved her coins from under the mattress and left the cabin. Let him worry. She had every intention of going to the card game and winning.

It was almost midnight and Justin lay awake, cursing himself for not tying Bree to the bed. He didn't have to go to Thurston's cabin to know she was there. He should never have agreed to bring Bree back to Virginia with him. She had been nothing but trouble from the very beginning and now she had deliberately disobeyed him. Didn't she realize the precarious position she was in? Without wind, the ship had been riding atop a glass sea and, if Tibbs ever sobered up enough to notice, Bree would be the first one to be blamed.

Justin pushed the coverlet aside and got out of bed. Even without the papers he held on her, as her husband, he had every right to go there and drag her back. And he intended to exercise that right.

He had no more than gotten dressed when he heard a knock. Expecting it to be a summons from the captain, Justin was surprised to see Higgins standing outside the door.

"What's she done now?"

"It isn't Miss Bree," Higgins said. "It be one of the mares. Miss Lucy."

Justin grabbed one of the lanterns and rushed out the door. "It's this damn heat. There's not a breath of fresh air to be had in the hold. If the wind doesn't pick up soon, we might lose every one of them."

"I don't think it's the heat," Higgins said. "Appears more like colic to me."

"Colic? You didn't give them any grain, did you?"

"No, I stopped it. Just like you told me."

"With the water as low as it is, I didn't give them anything yesterday."

"Then I don't understand. How could she have colic?"

"It's a head rubber, that's a fact."

"How bad is it?"

"Bad."

Justin was surprised to see Otis and Ned in the hold when they arrived. The situation was every bit as critical as Higgins had said. Miss Lucy hung limp, like a bag of feed in the stall. With her repeated kicks at the bellyband, the sling was the only thing that kept her upright.

Justin walked into the stall. Careful to stay out of the way of her hooves, he placed his ear to her stomach. Nothing. Higgins was right. It had to be colic.

"How long has she been like this?"

"She was fine when I checked on them after supper this evening."

Otis leaned over the stall door. "Ned and I were down the last bell. She was right perky then. Even tried to bite my hand."

Justin was aware of the interest the two sailors had developed in the mares. He turned to Otis. "You didn't feed her any of those dried apples, did you?"

"They've been gone for a week," Otis answered. "Nope, me and Ned, we only gave 'er a bucket of grain. Right pleased she was too."

"A bucket!" Higgins shouted. "You gave her a bucket of grain with no water?"

Justin touched Higgins's arm to forestall the setting down Higgins was ready to dispense. It hadn't been Otis's or Ned's fault. They hadn't known what the grain would do to a horse that wasn't receiving enough water, Justin told himself as he attempted to keep calm. "You say you gave this to her early this evening?"

"She seemed plenty 'ungry," Ned finally spoke up. "So I gave 'er a wee bit more later." He puffed out his chest proudly. "Miss Bree says as 'ow Miss Lucy 'ere always gets a bit more. 'Er always bein' so 'ungry and all."

"Horses will eat all you give them," Justin said between clenched teeth. "They're worse than pigs. If you let them, they'll keep eating until they swell up and burst."

Otis nodded sagely. "Miss Bree did say they had a pig's appetite. Didn't know Ned 'ad given 'er more grain or she wouldn't 'ave left the card game to come down 'ere 'erself. She's right partial to Miss Lucy, you know."

"Hell, did everyone feed her?"

Ned scratched his head a moment. " 'Pears so, Mr. Tyler." The comment earned him a punch from Otis.

There was no point in telling them that their generosity might very well kill her. "We can't cut her loose," he said more to himself than anyone who happened to be listening. "If she goes down, we'll loose her for sure."

Justin glanced up at the hatch overhead. He had removed the cover two days ago in hopes of capturing some fresh air for the hold. From the unmoving position of the stars, he could tell the ship still lay dead in the water. Another day would be breaking in a few hours and not a breath of air.

"If we could get her up on deck . . ." he said.

"Ned and me, we'll help."

There was no holding Higgins this time. "You've done more than enough of that already."

Justin quickly intervened. "Otis, gather up everyone you can. We'll have to haul her up on deck. Once we get her there, she'll need them to help keep on her feet."

They were gone before Justin finished. "Let's see if we can get some oil down her, before they get back."

Higgins held her head up while Justin sponged the oily water into her mouth, but without the proper equipment most of it ran down her neck.

Justin dropped the sponge back in the pail. "It isn't doing much good, I'm afraid. She appears to have given up."

"Can't say as it surprises me," Higgins said. "As rank as it is down here, she probably figures she's already dead."

Finally they heard the men working overhead and the ropes were lowered down into the hold. Justin didn't know how Otis had accomplished it, but he had gathered quite a few of his comrades.

Once they attached the rope to the mare's sling, the long process of hauling her up began. Her stall not being directly under the open hatch presented a new set of problems. The first order was to swing her clear of the other mares before they could pull her up. It took almost as many hands to steady her below as it did to pull her up.

After several tries and a few bruised ribs, the mare was on her way. Up through the hatch, then over onto the deck. They had her poised above the captain's cabin. All was going well until the rope slipped and Miss Lucy's delicate hooves made a frantic purchase on the top of the room. Shouting, accompanied by pounding on the door, sent Justin looking for the cause.

" 'Pears one of the casks of water got wedged against the captain's door," Otis said with a broad smile.

PIRATES AND PROMISES

Justin patted him on the shoulder. "Safest place for it to roll, wouldn't you say?"

"Thought ye'd see it that way."

Once free of the cabin, the men lowered Miss Lucy to the deck. After six weeks in the hold, there was no chance that she'd be able to keep to her feet and Justin knew it. The best he could hope for was that with Higgins's help and the outside rail, they could manage.

The moment Miss Lucy's hooves hit the deck, Justin had all the help he could need. "Watch her hooves," he shouted. "With the pain in her belly, she's liable to do anything."

Justin pulled on her halter while Higgins and the sailors kept her upright. It was the only time in days that everyone prayed that the sea would remain calm. Progress was slow, but the mare was moving and that was the only thing that would save her now.

From one end of the deck to the other, they urged the mare to keep walking. For the first time in weeks the sailors worked together with both discipline and determination as each took a turn at walking beside the mare. When she finally dumped her duty, everyone cheered.

Justin handed the rope to Higgins. "Take her around a few more times. Once she's finished, get her secured below, then have someone help you move that cask away from in front of the captain's cabin. I'm going to see about Bree."

When Miss Lucy was once more secured in her stall, Higgins, Ned, and Otis went to see about the cask. Careful to step around the numerous piles the mare had deposited on the deck, they scooted the water barrel away from the door.

Their hopes of not rousing the captain again were tossed aside when the door flew open. With a curse on his lips, Tibbs rushed out the door. "What the hell's going on here?"

Before anyone could answer, he hit the slimy substance on the deck. With a loud *whumpt,* his feet flew out from under him and his head cracked against the wooden floor.

For the first time in weeks, every man looked to his duties.

The captain sat up, then studied the fragrant globs hanging on the sleeve of his soiled shirt. "What the . . . ?"

He lifted an arm and took a healthy sniff. "Horse . . ." His indignant bellow echoed across the ship. "How'd this stable muck get on me deck?"

No one answered.

At the ominous quiet, Otis dragged Ned around the corner. Once out of sight, Otis glanced over at Ned.

The plump short sailor stared back. "I ain't cleanin' him up," Ned said.

"As short of water as we be, don't reckon 'e'll be doin' it 'isself either."

CHAPTER 14

Before dawn the door of Thurston's cabin slammed back against the wall and all eyes were drawn to the tall figure in the doorway. Bree took a deep breath. Seeing Justin every day, she had forgotten how intimidating he could be at times and this was definitely one of those times. The smug grin on Nicholas's lips didn't appear to help matters. Had Justin wished her to Hades, the murderous look he gave her would have been more than sufficient to send her on her way.

"You're coming with me," he said.

Bree looked down at the cards she held. The pile of coins out on the table was small, but she hated to give up that nice pair of boots.

"As soon as I finish this game," she said.

Justin reached down and grabbed her hand. "Now," he demanded as he pried the cards from her fingers, then threw them face up on the table. "I said no more gambling and I meant it."

"But the boots," Bree protested as he pulled her to her feet.

He didn't wait for her to collect her coins. "To hell with the boots!"

Bree stumbled behind him to the steps that led below. "But I—"

Justin stopped and turned to her. "If you need boots, I will buy them for you. You don't have to win them off some poor sailor. Now let's not hear any more about them."

Bree glared back at him. He was in one of his moods and Bree knew by now that it would do her no good to argue. The man was as unmanageable as a new maid on wash day. She'd have to wait until he got over this little tantrum, before she returned to the tables.

"You're not to be gambling anymore," he said.

Drats! Had he taken to reading her mind? "I see nothing wrong with it," she snapped. "There is certainly nothing else to occupy my time."

"You might try tending to your duties," he said. "Miss Lucy almost died from the grain everyone felt necessary to feed her."

"Miss Lucy sick? But I—"

"Yes, I know. If you had been helping Higgins as you should, he would have explained that he had cut the grain from the feedings. To make matters worse—"

The lecture went on and on, but Bree wasn't listening. She loved the mares and her selfishness had almost killed one of them. She would never forgive herself.

When daybreak came, Justin found Bree walking on the deck. She looked so forlorn standing at the rail, he wished he could cut his tongue out. He should never have come down on her so hard. He knew she cared for the mares every bit as much as he did.

Justin gathered her in his arms. "I'm sorry," he said. "I was worried, but I shouldn't have taken it out on you."

Bree pulled away. "I would never forgive myself if Miss Lucy had died," she said.

"Don't think about that now. What's important is that she didn't."

Bree cried then. Softly, as if her heart were breaking.

Justin held her close. There was nothing he could say. Placing the blame on her had been unforgivable.

They were interrupted when Thurston came to a stop beside them. "I have something for you," he said.

When Bree turned to him, he handed her a pair of boots—the ones she had hoped to win.

Rage curled around Justin's heart at the smile that came so easily to Bree's lips. How quickly she had put the incident of the mare aside at the sight of her precious winnings. He knew if he stayed, he would use his fist on Thurston's jaw again. He left to check on the mare.

Otis was chatting with Miss Lucy. The mare was doing well, considering the air in the hold was still rank.

However, as Justin looked around the cavernous room, none of the animals appeared to be faring all that well. He glanced up at the hatch overhead. What they needed was a good dose of fresh air, but until the wind picked up, they'd see none of that. Or would they?

"Otis, is there anyone aboard that is good with their hands?"

"W'at did you 'ave in mind?"

"Sewing."

"Ned ain't none too good, but 'e's the best you'll find."

"He'll do then. Fetch Bree from the cabin too. Tell her to bring her gown and all the needles and thread she can find. Higgins is in the galley cooking up a tonic he says will do wonders. If what I have in mind is successful, we'll have no use for it."

While Otis was gone, Justin knocked out the rails that separated Grump's stall from Aphrodite's. Finished, he knelt to stroke the pig's back. "Just because I've taken the barrier down doesn't mean you can treat Aphrodite as anything less than a lady," he told him.

It suddenly struck him that it seemed a lot like the speech he had been giving himself the last few weeks. "I know it will be difficult," he said, giving the pig another pat on the back. "Especially if she takes it in her head to wiggle her trim little butt at you. But be strong. The trip's just about over and then I'll see to it you have any amount of young ladies to tickle your fancy."

Grump grunted with pleasure.

"That plan interests you, does it?"

"Who you talking to?" Higgins said when he returned with the two sailors.

"Never mind that," he said a little too sharply, to cover his embarrassment. "Since Bree did not return with you, I'll assume she's still with Thurston."

Everyone's silence confirmed it. Let her stay with the bastard. "Did you bring the gown?"

Otis pulled it out from under Ned's shirt where they had hidden it. But he didn't feel comfortable about taking it from the cabin without first getting Bree's permission. "What we going to do with it?" he asked.

"We're going to build us the grandest lady's fan you'd ever hope to see."

"With Miss Bree's gown? Won't that upset her?"

Justin grinned. "One can certainly hope."

Otis took his turn at pulling the long hemp rope. Straw swirled at his feet as the huge frame, stretched with the skirt of Bree's gown, waved overhead. "Works right fine, Mr. Tyler," he said proudly.

Justin nodded. "It may not bring in as much fresh air as I'd hoped, but it certainly stirs up the stale. Almost makes it livable, doesn't it?"

One of the chickens, unsettled by the giant fan, flew from its roost atop the straw. Its squawk of indignation filled the hold.

"So it doesn't please everyone," Justin said to the ruffled hen.

Bree, who had grown tired of waiting on deck for Justin to return, made her way down into the hold. She heard him talking.

"What doesn't please everyone?" Bree asked, hoping he wasn't referring to her.

"Our fan—" Ned managed to get out before Otis backhanded him in the gut.

"Fan?" she asked, puzzled at the breeze that stirred the hold. She looked up. "What a clever idea. It's—"

Bree swung around. "It's my gown. You used my gown."

Justin hadn't missed the boots she was wearing. Thurston's gift. He tried to ignore them and continued to watch the material billowing overhead with each pull of the rope.

"It's a mite gaudy for my tastes, but the mares appear to like it," he said, trying to repay her for accepting the boots.

It was then Bree noticed the rest of the gown lying on the floor. She bent to pick it up. "You cut it up?"

No one said a word, but all looked to Justin for the answer.

"It fit better that way," he said matter-of-factly.

"You cut up my gown." She repeated the offense as if she hadn't heard his answer. "My one gown and you cut it up."

"Not in as many pieces as you did my shirt, but yes, I cut up your gown and for a much more noble cause."

"So that's it. You're still upset because I used your shirt. How petty."

Justin grabbed her arm. "Petty!" he shouted. "At least I didn't use it to curl my hair."

Otis pulled at the rope faster. Straw kicked up off the floor, setting the chickens off again. The more the anger grew in Miss Bree's eyes, the faster he pulled. When she stepped up to Mr. Tyler, he broke the fan. The frame hung overhead like the broken wing of a duck. No one appeared to notice.

"You're never going to forget that I cut up your shirt, are you?" Bree finally said. She pulled away from his grasp and started back up the steps.

"The fate of your gown shouldn't upset you," Justin taunted her. "After all, you have your boots."

Bree stopped. She had forgotten all about the boots. Up until now she had planned on returning the gift, but the pirate's obvious displeasure changed her mind. She turned and stuck her foot out. As if studying it, she turned it first one way, then the other. "They are nice, aren't they?"

"You'll be giving them ba—"

A loud creak of the ship halted Justin's tirade. Everyone looked up. As if someone had suddenly opened a door in the sky, great gusts of wind swirled down upon them. They headed up the stairs behind Bree, hope pounding in their hearts.

Groans sounded the length of the ship as the once limp sails took billowing shapes. It was the most glorious sight Justin could remember seeing. A shout rose from the crew. They were moving again.

Justin grabbed up Bree and swung her around. Then he recalled the boots she wore. Anger kindled anew and he set her down.

Puzzled at the abrupt change in him, Bree watched him walk away. Until Thurston stepped beside her, she couldn't imagine what had set him off again. Of course, the boots. If he was going to be such a bear about something she needed, then he could very well get over it without any explanations from her. She'd not give up the boots now for love or money. Tears burned at her eyes. Well, at least, not money.

The rain had stopped but the deck was still wet. Making his way along the rail, Justin came to the front of the ship. From his vantage point on the forecastle deck, he could watch the *Seahawk* slice through the waves.

"We'll be reachin' Virginia sometime today, Mr. Tyler," Otis said as he stepped up beside Justin. "Can't say as I'll be happy to see us land."

Justin knew the reason behind the words. Bree. Like the rest of the sailors on the ship, the man had fallen beneath her spell. Once they had gotten over the notion that Bree's presence had brought a curse down on them, they were more than willing to be distracted from their duties to watch her take her daily promenade around the decks.

Everyone but the captain. Tibbs just couldn't seem to accept a woman aboard his ship. He remained in his cabin for the rest of the trip, accompanied by his big black Bible and a jug of rum. No one was allowed near, except Samuel, the cabin boy.

Justin could almost understand what the captain was going through. Bree had torn up his own peace of mind on more than one occasion. But then, nothing seemed to make any sense where Bree was concerned.

She seemed to want him, yet it was Quentin's name on her lips. If Quentin was the one she wanted, why hadn't she stayed and married him? And what of the mysterious fiancé, Sir Henry? Had Bree some silly romantic notion that the great Lord Foxworth would be jealous enough to come after her? Justin wouldn't put it past her. She was young and naïve enough to believe Quentin would.

If he was of a self-sacrificing nature, Justin told himself, he would keep Bree as his wife to save her from his half brother, but he couldn't bring himself to do it. If Bree was to be his, it would be because he wanted it that way.

"There she be," Otis said, breaking into Justin's thoughts.

Justin had to squint to see the thin, dark line on the horizon. "Doesn't look like much from here, does it?"

"No, but she'll grow till land is all ye'll see."

"How long have you been on the *Seahawk*?" Justin asked.

"Nigh on nine years now. Me and Ned, we're thinkin' it's time we got us a place somewhere and put the sea behind us."

Justin's green eyes narrowed. "You thinking of any place in particular?"

"We was kind of partial to Williamsburg," Otis mumbled.

"Williamsburg." Justin wanted to grab the little man and shake him, but he managed to maintain a semblance of calm. "Did your decision have anything to do with Mrs. Tyler?"

Otis couldn't meet the tall man's eyes. "She did mention

as 'ow she would be pleased to 'ave someone to call friend there."

"Oh, she did, did she?" Justin no longer wanted to throttle Otis. Bree was his new objective. He didn't wait for an answer. He turned and headed for the cabin. "You need not worry your head over this any longer, Otis," he shouted over his shoulder. "Mrs. Tyler has someone. Me!"

Otis squared his shoulders. "Too many friends never 'urt nobody," he said to himself.

Justin didn't bother knocking. He shoved the cabin door open and walked in. The sight of Bree sitting in a copper tub of water stopped him momentarily, but his anger quickly took hold again. He marched over to her.

Bree refused to be intimidated by the dark gleam in his green eyes and sat up stiffly in the tub. Reaching over the edge, she scooped up her bath blanket. "Come in," she said, sarcasm cutting her words to a fine edge. "I don't mind performing my toilette in front of the entire crew."

Justin returned to the door and kicked it, but he was not to be put off. "You can bring every sailor aboard this ship with us," he said, "but it will change nothing. For the next seven years you belong to me. And if you have any thoughts of—"

Bree suddenly standing and stepping out of the tub cut short his tirade, but she appeared not to notice.

With a defiant frown on her face, Bree wrapped the bath blanket around her, then boldly stepped up to the pirate. Ignoring the warning in his stance, she tossed back her wet curls and stared up at him.

"My only thoughts are that you are a stubborn, arrogant, self—"

She never finished. Justin took her in his arms. Before she could protest, he covered her lips with his. His kiss was hungry—almost devouring her soul, leaving her breathless and shaking in his arms. When his fingers moved across her back with that sensual pattern she was beginning to recognize, Bree crushed her body against his naked chest. Before she could review the advisability of such a bold move, the bath blanket fell to the cabin floor.

Their bodies touched and a moan escaped his lips. His apparent agony was an echo to the terrible gnawing ache buried deep within her own heart. There was no way she could keep from answering it.

With a need not to be denied, Bree placed her arms around his neck. Even knowing she had no experience swimming in such treacherous waters, she did not hesitate wading in. Heart in hand, she willingly tumbled into the whirlpool of emotions he offered.

Justin shuddered with the hell of his own making. This was the last thing he wanted to happen and the first thing in his thoughts each day. The warm, wet temptation in his arms was almost too powerful for him to deny, but he knew for his own peace of mind he had to. Reluctantly, he released her.

Cupping her chin in his fist, he met her puzzled gaze. "Tell Otis and Ned to pick another port in which to retire," he said. "I'm the only man you need, Smythe. You may not believe that now, but then I have seven years to convince you, don't I?"

Bree swallowed the tears that scalded her throat and watched him leave. She refused to allow him to see how much he had hurt her, but she needn't have bothered. He didn't look back. It was more important than ever that Otis and Ned stay in Williamsburg. They were her only hope for a buffer against the pirate's attentions.

The big ship eased into the river. Most of the sails had been dropped and secured, but the *Seahawk* still presented an impressive sight as she made her way past the towns and plantations that lined the James River.

Virginia. Bree thought her heart would break. She had dreamt about this moment for so many years it was difficult to believe it had finally arrived. But to what? Certainly not the life she had hoped for someday.

Since meeting Justin, she had realized more and more that St. Clair might not be the man for her. Now she knew. She was in love with Justin and could never marry St. Clair. Unfortunately, there was also no changing the fact that the pirate was not in love with her.

All she had now was their partnership. If it didn't work out, the best she could hope for was that St. Clair would buy her papers and take her in until she could find suitable employment.

"Thinking of Sir Henry?" Justin asked as he joined her at the rail.

Bree nodded politely although she didn't know why. Justin had not asked the question out of courtesy, but merely to taunt her. But then Justin's manners had been anything but gracious for weeks now. It was as if he already regretted his decision to become an honest man. But it didn't matter if his nose were out of joint, Bree was going to see that he kept his word.

Now that she had accepted the fact that she had no other place to go, she needed to establish a profitable arrangement with Justin—a business arrangement only.

The duties of a horse breeder could not be so terribly difficult to learn. Her father's breeder had certainly managed quite well and Bree planned on being equally successful. Thank goodness Otis and Ned had accepted her invitation to help with the mares until they found employment elsewhere. Even Higgins had thought her plan had a lot of merit, so she hired on the two sailors. After the way Justin had treated her, she didn't care what his opinion was of the matter.

The trees along the riverbank parted and Bree's attention was drawn to the beautifully manicured lawn of a large white house. Huge oak trees lined the wide walkway leading up from a dock that stretched out into the water. If their venture proved as profitable as she hoped it would, someday she could own an estate such as that one. Yet what would be the worth of such a home without a family to share it with? For a moment, she wondered what St. Clair's estate was like. And what it would be like to have someone who loved her.

"Will you be going to see a solicitor when we dock?"

Justin studied her for a few moments. The breeze off the water was playing with the golden strands of her hair and he ventured to reach out and capture a curl. "It's what we agreed on, wasn't it?" he asked.

"Yes, but—"

Justin wrapped the curl around his finger. "Are you trying to tell me you've changed your mind and no longer want the annulment?"

Only a person bound for Bedlam would miss the obvious taunt and Bree wasn't about to let him know how much she had come to want the marriage. She'd cut her tongue out before she gave him a hint of what his touch was doing to her sanity.

Defiantly, she tossed her hair back over her shoulder. "I was merely asking to determine when you planned on inquiring about it."

"The ship will be stopping at Princess Anne's Port below Williamsburg. I've instructed Higgins to take you to one of the small inns there. Once I've seen to the unloading of the mares at one of the docks farther up the river, I will return. My solicitor is in Williamsburg."

"And the mares?"

"I know of a small cabin along the river that will suit our needs perfectly. There's plenty of grass for the mares." He leaned down and whispered. "And there's plenty of privacy for us."

Another reason to be grateful for Higgins's agreement to her hiring Otis and Ned, she thought as she lost herself in the passion of his dark green eyes. A person could drown in the emotions he summoned. A dangerous prospect for a woman who never learned to swim.

CHAPTER 15

FRANCIS Abrams poured his longtime client a cup of tea, than sat down to join him. "What brings you here, Adrian?"

The old man bestowed his solicitor with a wistful smile. "Justin has returned from England."

"I can see where your grandson's return would please you, but that doesn't tell me why you requested this meeting."

Francis knew that when Adrian Tyler took a sip of tea before answering, the old man was upset about something but was attempting to follow his physician's orders about remaining calm. Francis checked his pocket watch. He knew his client too well to believe the diversion would be effective. He'd give him three minutes.

Adrian suddenly sat forward and leveled a questioning glance at the solicitor. "Justin tells me he plans on paying you a visit."

"Did he tell you why?"

Tea splashed from the cup at the force with which Adrian returned it to its saucer. "Confound it, man, if I knew that, I wouldn't have had to come to you, now would I?" He knew immediately he had gone too far.

The solicitor glanced down at his watch. "One minute. You're doing better."

"I'm sorry, Francis," Adrian said with a smidgen of false humility. "I'm an old man and I worry about the boy. I might die any day and I want to see Justin settled with a wife and family before I do."

Francis smiled indulgently. He and Adrian had had this same conversation at least thirty times in the last five years. The best thing to do was to remain calm, but firm. Otherwise, Adrian would attempt to coerce him into any number of questionable situations. "You're not going to die anytime soon, old man. You know that and I know that."

Adrian coaxed a teasing smile from his weathered cheeks. "Could I talk you into believing me long enough to speak with Justin and tell him how much his marriage would mean to me? And don't bother mentioning Miss Wingham. I don't consider her a prospect."

"Adrian, you know what my answer has to be."

The old man leaned forward, the smile still on his lips. "A bright man such as yourself must want something. You do this for me and I'm willing to pay whatever you ask."

"I'm not going to take your money, Adrian. Justin will marry whomever he wishes and when he wants to, not before. Saying you're going to die is not going to change that."

Before Adrian could put forth another argument, a knock sounded on the office door. A young man with wire-rimmed spectacles perched on his thin nose entered the room. "Mr. Tyler is here to see you, Mr. Abrams."

Adrian looked to his friend. "This might be your last opportunity to make an old man happy."

Francis waved his secretary out. "Give me a moment, then have Justin come in."

Adrian set down his tea. "Can I go out through your apartments? I don't want Justin to know I was here. He might think I was meddling in his affairs."

"As you were," Francis pointed out.

"Yes, but he doesn't have to know of it."

Francis had been Adrian's solicitor for almost three decades. He had been there when his beautiful daughter had met and married the Earl of Foxworth all those years ago. He had witnessed the loneliness the old man had felt when she had left for England, then the joy when she had returned with his grandson. When his daughter had died two years later, Justin had become everything to the old man.

"As you wish, Adrian, but I'll warn you right now, I'll not be passing on this ridiculous story of yours. You're the picture of health. Justin wouldn't believe it anyway."

Adrian bestowed Francis with a parting frown and an exaggerated limp as he walked to the apartment's door. He had no more than started to close it behind him when Justin came in the other one.

"I need your help, Francis. I've gotten myself into a pickle of a problem this time."

Francis hadn't seen Justin in months and the change was evident. Something had happened to shake the man's normal calm demeanor. He waved to the chair Adrian had just vacated.

"You look more in need of a good night's sleep than you do a solicitor. What can I do for you?"

Justin ignored the chair and remained standing. "I've been forced into a marriage and I need a quick—and quiet—annulment."

Francis looked to his apartment door. It was open the tiniest bit and he could almost envision the grin on the old man's face if he had chanced to hear. There'd be no annulment if Adrian had any say about it.

Francis crossed the room to check. His hope that the old man hadn't heard was dashed when he grabbed the doorknob to find that someone was holding it firmly on the other side.

"Perhaps you would like to discuss this some other time," he offered Justin when he couldn't close the door—at least not without giving Adrian away. "After you've had some time to think about it."

"What's there to think about?" Justin almost shouted.

"Marriage to this woman would be impossible. She's not only too young for my tastes, but she has a way of driving me to distraction."

When Francis thought he heard a muffled chuckle coming from the other side of the door, he quickly crossed to his desk and sat down.

"She's a shrew?" he asked, hoping to find the fatal flaw that would dash his eavesdropper's hopes that the marriage was anything of permanence.

Justin raked his fingers through his hair as he paced in front of the desk. "No, not exactly. She's pleasant enough. But the marriage wasn't my idea. The captain of the ship took it into his head that Miss Smythe was in the family way and I was to make an honest woman of her." Justin paused and leaned down on the desk. "I tell you, I'll not stay married to the little minx."

Francis coughed discreetly. "And you've not bedded this Miss Smythe?"

"Hell, no!" he shouted, finally sinking into the leather chair in front of the oak desk.

"Oh, I see. So you're not the father of this child."

"No, I'm not. What I mean to say is that it turned out she's not in the family way."

"Now we're getting to the grist of the matter." It was certainly clear as to why Justin looked in need of sleep. Married, but not truly married. It was enough to drive any virile young man to distraction, even one who appeared reluctant to admit an attraction. Perhaps, if he could ask the right questions, he could at least get Justin thinking about the possibility that he might care for the young lady and save this marriage for both Justin and the old man.

Francis pulled out a piece of paper and dipped his quill into the inkwell in preparation of taking a few notes. "Now let's see. You say she is frigid and balked at performing her wifely duties and now you want the marriage terminated."

Justin sat straight up in the chair. "I didn't say that."

Francis calmly looked up from the blank sheet of parchment. Ah, so it was as he suspected. Justin wasn't indifferent after all. "Then you're saying you didn't perform your duty as a husband?"

"I'm saying the captain forced us into this marriage and neither one of us wants it."

"Did you bring the bride with you?" he asked quickly, hoping to cover the sound of Adrian's boot kicking the doorjamb. He'd have to hurry up this interview before the old man came tumbling through the doorway.

"No," Justin answered, settling back in the chair. "You'll have to take my word for it. We both want an annulment and I'm not leaving your office until you say you'll secure one for me."

Francis tapped the tip of his feathered quill against his chin. If he couldn't put Justin off, at least the right questions might discourage Adrian from interfering until Justin came to his senses.

"Then you must be ashamed of this Miss Smythe, Justin. Is that the problem? What I mean to say is she must be a trollop who would disgrace your family and send your grandfather to an early grave."

"The truth?"

Francis nodded. Justin was taking the accusation much more calmly than he had hoped.

Justin leaned close. "The truth is, Grandfather would probably fall in love with her the moment he met her."

With Adrian listening in the other room, that was not what Francis wanted to hear. But it was out now and he could do nothing more but bury his head in his hands and moan.

"That's the way I feel about it too," Justin said. "I don't care if Miss Smythe is the most sensual woman I've ever known. Before I met her, she was betrothed to my half brother. Just because I rescued her from marrying him, doesn't mean I have to be responsible for her the rest of my life." He stood. "Now are you going to help me, or not?"

Francis didn't bother looking up. "I'll see what I can do."

As soon as Justin closed the door to the outer office, a beaming Adrian stepped in from the apartment. "My grandson is married. I couldn't have hoped for more. Of course, you'll have to arrange for me to meet her."

Francis dropped his hands and met the old man's gaze. "Didn't you hear? Justin wants me to start annulment proceedings."

"Annulment is out of the question, Francis. Give me a week and I'll have him in her bed."

Bree hated having to lie to Higgins about having Justin's permission to rent a horse and carriage, but she knew of no other way of getting to Havenwood. After Justin's provocative declaration of his intention to seduce her, she had to find St. Clair. An illicit relationship was not what she wanted from the pirate and seeing St. Clair again might prove to be her only hope of putting the tempting thoughts of sharing Justin's bed out of her head.

Besides, Justin had refused to lift a finger to help her carry all the items she had won from the ship. If not for Otis and Ned, she would have had to leave most of them behind.

After having sold what she could, she found herself with a tidy little sum. Enough to purchase a faded but serviceable gown and rent for the carriage. Unfortunately, there was none left to redeem her papers. Unless she could convince St. Clair to loan her the funds, she would be forced to remain with the pirate a while longer.

The stevedore had said she need only follow along the James River. Havenwood was five miles to the north and west. He also informed her the narrow road was a bit marshy in places, but all in all she should have no difficulty finding the plantation. Even so, Bree was relieved to discover that a driver could also be hired for not much more than the price of a horse and carriage.

Bree leaned back in the seat. While there was no pattern of logic to the landscape, gently rolling hills made up the major part of sunlit grasslands and fields. One minute the carriage passed great fields of corn, wheat, and tobacco, the next they'd be traveling down a rutted road with tangles of weeds and marshlands covering the area.

Even this early in the morning the heat was already building. Steam rose like a warm fog off the lowlands and the fields appeared to shimmer in its wake. Bree made good use of the worn fan she had kept from her winnings.

They had been traveling for a while when their open carriage passed a small cemetery. Bree gazed out the window at the ruins of a large family home whose burned and blackened frame topped the hill behind the row of gravestones. It was difficult to imagine why no one had cared enough to clear the evidence of the past disaster and rebuild instead of letting the land fall to weeds and ruin.

When the carriage reached the overgrown drive, the driver flipped the reins along the nag's broad back and hurried by as if the ghosts of days past still haunted the gates of the old estate. The road was as narrow as the stevedore had predicted and she hated to think of what the driver would do if they happened to meet up with a carriage coming from the other direction. The water-filled ravines that appeared along the side of the muddy path were enough to give pause to even the most experienced of drivers.

Suddenly the path climbed to a small rock ledge and a cool breeze caught her damp curls. She almost gasped at the sight before her. Large oak trees bordered a broad sweep of lush green grasses that ran from a dock along the river to the double doors of an immense brick plantation house situated on the top of a hill. Its abundance of chimneys bespoke wealth and comfort.

"Havenwood," the driver announced.

Bree couldn't believe what she was seeing. The main part of the home stood three stories high with a spacious brick wing flanking each side. A wide circular drive took the guests up to the front steps or to the stables tucked away at the far end.

Bree took a deep breath of the jasmine-laden air and sighed. This was where St. Clair lived. She wondered what it would be like to wake up in the morning and step out onto the balcony at the window of your bedchamber and see the ships making their way up the river. It was no wonder St.

Clair hadn't returned to England. Havenwood offered all a man could want.

With her head full of dreams, it took Bree a moment to realize the carriage had stopped at the bottom of the broad staircase that led up to the double oak doors. A black man in yellow livery came forward to assist her. Bree touched her glove to his and stepped down. As soon as her feet touched the ground, he backed away. Bree made the long walk up the stairs by herself, knowing all the while that her progress was being closely watched by the other servants who had stopped their work at her arrival.

Visitors must be scarce, she concluded, for her appearance to cause such need for observation. She lifted her hand to knock on the great doors when they suddenly opened.

"May I help you?" a tall black man asked.

Bree knew she didn't look her best in the faded gown, but tried not to be intimidated by the butler's disapproving frown.

"Is Mr. St. Clair in?"

Bree hadn't thought it possible for the butler's frown to grow any deeper, but it did. Perhaps if she'd thought to hire an escort he wouldn't have turned his mouth down so.

"And you are?" Washington asked haughtily.

"Bree Smythe. A friend from England. But he doesn't know me by name," she rushed to add.

"Is Mr. ah . . . St. Clair expecting you?"

"No, not exactly."

The butler took a step forward. "Then I suggest you return when he does."

A niggling of fear began to twist at Bree's stomach. "And when will that be?" she asked, raising her hand to prevent him from closing the door on her.

Washington stared pointedly at her hand. "I couldn't say, miss, but I don't imagine it will be for some time yet. He's in England," he added firmly. He didn't feel the least bit uneasy about lying. Young women were forever putting themselves forward with Mr. Tyler.

"In England?" she whispered to herself as she dropped her hand. Had St. Clair come after her and she had missed him? What if he were to learn of the proposed marriage to Quentin? Bree had to speak with someone.

"Is his mother or grandfather home?" She said a quick prayer. "Or . . . perhaps his wife?" she added, her curiosity getting the better of her.

The tall man squared his shoulders and continued to glare at her over the arrogant bridge of his nose. Bree felt like an insect he was about to step on.

"Mr. St. Clair is not married and as for his mother, bless her soul, she died eight years ago."

"And his grandfather?" Bree persisted.

"He is in Williamsburg, consulting with his solicitor. Now if you will excuse me, I have duties that need attending to."

Before she could ask him where in England St. Clair might be, he closed the door in her face. Bree couldn't stop the tears that spilled down her cheeks.

She stumbled down the steps. St. Clair had not married. He had waited for her as he had promised. And she had let her lustful feelings for Justin cloud her loyalties.

She didn't see Justin until he had her by the arm, pulling her roughly down the rest of the steps. "Let go of me," she sobbed.

"Someone has to save you from yourself."

He didn't stop until he reached his closed carriage. He couldn't believe the hatred that filled his soul when he saw her on his doorstep. It was fate that he had come straight home instead of stopping to talk with Mr. Wingham. If he hadn't come along when he had, there was no telling what Bree would have tried next. She might have even managed to get an interview with his grandfather.

It didn't take much to come to the conclusion that Bree was trying to get word back to Quentin. Why else would she have come to Havenwood? Quentin must have told her about him. Only she didn't know the pirate and Quentin's half brother were one and the same and he'd see that she never found out.

Justin pulled her to the carriage. He'd have to remember to thank Washington for sending her on her way.

Bree tried to pull away. "What are you doing here? And where is my carriage? Where are you taking me?"

Justin shoved her into his coach and climbed in after her. "Have you forgotten, we have a bargain? Did you think to cancel it by returning to Quentin?"

With her last scrap of dignity, Bree gave him a haughty smile and then scooted to the far side of the seat.

"I asked you a question," he said when the coach started to move.

Bree looked out the window. She had no intention of talking to Justin while he was in another one of his black moods.

When she didn't answer, Justin's anger grew. Jealousy threatened to suffocate him and she didn't even appear to care. He had visions of wringing her pretty little neck. Instead, he reached over and pulled her into his arms.

When she started to protest, he covered her parted lips with his. She struggled against him, but it wasn't long before he sensed the change in her. She was no longer fighting him. There was no mistake. She might deny it to herself, but it was clear to him that she wanted the kiss also.

He lifted her onto his lap. The passion he had been holding back flooded his very being, drowning his anger. With a hunger that wasn't to be denied, he crushed her body against his. How could he toss something away that he wanted so terribly much?

Slowly so as not to frighten her, Justin raised the hem of her gown. Once under the material, he slid his hand up until he reached her breast. Her response was immediate. The kiss deepened. She was his for the taking. He was sure of it. He turned her in his arms so his thumb could tease the swollen orb he cupped.

It took a moment for Justin to realize the coach had stopped. When the door opened, he looked up to find himself looking into Higgins's face.

"What is it?" he growled over Bree's shoulder.

"The fence was down on the back side of the pasture."

"The mares?"

"They're gone. I've sent your men out on foot to look for them."

With a curse on his lips, Justin climbed from the coach. "My men?"

Higgins let his gaze drop. "Miss Bree hired Otis and Ned to help with the mares."

So she had done it despite his warning. But that didn't explain Higgins going along with her scheme.

"Since when is Miss Bree in charge of hiring my workers?" he asked as he glared back at the coach door. "Take the meddling Miss Bree on to the cabin," he told Higgins. "And make sure she doesn't leave."

Bree leaned back against the cushions. The passion he had stirred in her heart left her knees weak and trembling. Once again her traitorous body had betrayed her. How could she tell him she couldn't have run away if she'd wanted to?

They worked late into the night rounding up the last of the mares. When they had them secured behind the worm fence, Justin left Higgins at the cabin, then returned to Havenwood. He was too tired to deal with Bree's duplicity again tonight—nor his inclination to fall in with her schemes. It was best to keep one's goals in mind when dealing with women, he reminded himself as he climbed the stairs to the front door of his home. The butler opened the door when he reached it.

"Don't you ever sleep, Washington?"

The old butler nodded to the double oak doors down the hall. "Your grandfather," he whispered.

"I'm in the parlor, Justin," a voice rang out.

"You go on up to bed, Washington. I'll take care of the old man."

"Thanks, Mr. Tyler. He's in a right happy mood," he added in a whisper.

The butler turned and walked proudly down the hall. Justin watched until the man had gone through the door leading to the servants' stairway before he joined his grandfather.

Not wanting to face another bevy of questions without proper fortification, Justin walked straight to the sideboard and poured himself a brandy. "You shouldn't be up this late, old man," he said.

"Who are you calling old man? I could stay up all night, every night, and still be fresher than you."

Justin had no wish to argue the matter. He knew his grandfather was more than willing to do it just to prove he could. He took a seat across from him. "If you won't think of yourself, at least consider Washington. He needs his sleep."

Adrian brushed his concern aside. "That old priss needs to have his hair parted once in a while. He lords his training over the others too much as it is."

"Washington is excellent at what he does, Grandfather. His training, as you put it, has only made him a more valuable servant. It wouldn't hurt to consider training the other servants as well."

Adrian, who had been quizzing the black man for the past hour on their mysterious visitor, wasn't as generous in his opinion of the closemouthed butler.

"Educating Washington was your idea, not mine. Now you want a houseful of servants who think themselves above their station?"

Justin took a healthy swallow of the brandy. "I'm considering it," he said.

Adrian cocked his head and studied Justin a moment. "And what do you think Regina Wingham will have to say about that?" he asked, hoping to open the subject of brides and weddings.

"Until I decide to ask Regina to marry me, I won't waste my time worrying about it."

"I wouldn't be putting off asking the good lady, if I were you. That Leonard Atwater's been sniffing around her again, son. He plans on having those prime pasturelands for himself."

Justin set his glass down. "Regina's not about to accept that popinjay's proposal. Not as long as she thinks she has a chance at becoming mistress of Havenwood."

"And does she have a chance, son?"

Another trip to the sideboard to refill the crystal tumbler gave Justin the time to think over his dilemma. If he could stay out of Bree's bed long enough to secure the annulment, he had every intention of marrying Regina—but not anytime soon if he could help it.

"There's a few things that need working out first, Grandfather, but there's no doubt about it, I want those fields. With the land we have bordering her father's acres and the mares I brought back from England, I could have the largest stables in all of Virginia. Besides, if I have to marry someday, I might as well take the bride that has grace, charm, *and* land."

"You never thought of marrying for love, son?"

A frown settled on Justin's face. "Why worry about love? In the dark, it doesn't matter who warms your bed. But if you have to put up with a wife, she might as well be one who comes with something you can't get any other way. Old Wingham was smart. He knew I might not consider marrying his daughter if he sold me the lands I wanted outright."

"Even so, you can't expect him to wait around forever for you to decide to ask her."

Justin smiled down at the old man. "It was he who cut the bargain. He was so hungry for the alliance, I merely had to assure him that when I was ready to marry, Regina would be my first choice and he promised she would be waiting."

"And you're so sure she will?"

"Oh, I'll let Wingham worry over his decision for a few days more. With Regina growing older each year, it's got

PIRATES AND PROMISES

to be gnawing at his gut, but he'll not change his mind now. Regina would not let him."

"I hope you're right, son. I know how much you want that land. You have the mares now. Why not ask her? Waiting so long to wrap up your bargain could be risky."

Justin lifted a dark brow. "And how would it be risky?" The asking of the question brought an image of Bree dancing through his mind.

"Exactly!" the old man shouted as if he could read Justin's thoughts. "Not only could Regina decide Atwater is more to her liking, but some pretty little thing could cross your path and you just might end up marrying her instead."

Justin clenched his fingers around his brandy glass. "You need not worry, Grandfather, there's not a woman I know who could sway me from what I want."

Especially if she thinks only of Quentin, he told himself.

The light from a full moon peeked in through the many holes in the roof, casting a mantle of bright stars, like spots across the dirt floor. Bree had given up counting them hours ago and now tossed and turned on the bed. The brittle straw mattress was worse than sleeping with the horses. At least there the straw had been fresh.

Bree gave up trying to sleep and sat up. It wasn't the bed that was keeping her from sleep. She was worried about Justin. Their first night on shore and he was gone. She could only hope he wasn't out plying his skills as a highwayman while she was tucked safely away in this cabin.

What would she and the others do if he were caught? She'd be switched if she'd sell **any** of the mares to buy his way out of trouble. They were to be her future—their future. If he was out throwing it all away for a few coins, she'd not lift a finger to help him, she told herself. He deserved to hang and she'd be down front watching him swing.

The words sounded brave enough. Too bad the feelings she would need to back up the threats were sadly lacking. If all those years of reading had taught her anything, it was that the heroine always saved the hero with her love—and her hand in marriage. She had certainly proved a disappointment in that regard.

Perhaps she had been too hasty in agreeing to an annulment. Perhaps she should tell him she had changed her mind.

CHAPTER 16

BREE became more and more worried when Justin failed to make an appearance the next morning. A quick glance out the window told her Higgins was not about either. He must be out with the mares, she decided. She tried not to dwell on the possibility that he too had been worried about Justin and had gone out looking for him. She could only pray that neither one of them had been caught.

She quickly dressed behind the blanket Higgins had hung from the rafters for her privacy, then set about putting the small cabin in order.

She found a bucket hanging outside the door and carried it down to the small creek that ran beside the cabin. Having filled it, she went back to the cabin and began to wipe down the few pieces of furniture the previous owner had left.

The sun was high in the sky by the time Higgins returned with a wagon of goods. Bree ran out to meet him.

"Justin?" she asked, trying to appear casual with the question.

Higgins started emptying the basket onto the small table. "He will be here as soon as he's finished some personal business," he said.

She didn't ask more. From the careful way Higgins avoided meeting her gaze, she knew the personal business had to do with the annulment. She didn't know why the news should upset her so. They had agreed on the solution from the very beginning. It wasn't as if his feelings for her had changed in the least. In fact, his temperament of late clearly pointed to his displeasure with her company.

A small smile crossed Bree's lips as she followed Higgins out to the wagon. The pirate was making sure the annulment was carried out as soon as possible. Yet, he wouldn't relinquish her indenture papers in order to be rid of her for good. He had no qualms about keeping her under his thumb, only out of his bed. She'd have to see what she could do about that. He gave her no peace of mind and she'd see to it he had none either.

Higgins touched her arm. "Can you give me a hand? We need to get these things unloaded."

Bree looked over into the wagon. There were saddles, ropes, and two large covered baskets.

When they finished unpacking, the baskets proved to hold even more than Bree had at first thought. Their meager store of supplies had grown with the flour, sugar, salt, a jar of preserves, two smoked hams, five potatoes, and a handful of carrots tucked away beneath the blanket.

"Breakfast, miss," he said as he handed her one of the baskets.

One of the large lined baskets he carried held an odd assortment of plates, cups, and crude utensils. Nestled atop a large white sheet and a blanket was a covered plate. Bree could smell the fresh bread and sausages even before they were unpacked and her mouth began to water.

Once Bree had stored away the items on a wooden shelf along one wall, finished her breakfast, and cleaned the kitchen area, she once again found herself at loose ends. She went to the pasture with Higgins to check on the mares, but with the lush green grasses and another small stream running through the meadow where the mares grazed, there wasn't much that had to be done.

When Higgins said he was going to walk the fence with Ned and Otis to make sure further repairs weren't needed, Bree returned to the cabin and dug out the book Justin had found for her. She thought to keep her mind occupied, but the story failed to hold her attention and she found herself wondering where Justin was and what was keeping him so long.

Perhaps she should wash her clothes while she waited. They were certainly in need of it. Bree got out the piece of soap Higgins had brought her and began slicing it into thin shavings as she had watched her maid sometimes do for her bath.

Having reached the end of her block of soap, Bree looked down into the pot. Drats! She hadn't meant to carve up the entire piece, but the garments would no doubt benefit from the extra soap. After spreading the flakes out on the bottom, she grabbed up the kettle of water hanging on the fireplace hook only to discover that it was empty. The water she hadn't used to wash up her breakfast plate had boiled dry.

Bree fetched more water from the creek and put the kettle back on the iron arm and swung it over the coals. An hour later, the water wasn't much warmer than it was when she dipped it from the stream and the coals were just as cold. If Mr. Thurston were to see her now, he would not be so certain Lady Luck was sitting on her shoulder. She would have to wash her clothes in cold water.

Once she managed to stuff the garments into the pot of soap shavings, Bree poured the water over the clothes and stirred the mixture with a large spoon. The water first turned black, then took on a milky hue. She gave it a few more stirs, then lifted the items out. Bree smiled to herself. Other than being a bit slimy, the clothes were clean. She rinsed them at the stream, then spread them across the bushes to dry.

Now for something to eat. Bree stared at the things Higgins had brought. Up until now her culinary skills had been limited to the reviewing of the day's menus with her father's housekeeper and it was difficult to imagine what she was expected to do with the smoked ham and the variety of iron pots. She wanted to learn how to cook, but it didn't appear anyone was going to teach her, and left to her own, she would more than likely poison someone.

Bree smiled to herself. Did she truly care if her cooking made Justin ill? After keeping her waiting all day, he deserved to suffer too. So when late afternoon arrived and he still hadn't come, she asked Higgins to show her how to cook in the stone fireplace.

More than happy to be rid of the task, Higgins quickly instructed her in the rudimentary skills of building a cooking fire, then made his escape. There wasn't a woman he knew who wanted a man looking over her shoulder while she cooked. He'd make another trip up to the big house. By the time he loaded the rest of the things they would need, supper should be ready. He could almost smell the ham and potatoes now.

"Who-o-o wee!" Higgins said to himself. What was that awful smell? Even his old mare, Mable, shook her head in protest against the noxious odor. It was sharp enough to set one's nose to stinging and his eyes to burning.

Higgins lifted his gaze from the narrow lane to check the sky overhead. He couldn't see any smoke, but then the tall trees blocked his view in too many spots to discount his suspicions.

Burning! He had forgotten about Miss Bree cooking. Higgins slapped the reins across Mable's broad rump.

He rounded the corner and saw the cabin, a cloud of smoke rolling from the top of its open doorway. Before he could bring Mable to a stop, Bree stumbled out, a blackened oilcloth trailing from her fingers. From the sad condition of the slicker, it was apparent she had used it to try to put out the flames.

Higgins jumped down from the wagon, grabbed the bucket hanging beside the door, and ran down to the creek. It took him three trips before he was able to put out the fire on the hearth.

PIRATES AND PROMISES

"Thank goodness it didn't do much damage," he offered as he gazed down at her singed dress. "You could have been hurt."

She knew it would be best to appear contrite, but it was difficult when you were still angry and the reason behind your folly was still absent.

"What happened?" Higgins finally asked.

"Yes, what happened?"

They both turned in unison to see Justin dismount beside the wagon. Bree ran to him and threw herself into his arms.

"I wanted to cook your supper and now everything is ruined," she sobbed dramatically.

Justin patted her soothingly on the back. "Cooking his supper" sounded suspiciously like Bree was becoming domesticated and that made him uneasy. From the garments scattered across the bushes, it appeared she'd even tried her hand at washing.

"Now, now," he crooned as his gaze kept returning to the garments. Not a single shirttail fluttered in the breeze. "Perhaps Higgins can help make something out of it."

The solemn shaking of Higgins's bald head told him there was little hope, but Bree crying her heart out touched him. He couldn't stand by without at least attempting to ease her disappointment.

"Don't cry," he said, putting his arm around her shoulders. "Higgins will bring our supper out here and we'll have a picnic out on the grass. Would you like that?"

The solemn shaking of Higgins's head was vigorous enough now to scramble the man's brain. "Bring one of the blankets out, Higgins," Justin said sternly, ignoring his manservant's wild gesturing. "We wish to eat our supper out here."

The smile that broke out on Bree's smudged face more than made up for the disapproving frown Higgins gave him before he left to fetch the blanket. Once Justin had Bree busily arranging the dishes on their blanket, he snatched the stiff garments from the bushes and quietly returned to the cabin to speak with Higgins.

The smoke had cleared and other than the blackened hearth there didn't appear to be any damage. "What started it?" Justin asked, setting down the clothes. Most of them stood stiffly on their own.

Higgins poked around in the soot. "Danged if I know."

"What's that awful smell then?" Justin whispered aside to Higgins once he was sure Bree hadn't followed him into the cabin.

"That's your supper."

"Are you sure? I've never known food to smell like that before."

Higgins speared the ham out of the iron pot and lifted it gingerly to his nose. The pungent odor brought tears to his eyes and he quickly dropped it back in the pan.

"It's your supper all right. And don't say I didn't try to warn you. I'll have to throw this out and start over or we'll have no supper tonight."

Justin looked down at the charred ham and potatoes floating in the creek water. "That's all well and good, but what about Bree? Isn't there something you can do to save what she cooked?"

Higgins studied the fare for a moment. "I could shoot it," he said, "but I reckon whatever Miss Bree did killed it good enough for me."

"She'll be so hurt if we don't eat some of it," Justin said half to himself.

While Justin was always the gentleman, Higgins had never known him to be overly concerned with a woman's feelings before, and with the smell of Bree's culinary endeavor fresh in his nose, this was not the time for Justin to mend his ways.

"You go out and take Miss Bree for a nice walk along the creek," he finally said. "I'll take Mable back up to the big house and see if I can talk Cook out of something decent."

Justin paused in the doorway, his chest tightening at the sight of Bree on the blanket. She looked so forlorn and he wished there was something he could do to cheer her up. Perhaps . . .

Justin signaled to Higgins. "Have Cook make up a pan of ham and potatoes," he whispered. "If we don't tell Bree any different, perhaps she will think it was her supper."

"You plannin' on lying to her, Mr. Tyler?"

"It's either that or we find some way to eat what she did cook."

Higgins grabbed up the iron pot. He didn't feel right about their deception, but he wasn't about to sacrifice his stomach for anyone.

"You keep her entertained," he said. "I'll give this a decent burial and be back with our supper before you know I was gone."

"Take the clothes with you too. They'll need to be rewashed."

Higgins gave the shirt tents a sideways glance, then shook his head in amazement. "If I didn't think she'd burn down Williamsburg within the week, I'd say you'd be better off givin' her her papers and sendin' her on her way."

Justin was inclined to agree.

Justin walked Bree across the meadow for what seemed the tenth time. Where was Higgins? It had been almost two hours since he left and Bree was beginning to ask questions. If his manservant didn't return soon, there'd be no hiding the deception.

"I think we should go back," Bree said. After the solicitous manner in which he was treating her, she almost felt guilty about ruining his supper. "We've walked this same area no less than four times. If supper isn't ready by now, Higgins must need our help."

Justin did not miss the touch of defeat in her voice. "He said the ham needed to cook a little longer and he'd call when it was done."

Bree allowed herself a wan smile. "Even so, I think I'd like to go back."

Justin tucked her arm in his and turned back along the path they had worn beside the creek. "As you wish," he said. "But don't be surprised if Higgins gives us a scolding for not obeying his instructions."

"I'm so hungry now, I'm willing to take my chances."

That was easy for her to say, he thought. She hadn't gotten a whiff of the ham. He slowed his pace in hopes of giving Higgins more time to return.

When they reached the cabin, they found Higgins placing a small vase of wild flowers on the blanket. Justin breathed a long sigh of relief. Supper at last.

"The cabin's still a mite smoky, but I managed," Higgins said to the question he could see on Justin's face. "A nice idea, the blanket. Makes it a touch more romantic out here."

Justin frowned. Romantic? What had gotten into Higgins? He'd even brought a blush to Bree's face with his comment. Oh well, he might as well follow suit.

"Then I think since the lady fixed us such a fine meal, she ought to take her seat and we will serve her."

Once he had Bree seated on the blanket, he grabbed Higgins by the arm and pulled him to the cabin. "You were able to get the ham and potatoes, weren't you?"

"Yes, but . . ."

He knew that look. Higgins had taken his orders a step further than Justin had requested. "But what?" he growled.

"It's not my fault."

"Out with it. What did you do?"

"I only asked Cook for the ham and potatoes . . . just like you said."

Justin was fast losing patience. "And?"

"Well, somewhere in the cooking, she came up with gravy and a loaf of bread."

"So throw out the bread and let's eat."

"But it's out on the—"

"Fresh bread!"

At the exclamation, they both ran to the door. Bree sat perched on the blanket with a large slice of bread. Preserves dripped freely from the bite she had taken.

"I'm sorry to have started without you," she said after swallowing, "but it's absolutely delicious. Higgins, you will have to show me how you made this. I've never tasted anything so good."

"Higgins is quite the little cook, when he takes the notion," Justin said as he waved Higgins back into the cabin to get the rest of their supper. "He'll be out with the ham and potatoes in a moment."

Bree smiled up at him. "It was so nice of him to finish up after the awful mess I made of the fireplace."

Justin sat down and took her hand. "Think nothing of it. After all, you had done most of the work. He merely kept an eye on it."

Higgins returned in time to hear Justin casually dismiss his efforts. Upset, he plopped the bowls down on the blanket and left. Let Mr. Tyler explain the miracle cure the meal has undergone, he thought as he walked away.

Bree eyed the ham suspiciously. There was no way this could be the same piece of meat. She might not know how to cook, but there was nothing wrong with her nose and it told her this ham had not had a sailor's slicker melted to it.

"What happened to the blackened crust?" she asked.

Justin unfolded his napkin and laid it across his knees. "It was merely a matter of trimming off the part which had gotten burnt."

Trimmed, my eye! Somehow Higgins had managed to procure another one. "And the gravy?"

"If cooked properly, meat makes its own gravy," Justin answered with total disregard for the truth.

"Oh! Well, it certainly looks tasty," she said, picking up the spoon to serve. "I guess I'm a better cook than I thought."

Justin smiled over at her. "So it would seem."

With each bite, he could see her confidence returning. He'd have to remember to thank Higgins.

"Maybe it's eating outside," Bree said as she stared down at her plate, "or just that I'm hungry, but I do believe this is the best meal I've had in a long time. I think I'm going to enjoy cooking our meals."

Justin nearly choked on his bite of ham.

"You needn't think you have to do all the cooking, Bree. Higgins is perfectly capable of doing his share." He laid his spoon down. "In fact, I think he's growing lazy with all the work you do for him."

"That's nonsense and you know it. Higgins does more than his share and I'm sure he'd be happy to have me take over the cooking for him. Why, I . . . Where are Otis and Ned?" Bree asked, suddenly aware that she had seen nothing of them since noon.

"You were just complaining that there's not enough for you to do. The same thing occurred to me and I thought you might like helping Higgins exercise the mares." The smile that had sprung readily to her lips quickly faded. "You don't want to ride?"

"It is not that, for you know I would love to ride. It's . . . it's that I don't wish to take the task away from Otis and Ned."

"You don't have to worry about that. They no longer work for us."

Bree clutched her napkin. "But what will they do to survive?"

"You need not trouble yourself over their welfare." From what Justin had ended up paying Kelly at the Rosewater Inn to take on the two sailors, no one should have to worry. "I have found them positions elsewhere."

"And where might that be?" she asked with a great show of innocence.

"Oh, no you don't. You'll not be getting that information from me."

Bree smiled up at him. "Don't you trust me?"

"No, I don't," he stated. "If I told you where they were, it wouldn't be two days and you'd be knocking on their door."

"You deliberately got rid of them, didn't you?"

He grinned. "I thought it best.

Bree stood and started clearing the plates. *He thought it best.* Well, she'd soon have him reviewing that decision. They could not avoid eating her cooking forever. Sooner or later, the pirate was going to reap the punishment she had planned for him.

* * *

Justin couldn't understand it. Although Bree continued to fail at cooking, she hadn't appeared to lose any of her enthusiasm for trying and Higgins swore his stomach couldn't take any more of her experiments. He was threatening to quit.

Justin had to admit he wasn't faring too well with the concoctions himself, but Bree took such delight in preparing the meals he hated to tell her how unpalatable they were.

Bree had no such illusions about her culinary skills. She was a terrible cook and she knew it. What's more, she had no wish to become any better.

Oh, she'd known the pirate's plan from the very beginning. He thought to stick her out here in the middle of nowhere and forget about her until he had his annulment. Well, Bree had other plans for how she should while away her hours until St. Clair returned from England.

It galled her to think Mr. Thurston was free to spend his time amassing a fortune at cards when she was the better player. It was all Justin's doing. He wouldn't give his consent for her to go into Williamsburg, let alone allow her to gamble. It just didn't seem fair.

She had done everything to convince him to allow her to leave, but Justin ignored her hints. It was difficult to believe the lengths Higgins and Justin were going to not to have to tell her how terrible a cook she was. She would have thought that almost burning the cabin down would have had them putting their heads together to keep her occupied with other endeavors. Instead they were going to force her to poison one of them before they came to their senses.

Bree continued to cook for one reason only—her freedom. As long as Justin was determined to keep her a virtual prisoner in this leaky cabin, she would continue dispensing her own brand of revenge.

Bree eyed the bowl of dried beans she had set to soaking yesterday. Higgins had told her no one could ruin ham and beans. With a grim smile on her lips, she scooped up the beans and dropped them into the caldron of water. Next she gathered up all the herbs, roots, and spices Higgins had collected for her and tossed them in.

She was about to turn away when she spotted the small bottle of liniment Higgins used for the mares. She uncorked it and sniffed. The pungent odor brought a smile to her lips. Without another thought, she tipped the bottle over the pot and emptied it. Once the pirate tasted this, he would be more than happy to be rid of her.

"What do you mean, it will take a while? I want an annulment, not the Constitution changed."

Francis wished, not for the first time, he hadn't let Adrian talk him into this delay. What he hoped to gain in the few extra weeks was beyond him. Justin had made up his mind and there was no changing it.

"We can't rush these things," Francis said. "I'm sure you'll agree that secrecy is your utmost concern. We wouldn't want this to go any further than this room."

Justin had to agree. Regina was not known to be of an understanding nature. If she were to hear of the marriage, she was likely to accept Atwater's offer out of spite.

"Do the best you can to hurry things along. If this is not resolved soon, you may not have to worry about how to quietly secure the annulment. I'll have either bedded the minx or murdered her."

With a gasp from the solicitor still ringing in his ears, Justin left the office.

Justin took one spoonful and spit the soup across the table. "Damn!" he cursed, daubing his mouth with his napkin. "This is the worst thing ever."

Bree couldn't believe how easily the tears came to her eyes. "You don't care for my soup," she blustered accusingly.

Justin stood and took her in his arms. He hadn't meant to hurt her feelings. After all, she tried so hard.

"I'm sorry," he said as he held her close.

She buried her face in his shirt. "And I spent the entire day preparing it," she sobbed.

"Now, now," he crooned. It seemed like he was spending more and more of his time soothing Bree's tender feelings, but it was a role he was growing more and more fond of. "Until you learn how, perhaps you should have Higgins do the cooking."

Bree pushed away from him. "And what would you have me do then? Cooking is the only thing I have to occupy my time."

"How are you at mending?"

Mending! She had no plans of sitting calmly in a rocker with all manner of silk threads and sharp needles spread about her. She wanted excitement and adventure . . . perhaps a card game or two.

"My skills with a needle are worse than my cooking," she stated, hoping that would quash any plans he might have in that direction.

Justin opened his mouth to argue that nothing could be worse than her cooking, but he quickly closed it. He didn't need to upset her further.

"I could ask Higgins to bring you a proper saddle and you could begin helping him exercise the mares."

When a smile lit her face, Justin felt all the more guilty for not having followed through with his earlier idea. "But you must keep in mind that you will have to stay close to the cabin."

When the smile just as quickly slipped from her face, he added, "You wouldn't want anyone to see you and start asking questions. As unconventional as most would think Virginia, a young lady's reputation is still something to be protected."

Bree looked down at the white shirt and black breeches she had to wear every day now. "You need not worry on my account. Dressed as I am, I have no more wish to be seen than you have of someone seeing me."

Justin had to agree with her. If someone were to see her, the men's attire would raise more questions than the fact that she was staying in the cabin. He didn't know why he hadn't thought to replace her pink gown.

"Come here," he said.

Bree studied him a moment. "Why?"

"I won't eat you up. If I'm to bring something from town for you to wear, I need to have some idea of your size."

Bree stepped up to him. "What will you get?" she asked excitedly. "A riding habit?"

"Perhaps," he said. He couldn't keep from smiling at her enthusiasm.

"Oh, and I will need a few day gowns," she added. "Then there's the matter of a decent comb, a hand mirror, and—"

"Enough!" he shouted. "For now it's to be a day gown."

Before she could protest, he spanned her small waist with his hands. "About so, I would say."

At his touch, Bree could no longer hold back the smoldering embers of desire that sprang to life. With the endless days of boredom she had been forced to endure, she found herself welcoming the flames. When he ran his hands boldly up her sides, she held her breath, then nearly swooned when his long slender fingers fanned out along the sides of her breasts.

He was taking control of her body again. Why couldn't she manage to banish this terrible, undeniable attraction that seemed to grow whenever he touched her?

As if the actions had affected him also, Justin quickly pulled her to his chest and made a great do about where her head came to.

"So tall," he said evenly, but the huskiness of his voice gave him away. No matter what he tried to tell her—or himself—it was clear that he was every bit as drawn to her as she was to him. The knowledge gave Bree courage. She stepped back and took his hands. With her gaze locked with his, she placed them back high on her sides.

"I have the most difficulty with the fit here," she said with a shy smile.

Justin knew it to be true. Hadn't he purposely avoided letting his gaze fall to the snug fit of the shirt? Up until now, that is. Just looking at how the linen stretched tight across her already taut nipples brought an ache to his loins that was matched only by the wild pounding of his heart. He hadn't felt like this since he'd plopped down his hard-earned coin for his first light-skirt at Ma Yancy's place. He'd near split his breeches before she'd got them off him. Heaven help him, but they were every bit as tight now.

"Do you know what you're asking?"

"Yes," she breathed. "I'm asking you to take me as your wife."

Justin could feel the tight hand of logic slowly closing around his chest. His reluctance had nothing to do with her obsession with his half brother, he told himself. It was Regina Wingham and the land. He mustn't forget his plans for Havenwood. There was no denying he wanted Bree, but there was a quick cure for what he was feeling if you had the coin to pay. If he gave in to the lustful yearnings she was stirring in him, he might as well say farewell to the goals he had set for himself ten years ago.

Mr. Wingham had made it perfectly clear no amount of coin could purchase the land. There was only one way to acquire the prime piece of pastureland Justin coveted and that was to marry Regina.

Damn Francis and his refusal to rush things. He needed that annulment. Taking Bree to his bed before he secured it would cost him his carefully laid plans and that was too high a price to pay. Especially when he had every confidence Bree would succumb to the desires that plagued them both after the annulment. It wasn't as if there was any love to be considered between them. Hell, she was more than likely trying to seduce him to ensure her share of the profits from the mares. If that was the case, it was time to remind Bree of her prior commitments.

"We wouldn't want to upset Quentin, now would we?"

Bree pushed his hands away. "I hate Quentin," she said. "How many times do I have to tell you that before you will believe me?"

"Perhaps I would have, had you told me why you went to see his brother when I asked."

Bree pursed her lips tightly together. She refused to defend herself by telling the pirate of their promise or her dreams. He would only ridicule her for being so naïve as to think St. Clair would wait for her.

If it weren't for her promise to honor the terms of the indenture papers, she would abandon everything and look up Maddie's cousin. Surely a family that had enough funds to travel all the way to England to bring back a governess would not be so difficult to find. But she could never ask Justin if he knew of the Winghams, for if she ever found the need to put an end to this torture he was putting her through, he might think to look for her there. No, she would wait until he left for Williamsburg and she would ask Higgins.

CHAPTER 17

"IT wasn't my fault," Higgins shouted as Justin pulled his mount to a halt beside the narrow path leading to the cabin. Higgins had been waiting beside the road for over two hours to catch his employer. "Not a word slipped from my lips."

"Whatever are you babbling about?"

"Miss Bree," he said. "She's been askin' about Miss Wingham."

Justin dismounted so he wouldn't have to shout. "How did she learn of Regina?"

"I don't know, but as soon as you left for town, Miss Bree come lookin' for me. Wanted to know if I had ever heard of the Winghams."

Justin clenched his fist tight around the reins. Bree! No matter which way he turned, she always managed to hurtle a stone onto his path.

If Bree were to tell Regina of the marriage, she could ruin his chances of ever getting his hands on the land he wanted. Regina might not require that love go hand in hand with her marriage but she was a lot like Justin in one respect—pride would never allow her to accept what the town gossips would consider the leavings of another.

Despite his growing anger, Justin calmly handed Higgins the reins. "What would you suggest I do with her?"

They started walking along the road toward the cabin and it was several minutes before Higgins answered. "Other than hog-tyin' her and puttin' a ring in her nose, I don't know how you're goin' to be keepin' her to home."

The suggestion tickled Justin's fancy and he laughed. "I take it she served you some of that soup she tried to get me to eat."

"I've swallowed wash water that was better than that." Higgins raged at the memory. "She nigh poisoned me."

"That's the same stuff all right."

"Well, all I can say is you'd best be takin' her in hand before she kills the both of us or you wake up to find her on Miss Regina's doorstep bellowin' to all of Williamsburg that she's your wife."

Justin nodded his agreement. With the way Bree had been acting of late, coupled with her sudden interest in Regina, he might do best to reconsider his decision to have her assist with the exercising of the mares. Merely having her riding them was risky enough; but now that she had found out about Regina, the risk was greater that she might decide to take it upon herself to pay a visit to the Winghams. All she needed to get there was one of the mares and he had just put all of them at her disposal.

Justin stopped in the middle of the road, pulling Higgins and the mare up short. One thing for sure, it'd be a mistake giving Bree the new riding habit he'd purchased in town.

"Hold the mare. I have to get something out of one of the packages behind the saddle before Bree discovers the surprise."

Bree stood in the shadows along the road. A surprise? Justin had brought a surprise for her?

A smile curved the edges of her lips as he placed the package on the ground and started unwrapping it. He had talked of bringing her a day dress, but the dark blue riding habit he pulled from the paper was more than she could have hoped for.

"Oh, Justin," she gasped before she thought and both men turned to her.

Before Justin could stuff the dress back into the paper, Bree was kneeling beside him. She threw her arms around him, almost knocking the two of them over in her enthusiasm to thank him.

Higgins gave Justin a smile and a wave, then left with the mare. Why did his luck always seem to fail him where Bree was concerned?

"Oh, thank you," Bree said again, clinging to him as he tried to stand. "Now you will be able to take me with you without the shame of being seen with a ragamuffin."

Justin took her by the arms and held her from him. "I will not be able to have you ride with me."

"Why not?"

Hoping to placate her, Justin placed a kiss on her forehead. "The sight of you in that habit will draw every man's eye to us."

"Oh, I forgot," she said with a pout as she stooped to pick up the gown. "You are still the pirate and someone might recognize—"

Bree suddenly stopped in her speech and glared up at him. "How did you manage to buy this without being seen?"

"I have my ways," he said, failing to point out that the pirate had yet to make an appearance on Virginia's shores.

Bree didn't care for the smug grin on his face. "You didn't steal it, did you?"

"A reformed highwayman like me? Never! I paid good coin for those things."

Bree hugged the dress to her and smiled up at him. "Then we shall not waste your money. We will ride at night."

"The highwayman rides at night," he reminded her. He'd say anything to keep her from crossing paths with Regina. "Won't I be more easily recognized then?"

"Not if you have a woman with you. No one would ever suspect you of being the pirate then."

He had to give her credit. Although no one in Virginia knew of the pirate, her logic did make sense. Besides which, as long as she was with him, he could insure that she kept her distance from the Winghams.

"I will take you with me on two conditions. One is you are never to ride without me. Two, if we meet anyone on the road, you are to keep your pretty little mouth shut. And," he added, "you'll turn all the cooking duties over to Higgins."

"That's three conditions," she pointed out. "Which two am I to agree to?"

"All of them! And any others that might occur to me."

Bree glared up at him. "That hardly seems fair."

"As long as I'm the major partner in this relationship, I don't have to be," he said smugly. "Now what say you we exercise a couple of those mares this evening?"

A smile lit Bree's face. "As soon as I change," she said.

Justin watched her run down the path and a sadness suddenly took him by surprise. If not for Quentin, he would welcome Bree as his bride. She was not only beautiful, but innocent, untouched by the ugliness of others.

Moonlight trimmed each wave in an iridescent liquid silver that washed against the great ship's sides. Quentin leaned on the rail of the deck and cursed his bad luck. The calm winds of the last two weeks had delayed their time of arrival in Virginia and it would be a good ten days before they landed. The pirate could be anywhere by now. And Bree?

His gray eyes clouded with thoughts of her. The ache in his loins was almost unbearable as he pictured the ravishment she would have had to endure at the hands of the pirate. She would lie stripped and whimpering on the bed, waiting for her tormentor to have need of her body once more.

Quentin's breath quickened and his eyelids grew heavy

with passion. "I'm coming, my dear," he whispered, bitterness lacing each word. "I'm coming and, once we're married, you will feel more than the pain of a man between your beautiful legs. You will feel the sting of my hand and the cut of my whip. You will cry for mercy where there is none, then you will beg for your death."

The darkness of the riding habit only emphasized the fairness of her skin against the black tie at the throat of her white shirt and the blondness of her hair as it reflected the moon's soft glow. Justin had to steel himself against the hypnotic pull Bree had on him. He ordered her to keep her mount next to his as they approached the outskirts of Williamsburg. He had not planned on taking her so far, but seeing her obvious pleasure at their moonlit ride, he was even more reluctant to turn around.

"Why did you buy the gown?" she asked, breaking the silence that hung like a cloud between them.

"As a sort of celebration."

"A celebration?"

"Our annulment was granted today," he lied, hoping the announcement would put a halt to any ideas she might have of telling Regina of the wedding.

Bree didn't say a word, but the lie seemed to burn a hole in his soul. It wasn't too late to confess it as a lie, he told himself. The creak of a carriage wheel brought Justin to his senses before he weakened.

Lowering the brim of his hat, Justin nudged his mount against Bree's. Like a well-seasoned thief, she took her cue and guided the mare into the woods beside the road. Once safe, they both turned and waited for the carriage to pass.

The man driving lifted his whip and brought it down on the back of the black child running beside the carriage. "I say the coin is mine," he shouted down at the child.

"I . . . got no . . . coin, master," the boy said between ragged gasps.

"That woman gave you a coin all right and I'll have it before this night is out."

Justin leaned toward Bree. "Give me the tie on your shirt," he whispered. "I'll need it to cover my face."

"The pirate?" she gasped.

He nodded.

Bree quickly untied the wide black scarf that hung in folds down the front of her ruffled shirt and handed it to Justin. She worried about the pirate, but the stranger's shocking behavior warranted whatever Justin had in mind for him.

Once she helped him secure the tie about the lower half of his face, Justin spurred his mount and chased after the carriage. Bree kept to the trees and followed. By the time she caught up with them, the drunken man was lying on the ground, the carriage gone. As she watched, Justin leaned down and offered the small boy a hand up. The child stepped back in alarm.

Bree had forgotten how intimidating the pirate could be. The tall figure in black was enough to make most men quake in their boots, much less a young boy. Her heart swelled with pride. It was no wonder his reputation had spread so quickly in England.

"You can't take the boy," the old man bellowed as he struggled to get back to his feet. "No one steals a man's slave and gets away with it."

At his master's outburst, the child quickly swallowed his fear and grabbed Justin's outstretched hand.

"I can and I will, Mr. Vickers," Justin said as he swung the child up onto the horse behind him.

The stranger squinted as if to see whose face was hidden behind the scarf. "You know who I am?"

"It didn't take any great guesses. There aren't too many men I know who would sink low enough to steal from one of his own slaves, and a boy at that."

Vickers stepped closer. "And who are you that you think yourself above Virginia's laws?" he growled in reply.

Justin leaned forward in his saddle, a hard twist curving his lips. "Some call me the pirate, but I'm better known as Death."

PIRATES AND PROMISES 243

Vickers stared belligerently at the highwayman for a moment, then as if the fog of liquor had finally cleared, the old man suddenly paled and slowly backed away. "You may keep the boy," he rasped. "Just let me pass unharmed."

"I somehow thought you'd see it my way," Justin said, then held out his hand. "And now your purse."

"My purse?"

"You need not waste your time or mine with your senseless sniveling," he said, nudging the mare closer.

Bree gasped when Justin pulled a knife from his boot and held it menacingly at the old man's throat. Surely he didn't intend killing Mr. Vickers.

"It's your purse or your worthless life."

The man handed it over to Justin, then backed up a few steps before he turned and started running after his carriage.

"I'll be by soon to collect the papers on the boy," Justin shouted after him.

Bree started to join them when the pirate waved for her to stay in the trees. For once, she obeyed.

Justin dismounted. "Do you know where Havenwood is, lad?" he asked, handing the reins to the boy.

"Over past Cottonwood Grove?"

"That's the place. Now I want you to take my horse and go there. Talk to the old viscount and tell him to hide you until I can send someone to help you escape." Justin tossed the leather purse up to the boy. "And don't you go giving him any trouble."

The boy grinned down at the pirate. "I'll be real polite, Mr. Pirate."

"See that you are. Now be off with you, before Vickers comes back looking for you."

Bree waited until the young man was out of sight before she nudged her mare out onto the road again. Her heart was still thundering wildly against her ribs.

"Do you always give your take away?" she asked when she pulled her mount up beside the pirate.

"Let's just say I put it where it's needed most," he said as he removed her tie.

She gazed down into his face. "Then you weren't lying when you said you didn't use the money for yourself."

Justin gave a short laugh. "After all this time, you finally believe me?" he asked with a grin.

"Oh, yes, and this is all so wonderful. The way you handled that rude man was truly magnificent."

Heaven help him, she thought him some kind of hero. "I stole a slave, Bree. By tomorrow morning this place will be crawling with dogs and slave hunters. They won't leave a stone unturned until they've found him. And when they do, old man Vickers will beat him to within an inch of his life."

"Then we'll catch up to him and hide him."

Justin grabbed the reins of her mare and mounted behind her. "There's no we to it. I'll send Higgins north with him as soon as I get you back to the cabin."

They rode in silence the rest of the way. Bree settled back against his broad chest. It was wonderful having his arms around her again. She was so proud of him. What he had done was the most noble thing she had ever seen. He was so gallant, just like the heroes in her books. There must be all kinds of injustices she could make right with the pirate's help. One thing for sure, she'd not let the matter lie until she talked him into it.

"I said no and that's final!" Justin stated.

Bree folded her arms over her chest and glared up at him. She couldn't understand why he was being so stubborn. Robbing Mr. Vickers was the most exciting thing she had ever seen. The pirate was acting less and less like one of her heroes.

"I don't know how I ever imagined for a moment that you could be one," she mumbled under her breath.

"What?"

"Never mind. I say we take to the road . . . or whatever it is that you call being a highwayman," she said firmly. "And if you won't, I'll find someone who will."

"You might find that a bit difficult with your hands tied to the bedpost."

Bree ignored the black scowl on his face. Frustrated with his lack of cooperation, she paced across the room and back. "Why must you always choose to be the toad when you could just as easily be a prince?"

Justin didn't know what she was talking about, but it was evident that his character had sunk beyond all redemption with Bree. He didn't know himself why he was being so stubborn about her scheme. Bree had handled herself as if she had been born to the life of a highwayman's accomplice. And there were certainly enough gentlemen of his acquaintance who were just as deserving as Quentin's friends had been.

In fact, if the gossip he had heard only last week was true, there was a gentleman in Alexandria who needed a taste of the pirate's type of justice.

"If I agree to this," he said slowly, "and I'm not saying I do, you'll have to promise to stay out of sight."

Bree was almost afraid to breathe lest she do it wrong and give him an excuse to change his mind. "I promise," she said calmly.

"You'd have to allow me a few days. There's some information I need to verify. Then, come Saturday night, be ready to leave at sunset."

Quentin wondered what he would do if the pirate had disappeared with Sabrina once their ship landed in Virginia. The possibility had plagued him more than once since leaving England. From all he'd heard, America covered vast acres of land and the pirate was his only clue to finding her.

Suppose no one had ever heard of the pirate? If he didn't find Sabrina and marry her, he'd never get control of the rich inheritance Lord Smythe was certain to have left his daughter. More wealth than Quentin had ever known. Even Henrietta's inheritance paled when compared to the one which Sabrina would lay claim to.

Quentin smiled for the first time in days. The best part of all was that if she gave him too much grief after the marriage, he could always leave her here in Virginia and return to England. With the necessary papers to show proof of the wedding, a husband was entitled to claim his wife's estate.

When Justin arrived late Saturday afternoon, Bree was dressed and waiting in the shirt and breeches she had won off one of the sailors. The tight breeches once again clung tightly to her curves and Justin was instantly aroused.

"Afraid I would leave without you?" he asked as he nodded to the saddled horses tied beside the cabin.

Bree smiled up at him. "Merely assuring that you have no excuses for not including me."

He curved his fingers under her chin and returned her smile. "I do believe if I'd have been late you would have come looking for me."

She frowned. She had forgotten how insufferably arrogant he could be at times. Lifting a delicate brow, she met his eye.

"You flatter yourself," she said. "I don't need you or anyone else to point out a man in need of a comeuppance. What little I've seen of the Virginians, they are all in need of instructions on the fine art of good manners."

Justin took her by the arm and pulled her up against him. She may not love him but she had woven a web around him nonetheless—a web he meant to wrap around her as well. "If that is what you truly believe," he said with a wicked grin, "then as a *Virginian*, I need not be restricted by what you deem acceptable manners."

Before she could pull away, Justin brought his lips down on hers. Lord help him. Her struggles only made him all the more determined to give her a taste of what he wanted. He deepened the kiss until he was more than a little drunk himself from the effects of it.

With passion clouding his earlier convictions to keep his distance, Justin crushed her against the length of him. She no longer resisted, but slid her arms up to embrace him. Heat like thick hot syrup poured unchecked into his veins and throughout his body, burning a sweet trail of desire to his loins . . . and to his heart.

Suddenly nothing mattered to Justin but quenching the fires she so easily lit within him. Not the annulment. Not Regina or the land. It was more important to follow his heart into this heaven she tempted him with than it was too fret over what he might be throwing away.

With one fluid motion, he swept her up in his arms and carried her to the bed. Reluctant to release her, he lowered her gently down the front of him. Bodies swayed and clothes ripped as they struggled to get closer.

Bree buried her face against the rough hairs on his broad chest. The feel of his rough skin next to hers sent a wave of desire washing over her. When his hold tightened, she pressed her body wantonly to his.

As if he sensed her need, he lifted her onto the bed, then joined her. With each kiss, his touch grew bolder, moving from the hollow of her back to the curve of her breast. Bree held her breath when he lowered his head to suckle what he had captured.

His lips teased the nipples of her breast while his free hand massaged slow sensuous circles down her back. With each stroke, passion laced her body with a warmth that threatened to burn a hole in her soul. As if he could not get enough of her, his arm circled her waist crushing her body up to his. Bree gloried in the desperation she sensed in him. Finally, someone wanted her. Just her. Her heart jumped at the thought.

With slow deliberation, Justin ran his hand down her body—touching—discovering—exploring. Her skin was warm satin; her lips, the softness of rose petals. She trembled when he parted her legs, then moaned when he traced the valley of her womanhood. She was the virgin and the vixen—a dangerous combination.

Justin lifted his head and gazed down at her. Her eyes were soft blue pieces of heaven. A heaven she was offering him. She was like a delicate flower lying waiting—trustingly in his grasp, her blue eyes glazed with the same passion that burned within him.

"Slowly," he warned. "I don't want to hurt you."

"But the need," she whispered. "The fire."

A knowing smile curved the lips he lowered to hers. She may not love him, but she wanted him. "May I fan the flames?" he asked.

Passion had given his words a huskiness that left Bree's knees trembling. "Only if you'll show me how to survive heat," she answered against his parted lips.

Justin knew he would be forever damned for what he was about to do, but he hadn't the strength to turn back now. The soft moan that escaped her lips tore the last chains from his doubts. Roughly, he gathered her in his arms. He could no longer deny his need for her. Fulfillment for both of them was but a tender plunge away, he told himself as he settled between her legs.

"Oh, Bree," he whispered, his breath a ragged rasp against her hair.

Bree dug her nails into his back when he entered her, gasping at the pleasurable pain. With care and soft-spoken words, he began to move slowly within her. The sensuous pleasure-filled rhythm warmed Bree, bringing all her fantasies to life. Lying in the pirate's arms was everything she had imagined it would be.

The strong blade of a knife, yet warm silk and honey. He was the hot desert sand tempered with cool spring rains. A wild wind-tossed sea bordered with smooth sandy beaches.

He was love . . . her love.

"If anyone touches Bree, I'll kill them," said the querulous man bundled under the blankets. "When I find her, she better still be the sweet innocent child I loved so much."

Maddie changed the wet cloth on Edward's forehead, then spooned out another dose of the laudanum. She thrust the spoon at him.

"You'll have to get a sight better before you can hope to do Quentin any harm," she said, deliberately baiting him when it looked as if he were going to refuse his medication.

PIRATES AND PROMISES 249

Dr. Jones had warned her not to coddle Lord Smythe. His hatred for Quentin appeared to be his only hold on life for weeks now and they would not take that from him.

She smiled when he swallowed the pain medication. It would put him back into the restful sleep he needed for recovery. "I think we'd best start our search with St. Clair," she said. "If Bree reached Virginia, Havenwood would be the first place she is likely to go."

They had discussed this same strategy no less than once a day since leaving England almost five weeks ago, but it never failed to calm her patient. Maddie wiped the beads of perspiration from his brow. If only the fever would go away and stay away. The unbearable heat they had had to endure for the past week seemed to drain what little energy the earl had left.

"I wish the pirate had planted that dagger in the bastard's heart when he had the chance," Lord Smythe said so low Maddie had to lean down to hear.

Maddie gave his hand a squeeze. She only wished she could put her own worries on the matter aside. As young and naïve as Bree was, she hoped she didn't fall for the romantic figure of a man the pirate had become to the ladies.

Silence hung like a heavy cloud between them as they turned their mounts toward Alexandria. Bree's head was filled with romantic notions of love and commitment. She tried not to think of the pleasurable pain she felt between her legs with each stride of her mount, but hurried to catch up with the pirate.

Justin had voiced no regrets about their marriage being annulled, but Bree had read enough books to know that what had happened between her and Justin proved that he loved her and no amount of pain was going to take the joy away from her.

Justin ventured a glance at Bree. He knew he had hurt her, but she never said a word. Afterward, she had lain in his arms sated with their lovemaking, a smile of contentment on her lips. He couldn't believe he had thrown away all his plans in a moment of passion.

And he hadn't even cleansed his soul of Bree as he had hoped. Heaven help him but he wanted her now more than ever before. It was something he had to put a stop to now.

"We cannot allow this to happen again," he said. The words sounded gruff and unfeeling, even to him. But when she turned her head toward him, there was a soft smile on her lips.

"If that is what you wish" was all she said. It was as if she knew he had lost his heart to her. How had he let himself fall under her spell like this? All this time he had thought her the innocent, but he was wrong.

Most women collected jewels and trinkets. It was clear to him now Bree collected hearts. First, the mysterious Sir Henry, then Quentin and Thurston, and now she had taken possession of his.

Justin nudged his horse ahead. He hated having to lie to Abrams about consummating the marriage, but it was imperative that Francis secure the annulment tomorrow. After what had happened between them, it was the only thing he could hope to save his sanity.

Bree followed him in silence. Justin seemed unusually quiet himself, but for what they had experienced words were not necessary, she told herself.

Of course, marriage would come in time and, unlike the last time, the pirate would want it. She smiled. It would merely take him a while to grow accustomed to the idea.

Bree hung back in the shadows. Their third night and Justin had taken her to his bed before each raid and made love to her. Tonight had been no exception, unless you counted the fact that the pirate had chosen Thurston as their victim.

It took all of Bree's control to keep from giggling at the anger she saw on Nicholas's face when Justin demanded he hand over his night's winnings. The pirate claimed Thurston was a disreputable gamester who had cheated an elderly gentleman out of his plantation, but Bree suspected his reasons for picking the gentleman for this night's raid had more to do with Justin's dislike for the man than any crime Nicholas might have committed.

"I said to hand over your winnings," the pirate repeated.

Thurston lifted his chin defiantly, but tossed his purse up to the highwayman. "So we meet again."

"Ah, but the last time I spared you."

"You could always find it in your heart to do so again."

The pirate laughed good-heartedly at the suggestion. "But now it is different, is it not?"

"What do you mean?"

"Do not play the innocent with me, my friend. We both know you have now cheated at cards enough to make it worth my while."

When Thurston didn't argue his innocence, Bree had thought that to be the end of it, but when she saw the devilish grin spread across the pirate's face, she knew he wasn't finished with Thurston yet.

"If I could, I would demand the papers on the land you took from Wilcox," she heard him say, "but for now I will settle for the purse you carry inside your shirt."

Even hidden as she was, Bree could see the flush creep up Thurston's neck, but he quickly recovered.

"In my shirt?" Nicholas mocked, holding his arms out wide. "As you can see there is no room to hide one in my shirt."

Justin shoved his pistol in Thurston's face. "You can either hand it over or I can take it off your body after I shoot you."

Bree now wished she'd never told Justin about the other leather purse Thurston carried. Her heart seemed to stop when she saw Nicholas studying the pirate. Surely he hadn't recognized Justin. He was more than likely wondering how the pirate knew of the hidden purse's existence.

As far as Bree knew, she was the only one to have discovered its hiding place and she had found it when

Thurston had forced his attentions on her. But then, she couldn't have told Justin that. He was already displeased enough with Nicholas at the time and she hadn't wanted to be the cause of a fight that would have only angered Captain Tibbs more.

Thurston slipped his hand inside his shirt to get to the pocket sewn under his arm. "I'll see you hang for this," he vowed.

"But then you would have to catch me, wouldn't you?"

Thurston dropped the purse into the pirate's hand. "I'll catch you. Have no doubt about that."

"I wouldn't be so anxious to do that if I were you." He eased the hammer back on his pistol. "The next time you cheat someone and I hear about it, I'll be coming after more than your winnings."

"Such an unpleasant man," Bree suddenly announced.

Justin turned to her. "I thought he was your comrade."

"Ah, but that was before I discovered he was a thief." She shifted in the saddle to see Justin better. "And when you confronted him, he didn't even deny it."

"He did appear to be more concerned with being caught than he was over his crimes."

"You should have shot him," Bree stated.

Justin eased his horse over next to hers. "You've become such a bloodthirsty little thing, haven't you?"

She smiled up at him. "Perhaps, but he most certainly deserved our punishment."

Her face glowed with their success and it took all Justin's willpower not to take her in his arms. Three nights together. Three nights and still his need for their lovemaking had not lessened, and Justin was beginning to believe he would never be able to quench the fires for her from his body—or his mind.

Bree didn't make it any easier. She appeared entirely too content with their new relationship, and that drove him closer to madness than had she begged for him to repeat his attentions. The rides as the highwaymen appeared to give

PIRATES AND PROMISES 253

her all the excitement she craved.

Instead of scaring Bree, each new escapade only served to excite her more. She was growing more and more bold. She'd even taken to wearing a mask, riding astride like a man and joining him in the thefts. He had to admit she had grown quite good at it and he was beginning to look forward to their little forays, but he had to think of Bree's safety.

The pirate's legend was already growing and it wouldn't be long before the militia were brought in. If they continued with the robberies, he had no doubt they would be caught. What Bree needed was a good scare and he knew how to give it to her. With a little bit of help from Higgins, the next place the pirate and his lady would strike would be Havenwood.

CHAPTER 18

"HAVENWOOD!" Bree gasped. "Have you taken leave of your senses?"

Justin continued to clean his pistol. "Do you think the noble St. Clair above reproach?"

Bree was happy to see his attention claimed elsewhere, for she knew her flushed face would give her away. "If he is anywhere near as unscrupulous as Quentin, I imagine he would deserve our justice," she said innocently as she sipped at her tea.

Justin watched her out of the corner of his eye. "I hear he came here ten years ago," he said. "Now he devotes all his time to building his grandfather's estate."

Bree's heart sank to her toes. How was she to explain that it had been St. Clair's dream when she couldn't even explain why she still cared. She had accepted weeks ago that her foolish dreams for St. Clair were only that—a child's fantasy.

It was the pirate she loved. But it still hurt to discover that St. Clair had fulfilled his promise to himself, but not to her. Or had he? Was that the reason behind his recent trip to England? But then, she couldn't let herself dwell on that.

"I would hardly consider helping his grandfather a crime," she said with a steadiness that belied the turbulence that battered at her heart. "Besides, I was told St. Clair was in England."

"He's returned," Justin stated as he rose from the table and walked to the door.

"He's . . ." Bree left the question unasked. If St. Clair had gone to England only to find her gone, how would she ever forgive herself? She was not worthy of anyone's love.

"He's no better than his brother," Justin said, hating himself for the bargain he was about to strike with Mr. Wingham. But did he really have a choice? He had tried shutting Bree out of his mind, but one touch from her and he fell into her bed again. Bree was in love with Quentin, he told himself for the hundredth time, and the only way to get her out of his heart was to finally close the door on any hope of her returning his love.

Justin paused, then turned back to her. Glimpsing Bree's pain, he wished he'd kept walking. The sadness in her face was like a giant hand closing around his heart. It was clear she regretted what had happened between them and there was nothing he could do to take it back. He was more certain than ever she'd never get over her feelings for Quentin. Justin felt as if he were a hundred years old.

"I leave at midnight tomorrow," he said brusquely. "If you wish to accompany me, be ready."

Bree wanted to go after him and make him say he was wrong about St. Clair, but she couldn't move. Her heart was too heavy to carry.

"Well, well," Quentin said as he turned slowly, taking in the rich furnishings of Havenwood. "So all this belongs to my dear little brother, does it?"

Adrian stiffened. "It will one day," he corrected his rude guest. "When I'm dead."

"Charming. Of course, it's not quite up to the standards of Foxworth. But charming."

Adrian found himself disliking the arrogant lord every bit as much as his grandson did. It was no wonder his daughter had returned to Virginia with Justin rather than suffer the *generosity* of this popinjay.

"I'm pleased it meets with your approval. Now what may I do for you, Lord Foxworth?"

"You may offer me a drink, then tell me where I might find Justin."

If not for satisfying his curiosity as to why Lord Foxworth would visit after all these years, Adrian would have been tempted to toss the gentleman out on his ear. Instead, he rang for the butler.

"Justin will be away for a few days," he said.

Quentin frowned. "I had hoped to enlist his help, but if he is unavailable, then I must insist on speaking with your constable."

"He's a very busy man."

"He will speak with me. I have information about this highwayman they call the pirate. You see, the man was in England before he found his way here."

"You know who it is?" Adrian asked. He had his own idea as to who the pirate might be and he'd not be sharing it with this man.

"I hear he has been making a pest of himself here in Virginia. Pillaging . . . looting . . ."

Quentin paused when Washington entered. "We'll have a brandy," he told the tall black man. "Then you may leave."

Adrian would have called him on his bad manners, but he knew it would be wiser to hear what Lord Foxworth had to say. He waited until his guest received his drink. He then leaned back in his chair, a smile on his lips.

"I was under the impression this pirate only bothered those in need of his special retribution," Adrian said, hoping to annoy Foxworth with his opinion.

"The man is a thief!" Quentin stormed, almost spilling his drink in his anger. "He not only stole the jewels that had been in my family for generations, but he forced my fiancée to accompany him when he left England."

PIRATES AND PROMISES 257

Ah, so his suspicions were not so farfetched as he imagined. Justin was the pirate. And his bride? She had to be the woman Quentin sought.

"I am sorry for your loss," Adrian said. "And you are correct. I think a matter this delicate would be best handled quietly among family. If you will but leave directions with my butler, I will see that Justin is informed that you are in need of his help."

"You don't understand, old man. I will be staying here until I return to England with my fiancée."

Ira Wingham hurried into the study. "Good afternoon, Justin," he said.

"I'm sorry if I've come at a bad time."

"Nonsense," he said, taking a seat opposite Justin. It was about time Justin came calling about Regina's hand. Everyone knew the young man had been back for weeks. With the likelihood of Atwater making an offer of marriage, Ira had expected to hear from Tyler sooner. "We heard you were back."

Justin didn't miss the unasked question in the big man's voice. Mr. Wingham was one who was used to having his way in most matters and it didn't sit easy with Justin to feel the need to explain his reasons for not paying a visit before now. It would do Wingham good to wonder.

"The trip proved to be most successful, Mr. Wingham. Lord Montgomery was willing to part with more of his mares than I had hoped."

Ira offered Justin a cigar. "You'll be needing land more than ever now, won't you, lad?" he said.

The smug grin on Wingham's face irritated Justin. He knew what was expected, but something inside him refused to give in to the bribe. "Thought I might see what your price was for that piece that borders Havenwood."

Wingham frowned. Normally, the courting ritual young men put themselves through lent a side to it that he found amusing, but Tyler's manner of approach bordered on insolence. Perhaps he was shy after all. Not wanting to jump to the wrong conclusion and lose the opportunity of securing the young man for his daughter, he pasted a pleasant smile on his face.

"Now you haven't been gone that long, Justin," he said with a hint of a laugh. "That land is just like the hand of my daughter. I could never put a price on it."

But you just did, Justin wanted to point out. "Regina is a beautiful young woman," he said instead. "I can certainly see how you would consider her priceless."

Justin had come to settle the bargain for Regina's hand, but suddenly he couldn't get past the fact that he would be marrying her for the land and not for love. And then there was Bree.

"The land . . ." Justin paused, then plunged forward. "Sir, the land should be different. I don't imagine Regina approves of someone marrying her for a piece of land."

Wingham suddenly smiled. So that was it. Tyler was concerned with Regina's feelings. Hell, Regina didn't care what it took to get the elusive Mr. Tyler to the altar, but if that was the way Justin wanted to do it, he wasn't averse to having the young man pay for the land.

"These things are done every day but I can see where you might think it would cause undue embarrassment for someone as delicate as my Regina. There will be some details to work out so let me have a few days to think on it."

Justin stood. "I was hoping you would see my way of it. Give my regards to Miss Regina and I'll be waiting to hear from you."

The man walked with Justin to the door. Normally he would have asked Tyler to lunch but he knew Regina and her mother would be waiting upstairs to hear all the details of Justin's visit. It had been a strange conversation to be sure, but what did it matter? Justin Tyler would be marrying his daughter.

Once at the door, Ira shook Justin's hand. "I'll try not to keep you waiting long. I know you'll be wanting to move those mares onto the meadow as quickly as possible."

Justin felt much better when he left. Wingham would now sell him the land, and if he was to offer for Regina's hand now, he could tell himself it wasn't for her dowry.

Dressed as a young man, Bree sat in the dark cabin and waited for Justin to arrive. In her hand, she held the locket. It felt good to hold it after hiding it away. She had spent the entire day wondering what awful crimes St. Clair had committed to have the pirate select him as one of their victims. But she could think of nothing the young boy she had carried in her heart for so long could have done.

The years of holding to a promise left her with no choice. She had to accompany Justin on his visit to Havenwood. She had to see St. Clair even if it was only to say she was sorry for not waiting. She knew it was the only hope she had of banishing him from her thoughts forever.

It would be for the best, she told herself. Then the knock on the door set her heart to racing once more. It was time.

"Bree?" Justin called as he opened the door. "Are you ready?"

Bree slipped the locket back over her head, then picked up her mask. All her years of waiting would finally be over. In a little while, she would come face-to-face with her promise—and her failure to abide by it.

"I'm ready."

Bree felt as if she were on her way to her hanging. What was taking so long? Would they never reach Havenwood? If she didn't know better, she could swear they had been traveling in circles for the last hour.

"What crimes has St. Clair committed?" she finally asked.

Justin found himself studying her for a moment. "If you must know, St. Clair's crimes are probably the most shocking of all. Don't ask me to soil your ears with the details."

A part of her wanted to scream it was all lies. St. Clair could never do anything dishonorable. Another part of her wanted it to be true so she could put the past behind her and build on a future with Justin. Either way, she had to hear.

Taking a deep breath, Bree summoned up her courage. "I need to know," she stated firmly.

Justin merely stared at her. As far as he knew, Bree knew nothing of him as St. Clair. So other than being Quentin's half brother, why was she so concerned? Did she think the crimes he was guilty of would somehow taint Quentin? He couldn't hold back the old bitterness that rose like sour bile in his throat. Little did she know she was encouraging St. Clair's greatest crime—that of being the pirate.

"You need not worry that Quentin will learn of this," Justin said, his hate for his half brother almost choking him.

All of a sudden he wished he had never thought of this farce. He could just as easily have insisted their days as highwaymen were over. But it was too late now. He could already see Havenwood through the trees.

Justin stopped his mare beside the road. "We'll leave the horses here," he said. "I don't want them giving us away."

Bree's hands were like blocks of ice when she tried to tie her mount to the tree. It seemed to take a lifetime to secure the knot—almost as long as she had waited for St. Clair to return to her.

Justin took her by the arm and she didn't object when he led her to the back of the house. If St. Clair had grown as evil as the others they had robbed, then he wasn't deserving of her concern or her promise.

"I'm told St. Clair will be out for the evening," the pirate told her. "That should give us plenty of time to search the house."

Somewhere in her mind she heard his words, but it was as if he were shouting them to her from the bottom of a well. Instead she spent all her efforts concentrating on putting one foot in front of the other. When they finally reached the study door, the pirate eased it open and they slipped through. With measured steps, he led her across the room to a hidden cubicle tucked behind one of the many paintings hanging on the wall.

"How did you know about this?" Bree whispered.

A man rose from the shadows behind the desk. "I'd like to know the answer to that myself," he demanded. "What are you doing in my house?"

"St. Clair!" she breathed in shock, then everything went black.

Justin caught her before she hit the floor. Justin may have wanted Bree to have a scare, but having her come face-to-face with his grandfather was certainly not what he had planned. And why was his grandfather here instead of the man Higgins had set up to catch them?

Justin pulled the mask from his face. "What are you doing here, Grandfather?" he asked as he lifted Bree into his arms.

The old man folded his arms across his chest. "I could ask that of you also."

"Let me dispose of . . . my companion and I'll be back to explain."

Adrian hurriedly crossed the room to the window and blocked Justin's escape. He had his own suspicions as to who the companion might be. After unsuccessfully trying to meet with her for weeks now, he wasn't about to let his grandson whisk her out of sight before he could form his own opinion as to the young lady's worth.

"I want an explanation for your being here dressed like this," the old man said, "and now is as good a time as any."

Bree's inert form was growing heavy and Justin was forced to shift her in his arms. When he did, the mask on her face slipped.

"Ah!" Adrian said as he pulled the mask the rest of the way off. "What have we here? A woman, Justin?"

There was no hiding the innocence of youth on the woman's face. She lacked the polished, hard, cold look of Regina and that was sufficient for Adrian's approval.

"She's beautiful, son. Dare I hope she belongs to you?"

Justin cursed under his breath. If the old man was to find out about the wedding, he would tell all of Williamsburg to ensure it stood. Justin had to get Bree away before the old man had a chance to question her or all his plans would be for naught—the annulment and the salvaging of his heart.

"As you can see, she's in no condition to make your acquaintance at the moment, Grandfather." He had no intention of waiting for the objections he knew were on the tip of his grandfather's tongue.

"She's in no condition to renew hers with Lord Foxworth either," Adrian said.

Justin stepped back. "Quentin's in Virginia?"

"Quentin's not only in Virginia, he's upstairs sleeping off an overindulgence of your best liquor."

"Then I hope you understand when I say I'm unable to wait around until either Bree or Quentin recovers."

Justin pushed past Adrian and was out the window before the old man could stop him.

"I still want an explanation, son, and I want it before morning," Adrian shouted after him.

If I can think of one we can both live with, Justin thought to himself. By the time Justin reached the horses, Bree was coming to.

"Can you ride?" he asked.

Bree wiped her hand across her face. What was he talking about? Of course she could ride. Then like a bolt of lightning, the memory hit her. They had been caught. She struggled to get out of his arms.

"St. Clair? What did you do to St. Clair?"

Justin was taken aback for a moment. How did she know about Quentin? Then he recalled the darkness of the study. Was it possible she had mistaken Adrian for the man she sought?

"I did nothing to him. Now quit squirming before I drop you." Justin set her on her mare, then mounted his own. "You'd do better to wonder if St. Clair thinks it necessary to send someone after us."

Bree turned to look over her shoulder. The night was too dark to see much, but that shouldn't deter anyone from following them. Her heart alone was beating loud enough to alert the entire countryside as to their whereabouts.

"Do you think he will find us?" She couldn't face St. Clair now. She just couldn't.

He didn't need to see her face, he could hear the fear in her voice. "If we don't hurry, he very likely will," Justin lied.

They rode on in silence, Justin leading the way down the dark paths. If he had thought to scare Bree, it would appear he was successful. He hoped the lesson stayed with her.

After a sufficient roundabout way, they arrived at the cabin on the edge of Havenwood. Bree was still trembling when he helped her down from her mount. Justin felt like the worst of villains, but he kept telling himself he had done it for her own good.

"Wipe the horses down, Higgins, then go on home to bed," he said, his green eyes narrowing.

It was almost as if Adrian had been expecting them tonight. The fact that his manservant carefully looked in every direction but his, told Justin Higgins was the informant. It wouldn't be the first time his manservant had given in to the old man.

"Be back by morning," he added in a harsh whisper. "We'll need to talk."

He took Bree's arm and helped her to the cabin door. He was worried. She hadn't said anything the entire trip home. It was almost as if she were walking in a fog and couldn't find her way out.

"We'd best not press our luck again for a while," he said as he followed her in.

Bree suddenly turned and threw herself into his arms. "I never want to do something like that ever again. God is the one to mete out justice. We shouldn't take it upon ourselves to do his work for him."

Justin rested his chin on the top of her head. He couldn't contain the smile that nudged at the corners of his lips. "I think that's wise," he said solemnly. "Who knows? The next time we might not be so lucky."

Lucky! What was he thinking? His grandfather waiting there instead of one of the servants was enough to have *him* rethinking his role as the pirate.

"Justin?"

It was almost a whisper. Like the soft rustle of a summer breeze. Justin could feel his body's immediate response.

"Hold me," she said. "Love the fear away."

It was the first time she had asked him to make love to her. He didn't want her if it was Quentin who was on her mind, but the feel of her body pressed against his was enough to have a priest questioning his vows, let alone a man who could easily lay claim to what he held. Justin held his breath as desire climbed him like honeysuckle, twining its vines in and out of his heart.

But you're stronger than most men, he told himself. A man would have to be a fool to torture himself for a night with someone whose heart was given to another. She didn't love him and she didn't want him. He was merely a substitute for the one she truly loved—Quentin.

But when Bree shifted in his arms and started unbuttoning his shirt, Justin stopped fighting the attraction. Let her fall into her own trap trying to change his mind. He could handle whatever she was willing to give.

Once she had the buttons undone, she moved the edges of his shirt aside. When her tongue circled his taut nipple, there was no holding back the gasp her action tore from his throat. Damn! The honeysuckle that had trapped him was now starting to bloom.

Heat soared through his loins and his heart felt like a stone lodged in his throat. There was only one cure for what ailed him. Bree.

Without another thought to the pain it would cost him, Justin kicked the door shut behind him, then scooped Bree up in his arms. To hell with everyone. To hell with fighting what God had meant to be. A man needed a woman and he meant to have his.

"Look for me among the fools," he said to himself as he carried her to the bed. With care, he stood her in front of him. The light from the fire on the hearth told him all he needed to know. She wanted him.

Each kiss, each touch fed the flame growing between them. They slowly began to undress each other. Once finished, Justin stepped back.

A sensual pattern of firelight and shadow flickered across the generous curves of her body, releasing any doubts he might have had about what he was doing. The warmth of the room was nothing compared to the heat that raged within him. He was burning up and he knew of only one way to put out the flames that licked at the door to his soul. He held out his arms and Bree stepped into them.

Without a moment's hesitation, he swept her off her feet and placed her on the straw mattress. She looked up at him when he joined her, her eyes heavy with a passion that matched his own need. She trustingly laid her head on his chest.

Justin lifted himself up on his elbow and leaned over her. Once placing his hand on the far side of her, he did not hesitate. Years of experience had taught him the ritual of lovemaking and he knew it well. He started at her lips and kissed his way down her slim neck. Her breath was ragged and she arched in need.

"Yes," he murmured against the base of her throat. "You remember the way of it."

Bree gasped as he caught her nipple between his teeth. The sharp little pains were nothing compared to the effect his hands were having on her as they glided down her ribs, past her waist, then to her hips. He was like a blind man and she, his path home. With slow deliberate care, he searched all the ways he might travel. By the time he raised his hands back to her breasts, she knew the map would be etched into her flesh for all time. She would treasure it forever.

When he suddenly released her breast, an ache filled Bree and she cried out with the cold emptiness.

"I'm here, Bree," he whispered. "I won't leave you now."

Justin kissed her again as he settled between her legs.

She didn't protest, but instead rose to meet him. He knew then he was no longer the casual lover intent on giving satisfaction as well as receiving it. All the chains he placed on his control had broken. The tide was coming in and his shorings were beginning to slip in the sand. He was going to drown and he had no intention of signaling a distress call. When a man was meant to die, he did, and Justin was more than prepared to enjoy his death.

He took her then. She cried out, but neither of them pulled away. Without hesitation, she rose to meet the thrust after thrust of their relentless passion. Nothing mattered but their need for each other. Release came with an explosion of both their hearts and their souls.

Afterward, they lay in each others' arms, each wrapped up in their own thoughts. The pirate lifted the locket lying between her breasts and studied it.

At the frown on his face, Bree took a deep breath. The time had come to tell him everything. "Justin?"

His name on her lips had an uncanny effect on Justin's heart. He kissed the top of her head. "What is it?"

"When I went to Havenwood . . . the first time . . ."

Justin stiffened. Quentin! He could feel the jealousy returning, creeping up to suffocate him. "I'd rather not discuss him now."

Bree raised up so she could see him. "It was not Quentin I sought, but his brother."

Justin was strangely silent, but she knew she had to explain. She had betrayed St. Clair. She couldn't betray Justin as well.

"Quentin's brother was the one I was betrothed to."

Justin raised up on one arm and looked down at her. "What are you saying?"

At the coldness in his voice, Bree almost changed her mind, but she knew there could be no more secrets between them. "When I was young, I met St. Clair in England. I was a child and like a child who has found her hero, I fell in love with him."

Justin listened with a growing dread as she explained

about the secret place, the proposal, and the promise. Then she told him about losing her father's love and how St. Clair was the only one she had left, but Justin didn't want to hear that. It only made it all the more difficult that he would prove to be her biggest disappointment.

He remembered the little girl on the rock. He also remembered the locket Bree treasured so much. It was the one he had intended for Henrietta Parker. But he remembered no promise except the one he'd made to himself—a promise he had spent the last ten years achieving.

"What of Sir Henry?" he asked her. What of Quentin? he asked himself. His half brother was here to take Bree back.

"When you insisted on knowing my fiancé's name I borrowed him from a book I had once read. It was St. Clair from the very beginning. He was to come back to England to get me. Do you see now why I had to beg Quentin to call off the engagement? St. Clair had told me how cruel his brother could be. I couldn't have St. Clair arrive only to find me married to the man he hated most."

"If St. Clair loved you, why didn't he return for you before now?" he asked in hopes of her seeing the folly of her argument. How could he tell her he remembered no promise—that she would have waited forever and he would never have returned?

"St. Clair came to Virginia to make his fortune so we could be together."

Ah, so that was why you waited so patiently, he told himself. She was just like Henrietta.

"You hoped to share in his wealth?" he asked bitterly.

The contempt on the pirate's face frightened her. "You make it sound so ugly," Bree whispered, fighting back the tears that threatened. "It wasn't like that at all. St. Clair loved me. He gave me this locket."

Justin pulled the locket from her throat and tossed it across the room. He had never promised her anything. This love she professed to have wasn't for St. Clair. It was for the wealth she hoped he had accumulated. She didn't even love the pirate. She loved this fantasy—this dream. Well, he had his dreams too and she wasn't going to take them away from him with this silly little lie of hers. He wouldn't let her.

"If my solicitor questions you about our marriage, you mustn't mention what happened between us tonight," he stated firmly. "Nor the other times."

Bree met his gaze. What was he saying to her? "I thought it all settled," she managed to get out despite the lump in her throat. She didn't understand. "Didn't you get the annulment?"

"I did," he said without a thought to the lie he was telling. He reached for his breeches. "It's merely a matter of the papers being signed."

Bree waited until he was dressed and gone, then crawled out of bed and retrieved the locket from the floor. Desperately, she clutched it to her. After all that had happened, it was all she had left and even that was a lie.

She might as well admit it. St. Clair had forgotten about her and the promise. He had never loved her and had no intention of ever returning for her. She had been lying to herself all along, hoping if she stood by the fantasy somehow it would come true.

But now she loved Justin and, like St. Clair, he didn't love her. She didn't know why she had ever hoped for anything different. If her own father could not find it in his heart to love her, how could she expect anyone else to?

"You needn't worry," she said to the closed door. "I'll sign the papers."

Justin kept his horse to a walk as he headed down the dark, lonely road. Francis would have the annulment papers by the end of the week. It was for the best, he told himself. Loving Bree the way he did would only cause him more hurt. Besides, when did love ever help anyone? Perhaps he could take her to his aunt in Richmond. She could help Bree find a husband. One that would provide her with the wealth she wanted.

Come morning, he would tell her the partnership was off. He was even prepared to relinquish her indenture papers. Once free of him, she could do what all young girls did—find a husband.

He didn't know why the decision left a bitter taste in his mouth, but it did. A bitter taste in his mouth and an ache in his heart. Hearing about her uncaring father, he could well understand why Bree had clung to her dream of marrying St. Clair. It was all she had thought she had for all those years.

Suddenly, the realization that Bree loved *him* and not his wealth crashed in on him and his heart felt lighter than it had in months.

Bree would not be going to Richmond to seek a husband. She had one right here. Him! As far as he was concerned, the annulment was off. He turned his horse and headed back to the cabin.

Justin smiled to himself. The old man might be pleased with his decision, but Bree would probably break his nose. Right after she kissed him. One thing was certain, she was going to be surprised to find she was not only still married to the pirate, but to St. Clair as well.

The morning sun filled the small cabin, waking Justin from his sleep. He stretched lazily and reached for Bree, but found only an empty pillow. He had returned hoping they could continue where they had left off before Bree's confession, but she had been sound asleep when he had returned and he didn't have the heart to wake her.

Justin yawned. He might as well get up. It didn't look as if she were going to join him. She was more than likely pouting somewhere, planning some diabolical domestic duty as his punishment. With an indignant groan, he sat up on the edge of the bed. If she had broken her promise and was cooking breakfast . . .

Justin looked around the cabin. Odd that he had slept so soundly he had not noticed her leaving. His gaze went to the wall beside the bed. The empty pegs seemed to jump out at him. Where were her clothes? The new comb and hand mirror were missing also. Fear closed like a vise around his chest.

A few strides and he was across the room. Unconcerned with the fact that he was naked, Justin threw open the front door and raced to the road.

"Bree!" he shouted. "Bree!"

"Is that how you planned to greet her?" a voice from behind him asked.

Justin spun around. His grandfather was sitting on a long wooden bench under one of the tall oaks beside the cabin.

"What are you doing here?"

Adrian got to his feet. "I was waiting until someone woke up," he said, then took a watch out of his vest pocket and flipped open the gold cover. "Slept rather late, didn't you, son?"

"I was up late," he growled. "How did you find me?"

"I'd like to say it was because Higgins was in need of a good meal and I bribed him with Cook's biscuits and gravy, but . . ."

Adrian paused and stared at Justin. "For a skinny little man, your manservant can sure put the victuals away. You'd have thought he was starving to death."

Bree's cooking had that effect on both of them for a while, but Justin didn't feel it was the time to bring that up. "That doesn't answer my question, Grandfather."

"Oh, yes, you wanted to know how I knew you were here." Adrian frowned. "Do you think you could manage to at least make yourself decent first?"

Justin strode back to the cabin and grabbed up his clothes from off the floor. "I'm putting my clothes on," he shouted over his shoulder only to find his grandfather standing in the doorway.

"Out with it, Grandfather! I don't have time to play these games, I have to find Bree before she lands herself into something too large for even me to handle."

Adrian didn't want to play games either, but he also didn't want to admit that he had had one of the servants follow Justin when he had left Francis's office. It wasn't until later that Higgins finally agreed to help him.

There was only one way to get out of this mess. "If you had taken me into your confidence from the beginning, you would have known your half brother arrived before you almost walked in on him," he said with a feigned casualness.

Justin's gut twisted in a knot. "Did he tell you why he was here?" he asked. "What does he want from me?"

"Doesn't appear he wants anything with you, son. His bone of contention seems to be with this pirate. You know, the one who has been robbing the good citizens of Virginia. Well, if truth be told, his interest is in the highwayman and his companion, Miss Smythe."

Justin finished buttoning up his shirt. "You didn't tell him she was with me, did you?"

"Now why would I be telling that pompous ass anything? It's bad enough manners dictate that I open my home to him, I'll not be assisting him in finding your wife too."

Heat crept up Justin's throat. "My wife? Then you know."

"For some time now," the old man answered as he pulled out one of the chairs and sat down. "But more importantly, why the highwayman?"

A smile tipped the corner of Justin's lip. "I thought a few Englishmen needed a lesson in justice. Even so, a lifted purse here and there dropped into the hands of an ill-treated servant was little compensation for the crimes."

"And Bree?"

"Quentin had taken it in his head to marry the girl. Unfortunately her father was not opposed to the arrangement. I merely took it upon myself to cancel the wedding plans."

"So you married her?"

"No, that came later when Captain Tibbs decided greed was a sin and providing the young lady with a husband would save his depraved soul."

Adrian set his cane on the table. "And do you love her, son?"

Justin ran his fingers through his hair. "Bree is the most demanding, frustrating . . ." He paused. "Yes, I imagine I do love her."

"Quentin knows she's with the pirate and he says he means to have her back." Adrian waited for Justin's reaction to the announcement. With all the complications Quentin's arrival carried with it, he had to be certain the boy loved Bree enough to fight for her.

One look at the hate in Justin's green eyes was all he needed. "Quentin's determined to take her back to England," Adrian added. "He says he loves her and still wants her for his wife."

"Quentin loves no one but himself. If he means to take her back to England, it would be for one reason and one reason only. He plans to punish her for escaping him." Justin strode to the door. Once there he paused and turned back to his grandfather.

"Have Higgins keep an eye out for Bree. She's not here and I don't know where she might have gone."

Adrian arched a gray brow. "Missing?"

"We had a small disagreement last evening," he admitted. "I'm afraid I said some things I shouldn't have."

"Your fool pride again?"

"The reasons don't matter. If she has left me, she may decide to visit Havenwood. Before she does, you'd best be sending Quentin on his way, because I'll cut his heart out before I'll let him take Bree from me."

Adrian had no doubts that he would, but the boy wasn't thinking properly. If Bree was truly missing, the best place to have a pesky polecat was under your nose.

CHAPTER 19

THE servant showed Bree into the back parlor, then left. Clutching her new gloves tightly, she glanced around. It was apparent by the quality of the room's furnishings, Maddie's cousin was employed by a very wealthy family. The room, though large, was filled with an overwhelming amount of chairs, sofas, and tables. Although the arrangement was pleasing, Bree much preferred to have a clear path to pace while she waited for Miss Vye.

Pamela Vye. The name seemed a bit frivolous for someone who spent their days as a prim and proper governess. Bree hoped Pamela could help her find employment. Since she had walked out of her partnership with Justin, acquiring a position was the only hope she had to earning enough to purchase her own papers.

"Miss Smythe?"

Bree spun around. A short woman with a head of bright red curls and a face covered with freckles stood just inside the door. She looked much too young to be a governess, let alone be of any assistance in helping Bree find employment. "Miss Vye?"

"Yes," the young woman answered shyly. "I do apologize. I did not mean to put a scare in you."

Bree liked the governess immediately. "It's not any fault of yours. I guess I'm a bit preoccupied."

Pamela waved Bree to one of the chairs, then sat opposite her. "I was told you wished to talk with me."

"I've come to ask for your help." At the affirmative nod that sent the girl's curls to bobbing, Bree continued. "Your cousin Maddie wrote to you of my coming."

"Oh, yes, you're the one who asked about St. Clair. Well, I must tell you I had a devil of a time locating him until I got the last letter from Maddie. You see, it seems the man no longer calls himself St. Clair. It wasn't until she mentioned Havenwood in the correspondence I received a few days ago that I realized who it was that she was inquiring about."

Pamela reached out and touched Bree's arm. "You realize she was terribly upset that you had disappeared and might be on your way here. I'm afraid my answer to your inquiry would have been too late to reach you in time to save you the journey here."

"Save me the trip?"

"Yes, you see, St. Clair was here this afternoon past to speak with Mr. Wingham about asking for Miss Regina's hand in marriage. Miss Regina and her mother are nigh walking on a cloud, they're so pleased." Pamela leaned forward, a knowing smile pursing her lips. "Of course, Miss Regina has been after him to marry her for the past two years. More's the pity too for he wouldn't have given in had Mr. Wingham not dangled that piece of land under his nose as if he were some rabbit after the garden greens."

St. Clair engaged? She didn't know whether to be relieved or upset. The arrival of a tea tray called a halt to the conversation, but not her thoughts. Somehow Bree managed to accept the cup poured for her and a small biscuit while she waited for the servant to leave. It seemed forever before he closed the door. Although she would have sworn to have lost her appetite, Bree discovered she had eaten all of her biscuit and drank half her tea.

"Havenwood looked to be most prosperous," she said. "Why would St. Clair need to marry to acquire more land?"

"It's said he and his man returned from England with a shipment of prize mares. The land was to be—"

"Prize mares?" Bree interrupted. A shiver of apprehension slid up her spine. Could there have been two such shipments over the last few weeks?

"St. Clair has the finest racehorses in all of Virginia," Pamela said after taking another sip of her tea. "There isn't a plantation to compete with his horses. With the new mares he's brought over from England, Havenwood will soon draw buyers from all the states."

Was it possible that the pirate had lied to her about buying the mares? Could they have, in fact, been purchased for Havenwood? It would certainly explain where the money had come from. And even Higgins claimed Justin had no intention of keeping the mares. The original plan was for them to be sold down in New Orleans.

Had Justin acted as St. Clair's agent to purchase the mares in hopes of stealing them once they arrived in Virginia? If so, he had more than likely lied to her about his reasons for robbing St. Clair. The pirate was no more than a common thief—a thief she had believed in. The pain was so intense, she could almost hear her heart rip.

There was only one way to find out for sure. She had to ask St. Clair.

"Good morning, Quentin," Justin said as he took a chair across from his brother. He was not in the best of moods and all he wanted to do was rid himself of his brother so he could search for Bree. "I trust that the servants have taken care of your needs."

"Adequate," was all he would say as he looked around the great room. "You've done quite well for yourself, brother. Heir to all this. I rather think I might have been tempted to cater to the old man's wishes myself if this were to be the reward for my efforts."

"Why are you here, Quentin?"

Pretending an interest in one of the figurines on the table beside him, Quentin picked the shepherdess up. Turning it to catch the light, he made a great show of studying the porcelain piece. "My fiancée took a fancy to seeing Virginia and I've come to fetch her home," he finally said. "Her father, God rest his soul, had passed on and we must go back and settle the estate."

We? So that was it. Bree was an heiress. Justin gave in to a smile. He'd give a hundred pounds to know if it was her inheritance or revenge that had played the greater part in prompting his half brother to travel all this way to retrieve his runaway bride.

"A shame to have lost your little Miss Southampton and her inheritance, isn't it?"

"It's merely a temporary setback, I assure you," Quentin said politely despite his displeasure at Justin's accurate assessment of the situation. "She'll be returning to England with me soon enough."

"Then you know where she is."

"No, not exactly. But I do know who she's with. Once I find them, he'll be dead and she . . ." Quentin replaced the figurine. "Well, let me just say, she will have the rest of her life to redeem herself."

"She left you for another?" Justin asked calmly despite the urge to reach out and throttle his half brother.

"She did not leave willingly," Quentin quickly pointed out. "This highwayman abducted her."

"The pirate took your bride. How devastating for you. And the wedding . . . I would imagine you have called it off."

Quentin lowered his gaze from Justin's. "One in my position would not ordinarily marry such a woman, but certain things make it worth a man's efforts."

"The inheritance? Of considerable consequences, no doubt."

The question brought Quentin's head up. His thin lips spread in a grin. "Quite considerable. Lady Smythe is the Earl of Roxbury's daughter."

"*Lady* Smythe?" Justin managed to ask past his astonishment. Bree had failed to mention that little detail. Yet, was that so surprising when she only knew him as the pirate? "This is why you want her for your wife?"

Quentin nodded. "Being the *late* earl's daughter is more than enough to convince me to put her past indiscretions aside and take her as my bride instead of merely my mistress. Lady Smythe may be soiled, but no man would be fool enough to turn his back on such a fortune. I can say with all confidence, I am truly looking forward to the marriage . . . and breaking her to my pleasures."

Justin wanted to cut his heart out and stuff it down his arrogant throat. "And this highwayman who has taken her, won't he have anything to say in the matter?" he asked instead.

"Once he is caught and hanged, Sabrina will be without a protector. She'll come back to me soon enough then."

"Isn't it likely she will be hanged as well?" Justin asked the question that had been haunting him for the past few weeks.

Quentin smiled indulgently. "I carry papers from her father stating how the pirate abducted her, forcing her to do his will. By the time I finish explaining everything to the constable, she will be mine."

"I thought you said her father was dead."

"All the easier to have someone forge the documents."

Justin did not challenge the statement. Quentin might be cruel, but he was not a fool. His half brother had decided on a plan of action and there was no deterring him from it. No one was more aware of that than Justin. A few clever questions to the right people and his half brother would discover that Bree had arrived on the same ship as Justin. It wasn't a giant leap of thought after that to conclude that Justin was the pirate.

"It would appear you'll have to find this highwayman first," Justin said, attempting to keep the skepticism out of his voice. "I wish you better luck at it than the others who seek to collect the price on his head."

"Ah, but then they don't know how to flush out his little cohort and I do."

"And that would be?" Justin gently prodded.

"All in good time, dear brother. All in good time." He bent to pick up his hat. "Now if you'll excuse me, there are things that must be taken care of in town if I'm going to catch this villain."

Justin stood and watched Quentin leave. He may not know what plan that arrogant bastard was stirring up in that evil mind of his, but he couldn't take the risk that the plan would be successful. He had to find Bree and fast.

It had taken some persuading but Pamela had finally promised to ask the Winghams if there was a position open for a maid. The thought of working from morning until night did not appeal to Bree. But it was best not to dwell on that now. She was too tired, too hot, and too hungry. Besides which, she needed a place to live.

The afternoon sun overhead beat down mercilessly on the tobacco fields as Bree sat on the rock beside the road and rubbed her sore feet. The new shoes Justin had purchased for her lay on the ground, beside her bonnet.

She had been walking for hours and still no sight of Havenwood. She looked down the long road. Surely she hadn't come the wrong way. The sight of a carriage in the distance had her wondering if she should stop it and ask for directions, but the loneliness of the countryside left her apprehensive about being so bold.

Picking up her shoes and hat, she crawled back into the bushes that bordered the road. Sitting amidst the branches and leaves, Bree swatted at a cloud of mosquitoes. She would have ventured a deep breath had she not suspected the effort would do no more than net her a mouthful of the pesky insects. The air was stifling, but she remained hidden until the carriage passed.

Justin would be proud to learn that his constant nagging for her to be more cautious was finally proving to be effective. But she mustn't think about him, she told herself. That part of her life was over. The mere thought of lying in his arms brought a bittersweet ache to her heart. Until he had walked out on her last night, Justin had been her love—the mares their future. She had to know if the horses rightfully belonged to St. Clair.

When she could no longer see the coach, Bree returned to the road and continued on her way. Clouds were gathering overhead, giving short moments of respite from the sun. She fanned herself with her bonnet. If she didn't reach Havenwood soon, when the coach returned, they would find her melted into a little puddle along the roadside.

So intent was Bree on watching the road lest she step into a hole and twist her ankle that she almost missed the drive leading up to Havenwood. Taking a deep breath, Bree strode up to the front door and lifted the brass knocker.

The butler who had treated her so rudely on her last trip opened the door. "Yes?" he asked arrogantly. "May I help you?"

Bree squared her shoulders and glared back at him. "I wish to see Mr. St. Clair."

"Is he expecting you?"

"Yes," she lied, pushing past him. "And I will await him in the parlor if it's all the same to you."

"You can't go in there," he called after her.

Bree opened the first door to the left and walked in. Her unexpected entrance brought the heads of the two men around.

Bree gasped at Justin in casual conversation with an old man. St. Clair's grandfather? How could this be? What was Justin doing here?

Everything was suddenly clear. The partnership with the pirate was all a sham. The mares never belonged to the pirate. They were St. Clair's. It was the only rational explanation for the pirate's presence.

"I'm sorry, Mr. Tyler," the butler said behind her. "I tried to stop her."

Justin rushed across the room to Bree. "Where have you been? I've been worried sick."

Ignoring him, Bree turned back to the butler. "I need to speak with St. Clair," she said.

Justin knew the time had come to explain a few things of his own. "That's quite all right, Washington. I will take care of the young lady myself." Justin took her hand and walked her across the room. "Bree, please have a seat. There's someone here I want you to meet."

Bree ignored the command, but stood looking from one man to the other. The resemblance between them suddenly struck her. In the afternoon sunlight, it was easy to see the similarities. She should have noticed them before. The eyes. St. Clair's eyes. Could it be that the pirate was also related to the old man?

"What are you doing here?" she asked, knowing she didn't want to hear the answer.

The old man quickly crossed the room to the door. This was one time he wouldn't interfere. If there was to be a reconciliation, they would need time to talk.

"I'll inform Washington to call back the men, son," he said to Justin before leaving the room.

"Son?" Bree asked.

"Actually, grandson."

"Then you are . . . a cousin of St. Clair's?" she managed despite the lump in her throat that threatened to choke her.

"No, I am St. Clair," he answered.

Bree clutched the back of the chair. No, this couldn't be. He couldn't be St. Clair. St. Clair was to marry Miss Regina. But if the pirate was also St. Clair, then that would mean . . .

Now it all made sense. The annulment. The land.

"Does that upset you?"

The question seemed to come from somewhere off in the distance. Bree couldn't bring herself to answer it.

The tears that welled up in Bree's blue eyes surprised Justin. Afraid she would run from him again, he took her hand. "Let's not argue over what we cannot change. What's important is you've driven me nearly mad with worry. Where have you been?"

"Me? I've driven you mad!" She pulled from him. "What of you? I walk in here to find you are St. Clair. I've waited ten long years. Where were you?" she demanded.

"Bree, I'm sorry. That day in England... when we talked, I was upset. Somehow you misunderstood something I said for I would never have made such a promise."

"So now it's that I misunderstood." She paced the room and back, her hurt and her anger not allowing her to accept his apology. "And to think I worshiped you," she muttered to herself. She knew she was being unreasonable, but she didn't care. All the weeks she had questioned her attraction to the pirate—all the frustration and soul-searching of her disloyalty to St. Clair—finally boiled to the surface.

Bree came to a halt in front of him. "What have you to say for yourself?"

Justin was so happy to see her again, he wasn't going to allow this to come between them now. He cupped her chin in his hand and forced her to look at him.

"It doesn't matter whether I made the promise or not. What matters is that I kept it," he said. "I married you."

"And sought an annulment at the first opportunity." She couldn't bring herself to mention what she'd learned of his upcoming marriage. "Let me make one thing clear, Mr. ... whoever you are. I have managed to get by for seventeen years without anyone's love, and I can make it through the next seventeen with as much ease."

With shoulders squared proudly, she walked to the door. "You forgot about me," she said without turning. "I intend to forget about you."

The hurt and the bitterness behind her speech swept over Justin as he watched her walk out. He had hurt her again. He felt as if she had looked into his soul and found him wanting. He had lost her. She had walked out. And taken everything that meant anything to him.

"Bree!" he shouted, running for the door. He had to catch up with her and explain.

* * *

Bree blinked back the tears as she stumbled blindly through the trees. She could hear Justin calling, but she refused to turn back. The shouts only served to push her onward. Her heart was pounding, her lungs near bursting, and still she ran.

She refused to think about the pirate or the fact that he was St. Clair. To dwell on it would mean acknowledging the fact that St. Clair had rejected her not only as himself but as the pirate as well. But then after seventeen years, she should have grown accustomed to being unwanted. For when had she ever been loved?

It wasn't until she reached the burnt-out house on the hill with the tiny graveyard beside it that she knew she had to stop and rest. Her legs refused to go any farther and she collapsed in a heap on the hard ground.

A small rest was all she needed, she told herself as she scooted over into the shadow of what was left of the chimney. Once out of the hot sun, she leaned her head against the cool brick. As soon as she caught her breath, she would be on her way back to the Winghams. Justin would never find her there. Besides, Pamela was her only chance of finding a position.

She closed her eyes and let the warm breeze wash over her. Just a wink or two and she would be on her way.

Where was she? He had reached the old Merritt plantation and still he had not found her. It was difficult to imagine he had passed her in his haste, but it was more difficult to believe she had gotten this far.

Justin's eyes were drawn to the hollow shell that had once been the home of a proud family. A few burnt timbers and a fireplace with its towering chimney were silhouetted against the setting sun. Weeds now choked the lawns that were once well-tended flower beds. But the pastures that had held Merritt's thoroughbreds were still beautiful enough to set the most pious of hearts to coveting. Odd, all these years and no one had laid claim to the estate.

He nudged his mount on. He had to find Bree before Quentin returned. His half brother wasn't one for giving up where such a promise of wealth was involved. He'd search all of Virginia before he'd let Bree get away from him. Justin would kill the bastard himself before he would allow him to touch his wife.

It was dark when Bree woke. She had fallen asleep leaning against the chimney and it had extracted a generous payment for the privilege. Not only was she hungry and thirsty, but sore. She sat up and stretched. With the bold imprint of the rough brick stamped on her back, it didn't do much good. Every bone in her body ached.

What she needed was a hot meal, a cool drink of water, and a warm bath. With no friends in Virginia, there was little chance of having any of those wishes fulfilled.

Using the chimney to balance herself, Bree got to her feet and looked around. Not even the moon cared to share its light with her tonight. But enough feeling sorry for herself. No one was going to come to her rescue. It was late and she had a long way to walk before she reached the Winghams.

The darkness, like a thick fog, seemed to boil across the fields. Nothing looked familiar. Walking the long lonely road was difficult enough during the day. At night, it would take her forever. But she had no choice. She couldn't risk waiting until morning. Justin might find her.

Justin paced the study. The men had been out half the night and still hadn't found Bree. He had sent Higgins to the cabin for the blanket from Bree's bed. If they hadn't found her by the time Higgins returned, Justin would fetch the hounds.

"What's this about an indentured servant running away?"

Justin spun around to see Quentin standing in the doorway. "There will be one less servant by morning if I ever find out who imparted the news," he mumbled to himself.

"Tut, tut. Let's not quibble over such a trivial detail," Quentin said as he made himself at home on the leather chair. "I need a brandy, then you can tell me why this particular servant was so important that all the others must desert their tasks to find her."

It was so like Quentin to want Justin to wait on him even when he could see there were more important matters on his mind at the moment. Any other guest and Justin would have offered the brandy, but with Quentin . . . well, old feelings died hard. Justin started to tell him to pour his own brandy, then decided he needed the time to change Quentin's interest to something other than Bree.

"You were out rather late tonight, weren't you, Quentin?" he asked as he poured them each a glass of brandy.

"I thought it wise to learn all I could of this highwayman," Quentin said with a frown.

Justin handed him the crystal goblet and took the other chair. "And did you discover anything of importance?"

"Only that these Virginians of yours have taken to romanticizing the bastard."

Justin dipped his head to keep Quentin from seeing the smile that curved his lips. "You can hardly expect anything else when the man chooses his victims so well."

"Only a rabble would think such a thing."

Justin's green eyes darkened. "Then count me among the rabbles, dear brother, for I too believe there wasn't a one of them that wasn't in need of having his purse lifted."

"Are you saying that I deserved to have the family jewels taken also?"

Justin lifted a dark brow. "The family jewels? I thought your fiancée was the only thing of value he took from you."

"It is the only thing I can hope to recover."

Justin was not fooled by the casualness of the answer. Other than Bree's inheritance his half brother stood to lose, Justin knew Quentin's pride was the only thing he was interested in recovering. And that meant taking his revenge out on someone weaker than himself. And that meant Bree.

Justin took the seat opposite Quentin. "This highwayman they call the pirate," he said. "I'm told he's not a man to cross."

Quentin paused before taking another sip of his brandy. "He does not frighten me. Men such as him rarely survive once they come up against the deadly end of a *gentleman's* pistol."

"An interesting theory, Quentin." Justin leaned back in his chair, then casually crossed one leg over the other. "So you plan on challenging him to a duel once you've found him, do you?"

"As much as I would like to, I feel such a punishment to be much too swift. No, I will see that the man is shipped back to England for a proper hanging."

"Ah, but then you must catch him first."

Quentin's thin lips stretched in a tight smile. "If what I have planned is successful, the two of them will be in chains before the week is out."

"Your plan?"

"Why, I shall help him decide on his next victim."

Justin hadn't realized he had held his breath until the answer released a sigh. It was a trap easily avoided. Since Justin had no plans of playing the pirate again, he knew the possibility of Quentin springing his trap was slim, but still he couldn't help but pause at the thought of a rope slipping over his head. He could only pray that Bree didn't try anything on her own.

Given the early hour and the deplorable condition of her dress, Bree decided the back door of the Winghams' would be more appropriate. After she stated her business, the housekeeper sat her down at the kitchen table and gave her a cup of coffee. Bree sipped the strong brew while she waited for Pamela.

The warm fire and the smells of breakfast cooking reminded her of home—home when she still cherished her fantasies about St. Clair. But all her dreams of him had been shattered. Never would she have thought that all those years St. Clair knew nothing of the promise. She had put all her hopes into something that had never existed.

Maddie had warned her over and over again that she was only being silly. When had she begun to think she knew more than anyone else?

When a tear threatened to escape, Bree blinked it away. Maddie had been right all along. It had been a child's promise—a child's dream. Well, she would not make that mistake again. Not only had Justin taken the child's heart from within her and turned it into a woman's, but he had taught her there were no promises to be kept—no love to hold dear. It was a lesson she would abide by in the future.

"Lady Smythe?"

Bree was startled by Pamela's entrance and nearly spilled her coffee. "What did Mrs. Wingham have to say about my employment?" she whispered aside to the prim governess.

Pamela took her into the back hallway before answering. "Do you really think this wise?"

"I have nowhere else to turn."

"You could always return home," Pamela pointed out as she escorted Bree to the back parlor.

"Even if I had the funds, which I do not, after all that has happened, my father would never take me back."

Pamela studied the young woman. Perhaps she was right. A girl who runs away from home has lost more than her family, she has ruined her reputation as well. To return to England now would only cast her into scandal.

"Please have a seat." She waited until Bree was comfortable, then continued. "The only position available is that of a kitchen maid."

So it had come to that. A kitchen maid. Somehow it seemed inevitable.

"As long as I'm not required to cook I should do famously."

Pamela was pleased with her enthusiasm. "The housekeeper is with Mrs. Wingham now." Pamela leaned close.

"You've come at the right time. What with the wedding to be announced any day, they will be in need of extra servants to prepare for the upcoming event."

Knowing the wedding was to be St. Clair's, Bree only nodded.

"Of course, with Mr. Tyler making himself scarce of late, Miss Regina had best be looking more favorably to Mr. Atwater's offer if she wants a husband anytime soon."

"Mr. Atwater?" Bree asked, her heart in her throat. "I thought she was to marry St. Clair."

Pamela was not normally one to gossip about the family, but Lady Smythe seemed in need of something to take her mind off her own situation. "He's certainly the one Miss Regina has taken a fancy to having for her husband. She near drives us all mad with her efforts to wring a proposal from him, but it's only Mr. Atwater who has asked for her hand."

"Some men will never marry," Bree stated bitterly.

Pamela shook her head. "It's what I would have said myself, but Miss Regina may get what she wants. Mr. Tyler does want that parcel of land Mr. Wingham holds title to and it's said Mr. Wingham has refused to sell. He thinks Mr. Atwater's offer may be all Miss Regina needs to bring Tyler up to scratch."

"And you think he will marry to get it?"

The painful bitterness in Bree's voice was almost as disturbing as the sadness Pamela had witnessed earlier. She was at a loss for what to say. "It will be a good arrangement for both. Mr. Wingham plans to pay a visit to Havenwood today."

The final sword of truth twisted in Bree's heart. It was no wonder Justin wanted the annulment so very badly. He would take her body, but he wouldn't surrender his heart. Now she understood why. It had already been spoken for—sold for a piece of land.

Justin was frantic. The dogs had picked up Bree's scent, but had lost it again along the streets of Williamsburg. Where could she go? As far as he knew, she had no acquaintances in Virginia.

Justin pulled his mount up, his green eyes narrowing in thought. Except the Winghams! She had asked Higgins about the family. Could she have gone there?

Justin spurred his mount. Heads turned as he made his way around the wagons and carriages that clogged the street. His horse had no more than come to a stop in front of the Winghams' when he dismounted and handed the reins to the startled footman.

Justin pushed past the man. "I wish to speak with Mrs. Wingham."

"Mrs. Wingham, she still be to bed," the black man protested.

"What's all this racket, Ulysses?" Mr. Wingham shouted from his study.

"I-it be Mr. Tyler," the butler offered humbly.

Justin hurried down the hall. "I didn't mean to bother you, Mr. Wingham. I—"

"Nonsense, son, I was planning on making a trip to Havenwood later today. Let's go into my study where we can talk."

Justin followed him down the hall. "I came on a very important matter."

With a wave of his hand, Mr. Wingham indicated one of the chairs in front of the desk. "I've been expecting you, son."

"She's here?"

"Of course she's here. Didn't think I would let her just run off with Atwater, did you?"

Justin felt he was fast losing the thread of the conversation. "Atwater?"

"Don't look so upset, son. Thought you knew. Atwater proposed to my little girl yesterday."

It was difficult to describe the relief the news brought. With the old man's temper, he had not been looking forward to telling Wingham that he was declining his offer for the land—and Regina's hand.

"I must remember to extend my congratulations to the groom," Justin said. "Now, Mr. Wingham, the reason—"

"Call me Ira, son. You thought I had forgotten about our little agreement, didn't you? Well, set your mind at ease. I had no intention of accepting Atwater's offer without consulting you on your intentions first."

Justin didn't have time for this now. He had to find Bree before Quentin did. "Ira, all I wish to know at the moment is if you have seen a young woman. Her name is Smythe. Sabrina Smythe. She's . . . a distant relative and might have come to visit Regina."

"Don't know the name. What does she look like?"

"She's young with blue eyes, but it's her hair you'll remember. It's the color of golden moonlight."

Wingham's eyes narrowed. It was apparent Tyler's interest was more than casual. Relative indeed! If he didn't miss his guess, the woman Tyler was seeking was their new maid. Although he couldn't recall her name, she certainly fit the description. But he'd not be letting Tyler know of that. From the manner in which he was behaving, Ira wasn't about to take the risk that she meant more to Tyler than he was admitting. After all, his daughter's happiness had to come first.

"Can't say as I've seen her," he lied. At the disappointment etched clearly on Justin's face, he knew he had made the right decision. Regina would not be pleased to discover Tyler was in love with the new maid. Wingham smiled to himself. Pretty little thing she was too. Wouldn't mind a little time with her myself.

"If she should come to see you, would you please send word to Havenwood?"

"Certainly, son."

As soon as Justin closed the door behind him, Ira rang for the butler. "Tell the cook I wish to talk with her."

With a confident smile on his lips, he leaned back and folded his arms across his broad belly. He'd give her a week of Cook's heavy hand, then he'd set his proposition before the lovely little wench. If she and Tyler had had a lover's spat, becoming Ira's mistress might appeal to her by then. His smile deepened. The mere thought of having her in his bed brought a pleasurable ache to Ira's loins.

Bree shifted the basket of fresh fish to her other hip. The wharf was especially busy today as she made her way through the throng of servants sent to collect their house's share of the morning's catch. Once she dropped her basket off at the wagon and negotiated a price on the shrimp Cook wanted for supper, she could be on her way home.

Clovis was waiting patiently beside the horses. Clovis was the only servant Cook would spare to help with the tiresome task and he had been instructed to stay with the wagon at all times. Bree was expected to carry the purchases herself. She had allowed one of the sailors to assist her only once and the scolding she received from Cook was enough to know she'd not risk the luxury again.

The manner in which Cook treated her, Bree was surprised she was allowed to take charge of the coins needed to purchase the day's fish at the wharf. Yet, even that had proved to be a trial. It hadn't taken long to discover from the other kitchen maids that Cook gave her fewer coins than any of the other servants, but expected her to purchase the same amount of food.

It only took Bree one day to learn how effective a smile could be on the price of fish. The coin she saved on the fish was safely tucked away for the occasions when she might not be able to achieve an equitable price.

She had been doubly fortunate today. Not only had she gotten a fair price for the fish, but the merchant had readily accepted her offer to wager the price against the outcome of a fight that had broken out on the docks. Having observed her choice of winner on a previous occasion, Bree wasn't concerned with the possibility of losing. Two well-executed punches and Bree walked away with her fish and all her coins.

After leaving her purchase with Clovis, Bree next checked the day's catch of shrimp. As Bree walked among the stalls, she examined the shrimp for size and freshness. Once she found the ones she wanted to purchase, she began her bargaining, but it was soon evident the catch was slim today for the price had not only risen accordingly, but the merchant was unwilling to bargain with her on the price. Not about to give up the large margin of profit she had hoarded from the fish, Bree dropped her hand to her side and gave her leg a healthy pinch, bringing tears to her eyes.

"But if I don't bring home the shrimp, Cook will beat me something fierce," she said through her tears.

The merchant frowned. He was not usually moved by such emotions, but the young woman *was* pleasing to the eye. He reached out and tweaked her cheek.

"We might be able to work something out if you are willing, dearie."

His smile exposed a row of black rotting teeth. If Bree had had a choice, she would rather have barfed on his boot than purchased his shrimp. But she didn't. Company was expected for supper and Mr. Wingham had requested the ugly little shrimps specially.

"All I have are these few coins," Bree lied. If she was going to have to put up with this toad's attentions in order to get the shrimp, she was going to make it worth her while.

"Ye'll 'elp me fill yer basket?"

"Of course," she said with her sweetest smile.

Once they settled on a price, the merchant quickly pulled her behind his booth. "Ye can keep yer coin," he offered with a wink as he took her basket and began filling it.

"I will do it myself," Bree said as she continued to smile at him. "You take care of your other customer. I won't be long," she added.

While he haggled on the price with a wrinkled old lady, Bree quickly gathered up the plumpest shrimp. In a few moments, the merchant was back and she could tell from the scowl on his face, he wasn't pleased with her selection.

Taking great care, she placed her basket on a wooden keg, then turned to face him. She almost gagged at the sight of him fumbling with his pants. His grin was even more revolting than it had been when he proposed the deal.

Bree wasted no time, but tossed her coins on the ground. "I pay for what I get," she stated firmly, then pulled back her fist and punched him in the nose.

With the merchant's wails ringing in her ears, Bree picked up her basket and left. She could hear the man all the way back to her carriage. "All of Virginia can hear him," she muttered to herself. He squealed like a stuck pig.

As Bree passed the last stand, someone stepped aside to let her pass. She hoped it wasn't the constable.

Quentin couldn't believe his good fortune. Bree didn't even know it was him, he mused. He had almost failed to recognize her, himself. Gone was the young girl who had run from him, he noticed with a thoughtful smile and a beautiful sensuous woman had taken her place. He quickly mounted his horse and followed.

CHAPTER 20

THE hoofbeats of a lone horse echoed each step Bree took and she quickened her pace. A quick glance over her shoulder confirmed her suspicions. Someone was following her. She glanced again. There was something familiar about the rider, but the black beaver top hat shadowed his face. Justin? No, the rider didn't have the arrogant tilt of the pirate's head, nor the broad shoulders.

Bree's legs were beginning to ache. She couldn't shake the awful feeling that she knew her tormentor. If only she could get a closer look at the man without being caught. The thought had no more than crossed her mind when a carriage coming from a side street cut between her and the horseman, giving Bree the opportunity she needed. She turned and faced the man over the traces of the carriage horses. What she saw chilled her to the bone.

Quentin! He had found her. Bree dropped her basket of shrimp and ran. Clovis was curled up asleep on the seat when she reached the cart. Bree wanted to strangle him for his laziness. Instead, she climbed in beside him, grabbed the reins from his hands, and slapped the leather lines across the broad backs of the horses.

With the lurch of the wagon, Clovis awoke with a start. "Miss Bree," he wailed.

Odd how her position as kitchen maid had not kept the other servants from treating her like a lady. It was as if they sensed she did not belong in their ranks.

"Hang on, Clovis," she shouted as they headed home.

The horses, not bred for speed, lumbered clumsily along the well-traveled road into town. So ungainly were they in maneuvering the winding curves that Bree nearly overturned the small cart in her haste.

How had Quentin found her? Like one of Cook's chickens with its head cut off, the question kept flopping around and around in her head. Bree held her breath and leaned with the sway of the wagon while Clovis moaned in fear on the narrow seat beside her. Quentin had to have learned of her sailing with the pirate. Otherwise, how would he have known she had come to Virginia? Her fingers tightened on the reins. If Quentin knew about her, did he also know Justin was the pirate?

Bree couldn't allow herself to dwell on that awful prospect. Warning Justin was out of the question, for she might very well lead Quentin to him. She could never take that risk. As much as she told herself she didn't care, she knew she did. She loved him with all her heart. Not even knowing that he didn't love her in return could change that fact. If need be, she would lay down her life for him.

The sound of hoofbeats approaching told her the time to put proof to the boast might be sooner than she thought. She slapped the reins and shouted to the horses, but she knew their burst of speed wouldn't be enough to hold off Quentin for long.

The plodding workhorses were no match for the one the Earl of Foxworth rode. Her weaving the cart back and forth across the narrow road was the only thing that kept the earl from bringing his mount alongside. Bree prayed she would reach the town center soon for the horses could not be expected to keep up the fast pace for much longer.

As if in answer to her prayer, the stables that marked the town's boundaries loomed ahead. Once again, she slapped the reins along the horses' backs, but there was no response of a faster speed. As they reached the edge of town, one of the nags stumbled in his traces, almost bringing the other one down also. Bree pulled his head high and his gait smoothed out, but she had lost her domination of the road. Even now she could hear Quentin's horse moving up beside the wooden cart. She waited until he was alongside, then tugged hard on the reins, turning the horses aside into a narrow alley.

Clovis was thrown up against her as the cart negotiated the sharp turn. It took all Bree's efforts to keep from falling, but her plan had worked. A coach coming up behind them prevented Quentin from turning his mount. For the moment, they had lost Quentin. Another tight turn and they were hidden.

Bree brought the horses down to a walk. The most crucial part of their escape was yet to come. Somehow they had to get back across the main street without Quentin seeing them. She handed the reins back to Clovis and climbed over the seat into the back of the cart.

"Drive!" she demanded in a harsh whisper, then knelt down among the baskets of fish and produce and covered herself with an old canvas throw.

With the reins lying loosely in his hands, Clovis sat wide-eyed and staring. Bree raised up and nudged him.

"Drive, I said. Drive, or when he catches you, he'll cut off your ears and feed them to the pigs."

Clovis needed no more encouragement. He grabbed the leather reins and clucked to the horses. Although they didn't refuse to pull the cart, neither did they acknowledge Clovis's frantic urging for a greater speed. With sides heaving from the long run, they plodded around the next corner and down the street at their own leisurely pace.

Bree raised her tarp-covered head and peeked out over the edge of the wooden sides. Quentin was nowhere in sight. Still she huddled under the stifling square of canvas. She didn't have to worry about whether she remained in the Winghams' employ or not. Once Cook learned that she had lost the shrimp, she would be dismissed. It was probably for the best. If by some miracle she was allowed to stay, Cook would only send her back to the wharfs for the fish tomorrow and Quentin would be there waiting for her. As much as she hated to, she was going to be forced to ask for Pamela's help yet another time.

Justin stood hunched in front of his mirror, his fists placed firmly on each side of the ceramic washbowl. Another long night spent looking for Bree had not put him in the best of moods. Slowly he lifted his head to peer into the mirrored glass.

"Why didn't you tell Bree you loved her?" Justin asked his haggard reflection.

As soon as the words were out, he lifted a dark brow and stared at the mirror in surprise. The startling revelation was almost as puzzling as it was filled with frustration. Without fear, without reservations, he had actually said it. But now Bree was gone. Vanished.

If he could go back and relive that night again, he knew he would wake her and tell her they were still married and he no longer wanted the annulment—that, given a choice, he would never let her go. But God rarely gave fools a second chance and there was no doubt about it. He had been a fool more than once where Bree was concerned.

Somehow Justin managed to finish shaving. Thank goodness, Quentin spent most of his time away from Havenwood. It was difficult to be civil to his half brother knowing that he also sought Bree in his quest for revenge.

Justin raked his fingers through his hair. Each day was much like all the rest. He rose. He dressed. He looked for Bree. He returned home alone. He couldn't remember when he'd been so tired, but he couldn't give up now. He had to find Bree before Quentin did. If not for Quentin, he would post a notice on every tree—on every building in the area—begging Bree to forgive him and come home. Home to Havenwood where she would be mistress of his house for she was already master of his heart.

* * *

Nicholas Thurston leaned back and sipped his tankard of ale that Otis had watered down again.

A well-dressed gentleman had entered the Rosewater Inn, but Josh kept his taproom too dark to enable Nicholas to guess at the man's identity. He considered approaching the gentleman about a game of cards, when the stranger turned.

Seeing Lord Foxworth, Nicholas nearly choked on his ale. Hoping to stifle the sound of his coughing, he pressed his handkerchief firmly to his lips. What was Quentin doing here?

Not one to rush into a situation before determining if it held possibilities he might be able to use to his advantage, Nicholas pulled his hat low and waited. When he observed Quentin slip a few coins to the barmaid then leave, he was glad for his patience.

Nicholas forced himself to curb his curiosity until he was certain the earl was out of earshot, then signaled the barmaid. "Molly," he called in a sharp whisper.

She sauntered slowly over to him, her face aglow with the seductive smile she reserved for her special patrons. "What can I do for you, Nicholas?" she asked, leaning close.

"What did the gentlemen want?"

Molly grinned. " 'E wanted ta know if I knew where 'e could find the pirate. 'E and every constable in Virginia," she said with a laugh.

The pirate? What would Foxworth be wanting with the pirate? Nicholas pinched the nipple she poked at him. "You playing false with me, Molly?"

She winced at the pain. "No, Nicholas, you're the only one I'm bedding now."

"I saw the coins," he told her as he twisted the firm bud between his fingers.

Molly pulled away. "A girl can make 'erself a living more ways than 'aving ta please a man."

"But I please you too, don't I, Molly?"

Although he sometimes hurt her bad, Molly couldn't deny him. She wasn't getting any younger. It wasn't often she got a gentleman for a patron anymore . . . and a clean one at that. No, she'd not risk angering him. Not for the measly five shillings the gentleman had given her.

She offered her breast to her lover again. "You please me real good, Nicholas."

He swept her down onto his lap. "Then tell me what the gentleman wanted."

Molly ran her tongue over his ear. "Seems this pirate ran away with 'is lover. Brought 'er all the way from England, the pirate did."

"Everyone is looking for the pirate. How did he think you could help?"

"'E caught a glimpse of 'er down on the docks and wanted me ta send someone to 'Avenwood, if I should see 'er. 'E's offered me a whole crown if I'm to find 'er for 'im."

Havenwood? Molly had begun to nibble on his ear and Nicholas was finding it difficult to concentrate, but curiosity had gotten the best of him. "And are you going to do as he asked?"

"That depends—" she whispered.

"—on whether you are able to spot a woman on the docks?" he finished for her. "I hope he gave you the woman's description."

Molly moved to the curve in his neck. "That 'e did, love. Blond hair and bright blue eyes. Name's Sabrina."

Nicholas drew back, almost dumping Molly on the floor. "Sabrina Smythe?"

"I think that be 'er name."

Thurston's anger quickly changed to greed as a hungry grin slowly made its way across his face. Bree had come over with Tyler. Then that would mean the noble Mr. Tyler was the pirate. He was the one who had robbed him! He wondered how much Foxworth would be willing to pay to learn the pirate's true identity.

"Don't say a word to Otis or Ned," Nicholas warned.

One thing for certain. It would cost Lord Foxworth more than a mere crown.

The old woman patted Bree on the hand. "Do not worry so over your lack of experience, young lady. If you treat Willow Cottage as if you were its mistress, that is all I can ask."

Bree returned Mrs. Monihan's smile. "I will do my best," she said, then asked the question uppermost in her mind. "How often will you require me do the shopping?"

"I'm afraid Cook insists on doing all her own. Is that a problem?"

Bree didn't realize she had been holding her breath until she released it. "No," she said with a smile. "Not at all."

Willow Cottage was a small home on the outskirts of Williamsburg with only the cook and herself to see to the needs of the elderly couple. No one would find her here.

Over the next few days, Bree threw herself into the daily tasks of cleaning. She knew she could never repay Pamela for helping her find this position when Cook dismissed her without notice, but at least she could show Mrs. Monihan that she had made a wise choice in hiring her.

Now if only she had some equally easy way to deal with the memories of the pirate.

Nicholas walked back to the inn where he had been staying. "Damn!" he cursed to himself. The third day in a row that he'd missed Foxworth. If he wasn't so certain Tyler would refuse to see him, or worse, shoot him, he'd give up getting money from the earl and take his proposition to the Virginian. But instead, he would bide his time and wait until he could catch Foxworth alone. He only wished there was some way he could find out why the Earl of Foxworth would travel so far to bring back Miss Smythe.

A commotion down the way captured Thurston's attention and as was his nature he sauntered along the walkway to see if the arrival of the grand coach would be of any benefit to him.

"Careful of his shoulder," a woman in a sturdy black bonnet told the stableboy as he opened the door to help her companion from the carriage.

The tall man shrugged the lad's offer aside. Using a cane, he stepped down. "Now, Maddie, I'll not have you mothering me anymore. I'm fine, I tell you."

The woman called Maddie took the gentleman's free arm and guided him up to the steps of the inn. "You may be fine for now, Edward, but what happens when Lord Foxworth discovers you didn't die?"

"I'll not be agreeing to another duel with that bounder anytime soon, so that should keep me safe for the time being. Now where have you sent Grant off to?"

"He's on his way to Havenwood. Now let me get you inside. Dr. Jones has procured a lovely room for you with a . . ."

They disappeared through the door, but Nicholas had heard enough. The knowledge brought a smile to his lips. He'd not wait around any longer. The price for his information—and silence—had just gone up. He'd dash off a note for Foxworth then he'd pay a visit to Molly.

Higgins slipped through the study door and shut it quickly behind him. "Another note's come for your half brother," he said, waving the paper before him.

Justin reached for the parchment. "And?"

"You didn't tell me to read it."

"Did you remind Washington not to mention its arrival to Quentin?" he asked as he carefully slipped a thin stiletto under the seal.

"I doubt Washington would feel the need to inform your brother if the house was on fire, let alone if a message had come for him."

Justin scanned the missive. "Quentin appears to have finally gotten what he bargained for. A nibble about the pirate. It says here he is to meet with a barmaid at the Rosewater Inn. That's where Otis and Ned are. The note says it will cost him more than the crown promised."

"A crown? A right generous gentleman, your brother is," Higgins said.

Refolding the note, Justin dripped a fresh bit of wax on the edge and carefully pressed the original seal down to cover it. "Tell Washington to have my horse saddled and waiting. When Quentin pays his little call on his informant, I want to be there."

"You think this woman knows you're the pirate?"

With a soft chuckle, Justin handed him the missive. "The pirate's identity will not be in jeopardy, my friend. It matters not what he discovers. My dear, generous brother is about to receive more than he bargained for—a visit from the pirate."

Justin took the chair across from Quentin. "Washington tells me you've been staying in Williamsburg. Were you successful in your plan to trap the pirate?" he asked over the rim of his cup, hoping to learn something of Quentin's plans.

Quentin grimaced. "No, but I found Sabrina."

Justin was forced to take great care in setting down his cup calmly. "And what did she have to say for herself?"

Quentin broke off a piece of bread and slathered it with butter. "She got away before I could ask her," he admitted grudgingly. "But make no mistake about it, I will find her again and when I do, I'll have my questions answered."

"Where was she?" Justin managed to ask around the anger building in him.

Quentin looked up from his plate. "At the wharf, squabbling over the price of shrimp with some poor merchant. She must be working for one of the houses in Williamsburg for she was dressed as a servant. I followed her but she got away."

Relief washed over Justin like a giant wave across the deck of a ship. "Perhaps you should give up and return to England. A woman such as this isn't worth your efforts."

Quentin's gray eyes hardened like granite. "She's worth the effort and if she's in Williamsburg, I'll find her. When

I do, she'll pay for all the trouble she has caused me. And she'll pay well."

"Why blame her? After all, I doubt that it was her idea that you sail halfway around the world," Justin pointed out. "That was your choice."

"It was her father's."

"Her father's?"

Quentin pushed his plate aside. "The man blamed me for Sabrina running away with the pirate. Said I must have done something to frighten her, then the fool challenged me to a duel." Quentin's lips thinned in a smile. "But then it did him no good in the end. I shot h—"

The confession was interrupted by Washington. He held a silver salver out to Quentin. "A note for you, Lord Foxworth."

Justin waited a few moments for his half brother to read the note. He didn't need to hear the rest of Quentin's tale to know Lord Smythe's death had been at Quentin's hands. It was why Quentin was determined not to leave until he had married Bree. If word of the duel had become public, his only hope to give credence to his innocence was if he were to return to England with Lord Smythe's daughter on his arm. He was at the point of opening his mouth to tell Quentin to leave Havenwood and never return, when the earl tossed down his napkin.

"At last, someone who knows where to find the pirate."

Justin let him leave. He no longer cared what Quentin discovered of his role as the pirate. If worst came to worst, he would take Bree and flee. But first, he had to find her—before his half brother did.

Justin stood. His plans for Havenwood meant nothing if he didn't have Bree. Without his wife, nothing mattered. Not the scandal of the marriage that had been forced on them, nor the people they had robbed.

He had wasted enough time worrying what others would think. It was time the pirate took care of Quentin. With his half brother out of the way, he would find Bree if he had to send his men knocking on every door in Williamsburg.

Washington met him at the door. "A Mr. Grant to see you, sir. I've put him in the front parlor."

Although Bree rarely left the cottage in the week that followed, Justin's image followed her everywhere. In the turbulent clouds that billowed and banked before a storm. In the mischievous smile of the lad who cared for the Monihan's only horse. In the broad shoulders of the man who delivered the firewood each Monday. And in the stubborn pride of Mr. Monihan when he refused his medication.

With each new thought of the pirate that surfaced to plague her, Bree worked all the harder. Each night found her too exhausted to do anything but sleep.

Bree shoved the last chair off the floral carpet. With Mrs. Monihan's help, she had mended the parlor drapes yesterday. Today she would beat the rugs. Tomorrow she would start on the attic. Then when she finished, she would begin all over again.

Unfortunately, her body was quickly growing used to the demands she was placing on it and sleep no longer came as easily as it once had so Bree lay awake most nights, her mind reliving all that had happened with painful clarity. Each day had become nothing more than a series of hours made up of work and denial. Justin didn't love her. It was time she stopped loving him.

Justin followed Lord Roxbury's man of business up the stairs to the inn and down the hall. A soft knock brought a woman to the door. Justin recognized Bree's companion immediately.

"Maddie, I believe," he said with a polite bow, then stepped past her into the room.

Smythe sat in one of the chairs with a coverlet bundled about his legs. Another gentleman hovered over him as if he thought the earl was going to collapse at any moment. Quentin was going to be disappointed to discover the earl was very much alive. He wondered again what had prompted them to summon him. After all, he was not responsible for his half brother's actions.

"Are you St. Clair?" The voice seemed thunderous compared to the pale man in the chair.

Until Justin had some answers, he was more inclined to keep what he knew close rather than impart information which might put Bree in an unfavorable light. "In some circles, I am known as that," he said.

The earl stared thoughtfully at him a moment. "You're a handsome gentleman, St. Clair. I can see why my daughter maintained her fantasy all these years."

"I knew nothing of it until a few weeks ago."

Edward braced himself forward on one elbow. "Then you have seen Bree."

"Yes, I've seen her."

"Thank goodness," the earl said, slumping back in his seat. "Is she well? With her running away with that scoundrel of a highwayman and now with Lord Foxworth after her, I feared any amount of things might have happened to her." He paused when he got no reaction out of St. Clair. Had Bree been wrong?

"If you'll tell me where I might find my daughter," he said stiffly, "I'll not take up any more of your time."

Justin wasn't about to be dismissed so quickly. "Before I tell you what I know of Bree's whereabouts, I have a few questions of my own. The least of which is why you allowed yourself to be maneuvered into challenging my dear half brother to a duel."

"You know of that?"

"Only that one took place . . . and that Quentin thinks you dead and hopes to marry Bree for what he imagines she will inherit."

Edward shook his head sadly. "And to think I called this pirate the scoundrel. Yet I don't even recall him robbing anyone who I thought had not deserved the attention."

Although his physician protested that he needed to rest, Lord Roxbury spent the next hour telling Justin all that had happened. His abandonment of Bree, the marriage he had sought between her and Quentin, and the duel.

"I suspected as much," Justin said when Edward had finished telling of Quentin's behavior following Bree's disappearance. "It's another reason why he thinks to marry Bree. If he returns with her on his arm, he hopes to put to rest any suspicions that he had killed you in a duel."

"And we must stop him."

Justin stood. "Quentin will not be marrying Bree. He can't. She's already married"—he paused—"to me."

The announcement brought a gasp from everyone in the room. "You kept the promise?" Maddie asked with a smile.

"Nothing as gallant as that, I'm afraid. The captain on our ship thought to save her soul and his. He forced us to marry or be set adrift."

Edward raised up in his chair. "But Bree left with the pirate."

Justin gave Lord Roxbury a slight bow accompanied by a broad grin. "One and the same," he said.

Edward cleared his throat. "You don't appear to be apologetic about the affair, so I'll have to trust that you have a valid explanation. In any case, I will leave that for later. For the moment, I wish to see my daughter."

"I too! Unfortunately, Bree and I have had a small misunderstanding about that ridiculous promise and I haven't seen her since." Justin sat back down. His father-in-law was entitled to know the entire story and it was now his turn to do the telling.

By the time Justin was finished, the old man's physician was hovering over his patient with a vial of smelling salts. Edward waved him away again. "Do you have any idea where she might have gone?"

"I've searched everywhere, but I'm afraid with her being new to Williamsburg those choices are few."

"But Foxworth. You said he saw her purchasing fish. We can't let him find her first." Edward started to get to his feet, but Maddie's hand on his shoulder reminded him that he wouldn't be much good in his condition.

"You needn't worry about Quentin. Even if I didn't have my own man following his every move, the pirate will put an end to that threat tonight. With Quentin out of the way, I need not worry about Bree's involvement with the pirate's doings. Then if I have to, I'll knock on every door in Williamsburg until I find her."

Bree's heart cried out when she saw a black carriage stop in front of Willow Cottage. The night was dark and ground fog curled its way around the spokes of its shiny wheels. When the door opened, a man stepped down into the swirling, crawling mass. With determined strides he walked toward the door.

Instinctively she knew there would be no running this time. Justin had come to take her home. She opened the door to welcome him when she saw Quentin, a pistol leveled at Justin's back.

"No-o-o-o-o!" she screamed, but her warning was too late. Justin was falling.

Bree awoke with Justin's name on her lips. This was insane, she told herself as she tossed the coverlet aside. It was over. Justin didn't need or want her. It was only her imagination still hoping that he did.

But without Justin there was nothing left for her in Virginia. Mrs. Monihan was right. She needed to put her life with Justin away and look to what was ahead. Nothing would ever be settled until she wrote the letter to her father and told him she was coming home. She could do that now. Mrs. Monihan was giving her the money to leave on a ship due to sail the following week. Perhaps, if she promised her father she would never leave Roxbury Towers again, he would see his way clear to allowing her to return home.

At her desk she pulled out the piece of parchment Mrs. Monihan had given her. It had all seemed so easy when she had discussed it with her employer last evening, but now the blank sheet of paper stared hopelessly back at her, reminding her of the letters she had written her father when she was eight. What could she say so he wouldn't ignore this one?

Bree picked up the quill and dipped it into the inkwell. *I'm sorry you don't love me, Father, but I need to come home,* she wrote.

Quentin removed his dark brown coat. Looping the back of the collar with his finger, he swung the garment over his shoulder. Not even mid-morning and already it was muggy enough on the wharf to steam a clam.

When Molly had sent word that she wanted to see him, Quentin didn't allow his hopes to get too high. It had been weeks since anyone had spotted the pirate, and Quentin was beginning to think that the highwayman may have decided to ply his trade elsewhere—with or without Sabrina.

The door to the tavern had been propped open to try to catch the occasional breeze that made its way across the river and Quentin walked on in. Molly was busy with a table of customers and he was forced to wait.

He hated having to wait for anyone, much less a wench who more than likely had no new information. Well, she'd not see the color of his coin until he checked out her story. He had been given any number of false leads since the pirate's last caper. Even so, he couldn't afford to ignore the possibility that this one might prove fruitful.

"Are you still wantin' ta find that lady friend of yours?" Molly asked as she slipped up beside him at the bar.

"You know where I might find her?"

Molly glanced over her shoulder before she answered. "No, but a friend wanted me ta give ye a message. Said he knows where ta find the pirate—and Bree," she added, just like Nicholas had coached her.

Quentin grabbed her arm. "Where is she?"

Seeing the urgency in his eyes, Molly considered asking for a coin or two for herself, but decided to wait. Nicholas had told her, if what he had learned was true, there'd be a lot more than the crown Foxworth had offered. Instead, she stared down at the hand on her arm and refused to answer until he begrudgingly released her.

"That's better," she said, straightening the front of her stained blouse. " 'E'll meet ye behind Culver's warehouse. It's down by the ol' bridge. Yer ta be there at eleven o'clock and yer not ta be late."

"Why couldn't he have come here?"

It annoyed Quentin when Molly smiled for the first time since he had arrived and it had nothing to do with a growing attraction. If it was calculated to unnerve him, she was successful. When she finally answered, he was forced to lean close to hear her whispered message.

" 'E said as ye wouldn't be wantin' anyone else ta 'ear w'at 'e 'as ta say." Molly took a deep breath. This was the important part of the message. The portion that would make them both rich. "Said it was about a duel with some English lord . . . a marriage and . . ." She paused at the raw hatred on the earl's face. "And ye," she finished.

CHAPTER 21

QUENTIN purposely arrived late. Making certain he kept out of sight, he searched the shadows behind the warehouse in hopes of catching a glimpse of his blackmailer. Even if he had the funds to buy the man's silence, he had no intention of complying with the bastard's demands.

A flicker of movement caught his eyes. The man had taken to pacing the back doorway of the warehouse. Quentin smiled. As he had hoped, his late arrival had shaken the man's confidence and he was getting careless.

Quentin pulled out the knife he had hidden in his coat. Having viewed the man's broad shoulders, he was pleased he'd thought to bring it along.

He had, at first, thought it might be the driver who had brought Bree to the wharf, but the man pacing in the morning shadows was too light of skin. Quentin continued to wait. He had no intention of taking an unnecessary risk.

When the man stopped his pacing, Quentin knew the time had come. With careful steps, he edged along a pile of crates until he was directly behind his prey. He didn't hesitate. With his knife clutched firmly in his hand, he stepped forward. Quentin had only meant to threaten his blackmailer and was taken by surprise when the man suddenly spun around.

Instinctively, Quentin struck out with the knife, catching his opponent in the gut. As the man fell, he reached out and Quentin found himself face-to-face with an old acquaintance.

"Thurston," he breathed.

"I—I wasn't asking f-for that much," Nicholas said bitterly before he slumped to the ground.

Leaning down, Quentin grabbed the front of Thurston's shirt and shook him. "You can't die, you bastard," he shouted. "Not without telling me where I can find the pirate."

Nicholas opened his eyes and smiled up at Quentin. "G-go to Hades!"

Quentin dropped the dead man back onto the ground. His only lead and he had killed him. Quickly he glanced around to see if anyone had witnessed the murder. There was no one, but that didn't guarantee that when the body was discovered, he wouldn't be accused. Molly knew he was to meet Thurston.

Quentin retrieved his knife, then hid the body behind the stack of crates. He would return after dark to dispose of it in the river.

Calm. Remain calm, he told himself as he walked along the wharf on the way back to his carriage. Once he got past the merchants hawking what was left of their wares, he relaxed.

Justin waited until Quentin had left, then he climbed behind the crates. He had not planned on his half brother killing the man before he got the information he sought. Now he'd probably never know how the man had learned of the whereabouts of the pirate.

When Justin reached the body, he turned it over. Thurston! Once given the details that the pirate had come over on the *Seahawk* with a beautiful young lady, Thurston would have known. Quentin had stabbed the only man who could have told him the pirate's identity.

* * *

Once again, Quentin cursed his ill luck. He should have grabbed Sabrina that day when he had first glimpsed her bargaining for the shrimp. She would never return now. After a fortnight, it was obvious her employer was sending someone else to purchase the fish.

At the sight of a line of carriages, Quentin stopped. Sabrina might not come herself but he would be willing to wager they would continue to send the same driver. He wondered why this had not occurred to him earlier.

He quickly walked over to the carriages and carts pulled up by the warehouses. It didn't take him long to determine this would not be an easy task. All of Williamsburg appeared to have taken a liking to sending their servants to do the shopping in shiny black carts such as the one Sabrina had used. Other than a few differences, all of them looked to have been turned out by the same coachbuilder.

Although Quentin knew his chances of finding her driver were slim, he wasn't about to abandon the idea. He started at one end and walked along the row, asking each in turn about the whereabouts of a pretty little blond maid. It only took him five inquiries before someone pointed out Sabrina's driver.

Jubilation soared through him as he quietly walked the short distance to the cart. Careful not to disturb the sleeping driver, he climbed up beside him. Once Quentin was certain there would be no escape this time, he slipped his knife from his coat and woke the driver.

"Drive around to the road," he whispered, punctuating the command with the tip of his knife.

Clovis could hardly keep his knees from knocking as he coaxed the horses and cart down the narrow alley of carriages.

"I'm looking for Sabrina Smythe," Quentin snarled as he pushed the knife deeper into the side of the black man's cotton shirt.

Clovis stared wide-eyed at the man. "Don't know no Sabrina," he gasped.

"It doesn't matter what she calls herself now. She's the one you drove to the wharf a fortnight ago," Quentin stated firmly. "Surely you recall fleeing from me."

"T-that was no Sabrina," Clovis blurted out. "That be Miss Bree."

Realizing that the driver was in danger of impaling himself on the knife if he didn't quit his shaking, Quentin withdrew it. "Where can I find her?"

Clovis drew a deep breath. "Don't rightly know, sir. Cook up and dismissed her. Made Mrs. Wingham right upset with her too, it did."

"The Winghams." Justin had introduced him to the charming daughter only last week. Quentin laid the knife up under the driver's chin. "Where did she go?"

"I—I don't k-know."

Quentin placed the knife to the black man's neck and slowly carved a fine trail of blood along his throat. "Perhaps you should take a moment and think on it."

Clovis screamed, but fear of the stranger kept the other drivers from interfering. "She's a friend of Miss Vye's, the governess," he squealed. "She might be a-knowin' where Miss Bree went."

"And where would I find this Miss Vye?"

"She's taken the girls to Charleston. Heared Cook say she'd be back late tonight."

Quentin lowered the knife. "You've been most helpful. I trust you will continue to be so."

Clovis nodded.

"Then this little conversation should remain between the two of us," Quentin said with a cold smile. "Don't you agree?"

"Yes, sir."

Quentin handed the reins back to Clovis. "I trust you'll remember. I wouldn't want the surprise I have planned for her to be spoiled."

Clovis swallowed the lump in his throat and continued to shake his head as the white man walked away. He had no intention of saying anything to Miss Pamela, but Miss

Bree had to be warned. He only wished he knew where she'd gone.

"You look like death," Quentin said as he poured himself a brandy.

Justin ignored the comment. He knew how bad he looked. Weeks with little sleep did that to a man, but what did murdering a man do to a person? Apparently nothing if Quentin's smiling face was any example.

"What are your plans for this evening, Quentin?" Justin asked.

Having filled his glass, Quentin carried it and the decanter to the small table across from Justin, then sat down. A cold smile touched his lips.

"In a few minutes, I leave to meet with someone who knows where Sabrina is hiding."

Justin lifted a questioning brow. He had to be careful. He couldn't afford to rile Quentin now. Although Otis had told him of the meeting with Thurston, he hadn't obtained any information as to Bree's whereabouts. "And?" he asked.

"I am not selfish, brother. When I'm finished, I may even let you have a go at her."

It took all the strength Justin had left not to reach over and grab Quentin by the throat, but for now he needed him. "I thought you had given up on her returning to the docks."

"I had, until I found the servant driving the cart. Seems the governess of the house might know where Sabrina is hiding."

Fear tightened Justin's chest. "And was she of any help?" he asked.

The smile on Quentin's lips dropped. "Miss Vye should be returning from Charleston soon. I left word that I wished to speak with her the moment she returns."

The Winghams! Hope soared in Justin's heart at the possibility of finding Bree. He'd be there when Quentin found Bree. Soon, Bree would be back in his arms—his for all time.

* * *

Pamela stood in front of the open garden doors and studied Lord Foxworth with interest. So this was the other St. Clair. Although most would consider the man quite handsome, there was something undefinable about the coldness of his dark gray eyes that set Pamela's back up. She much preferred the brother who was to offer for Miss Regina's hand.

"What may I do for you, Lord Foxworth?"

"I am looking for a young woman who was once employed here. I'm told she was an acquaintance of yours and you might know of her whereabouts."

Bree had told Pamela of meeting Lord Foxworth on the wharf and fleeing from him. "It is my understanding that Bree has no wish to see you."

Quentin lowered his head as if embarrassed. "Sabrina and I were engaged to be married and I'm afraid we've had a misunderstanding."

Although Bree had not given Pamela her reasons as to why she might be hiding from Lord Foxworth, she would have been blind not to have noticed how much the encounter had upset her young friend. Was it possible that she had made a mistake and this was the St. Clair Bree had hoped to marry?

"I thought the engagement was between Bree and your brother, Mr. Tyler."

Quentin's head came up. He fixed her with a cold stare. "Now you have me at a disadvantage," he said. "I know of no other engagement. It has always been understood that Bree would be my wife."

"Oh, then you are the one she made that childish promise to?"

"Childish promise?" Surely Justin was not the one Lord Smythe had warned him held Sabrina's affections. "Again, I'm afraid I don't know what you're referring to."

Pamela smiled. "She said you didn't remember. As you can imagine, she was terribly hurt by that. That's why she ran away."

PIRATES AND PROMISES

Quentin knew nothing of what she was saying, but she had piqued his interest enough to want to know more. Hoping to charm the information out of the young woman, Quentin took her hand and looked deeply into her eyes.

"Could you possibly find it in your heart to forgive my deplorable memory of a promise which must truly be the bone of contention Bree is holding over my poor head."

Pamela coldly withdrew her hand. "It is Bree you should be applying to for forgiveness, not I."

"Surely you can see that until I know what it is that I have promised, I can never hope to mend this breach which has come between us. If you would only enlighten me of the details so when I find her I can remedy this awful misunderstanding, I would be truly grateful."

"I don't know," Pamela said, still not clear on her own misunderstanding of the situation. She knew how much St. Clair meant to Bree and she had been the one to tell her of his engagement with Miss Regina. Now it appeared as if she might have made a grave mistake.

"The misunderstanding may have been my fault," Pamela offered, then went on to explain about the locket and of how the forgotten promise had upset Bree. With not so much as a blink of his eye did the earl indicate whether or not he was upset with her.

"The Monihans were looking for a maid at Willow Cottage and I recommended Bree for the position. They're an elderly couple who live on the outskirts of Williamsburg. Bree has been working there since the day you last saw her."

Although a deep, consuming rage threatened to choke him, Quentin smiled sweetly, then stood. "How can I ever thank you for all your help?" he asked with a carefully measured touch of sadness. He would murder them both. "Rest assured when I find Sabrina, I will be more than happy to relay how much your assistance went toward returning her to my arms."

"Think nothing of it, Lord Foxworth. It was the least I could do after the unfortunate mistake I made. I shudder to think how I was the cause of Bree's poor heart breaking. I can only wish you success in convincing her that you return her love."

Quentin picked up his hat and crossed the room. He waited until he was at his carriage before he gave vent to his anger. Drawing back his fist, he drove it through the carriage door the footman held for him.

All Justin's questions. All his concerns. It wasn't a servant Justin had been searching for all this time. It was Sabrina.

"Take me to Willow Cottage at the west end of town. And hurry!" he shouted to the coachman. "First the harlot, then my dear brother! They will both regret the day they ever betrayed me."

The threat sent shivers scurrying up Clovis's back as he stood listening to the conversation. He had debated the advisability of listening at the parlor window, but now was pleased he had. While the carriage would be forced to take the roads through town, Clovis would be able to make use of the backyards and alleyways to arrive at the Monihans' before Lord Foxworth.

"I am not a runway," Clovis kept whispering to himself. "I am not a runaway."

A black man fleeing along the alleyways was more than enough reason to cause concern to anyone who happened to catch a glimpse of him. If he was stopped, he would tell them he was on an errand for Miss Vye. Nonetheless Clovis kept to the shadows as he made his way across town. Experience had taught him that Mr. Wingham didn't always take the time to listen to excuses before he dispensed punishment.

When he reached the Monihans' home, he skirted the front steps and kept to the narrow walk that led around to the back door. The home was smaller than the Winghams' with a cozy little garden tucked into the side yard next to a sizable apple orchard. Movement out of the corner of his eye stopped him dead. Expecting to hear a shout any moment, Clovis slowly turned to face his attacker.

"Lord a'mighty," he whispered in relief, to see that his assailant was nothing more than the neighbor's forgotten wash dancing in the wind on an old clothesline.

With his heart in his throat, he hurried to the back door. The light was on and he could see the cook cleaning up the last of the supper dishes. At his soft knock, she dried her hands and came to the door.

"Yes?" she snapped.

Clovis stepped back at the sight of the small woman brandishing her broom. From his place between the willow branches, he took a deep breath and stated, "I've a message for Miss Bree."

"Wha' you doin' hidin' back there, then?" the cook snapped. "You want to see Miss Bree, you'll have to come out of that there tree, and then no tellin' iffen she'll see you. We don't generally 'cept no callers this late."

Clovis stayed in among the branches. While uneducated, he was not lacking in intelligence. He merely had a tendency to take his time before speaking. He much preferred to think his answers through, greatly improving his chances of making the right decision.

"Visitors don't stand in the bushes," the feisty little woman said when he failed to come forward.

It was obvious to Clovis she wasn't inclined to wait for him to formulate his thoughts. He wanted to tell her he would answer if only she wouldn't rush him so, but he could tell she was upset enough without his criticism.

"Wha' kind of house you think this is?" she added with a stomp of the broom handle before slamming the door.

What was he to do now? That man with the knife was after Miss Bree and he'd be here any moment. Miss Bree had been right nice to Clovis and he couldn't bring himself to leave without warning her. There was no telling. The stranger might hit her like he'd done to that carriage door.

Clovis stepped around the corner and made his way back to the front of the house. The clothes flapping in the breeze sounded like a gun and his heart skipped a beat. While he disliked violence of any kind, he hoped the lazy servant who left the laundry on the line would get a beating.

Clovis suddenly stopped and turned. The clothes!

After searching the clothesline, he finally selected a simple blue dress and slipped it on over his head. Next he tied a bright scarf around his head and checked his reflection in the dark windows of the neighbor's house. Satisfied that his looks had changed sufficiently, he unpinned a lace-trimmed linen shawl from the line to complete his disguise.

He started around the back of the house again, but stopped and made his way to the front instead. He couldn't face dealing with the hostile cook again. He'd try his luck with the butler.

The front of the house was dark. Clovis lifted the brass knocker and let it drop. A shiver of fear skittered up his back. He'd forgotten to prepare what he was going to say. Of all the . . .

The door opened. Clovis could see from the dark outline behind the bright candle that this was no butler, but then neither was it the cook with her broom.

"I'm afraid the Monihans are out for the evening," the woman said.

"Miss Bree?"

Bree lifted the candle higher. "Yes?"

Clovis ripped off the scarf. "It's me, Miss Bree. Clovis."

"Come in. Come in." Bree stepped back from the door. "What are you doing here? And dressed like that?"

Clovis quickly reviewed all that had happened. "It's Lord Foxworth. He should be here any moment now," he added at her silence.

Bree remembered clearly what Lady Horace in *The Merry Widow* did when the villain discovered her place of hiding, but Bree had no wish to petition the convent. Unlike Lady Horace's situation, there would be no last-minute rescue from her hero.

"You're certain it was Lord Foxworth?" she asked, her mind still seeking a solution.

"That's what Miss Vye was forever a-callin' him."

This is all Justin's fault, she thought, giving wings to her anger. First he makes a promise he has no intention of keeping, then he abducts her and carries her off to Virginia—still with no thoughts of marrying her. Now Quentin was after her and there was no doubt in her mind but that marriage was the last thing in Lord Foxworth's plans for her either.

Well, she had had enough abuse from the St. Clairs. The pirate was responsible for this plight and she would see that he got her out of it. Bree grabbed Clovis by the arm and pulled him toward the kitchen.

Clovis held back. "Where are we going?" he protested.

"To force a toad to be a prince for once."

When the coach came to an abrupt stop, Quentin pulled the drape aside, then lowered the coach window. There were no houses, nothing but trees and a lonely road.

"What's happened, driver? Why have you stopped?"

The driver didn't answer, but handed the reins to the footman and climbed down. Quentin watched with dread as the dark figure moved to the door of the coach. Having heard how arrogant and unpredictable these Americans could be, Quentin had stuffed a pistol down between the cushions for just such a confrontation. The thought that Justin should be more careful in the hiring of his staff crossed Quentin's mind as his fingers curled around the cold metal. He barely had time to cock the pistol before the door flew open.

"Out!" the figure swathed in black demanded.

"The pirate!" Quentin breathed, then pulled the trigger.

Bree stumbled along beside Clovis. A heavy fog had rolled in, making the streets almost impossible to see, but she'd not turn back. Not even if it meant losing the money Mrs. Monihan offered to pay for her trip back to England. After tonight, she was going to demand that Justin either marry her again or send her back to England himself.

Even so, she was not looking forward to the long walk to Havenwood. Clovis suggested that they borrow the Winghams' cart and Bree readily agreed.

By the time they arrived at the Winghams', both were tired. Fortunately the stableboy was of an obliging nature and didn't question Clovis's need for the cart. Once the horses were secured in their traces, they were on their way.

The fog thinned a bit once they were away from Williamsburg, but Clovis kept the horses to a walk. Bree wished they could have driven at a breakneck speed through the streets. The leisurely pace of the horses gave her too much time to question what she was about to do.

She didn't relish a return to England, but she had come to accept the fact that England was her only choice. The best she could hope for was that her father would allow her to stay at Roxbury Towers.

A return to the solitary life wouldn't be all that terrible, she told herself. At least now it would be easier to accept for she would know that there were no more dreams of adventure . . . or love.

When tears leaped to her eyes, Bree raised her chin defiantly. She didn't need anyone's love. Not her father's. Not Justin's. She would have her books, Maddie, and her memories for company. That was all anyone needed. That and something to heal this awful ache in her heart.

A lone tear coursed down her cheek.

Water lapped hungrily at the sides of the small dinghy that slid silently up to the wooded shore of the James River. As the two seamen watched, a tall, dark figure stepped out of the trees and the fog. He pulled another man behind him. The silkiness of the black cloth that covered the man's eyes and encased the man's broad shoulders shimmered in the strange glow that appeared to take life from the swirling fog. The sailor had to take a deep breath and remind himself that they were only dealing with Mr. Tyler and not the devil himself.

"That you, Mr. Tyler?" Otis called across the narrow way.

"Yes."

PIRATES AND PROMISES

Quentin stopped, bringing the pirate to a halt also. "Justin?" he demanded.

Justin turned and made a deep bow to his prisoner. "At your service, dear brother."

Quentin gasped. "You're the highwayman. You took the family jewels."

"How very crass it sounds coming from your lips," Justin said as he removed the silk mask.

"You stole from me!"

"Not stole. You make it sound as if I were a petty pickpocket. I was a highwayman and a tolerably good one, I might add. Besides which, I would prefer to call it the redistribution of a few assets to pay your outstanding debts."

Quentin tugged at the ties binding his wrists. "I had no outstanding debts."

"Oh, but you did, dear brother. I doubted very much that those you owed would press for payment, so I took it upon myself to save your soul from debtor's prison."

Quentin stopped. "How admirable. Now let me go."

Justin pushed Quentin toward the shore. "All in good time. All in good time."

"I wish I had killed you."

"You would have if the gun hadn't misfired. Not as trusty a pistol as the one you fired at Lord Smythe, eh?"

"How did you know?"

"The gentleman told me himself."

"But he couldn't. He's—"

"Dead? No, he's very much alive and he approves of my plans."

"What are you planning on doing with me?" Quentin shouted over his shoulder.

"You've been looking a little pale lately. I thought a nice long sea voyage would do you good. Of course, you'll have company. Smythe's man of business is a most thorough fellow. He'll see that you tend to the delicate matters you left unresolved in England."

Quentin spun around. "You don't understand. I can't go back there now."

Justin's green eyes glittered like emeralds and Quentin took a step backward. "They'll hang me," he screamed.

Justin shoved Quentin down into the waiting boat. "If they don't, I will."

Justin had lost her again. She wasn't at the Monihans' and she wasn't at the Winghams'. The only thing he knew for certain was that one of the servants had taken a cart to escort a young lady home. Justin had been waiting for hours and the servant had yet to return her to the Monihans'. Another hour and it would be dawn. She was not coming back. He might as well leave.

The ride home was fraught with bouts of soul-searching. If he lost Bree, he had no one to blame but himself. She had let him know in many ways that she was willing to give up everything for him and he had ignored all the signs, misunderstanding, stubbornly holding to the meaningless ideals he had set for himself years ago.

What were all the riches he had accumulated worth without Bree at his side? What difference did owning a particular plot of land mean, if he had to be married to someone he didn't love?

To be certain, if he meant to raise champion thoroughbreds, he would need more land, but Virginia had more land. Perhaps not the ideal acres he had set his heart on, but surely he hadn't exhausted all the possibilities. Why, even the old Merritt plantation up ahead, while not perfect, was better than marrying Regina—and losing Bree.

He let his gaze wander over the burnt out house and the tiny graveyard as he passed. The fields, once dotted with rich crops, now lay untouched. Lush meadow grasses covered the scars once made by man and plow. Here and there young birch and pines joined them as if to lay their own claim to the land.

Justin stopped his horse at the end of the long lane. Under the grasses, the ground still lay in ridges, but here was land. It would take a lot of hard work to level the fields, but it was not impossible and, when he was finished, the pastures would be perfect for his mares. He had been a fool for not thinking to find the new owners and making an offer before. Justin headed his mount home. As soon as he found Bree, he would set Francis to look into the matter.

The sight of a carriage standing at the bottom of the front steps stirred Justin's heart with hope. With a touch of his whip, he urged the horse faster. Once at the door, he dismounted and tossed the reins to a stableboy.

"The cart. Who does it belong to?"

"That be Mr. Wingham's. One of his servants brought it in last evenin'. He had a lady with him, he did. Right—"

Justin was no longer listening, but started toward the house.

"—pretty, she was," the stableboy called after him.

Bree. The name carved a warm notch deep in his heart. It had to be Bree. God would not be so cruel as to allow it to be anyone else.

He mounted the steps two at a time and threw the oak doors wide. "Where is she?" he demanded of a startled Washington.

"Which—"

"My wife, man. Where is my wife?"

Hearing Justin's voice, Regina came out of the parlor. Her father had been right. Coming to Havenwood might be the only thing to save her hopes of marrying Justin. She only wished she had been able to change into the intimate nightdress she carried in her reticule, but with the old man in the study she had had to change her plans.

"I'm here, my love," she said.

Justin spun around. Regina? "Where's Bree?" he asked.

The fact that he had been asking about the maid did not sit well with Regina. "I don't know of any Bree," Regina lied as she sauntered up to him, a seductive smile on her pretty face. "But then we don't need anyone else but us, do we?"

Justin lifted a dark brow. "What are you doing here, Regina?"

"Now don't be upset with me," Regina said, stepping into his arms. Boldly, she ran a slim finger down Justin's clenched jaw. "When I heard you had been asking for me, I had one of the servants bring me by last evening. I know it was dreadfully forward, but as we are to be married soon, I saw no harm in it."

Justin took Regina by her arms and set her from him. "I don't know who told you we were to be married, but whoever it was, they made a grave mistake. I could never marry you, Regina. I love another."

"You can't mean that," she wailed, breaking free of his tight hold and throwing herself back into his arms. "I've waited for you all night. It's me you love."

With tear-filled eyes, she gazed up into his eyes. "What of the land? What of my reputation?"

"You might catch him with the land," Bree called out from above as she made her way to the stairs. "But I can attest to the fact that Justin cares for no one's reputation."

Justin watched Bree come down the stairs. She was dressed in one of his mother's old gowns. Her hair, unbound, fell to her waist in a mass of curls. She was beautiful.

"Bree," he whispered.

One look at Justin's face and Regina knew she was about to lose everything. Desperate, she rounded on Bree. "What would you know of it? Justin and I have been lovers for months. He would never leave me to face the gossips alone."

With her pride tottering on the brink of sanity, Bree summoned her last bit of dignity and looked Justin in the eye. Her heart soared with the love she saw displayed there.

"The past is not important," she said with her gaze never straying from Justin's. "What matters is that Justin Tyler St. Clair is pledged to marry me."

Regina looked from one to the other. "Justin, tell me she's lying."

"I'm sorry, Regina."

"Glory be!" came a shout from the study.

PIRATES AND PROMISES 325

"That's my grandfather," Justin offered as he took Bree's hand. He was staring down at her, but he couldn't help himself. He would never get enough of her beauty.

Bree met his gaze. "Yes, I know. We talked last evening."

Upset that things had failed to go her way, Regina bolted for the door. Bree was pleased when Justin didn't try to stop her.

He reached out and took her hand. This was not the time for explanations that the marriage had never been annulled. Even if it would satisfy his grandfather.

"Grandfather would be pleased to have a wedding at Havenwood."

Bree thought her heart would burst. She smiled up at him. "I missed you."

"Tell her, you fool!" came from the study.

Justin ignored his grandfather's outburst. This time was for Bree.

Justin took her in his arms. "Since we're going to do this up proper this time, shouldn't I be asking your father's permission for your hand?" he teased.

"My father's in England—"

"Your father's in Williamsburg," Adrian shouted.

Bree's puzzled gaze met Justin's. "Here?"

Justin curled his finger under her chin. "It's a long story and I think he should be the one to tell you about it, but he wanted you to know that everything he did was for his love for you."

"Me?" Bree asked. Her father loved her? It couldn't be. "And what of you?" she couldn't help but ask.

"Tell her you love her," came from the study.

Justin pulled Bree down the hall. "I would be pleased to have you as my wife," he answered in a loud voice as he slammed the study door. "There, old man, now let me get on with this."

Finally having Bree to himself, Justin gathered her into the circle of his arms. "What do you say, love? Will you have me?"

Bree wanted to say yes, but he still hadn't said he loved her and all of a sudden it was very important that she know. "Do you love me?"

He hugged her tight. He knew the hurt would be a long time in healing. Burying his face in her hair, he whispered, "When you were gone, it was as if you had taken a part of me with you." He lifted his head so he could see her face. "I'll love you for all time. Now, what will it take to convince you?"

"My birthday *is* tomorrow," she said coyly. "And I *will* be eighteen."

"Ah, the promise," he said with a grin. Stepping back, Justin gave her a deep bow. "A gentleman—and a pirate—always keeps his promise."

Letter to the Reader

As you were growing up, there were probably many loves in your life. But there will always be only one childhood sweetheart—that someone special you've carried in your heart and in your mind since the first time you fell in love. When I learned of the untimely death of Stephen Ben Tyler, my childhood sweetheart, I knew I had to do something special for the friend who had meant so much to me when I was growing up. *Pirates and Promises* is his book. I hope you enjoy it.

Anne Caldwell would enjoy hearing from her readers. You may write to her at P.O. Box 15621, Colorado Springs, CO 80935. For those who wish a reply, a self-addressed envelope would be appreciated.

Discover the passion, intrigue, and beauty of England

Tea Rose Romances

Enthralling new novels that will sweep you away to a time and place as glorious as love itself...

__PIRATES AND PROMISES 0-515-11248-8/$4.99
   by Anne Caldwell

Bree longs for something more than the wealthy man her family wants her to marry. And oddly enough, when she's kidnapped by a highwayman, her wish comes true. He's a pirate, a scoundrel, a handsome and arrogant rogue—but Bree's captor is also her childhood sweetheart in disguise. And the adventures they only dreamed about as children are now as thrillingly real as the fire in their hearts.

And don't miss the upcoming Tea Rose Romances...

__EMBRACE THE NIGHT 0-515-11373-5/$4.99
   by Elda Minger (May)

__SWEET IRIS 0-515-11381-6/$4.99
   by Aileen Humphrey (July)

Payable in U.S. funds. No cash orders accepted. Postage & handling: $1.75 for one book, 75¢ for each additional. Maximum postage $5.50. Prices, postage and handling charges may change without notice. Visa, Amex, MasterCard call 1-800-788-6262, ext. 1, refer to ad # 482

Or, check above books and send this order form to:	Bill my: ☐ Visa ☐ MasterCard ☐ Amex _____ (expires)
The Berkley Publishing Group	Card#_____
390 Murray Hill Pkwy., Dept. B	($15 minimum)
East Rutherford, NJ 07073	Signature_____
Please allow 6 weeks for delivery.	Or enclosed is my: ☐ check ☐ money order
Name_____	Book Total $_____
Address_____	Postage & Handling $_____
City_____	Applicable Sales Tax $_____ (NY, NJ, PA, CA, GST Can.)
State/ZIP_____	Total Amount Due $_____

Come take a walk down Harmony's Main Street in 1874, and meet a different resident of this colorful Kansas town each month.

A TOWN CALLED
⚘HARMONY⚘

__KEEPING FAITH by Kathleen Kane
0-7865-0016-6/$4.99 *(coming in July)*

From the boardinghouse to the schoolhouse, love grows in the heart of Harmony. And for pretty, young schoolteacher Faith Lind, a lesson in love is about to begin.

__TAKING CHANCES by Rebecca Hagan Lee
0-7865-0022-2/$4.99 *(coming in August)*

All of Harmony is buzzing when they hear the blacksmith, Jake Sutherland, is smitten. And no one is more surprised than Jake himself, who doesn't know the first thing about courting a woman.

__CHASING RAINBOWS by Linda Shertzer
0-7865-0041-7/$4.99 *(coming in September)*

Fashionable, Boston-educated Samantha Evans is the outspoken columnist for her father's newspaper. But her biggest story yet may be her own exclusive–with a most unlikely man.

Payable in U.S. funds. No cash orders accepted. Postage & handling: $1.75 for one book, 75¢ for each additional. Maximum postage $5.50. Prices, postage and handling charges may change without notice. Visa, Amex, MasterCard call 1-800-788-6262, ext. 1, refer to ad # 489

Or, check above books and send this order form to: The Berkley Publishing Group 390 Murray Hill Pkwy., Dept. B East Rutherford, NJ 07073	Bill my: ☐ Visa ☐ MasterCard ☐ Amex (expires) Card#_____ ($15 minimum) Signature_____

Please allow 6 weeks for delivery. Or enclosed is my: ☐ check ☐ money order

Name_____
Address_____
City_____
State/ZIP_____

Book Total $_____
Postage & Handling $_____
Applicable Sales Tax $_____
(NY, NJ, PA, CA, GST Can.)
Total Amount Due $_____

Winner of the Golden Heart Award

ANITA GORDON

__THE VALIANT HEART 0-515-10642-9/$4.95

By birthright, Brienne was Baronne de Valseme–but the black-haired maiden was robbed of her legacy by plundering Norsemen. Offered against her will as a bride to Rurik, the enemy, their people are joined in a delicate and uneasy peace–but destiny decreed that Brienne and Rurik would join an everlasting, enthralling life...

"Anita Gordon gives the ring of authenticity to her first Medieval Romance."–LaVyrle Spencer, *New York Times* bestselling author of *Bitter Sweet*

"An exciting confection; I read it with avid enjoyment!" –Roberta Gellis, bestselling author of *Fires of Winter*

__THE DEFIANT HEART 0-425-13825-9/$4.99

A fiercely handsome Norman lord stole the ravishing Irish beauty from a life of slavery, angered to see the lovely maiden treated as a possession. But soon there stirred within him a powerful desire to possess her himself–as only a lover could...

Payable in U.S. funds. No cash orders accepted. Postage & handling: $1.75 for one book, 75¢ for each additional. Maximum postage $5.50. Prices, postage and handling charges may change without notice. Visa, Amex, MasterCard call 1-800-788-6262, ext. 1, refer to ad # 459

Or, check above books   Bill my: ☐ Visa ☐ MasterCard ☐ Amex _____ (expires)
and send this order form to:
The Berkley Publishing Group   Card#_____
390 Murray Hill Pkwy., Dept. B   ($15 minimum)
East Rutherford, NJ 07073   Signature_____
Please allow 6 weeks for delivery.   Or enclosed is my: ☐ check ☐ money order
Name_____   Book Total $_____
Address_____   Postage & Handling $_____
City_____   Applicable Sales Tax $_____ (NY, NJ, PA, CA, GST Can.)
State/ZIP_____   Total Amount Due $_____